KEEPERS OF THE KALACHAKRA

BOOKS IN THE BHARAT COLLECTION

The Rozabal Line

Chanakya's Chant

The Krishna Key

The Sialkot Saga

Keepers of the Kalachakra

The Vault of Vishnu

The Magicians of Mazda

The Ayodhya Alliance

Praise for the Bharat Collection

***The Rozabal Line* (2008)**

'In *The Rozabal Line,* Ashwin Sanghi does a Dan Brown by mixing all the ingredients of a thriller—crusades, action, adventure, suspense—and pulling off, with dexterity and ease, a narrative that careens through cultures and continents, religions and cults.' ~*The Asian Age*

'*The Rozabal Line* by Ashwin Sanghi is a kickass thriller that forces you to re-examine our histories, our faiths.' ~Pritish Nandy

'Sanghi's flair for religion, history and politics is clearly visible as he takes the reader across the world, spanning different decades. A mixture of comparative religion, dangerous secrets, and a thrilling plot makes for an esoteric read.' ~*The Statesman*

'Sanghi has got the sure-fire formula right.' ~*The Times of India*

'A provocative, clever and radiant line of theology ... Sanghi suggests that the cult of Mary Magdalene has its true inspiration in the trinity of the Indian sacred feminine, thereby out-thinking and out-conspiring Dan Brown.' ~*The Hindu*

***Chanakya's Chant* (2010)**

'With internal monologues and descriptions as taut as a-held-by-the-thumb sacred thread, we have Ashwin Sanghi's cracker of a page-turner, *Chanakya's Chant*. Two narratives flow like the Ganga and Yamuna ... a brisk technicoloured thriller.' ~*Hindustan Times*

'I'm utterly enthralled. A delightfully interesting and gripping read. The historical research is deeply impressive.' ~Shashi Tharoor

'A gripping, fast-paced read, the novel is a true thriller in the tradition set by Dan Brown.' ~*People*

'Political grooming and conspiracy remain at the core of Ashwin Sanghi's historical thriller. Bloodshed, legal trials, betrayals, murders, assassination attempts make this into a page-turner.' ~*Sakaal Times*

'Released in India to wide acclaim, *Chanakya's Chant* is a political page-turner.' ~*Business India*

***The Krishna Key* (2012)**

'Why should racy historical thrillers or meaty fantasy sagas come only from the minds of Western writers? Ashwin Sanghi spins his yarns well and leaves you breathless at every cliff-hanger. No wonder his books are bestsellers!' ~*Hindustan Times*

'While the plot is set in today's world, one can expect to travel back and forth in time with generous chunks of history and nail-biting action.' ~*The Telegraph*

'An alternative interpretation of the Vedic Age that will be relished by conspiracy buffs and addicts of thrillers alike.' ~*The Hindu*

'Just finished *The Krishna Key* by Ashwin Sanghi. Rocking story and incredible research. Loved it!' ~Amish Tripathi

'Sanghi manages to blur the line between fact and fiction and give a whole new perspective to history and the Vedic Age.' ~*DNA*

The Sialkot Saga **(2016)**

'*The Sialkot Saga* moves at a breakneck pace, hurtling through time and space, uncovering ancient secrets and burying modern ones.' ~*The Hindu*

'The book spreads across decades and centuries, till it reaches present-day India and will sure have both historic and thriller readers in for a treat.' ~*The Times of India*

'There are books that take time to develop an interest and then there are books that grip you from the very first page. *The Sialkot Saga* is one such book that hooks you from the start.' ~*Hindustan Times*

'There's never a dull moment in the book. In fact, the story takes on such a pace that the overwhelmed reader is compelled to put the book down and take a deep breath on many an occasion.' ~*The Financial Express*

'Sanghi weaves a masterpiece building up the readers' involvement in the novel with every turn of the page.' ~*The Pioneer*

Keepers of the Kalachakra **(2018)**

'The book can't be put down till all pieces of the jigsaw puzzle are put together.' ~*The Financial Express*

'The author packs a powerful punch ... spicy and saucy, a survey of the past and the present ... without a dull moment, without a dull page.' ~*The Sunday Standard*

'Science and spirituality collide in Ashwin Sanghi's latest thriller.' ~*India Today*

'Spread over a vast canvas, the novel has an engaging plot laced with mythology, history and legends.' ~*The Hindu*

'Ashwin Sanghi's *Keepers of the Kalachakra* is as explosive as a time bomb ticking in your hand. Every chapter springs an unpredictable surprise.' ~*Deccan Chronicle*

'*Keepers of the Kalachakra* has it all: political characters that remind you of real-life politicians, a racy, complex plot and enough improbable twists to keep you hooked.' ~*Hindustan Times Brunch*

***The Vault of Vishnu* (2020)**

'In an enthralling alchemy of myth and science, Ashwin Sanghi gives us the sixth book in his Bharat Collection. As with all of Ashwin's books, the research is meticulous and the technical(ese) leaves one gasping as *The Vault of Vishnu* takes the reader through the highs and lows of history, myth, physics, warfare technology, artificial intelligence and biochemistry.' ~*The Times of India*

'*The Vault of Vishnu*, like all of Ashwin's books, is a heady mix of history, myth, science and thrills.' ~*The Hindu*

'A very interesting and intriguing thriller, thanks to the author's storytelling gift and painstaking research on Hindu metaphysics.' ~*The New Indian Express*

'Sanghi's latest work uses his favourite tool—mythology—and blends it with history to deliver some edge-of-the-seat action.' ~*Hindustan Times*

***The Magicians of Mazda* (2022)**

'*The Magicians of Mazda* is a deft blend of imagination, history and thrills.' ~*Deccan Herald*

'An excellent cocktail of a thriller that has lessons for the present time too.' ~*The New Indian Express*

'Hold your hearts and reading glasses in place, readers! *The Magicians of Mazda* promises to be Sanghi's best thriller yet!' ~*The Times of India*

'Ashwin Sanghi has an extraordinary talent for bringing ancient wisdom alive, then whipping up a fast-paced thriller by blending fact with fiction ... he doesn't disappoint.' ~*Firstpost*

'Sanghi's fascinating style of storytelling ensures that readers find a comfort spot on the very edge of their seats.' ~*The Telegraph*

KEEPERS OF THE KALACHAKRA

ASHWIN SANGHI

An Imprint of HarperCollins *Publishers*

First published in 2018

Published in India by HarperCollins 2022

This edition published in India by Harper Fiction 2025
An imprint of HarperCollins *Publishers*
HarperCollins *Publishers* India, Cyber City,
Building 10-A, Gurugram, Haryana – 122002, India
www.harpercollins.co.in

2 4 6 8 10 9 7 5 3 1

P-ISBN: 978-93-5629-247-5
E-ISBN: 978-93-5629-248-2

Typeset by Art Works, Chennai

Printed and bound at
Thomson Press (India) Ltd

This book is produced from independently certified FSC® paper
to ensure responsible forest management.

HarperCollins *Publishers*, Macken House, 39/40 Mayor Street Upper,
Dublin 1, D01 C9W8, Ireland

Disclaimer

This is a work of fiction. All names, characters, organizations, incidents, dialogues, and locations—whether historical, mythological, political, religious, or contemporary—are either products of the author's imagination or used fictitiously in an artistic and narrative context. Any resemblance to actual persons, living or dead, or to actual events, places, or institutions is entirely coincidental and unintentional.

References to religious, historical, mythological, political, scientific, or cultural figures, scriptures, texts, places, doctrines, practices, or events are made solely to enhance the thematic and dramatic fabric of the story. These references are fictionalized, speculative, and interpretative in nature. The author explicitly disclaims any intention to assert, imply, or represent accuracy. These portrayals are not intended to question, challenge, endorse, criticize, or validate any faith, ideology, belief system, political viewpoint, or cultural position.

This book does not purport to present authoritative or scholarly perspectives on any field of study, including but not limited to: religion, mythology, theology, history, archaeology, science, anthropology, sociology, psychology, philosophy, literature, geopolitics, political science, military affairs, strategic studies, cultural studies, or jurisprudence. The contents are presented strictly as a fictional narrative and should not be interpreted otherwise.

All quotations, verses, and imagery—whether textual, visual, or symbolic—should be understood as narrative devices within the fictional structure of the book and not as accurate or authenticated references. Any resemblance to real scripture, canonical text, or doctrinal literature is coincidental or creative in nature and does not reflect any claim to authenticity or endorsement.

Design elements such as internal images, section breaks, cover artwork, and maps, if included, are purely illustrative and are not intended to be geographically, historically, politically, or scientifically accurate.

Wherever appropriate, the author has provided notes, references, and citations at the end of the book for readers who may wish to explore contextual inspirations. These references are intended solely for background interest and are not necessary for the understanding or enjoyment of the story. The author makes no representations or warranties as to the accuracy, reliability, completeness, or credibility of any such sources, and disclaims all responsibility for how they are interpreted or used by readers.

The author unequivocally disclaims any and all liability—legal, civil, criminal, or reputational—arising from interpretations, misinterpretations, or actions based on this work of fiction. Readers are strongly advised to treat all content in this book as fictional and to exercise discretion in drawing conclusions or forming opinions based on this work.

ॐ पूर्णमदः पूर्णमिदं पूर्णात्पुर्णमुदच्यते
पूर्णस्य पूर्णमादाय पूर्णमेवावशिष्यते
ॐ शान्तिः शान्तिः शान्तिः

Om poornam-adah poornam-idam
Poornaat-poornam-udachyate
Poornasya poornam-aadaaya
Poornam-eva-avashissyate
Om shaantih shaantih shaantih

That is infinite
And *this* is infinite
From *that* comes *this*
If *this* is added or subtracted from *that*
That still remains infinite
Om! Peace! Peace! Peace!

—*Brihadaranyaka Upanishad* and *Ishavasya Upanishad*

Prologue

The last week of February

The young man lay on the floor, reaching helplessly for his left arm with his right. His howls were like those of an injured animal. Surrounding him were officers of the WHMU, the White House Medical Unit, as also agents from the Secret Service. Standing still, some distance away, was the President himself. The goggle-eyed guests who had been invited to the state dinner at the White House were ushered out with a minimum of fuss from the State Dining Room and into the adjoining Red Room. The support staff was at its efficient best, although no one knew what the hell was going on. The most they could conclude was that Jean Belanger, the Prime Minister of Canada, was in a bad way.

A medic held a cotton swab to Belanger's mouth as he coughed. There was blood in his sputum. Even in his semi-comatose state, Belanger felt a maddening urge to scratch his left arm, to rip his own skin off. One of the nurses from the medical team quickly snipped off his jacket and shirt to expose the arm that seemed to be causing all the trouble. And that's when they saw it.

It was a dark red and was twice the size of his other arm. All over his skin were scarlet blisters, pustules that oozed a strange mixture of blood and watery plasma.

'I think he's been poisoned,' said the WHMU Director, a man also designated as Physician to the President. 'There's no time to lose. His heart rate is rapidly dropping!'

Upon a nod, the Director's assistant hurried over with a defibrillator. 'Charge it to two hundred joules,' ordered the Director.

'Yes, sir,' answered the assistant, kneeling on the floor next to Belanger. He applied two gel pads, one on Belanger's upper chest, below the right clavicle, and the second below his left nipple. Pressing the paddles firmly onto the gel pads, he applied twenty-five pounds of pressure.

'All clear!' he shouted as he depressed the shock button on the paddles. Belanger's body jolted as the current hit. The Director stared at the monitor, hoping for a stable rhythm.

And then, Belanger retched. The vomit splattered over his tuxedo, trickled down and was slowly absorbed by the thick pile of the pale blue wool carpet on the State Dining Room floor. 'We must shift him to Bethesda immediately,' said the Director. He stole a glance at the President to seek his concurrence. The President nodded wordlessly.

Within seconds, an Air Force chopper landed on the helipad in the South Lawn and Belanger was efficiently shifted into it. As he was being slid in, the Director saw the next telltale sign.

Belanger's face, like his arm, was now severely swollen, but on the right side. It had ballooned to the extent that his right eye was no longer visible. The Director quickly got into the helicopter along with other medics. In the distance, he could see men dressed in bio-hazard suits running across the lawn towards the White House. They were carrying canisters of chlorine dioxide to fumigate some areas. They had to keep in mind the possibility that anthrax had been used. Belanger's symptoms of nausea, blisters, swelling and shortness of breath were similar to the effects of anthrax poisoning, but no one could be sure.

As the chopper took off, the Director glanced through the window at the President who was standing in his white-tie get-up on the South Lawn, his jet-black hair blown awry by the whirling rotors.

He was intently observing the helicopter as it lifted off the ground.

The twenty-four hours prior to Belanger's arrival had been utterly manic in the West Wing. The President, in his trademark style, had wanted to cancel the official programme. It was his way of announcing: 'Screw you, world. I'm the President of the United States of America and I can do whatever I want. And that includes cancelling a state dinner that has been fixed weeks in advance.'

The President had held office for just a month. And what a tumultuous month it had been, although none of those who had supported him had expected otherwise. Only a few deluded souls had expected him to change his ways after winning.

'Why the fuck am I meeting this bleeding-heart liberal?' he had asked, strutting around the Oval Office. He was fit for a man of sixty, and always impeccably dressed and groomed. His sharp features and lean frame gave him a bit of the look of a hawk, particularly when he put his glasses on his nose to read. But then, hawkish behaviour in politics could be a strategic advantage.

'An understanding and an alliance with Belanger would give more credibility to your executive actions, Mr President,' replied his Secretary of State. He was the second person to occupy the post in the thirty-odd days of the present administration. The first had been fired by the President within ten days. The current Secretary of State was constantly aware that he could meet a similar fate. He strained at every nerve to convince the President of the desperate need to keep the official programme intact.

'My voters don't need further proof of my credibility,' the President shot back. 'It's only those bastards—the left wing media and the peddlers of fake news—that are baying for my blood, because that's their fucking job. God knows they have little else to do.'

He was entitled to his opinions. This was a man who had won the elections against all contrary predictions by pollsters and media pundits, leaving each of them with egg on their faces. He was arrogant, brash and politically incorrect, and those were precisely the reasons why he had won.

During his first month in office he had placed curbs on Muslim immigration, doubled defence spending, pooh-poohed climate change prophecies, reviewed and reversed international alliances, taken steps to cut taxes, and fired several more people along the way.

When it had been nervously pointed out to him that he was creating enemies, the President had replied, 'Churchill once said that if you have enemies it indicates that you've stood up for something, sometime in your life.'

'But you have four years as President,' argued the Secretary of State, 'all the time in the world to make enemies. Why the impatience?' He bit his lip, worried that he had gone too far.

'I don't need four years to set things right,' said the President emphatically. 'Just one year, and I will have cleaned up the mess my predecessor left behind. By that time, no one will need any more convincing.'

'And that's the reason you need the Prime Minister of Canada on your side,' explained his Secretary of State. 'You are seen as far-right, and many people hold that against you. In popular perception, the only global counterweight to you is this man, Jean Belanger. He's the youngest Canadian Prime Minister ever. He also oozes charm—the world's female population is swooning all over him. It would be a publicity coup for you.'

'I hate what he stands for,' said the President, smoothing his perfectly parted black hair. He knew that Belanger had far better looks. He did not like the idea of standing next to him and falling short in anyone's opinion. He hunted quickly for a point of attack, and came up with one. 'He's soft on immigration and terrorism. He's a fucking idealist,' he said with satisfaction.

'I know, but you do need him.'

'Why?'

'Because, globally, he is the last liberal left standing. Everyone else seems to be either irrelevant or…'

'Or?' asked the President icily.

'Dead.'

The State Dining Room was the larger of the two banquet halls on the State Floor of the White House. The previous First Lady had personally looked into its refurbishment and a massive new carpet covering twelve hundred square feet had been installed to match the design of the ceiling. The room could seat up to a hundred and forty people, but the dinner organized for Belanger had been for only thirty-four. The President had decided to limit the guest list to selected diplomats and certain members of his Cabinet, Senators and Congressmen.

The Belangers arrived in a motorcade from Blair House. The President stood at the North Portico along with his wife, the perfect political spouse with a suitably aristocratic lineage. The First Couple waited to greet Prime Minister Jean Belanger and his simply yet elegantly dressed wife. After a brief slowing down in the formal welcome, glittering with photo-ops, the other First Couple were escorted to the Yellow Oval Room for the reception.

Reception concluded, the two couples walked down the Grand Staircase where the United States Marine Band stood at attention. The routine was predictable: *Hail to the Chief* followed by the Canadian national anthem, *O Canada*, and ending with the *Star-Spangled Banner*. Finally, they headed down Cross Hall and into the State Dining Room where a five-course meal awaited them.

The President rose to deliver a short welcome address. As usual, he ignored the text that had been painstakingly prepared by his staff. Deviating from the norm was this President's norm. The problem was that he always managed to create a crisis with his off-the-cuff remarks. It was almost as though he went searching for minefields that he could step on.

Today was different, though. He was like a well-behaved schoolboy. Although he departed from the written address, he said nothing that could be considered controversial. 'And in conclusion, I would like to say that my wife and I are deeply honoured by the visit of Prime Minister Belanger and his lovely wife. The United States of America and Canada stand together and our friendship shall strengthen and endure.' There was applause, mostly emanating from immense relief that nothing contentious had been said.

Then Jean Belanger stood up to deliver his speech. 'Thank you, Mr President, for the gracious welcome that you have accorded us. At heart I am a liberal. I believe in the value of democracy, freedom of speech, and the equality of genders. I believe that no person should be discriminated against on the basis of race, religion or sexual orientation…'

He paused. The audience assumed that he simply needed a few seconds to collect his thoughts. Belanger reached for the glass of water before him with trembling hands. He continued, shakily. 'B-but there is an unhappy thing, too, that we agree on ... th-that we live in a dangerous world. One in which innocent lives are lost daily. It has to be our mutual resolve to leave this w-world a better and safer place for our ch-ch-children...'

Sweat was pouring down his face. His eyes had taken on a glazed look and his eyeballs seemed to be rolling back. He swayed a little. And then he fell backwards, toppling his chair over as he went down. There was a collective gasp from the assembled guests.

Luckily, the mottled blue carpet installed by the previous First Lady absorbed the impact of his fall.

The Walter Reed National Military Medical Center, located in Bethesda, Maryland, was abuzz, given the profile of its latest patient. The hospital was renowned for the number of famous people who had been treated there. The staff had long grown used to the arrival of powerful people. John F. Kennedy had been rushed there after his assassination. Ronald Reagan had undergone surgery for his prostate cancer at Walter Reed. George Bush had been taken there for treatment of his atrial fibrillation. But the arrival of any President or foreign head of state in critical condition was always a cause for madness to prevail.

The WHMU Director quickly briefed the doctors as Belanger was wheeled into the Intensive Care Unit. 'His pulse is erratic, his left arm and the right side of his face are swollen. He has developed bright red pustules on his arm and his heart rate has been in decline. He's thrown up several times. We've taken blood samples during the chopper ride. How quickly can you get me a toxicity report?'

'It's done,' said the senior pathologist on the scene. The newest machines at Bethesda spat out such reports almost instantly. 'It's crazy but he has all the symptoms of snakebite. But there aren't any snakes in the White House and there is absolutely no poison in his system.'

No snakes in the White House? wondered the WHMU Director. *I'm not sure the President would agree. He seems to think that everyone around him bears shades of the reptilian.*

'I have bad news and worse news,' said the young US Navy Commander who was also the on-duty doctor at the ICU. 'Which will it be?' he asked as he scanned the reports.

The WHMU Director brusquely replied, 'Both!'

'The bad news is that his kidneys seem to be shutting down for no apparent reason. The worse news is that intravascular coagulation has begun impeding his blood circulation. If we do not figure out a course of treatment, he will soon go into coma.'

The words, 'Death will inevitably follow', were left unsaid.

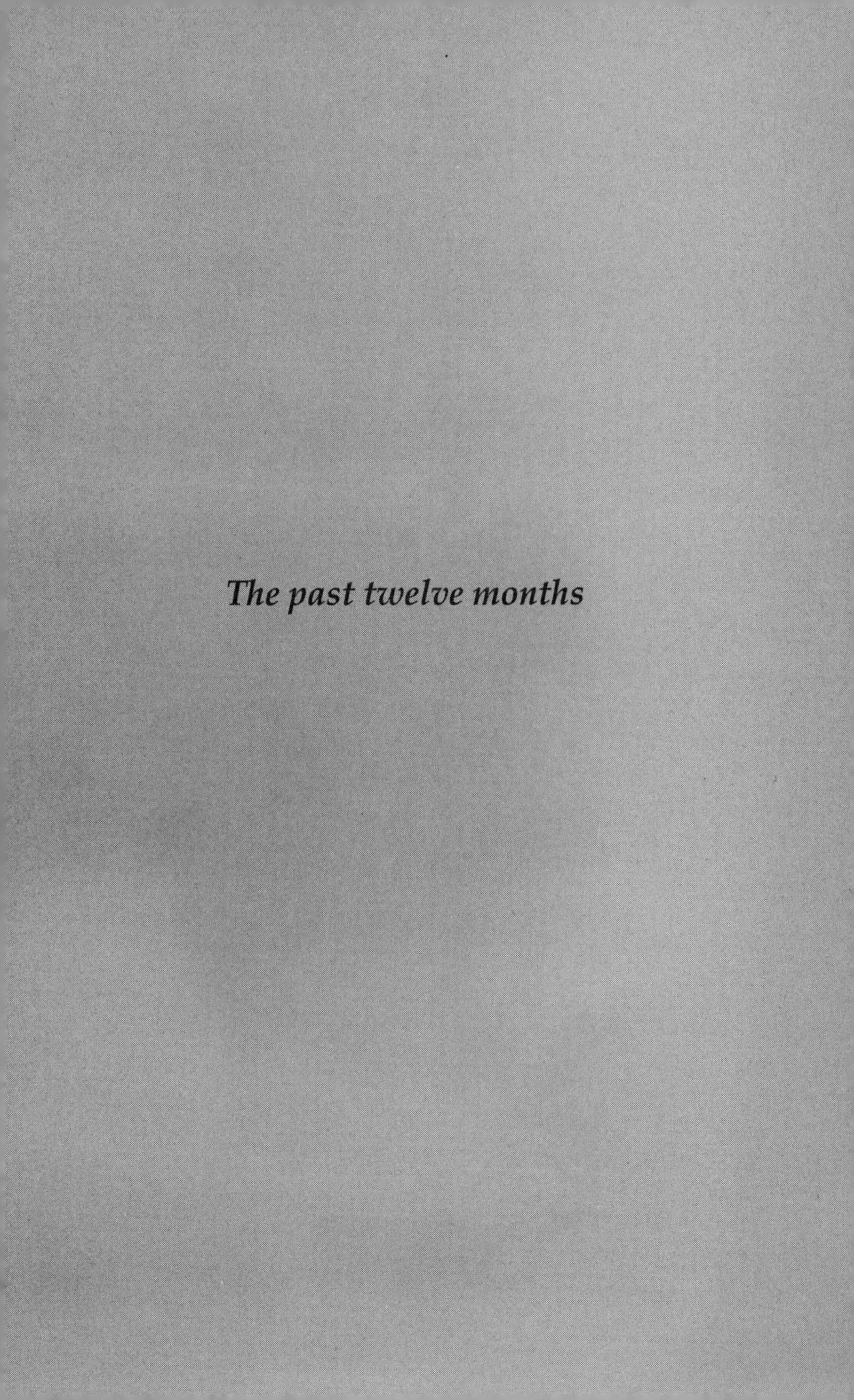

The past twelve months

1

The room was ordinary and windowless, and its walls had been painted bluish-green. The air-conditioning hummed softly to keep out the heat of the Jordanian desert. In the centre of the room was a round conference table surrounded by four hardback chairs. On the table were cups, the coffee half-consumed, water bottles and sandwich wrappers. By way of routine, the first ten minutes had been devoted to sweeping the room for listening devices.

The four people seated around the table seemed a strange assortment. In ordinary course, they would probably never have socialized with one another. Judith Frost was a CIA operative, Yuri Petrov was on deputation from Russia's SVR—the Sluzhba Vneshney Razvedki, Rakesh Sharma was from India's Research and Analysis Wing, or RAW, and Jin Zhang represented China's Ministry of State Security, the MSS.

But the combination wasn't that odd, when one considered the reasons for the existence of the group, informally christened IG4.

Meeting locations of IG4 were never constant. The four members travelled around the world to secret rendezvous points that were usually fixed just a day or two in advance. This time, it was the capital city of Jordan, Amman.

In her early fifties, Judith was considered one of the best counter-terrorism experts in the world. She was dressed simply in beige slacks and a linen top. Thin rimless glasses sat unobtrusively on her pert nose. Her tightly tied-back hair gave her a somewhat schoolmarmish look.

A large, flat-screen monitor had been mounted on a wall and hooked up to a high-encryption notebook computer. Judith tapped a key on the computer to bring up a slide that showed photographs of three people.

'So here's our list,' she began. 'The British Foreign Secretary, the German Chancellor and the American Attorney-General. All three have died within a period of two months.'

She paused to get her thoughts in order. 'Now, let's quickly review what we know. In all three instances there were no security breaches. Symptoms *did* appear but they disappeared just as quickly. By the time these people died, there was nothing to suggest anything other than death by natural causes. What was particularly strange was that all three individuals were young and healthy, and did not have any serious medical ailments to speak of.'

She took a sip of water from the bottle in front of her and continued. 'The truly odd angle in this story is that the symptoms prior to death of each of these three people were almost identical. Swelling of one or more of the limbs or face, severe rash, vomiting, reduced heart rate, shutting down of the kidneys, intravascular coagulation, and finally, coma. Almost all the symptoms one would see in cases of poisoning. Except for one thing. None of them had been poisoned.'

Rakesh Sharma from RAW spoke. Sharma had originally been an army man who was subsequently absorbed by military intelligence and then RAW. His bearing and demeanour were those of a man brought up in the armed forces. His bushy moustache and impeccably knotted regiment tie were dead giveaways. Tall, fair and with an imposing hooked nose, Sharma automatically commanded the attention of those around him. The only part about Sharma that could not be discerned, unless one looked very closely, was a prosthetic leg, a legacy of the Kargil War.

'Having one or two symptoms that match could be passed off as coincidence,' said Sharma. 'But so many commonalities and that too across powerful political leaders? All within a few months? These cannot be swept aside as coincidence.'

Judith nodded in agreement. 'Let's keep one more detail in mind. Each of the three individuals was surrounded by several layers of security. It would have been exceptionally difficult for anyone to breach the protective ring around these leaders. Assassination was almost impossible. Their autopsies did not show needle marks or ingestion of toxic substances. In fact, pathology reports showed no toxicity at all.'

'We need to think beyond such commonalities,' interjected Yuri Petrov as he drained his coffee cup. 'What we need to find out is what links these people together other than the symptoms of a disease. If we find the link between these three leaders, we will be closer to figuring out what actually happened.'

Petrov was a beefy man who looked like he worked out at the gym for several hours each day. On his head was a mop of reddish hair that seemed to be thinning in places. His red hair contrasted with his eyes, which were bright blue, an extremely rare combination.

Petrov was the youngest in the room but possibly the most powerful among the four. The Russian SVR was dominated by men whose fathers and grandfathers had been operatives in the erstwhile KGB. Petrov was an exception. He had proved himself to be incredibly adept in negotiating anti-terror alliances. He had also managed to make himself indispensable during Russia's annexation of the Crimea. It was whispered in the corridors of power that he had access to the President of the Russian Federation through his immediate boss at the SVR.

Petrov lit up his Belomorkanal, ignoring the dirty look that Judith threw his way. 'Let's examine their finances, marriages, political connections, friendships, business dealings, enemies, sexual liaisons, travel schedules, legal disputes and everything else that bears scrutiny,' said Petrov. 'That's the only way we will find the elusive link.'

'It's like searching for a needle in a haystack,' said Zhang, adjusting his thin, metal-framed glasses. He was a petite man, always perfectly groomed and attired, his black hair neatly gelled back to reveal a wide forehead.

'Correction,' said Judith. 'It's one needle hidden among millions of haystacks.'

Petrov was quiet. He knew that a meeting with the Director of the SVR was in order.

2

Vijay Sundaram walked towards his lecture hall on the sprawling 325-acre campus.

Located in Hauz Khas, a prime South Delhi locality, the IIT Delhi campus boasted abundant lawns, generous residential facilities and wide roads. The Indian Institutes of Technology, or IITs, were the most sought-after universities in India. Among the twenty-three IITs scattered around India, IIT Delhi was one of the best. The leading global technology giants recruited engineers from here for jobs around the world.

Vijay sighed as he made his way in the blazing hot sun across the campus. He was deep in thought. Twenty-eight years old, he had never acquired a taste for appearances. He was habitually unkempt, his shirt hung sacklike on his thin frame while even his glasses looked like they hadn't been cleaned in days. His hair was speckled with dandruff and his shoes seemed like they would give up on him at any moment. Luckily for Vijay, his endearing smile, deep, penetrating eyes and caring nature compensated for everything else about him.

In short, his awkward looks were irrelevant. Vijay had just been awarded his PhD by IIT Delhi. It had been a slow and painful seven years to earn his doctorate, significantly longer than the average five. For a boy who had been brought up in an orphanage in Sringeri, a sleepy town in the south Indian state of Karnataka, the mere fact that he had presented a thesis was an achievement, let alone that it had been hailed as path-breaking within academic circles. It was testament to his brilliance and perseverance.

But the appearance of the end of the long road to his PhD was troubling Vijay. It implied the end of IIT life and the beginning of what Indian parents liked to call 'settling down'.

And then there was Sujatha.

In recent weeks, she had been dropping hints about their getting married. There was a part of Vijay that wanted to be with Sujatha for the rest of his life. And another part that wanted to run away. Hence Vijay's incessant sighs these days.

He felt his phone vibrate. He fished it out of his pocket and looked at the screen with a quiet smile of satisfaction. Milesian Labs. Probably calling about his job interview the next day. He took the call as he walked towards his final lecture.

Maybe the call would decide things for him.

3

Vijay Sundaram surveyed the classroom. It was packed to capacity. Vijay was one of the most popular teachers at IIT Delhi and among the youngest. The minimum requirement for teaching was a PhD, but the university had made an incredible exception for Vijay. He had been allowed to teach while working towards his doctorate. Teaching enabled him to meet his expenses while he continued with his research, but all that would soon be coming to an end.

'During this academic year,' began Vijay, 'I have taken you through the fundamentals of quantum theory. Given that today is my final lecture here, I thought that I should find a way to give you a different perspective on what we have learned.'

Vijay took off his glasses and used his handkerchief to wipe them, something he hadn't done in days. His students grinned.

Vijay put on his glasses again and continued. 'How many of you are familiar with *Vedanta*?' Only a few hands went up. Less than 10 per cent of the class.

'The word "Vedanta" literally means "the end of the Vedas", the oldest scriptures of Hindus,' explained Vijay. 'Originally, Vedanta meant the *Upanishads*, but eventually the definition was expanded to include the *Brahmasutras* and the *Srimad Bhagvatam*.'

There was silence in the class as his students attempted to understand where he was going with this. 'While quantum physics and Vedanta may seem poles apart, the truth is, both are attempts to understand the underlying reality of the universe,' continued Vijay. 'We refer to quantum physics as science and Vedanta as philosophy, but they are one and the same. From Aristotle all the way to the nineteenth century, the term "natural philosophy" was used instead of science. There was a reason for it. A good scientist has to be a philosopher and a good philosopher must also be a scientist.'

His students were all ears. This was not part of the curriculum, but they knew that the knowledge Vijay was imparting to them that day was priceless.

'Physics, as we know, can be studied in two phases: classical and quantum,' said Vijay. 'Sandwiched between the two is Einstein's Theory of Relativity. Isaac Newton is the starting point of classical physics, which focuses on macro objects and the rules that govern them. An example: for every action in nature there is an equal and opposite reaction. But Newton's classical laws were never concerned with atomic and sub-atomic. Classical physics believed that the world was little more than a machine and that all motions of various objects within this machine could be predicted by classical laws already in place.'

He paused to take a deep breath.

'The world of classical physics was turned upside down with discoveries in the twentieth century,' said Vijay. 'At a sub-atomic level, classical laws did not seem to work. One needed an entirely new set of laws. This led to the development of quantum physics.'

'The double-slit experiment,' said one of his students excitedly.

Vijay smiled. It was always nice to see enthusiasm. 'Precisely. In 1801, Thomas Young showed that light was a wave. In his experiment, he placed a light source at one end and a photographic plate at the other. Between the two was a barrier with two slits. Can someone please tell us what happened?'

A young man in the front row got up and spoke. 'Our natural instinct tells us that we should see two bands on the receiving photographic plate. Instead multiple bands are observed—an interference pattern. This shows that light is a wave, not particle.'

'Thank you,' said Vijay, bringing up a slide that showed the experiment on a roll-down screen next to the blackboard.

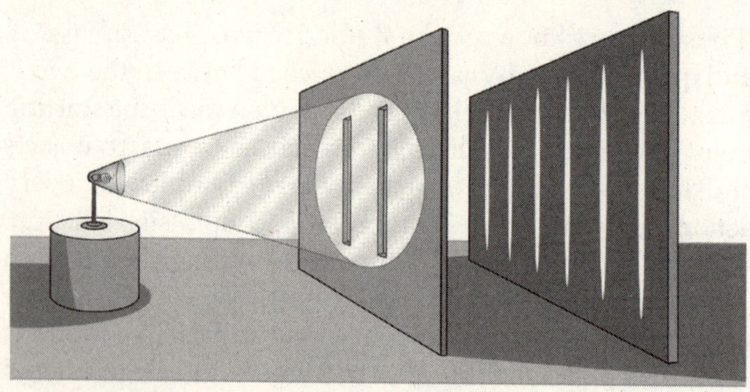

'Now can someone tell us how Einstein's discovery in 1905 ran contrary to this notion?' asked Vijay.

Several students put up their hands. Vijay chose a young lady in the third row.

'Einstein shone a light on photoconductive metal and found that it emerged on the other side of the metal as packets of fixed energy—photons,' she said. 'He concluded that light is a particle, not a wave.'

'What is light then?' asked Vijay. 'Wave or particle?'

'Both,' said the young lady. 'If we carry out the slit experiment with one slit instead of two, we find that light is received on the photographic plate as a single band. In this case, light behaves like particles. But with two slits, it behaves like waves.'

'Thanks,' said Vijay, clicking to the next slide that showed the single-slit experiment.

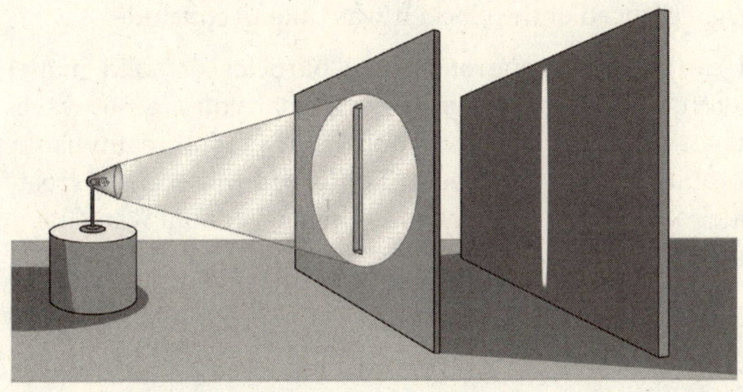

'So there is something that controls the way that light behaves. It sometimes behaves like waves and sometimes as particles. What determines its behaviour? That is the starting point of quantum physics. Now let us fast-forward to 1923. That was when the physicist Louis de Broglie theorized that not only light but *all matter* must have both wave and particle properties. The tree in your backyard may seem more particle-*ish* but it would necessarily have a wavelength. Six years later, Louis de Broglie won the Nobel Prize for this insight.'

Vijay quickly did a scan of the faces in the classroom. Not a single bored expression.

'Now what does Vedanta say?' asked Vijay. 'Vedanta tells us about *vrittis*. Anyone here who knows what those are?'

There was silence.

'Vritti literally translates to a mind wave,' said Vijay. 'I will not get into the details of the types of vrittis, but it is sufficient to know that these mind waves create the objects that we observe in our world.'

'Surely you mean *observe* the objects, not *create*?'

'It is our very act of observation that makes waves into objects,' said Vijay. 'And *that* is at the core of Vedanta.'

Vijay glanced at the clock. It was time to conclude.

'I can see each one of you as particles or solid matter before me, but how can I be sure that you are not waves when I turn my back on you? What we call reality is the combination of observer and observed. We seem to create our reality and that is precisely what Vedanta wants us to understand.'

4

Vijay left the classroom and headed to the main gate. There were hundreds of little errands that he needed to complete as part of his exit from IIT. He remained lost in his thoughts as he mentally ticked off points on a checklist. He watched a student sharing lunch with his parents under a tree. He tore away his gaze and moved on.

Vijay had no clue of who his parents were. He had been found abandoned on the steps of the Sringeri Sharada temple in Karnataka. The local police had placed him in an orphanage affiliated to the trust that managed the temple. The administrator of the trust was Mrs Srinivasulu Laxminarayana Venkata Rao. Because no one could really remember her name—leave alone roll it off their tongues—people simply called her Amma. She was a gentle lady who had overseen the passage of hundreds of children to and from the doors of her establishment.

The trust not only ran the temple and the orphanage next door but also a school and a charitable hospital. Amma herself had remained childless and came to view each child in the orphanage as her own. Each new entrant was randomly assigned a name and surname upon school admission. So each child knew he had an identity, just like everyone else in the world. His had been Vijay Sundaram. Amma had a secret place in her heart for the bright-eyed Vijay, but none of the children would know the difference. They all knew they were not destitutes cast on the dustheaps of the world, but beloved children who received the best attention to their health and education.

Vijay shared a dormitory with sixty other boys. A separate dorm accommodated the girls. The children led a busy and disciplined life and they were well looked after, with three square meals a day, clean clothes and a solid roof over their heads. The charitable hospital next door saw to their mildest discomforts, and a propitious outbreak of measles or chicken pox was cause for celebration because it meant a break from classes, fistfuls of grapes and rowdy games of carrom—all within wistful distance from their not-so-stricken friends. Their routine was hectic: early morning prayers, exercise, school, sports, homework and chores—with some laughter in between. Vijay was a loner, preferring to keep to himself, but distinguished himself through his academic performance, which was always stellar. It became evident early enough that he was destined for a career in science.

During his seventh standard exams, his mathematics paper included the question: 'Indicate which of the following statements are either true or false'. Vijay's answer was a single line that indicated his almost intuitive grasp of grammar as well: '*All* of the statements are either true or false.' He then proceeded to provide the usually expected answers overleaf.

Amma had a set of bookshelves in her office. Books donated by patrons of the temple were kept there and made available to the children. Amma was particular that the books be treated well and returned to her bookshelf within a reasonable period. Among the children, Vijay was the most frequent visitor to her office. He would often devour a book within a day and return the next day for replenishment. In the beginning, Amma often wondered whether he actually read the books that he borrowed.

A day after he had returned a book about the Big Bang, she asked him, 'Do you recall when the Big Bang started?'

Vijay knew the answer. '132, Amma,' he replied confidently.

132? That answer makes no sense, thought Amma.

After Vijay left, Mrs Rao leafed through the book to look for a clue to his strange reply to a question about what happened 13.8 billion years ago. Mrs Rao was confused. *Why had Vijay said '132'?*

Then her gaze travelled to the bottom of the page. It was page 132. The boy's memory took snapshots without cease, continuously camera-ready.

5

The Sringeri Sharada temple was famous for an ancient geometrical design called the Sri Yantra that had been installed there in the eighth century by one of Hinduism's most famous thinkers, Adi Shankaracharya. It consisted of nine perfectly interlocking triangles, with four of them pointing up and five pointing down. While many people could draw the design using various tools, most of them got it wrong. The Sri Yantra at Sringeri was considered to be one of the perfect examples of sacred geometry. Vijay would spend hours gazing at it.

One day Amma asked him whether he could draw the design. Vijay quickly drew a perfect Sri Yantra from memory, marking the key fifty-four points of intersection, something that even mathematicians could rarely achieve freehand.

6

A languid lake bordered the school and the children would often swim there during their free time. Vijay loved breasting the water and became a good swimmer.

One day, he noticed a girl of his age playing in the water with her friends. They were ducking each other into the water. Vijay watched with amusement until he realized that the girl had not reappeared above the surface. He jumped into the lake without a second thought, sliced through the water and emerged a minute later with her struggling in his arms.

After she had recovered, spluttering out the last of the water she had taken in, he asked her name.

'Sujatha,' she said shyly, grateful for what Vijay had done. 'Sujatha Iyer.'

7

The hotel in Manhattan had been lit up like a Christmas tree. It was top-billing night at the hotel, with a wedding, birthday party and a business conference all happening on the same day in various select public spaces. The hotel had 100 per cent room occupancy and the staff were putting in double shifts to cope. The hotel's General Manager was all over the place, ensuring that the guests were well looked after.

The main ballroom was stuffed to capacity and the band was in full form. The waiters and the guests had to literally shout to make themselves heard above the din. No one noticed the lone figure wearing an oversized blue blazer and shuffling his way towards the dance floor up front.

Suddenly, there was a dazzling burst of light, followed a nano-second after by a deafening blast. Then there came the low rumble of everything crashing to the ground—the walls and ceilings included. It was like a massive shockwave that dominoed down the entire hotel, shaking it to its very foundations. In the ballroom, the floor collapsed while the plate glass windows overlooking the street were blown out. The piteous screams that followed begged to be heard over the clamour. The suicide bomber in the blue blazer had tightly packed ball bearings, nails and crushed razor blades around the explosive material. These lethal bits of metal zipped through the hotel like supercharged projectiles, tearing through flesh and instantly killing or grievously wounding anyone in their trajectory.

Police and rescue workers landed up soon enough, but they were greeted by hundreds of corpses—bodies flung great distances, torsos with heads or limbs missing, and hideous chunks of melting human flesh. The first priority of the new arrivals was to locate survivors, people who had been knocked unconscious or were trapped under falling concrete. In parallel, they needed to ensure that there were no more timed devices in the area. It would be another twenty-four hours before the total count of dead and wounded would emerge.

The cold numbers came to 163 dead and over 200 wounded. It was one of the deadliest attacks since 9/11.

8

Abu Ahmed al-Mafraqi was dressed in sandals and a pilgrim's *ihram*—two pieces of white seamless cloth, one tied around his waist and reaching below his knees, the other draped over his left shoulder and knotted at the right side. His dark eyes framed by bushy eyebrows, and his black beard interlaced with streaks of white completed his look of sacrosanct authority.

Earlier that morning, he had washed, prayed and consumed a simple breakfast from the tent's buffet along with his companions, appreciating the sense of brotherhood that this communal eating afforded him. He had declined the offer of a swanky $2,700-room overlooking the Kaaba.

What was the point of performing Hajj as though it were a designer holiday?

It was the largest annual gathering of human beings and, for the moment, Mafraqi blended with the three million other pilgrims to the Hajj in the last month of the Islamic calendar. But he wasn't any other pilgrim. The Mabahith, the Saudi secret police, was keeping a close eye on him.

He was on his seventh and final *tawaf* circuit around the Kaaba, having effortlessly done the first three at a nimble clip as required by tradition, and slowing down for the next four. The crowds respectfully made way for the distinguished figure in their midst when he bent down during each circuit to kiss the black stone. Around him, his security detail also performed the tawaf in sync. Accompanying him was Habib bin-Wadih, his second-in-command.

Tawaf completed, the men prayed at the Muqam Ibrahim and made their way to drink water from the Zamzam well. Refreshed, they walked back and forth seven times between the hills of Safa and Marwah, close to the Kaaba. It was a comfortable walk because the entire stretch was now enclosed by the Masjid al-Haram mosque, accessed through air-conditioned tunnels. It was a respite from the forty-eight-degree heat of Mecca.

They headed back towards their tents to rest before embarking on the remaining stops on the Hajj route—Mina, Arafat, Muzdalifah and Jamarat. As they walked, Mafraqi turned to Habib.

'The timing is auspicious,' he said in a low tone. 'Our brother in New York has done us proud. After this Hajj is over, we will ensure that every Muslim brother around the world will rise up and defeat the Kafirs. This will, insha'Allah, lead to a golden age of the *umma* living under Sharia!'

'Khalifat Rasul Allah,' began Habib hesitantly. The title simply acknowledged that Mafraqi was already viewed as caliph by millions of Muslims around the world. 'What about those countries in which the majority is non-Muslim?'

'There are only two types of countries in the world,' said Mafraqi. 'The first fall under Dar al-Islam, or where Muslims rule under Sharia.'

'And the other?' asked Habib—a little unnecessarily, everyone knew the answer—because the boss liked to intone platitudes.

'Dar al-Harb, or lands of war, where we need to fight to establish Muslim dominance. Islam took over Mecca, Medina, Jerusalem and Constantinople. Rome is the last bastion. It shall eventually be the capital of my caliphate.'

'But we have many Muslims around the world who do not think alike,' said Habib. 'Our brothers living in America, England, France and Belgium have adopted new habits and rules. Many of them have become *murtadd*!' Apostates!

'It is their foolish desire to assimilate,' said Mafraqi. 'They want to be more like their hosts. To fit in! But what will happen when their hosts turn against them? They will have no alternative but to return to their Muslim roots. That is what we must accelerate!'

9

Mafraqi had been born in the city of Mafraq. Alim, for that was what he was originally called, had been a difficult child. His parents were ordinary working-class Jordanians; his father a municipal engineer and his mother a devoted housewife whose entire life was spent looking after the nine children she had borne her husband. Alim was the youngest.

The family lived in a derelict house that overlooked a garbage dump. It was the dump that became Alim's introduction to drugs, alcohol and crime. Alim dropped out of school and then succeeded in getting himself sacked from the job that his father had arranged for him. But he excelled in his chosen career as a street Arab instead. He rapidly progressed from petty theft to vandalism to drug-dealing and then eventually to rape and murder—none of these traceable to him. The feats of violence, which made him a byword in the small and secret criminal world he inhabited, included slashing the face of an old man for rebuking his ways, brutally sodomizing a boy till he haemorrhaged to death, and his indescribable cruelties to the hookers he pimped for.

And then something changed.

A new preacher moved into the neighbourhood and arranged for Alim—just the right age and with no known record of misbehaviour—to marry his niece. He nudged Alim towards religious classes at the local mosque, convinced that the young man would find role models in such places. The strategy worked like a miracle. Alim gave up drugs and booze and delved into Islamic studies with all the zeal that he had once reserved for crime. He became a permanent fixture at Qur'an discussions and prayer meetings. He eagerly consumed all propaganda videos and audio recordings of speeches relating to Afghanistan, Bosnia, Palestine, Kashmir, Xinjiang and Chechnya. When the imam asked for volunteers to fight the communists who were attacking Muslim brothers in Afghanistan, Alim's was the first hand that went up.

He reached the Afghanistan–Pakistan border a month later, just in time to be part of the action to drive the Soviets out for good. His bravery on the battlefield was often mistaken for foolhardiness, but it always seemed to work. It was as though he longed for death more than anything else.

Whenever he had free time, he would visit the mosques of Peshawar, usually moved to tears by the imam's sermons, fervently hoping for martyrdom one day.

10

By the time that Alim returned to Jordan a few years later, he was a battle-hardened mujahid whose mental circuits had been irreversibly altered by the Arab clerics of Peshawar. Alim found himself angry with the liberalism of Jordan. He hated the fact that women dressed however they wanted, that couples mixed freely at cinemas, that liquor stores and pimps flourished. The fact that he had once been part of that ecosystem only seemed to make him more determined to destroy it. Alim was convinced that divine intervention was possible. After all, a motley army of mujahids from Muslim lands had sent the Soviets packing. The very notion was unthinkable, unless one considered the Hand of God. If Allah led them towards that unbelievable victory in battle, why would He not help Alim establish a caliphate? One where His will would prevail?

Alim put together a plan to disrupt the Jordanian parliamentary elections, but there was an information leak. The notorious Mukhabarat, the Jordanian secret police, came knocking on his door and he was arrested along with seventeen others and taken to Al-Jafr prison, a fortress that lay in the middle of a searing hot and isolated baked-mud plateau. Not a blade of grass nor a human being was visible for miles around. It was the most dreadful place on earth. The prison was infamous. New inmates were routinely sodomized, administered electric shocks, burnt with cigarettes or suspended upside down from ceiling fans or hooks. Alim not only survived, he also became the undisputed leader among the inmates. He regularly led prayers, and his word was law.

Upon the death of the ailing King Hussein and the coronation of King Abdullah II, Alim was released along with two thousand other Jordanian prisoners, as part of a general amnesty. His group moved to a camp along the Iran–Iraq border from where they began plotting their next moves. They carried out petty terror attacks until the Americans handed them the perfect prize—the invasion of Iraq.

Alim undertook terror operations within occupied Iraq and caused massive losses for the Americans. During one particular operation, though, Alim was captured and he found himself in Abu Ghraib prison in Baghdad. He used it as a networking opportunity to expand the span of his web. He also let it slyly be known that he was descended from the Quraysh, the tribe of Prophet Muhammad.

By the time he emerged from Abu Ghraib, he was no longer Alim. His new name was Abu Ahmed al-Mafraqi. Instead of a trigger-happy thug, Mafraqi was now a soft-spoken teacher whose radical ideas had the devastating power of a thousand bombs.

One of the most short-sighted and self-destructive decisions that the American administration took was to disband the Iraqi army. The result was a quarter of a million unemployed Sunni fighters on the streets. Mafraqi capitalized on this. Thousands of former army officers joined him and brought with them millions of dollars' worth of equipment that they stole from army depots. The Americans helped things along by withdrawing prematurely from the mess that they had created.

The vacuum caused by American withdrawal provided the ideal environment for Mafraqi to flourish. He became notorious because of his ruthless terror attacks on almost everyone—Shia worshippers, personnel of the United Nations, even women and children. Captured prisoners would be crucified, flogged, stoned, drowned, skinned alive or set alight. Horrific videos were posted on the internet so that his macabre deeds could be viewed by everyone. It was shock and awe to the extreme.

Mafraqi became the most wanted terrorist on America's list and the authorities put a reward on his head. The unforeseen fallout was that Mafraqi's reputation surged and thousands of Sunni Muslims from around the world queued up to join him. His men cut wide swathes through Iraq and Syria, establishing their dream of a glorious caliphate on both sides of the Syria–Iraq border. It would only be a matter of time before Mafraqi was declared Caliph at the Great Mosque of al-Nuri in Mosul, having been duly elected by the *majlis al-shura*.

Mafraqi was certain the best was yet to come.

11

It was a clear day in Columbus, Ohio. More than fourteen thousand people were packed into the Greater Columbus Convention Center that had been decorated with balloons, bunting and posters of the candidate.

The crowd was restless. They had been waiting for over an hour for him. Suddenly, there was a roar of applause, as the candidate walked up to the lectern on the stage. He was wearing a dark blue suit with a golden-yellow tie. His black hair was perfectly parted and he was wearing rimless spectacles so he could read the teleprompter.

'Thank you, Columbus, for your very warm welcome. It's great to be in Ohio this afternoon,' he said, waving enthusiastically to the crowd.

'Today is a very important day on my campaign tour. It is the day I begin outlining my plans to make America secure. Our country has, in its great and valiant history, succeeded in erasing the evil designs of forces as malevolent as Fascism, Nazism and Communism. Today we are faced with a challenge that is far greater—yet another *-ism*. You know of what we speak—the hydra-headed monster of Islamism and terrorism. And let's call it what it is. It constitutes that most insidious threat to the home of the brave.'

The crowd was enthusiastic. It was refreshing to hear someone who wasn't afraid to give a monster its name.

'Just a few days ago, 163 Americans died in a New York hotel, in which another 200 were injured. Remember, ladies and gentlemen, that this incident is only one of many in a deadly pattern that started with 9/11. At that time, 3,000 were killed and 6,000 injured in one satanic swoop. They were our kin, our colleagues, our innocent civilians, people we loved, people who wanted nothing more in life than to work towards the safety of their families and the preservation of our hallowed shores.'

The orator paused for effect. 'And that was just the beginning, my friends,' he resumed with renewed energy, marking off his points on his fingertips. 'Since then, the Boston Marathon bombings wounded 264 people while another 14 blameless Americans were gunned down at an office party in San Bernardino at which 22 were injured. At the Pulse Nightclub in Orlando, 49 Americans were killed and another 53 were injured—it was the ghastliest mass shooting in America and the worst-ever attack on the LGBTQ community. Are we going to let all this continue?' He thumped the lectern in front of him in tandem with the applause and cries from the audience of, 'Never again, never again!'

The speaker decided it was time to address the wider audience television brought him. 'And the violence is not limited to America,' he began quietly, building up to a crescendo. 'In Mumbai, terrorists killed 164 people and wounded another 308 during a series of 12 coordinated shootings and bombings lasting 4 days. In Belgium, terrorists detonated a bomb inside Brussels airport killing 32 and injuring 340. Another crazy truck driver mowed down 12 and injured 56 in Berlin. In Bangladesh, 26 people were killed inside a café. *It never stops!*'

He took a much-needed gulp from the glass of water placed near him.

'In France, the office of the satirical newspaper *Charlie Hebdo* was attacked for publishing cartoons of the Prophet Mohammed. In that shocking blow to not only human life but to freedom of expression itself, 12 died and 11 were wounded. Later that year, terrorists went on a frenzied shooting spree in Paris that killed 130 people and wounded another 368. In the south of France, a terrorist mowed down 85 people and wounded 308 by simply and cold-bloodedly driving his truck into a crowd.'

The candidate's eyes swept over the assembled persons, which consisted of mostly blue-collar workers and white stay-at-home moms wearing t-shirts that had his name emblazoned on the front.

'Citizens of America, remember that those atrocities did not stop at killing and wounding. Children were kidnapped. Girls were sold into sexual slavery. Men and women were burned alive to the thrill of cheering multitudes. Crucifixions have been brought back as penal measures, in addition to beheadings, drowning and ritual disembowelling. Holy sites—ours, theirs—have been desecrated or bombed. Ethnic minorities have witnessed mass executions. Non-Muslim populations are being ethnically "cleansed".

'My friends, we will never again let such evil perpetuate itself. Nor can we let the vengeful ideology of radical

Islamism and its oppression of women, gays, apostates and non-believers be allowed to spread within our own borders. We must defeat this hateful ideology and the terrible creatures that it spawns. Just as we have exterminated such vermin in the past!'

There was a thunderous ovation and hoots of approval. One section of the audience began chanting his name. The candidate smiled and waited for the crowd to settle down. He had kept an important point till the last.

'There are political leaders in our country who wish to pussyfoot around the issue. They are unwilling to even name the enemy. They wish to close their eyes to the bloodshed that has been the direct result of this ideology. They mouth platitudes but are unwilling to call evil what it is.

'I stand before you today to tell you that enough is enough! I will not allow this to continue. If I am given a chance to serve as President of this great country, I will ensure that this threat is destroyed. Once and for all!'

The crowd went wild as he uttered those words. He was the messiah.

12

It was a serene setting. The monk was seated in a private garden in Dehradun, talking to an audience of around a hundred. People waited for weeks to attend one of his lectures because he usually remained isolated in meditation in the forests.

An elegant canopy shielded the attendees from the sun. Up front, a whiteboard and projection screen had been set up. A gentle breeze wafted through, bringing the scent of jasmine to the audience.

The monk was dressed in his usual saffron and vermillion robes. The expression on his face was one of immense calm. Everyone knew him as Brahmananda. On the table in front of him was a notebook covered in maroon fabric that went wherever he did. On its cover was a small embroidered lotus.

'Our Earth is 4,600 million years old,' he told his audience. 'Now let us imagine that those 4,600 million years are like the life of a forty-six-year-old woman. Each year of this woman's life represents 100 million years of Earth's existence.'

Some members of the audience tittered. No one had ever explained it like that to them before.

'By that arithmetic, animals appeared only during the last six years of this woman's life,' said the monk. 'And it was only a week ago that some apes began to take on human qualities. And taking it from there, it was just four hours ago that our own species, we homo sapiens, learned to hunt, gather and cultivate.' He smiled at the range of gob-smacked expressions. 'Isn't that amazing? But the one fact that should shock you is—'

The audience waited to hear more startling facts from Brahmananda.

'—that we started maintaining some semblance of historical records only during the last ten minutes,' he said. 'In that sense, our written record of history is pathetic and we only have scattered records for the last ten minutes of the forty-six years that Earth has been around.'

A well-dressed lady in the front row raised her hand.

'Yes?' asked Brahmananda, encouragingly.

'Isn't it possible that what we know is *all* that there is to know?' she asked.

The monk got up from his chair and walked to the whiteboard. He picked up a marker and drew a diagram.

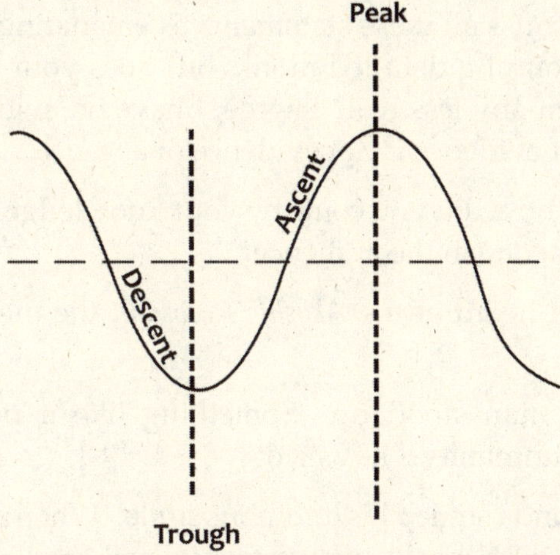

'We must remember that civilizations ebb and flow, much like waves do,' said Brahmananda. 'Our recorded history is simply the last cycle. It does not mean that advanced civilizations have not existed and died before. They have—repeatedly. It's simply that records of those civilizations have also died with them.'

He took a sip of water from the bottle that had been kept near his chair. 'So how is one to get an idea of history in the absence of a historical narrative? In the absence of archaeological evidence?' he asked. There were no volunteers to answer.

'If I told you about a lost continent called Lemuria, or another called Atlantis, continents that were far more spiritually and scientifically advanced than ours, you would say that I was propagating myths,' said Brahmananda. 'If I told you that the inhabitants of these civilizations had the ability to teleport and could live far longer than any present-day human; if I told you that they had intuitive knowledge that made languages, words and calculations irrelevant; if I told you that they needed very little food because they absorbed energy from the atmosphere around them … you would dismiss all these statements as emanating from the imagination of a deluded monk. But does your dismissal make them any less real? I agree, I have no evidence, but absence of evidence is not evidence of absence.'

'But then, how did you come by your knowledge of them?' asked someone in the audience.

'Have you heard of the *Akashic Records*?' the monk asked in return.

A young man stood up. 'Something like a permanent record of humanity?' he asked.

Brahmananda smiled his luminous smile. 'When an aircraft travels through the sky, you can see its trail. Similarly, every event, thought, action, intention, emotion or expression leaves a trail. That trail is compiled into the Akashic Records,' he explained. 'The Akashic Records contain the vibrational records of each and every individual soul in the universe and the journey that it undertakes. Hence, our understanding of Atlantis and Lemuria.'

'Where *are* these records?' asked the young man.

'That's like asking—*where exactly* is the information that I access on the internet stored?' shot back the monk. 'All the information that you could possibly want is out there on the internet but you need to know how to search for it. It's the same with the Akashic Records. Everyone has access to the records, but some people know how to search better.'

13

'Do you know where the name Lemuria comes from?' asked Brahmananda.

'No,' replied the young man, bemused.

'Well, in 1864, the zoologist Philip Sclater wrote an article titled "The Mammals of Madagascar" in the *Quarterly Journal of Science*,' explained Brahmananda. 'He was puzzled by the fact that fossils of primates that he called lemurs could be found in Madagascar and India but not in Africa or the Middle East. Sclater hypothesized that Madagascar and India would have been part of a larger continent that he called "Lemuria".'

'And then?'

'What Sclater did *not* know was that a fifteenth-century Tamil version of the ancient religious text, the *Skanda Purana*, had referred to an earlier continent to the south of India. In this particular work, it was referred to as "Kumari Kandam". Kumari Kandam and Lemuria, assuming they existed, were one and the same, stretching from India and Sri Lanka in the north, to Madagascar in the west and Australia in the east and south.' The monk clicked a button that brought up a map of the supposedly lost continent.

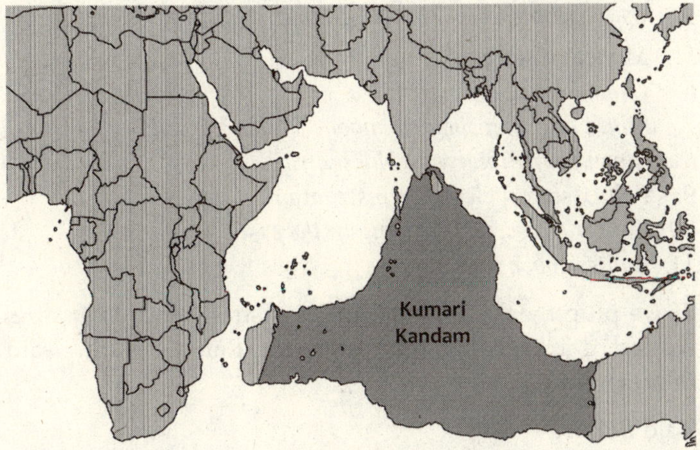

'The notion of Kumari Kandam explains many recent scientific discoveries,' said Brahmananda, turning back to the audience. 'For example, the fact that lemur fossils can be found in India and Madagascar but not in Africa. Also, the fact that there is a DNA link between Indians and the aboriginal people of Australia. In addition, the fact that the dingo dog is found both in India and Australia.'

'Sri Lanka would then have been part of this larger land mass?' asked a middle-aged lady in the fourth row.

'Yes, but rising sea levels would have altered that. By the time of the *Ramayana*, there was water between India and Sri Lanka and hence the need for Rama's bridge.'

'How long ago would that have been?'

'That answer lies in the *Ramayana* itself,' said Brahmananda. 'The epic gives us the planetary positions on Rama Navami, the birthday of Rama. Let's consider all the key astronomical signs.' He went to the whiteboard and wrote a list in his old-fashioned sloping hand.

1. *Sun in Aries*
2. *Saturn in Libra*
3. *Jupiter in Cancer*
4. *Venus in Pisces*
5. *Mars in Capricorn*
6. *Lunar month of Chaitra*
7. *Ninth day after the new moon, Shukla Paksha*
8. *Moon near Punarvasu Nakshatra*
9. *Pollux star in Gemini constellation*
10. *Cancer as ascendant rising in the east*
11. *Jupiter above the horizon*

'If we plug these elements into an astronomical software, we get a clear date and time for Rama's birth,' said Brahmananda.

'And that is?'

'The 10th of January 5114 BCE, at 12:30 p.m.,' declared Brahmananda.

14

'So the crossing to Lanka happened around seven thousand years ago?' asked the young man who had brought up the topic of Lemuria.

'Yes,' said Brahmananda. 'And this fits in with data from the World Oceanography Studies which shows that the rise in sea level in the region between southern India and Sri Lanka has been 0.2 millimetres to 1.29 millimetres per year. These annual increases aggregate to around nine feet over the period of seven thousand years.'

'Would a bridge like the Rama Setu have been necessary?' asked the young man. 'After all, the sea level was in fact lower in those times.'

'The residual stones of the bridge built by Rama's army to cross into Lanka can still be seen around six feet below sea level,' said Brahmananda. 'But seven thousand years ago, the sea level would have been nine feet lower than what it is at present. This means that the bridge would have been around three feet above water level, an adequate elevation for an army to cross.'

'Seems difficult to imagine that such a bridge could have been constructed at that time,' said someone.

'On the contrary, it would have been relatively easy,' said Brahmananda. 'There would have been portions that were above ground where nothing major needed to be added. The builders would have had to pile rocks only in those areas where the land had sunk significantly below sea level.'

'What happened to the bridge?'

'The bridge was used all the way up to 1480,' said Brahmananda, clicking on his remote to bring up a satellite image of the bridge. 'There are sufficient records that refer

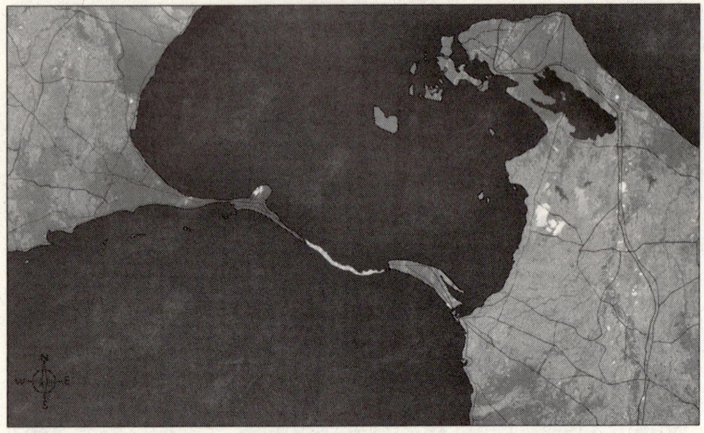

to the bridge up to that date. The bridge became unusable after a cyclone in 1480, but satellite images still show the outline of the bridge that once existed.'

'There are those who say that the idea of a bridge is fanciful at best,' said a woman. 'They say that what is seen on satellite images is a natural formation, nothing more than that.'

'The *Ramayana* informs us that the length to breadth ratio of the bridge was 10 to 1,' said Brahmananda. 'The current formation measures 35 kilometres in length and 3.5 kilometres in width. Thus the ratio is 10 to 1. How would Valmiki, the author of the *Ramayana*, have known this?'

'But do you also believe in the idea that Rama used monkeys, or *vanaras*, to fight in his army?' asked a young lady in bright red. 'Isn't that a little too fantastic?'

'They weren't monkeys,' said Brahmananda, shaking a finger in gentle admonishment. 'They were simply *Vana Nara*—or "people of the forest". The British did a great disservice to India by giving the tag of mythology to our history. Why would a mythological work have a family tree that details forty-five generations before Rama, and thirty generations after him? And while it is true that you could write up a fictional family tree, a fictional tree would not correspond with other ancient Hindu texts. But it does!'

'You are convinced that it is history, not mythology?' asked the lady in red again.

'Do you know the difference between mythology and history?' asked Brahmananda.

The lady expressed herself in a shrug.

'Mythology is a set of lies that people rarely believe,' Brahmananda said and paused.

'And history?'

'A set of lies that people have agreed to believe.'

The audience laughed.

'Both history and mythology contain embellishments and sometimes outright lies,' he said. 'But that doesn't take away from the fact that they also contain core truths. Ikshvaku, the head of Rama's lineage, is named in the Rig Veda; the town plan of Ayodhya is described in the Atharva Veda; the sages of the *Ramayana*—Vishwamitra, Vasishta and Bharadwaja—are cited in the Rig Veda. The consistency between the *Ramayana* and other texts of India is remarkable.'

'Would that be sufficient evidence?' asked an elderly gentleman who had been listening patiently.

'Fairly enough,' said Brahmananda. 'But let's look at geography, shall we? Two Chennai-based botanists carried out an extensive three-year study. They found that all the 182 plants mentioned during the fourteen-year trek undertaken by Rama corresponded with the local flora and fauna of the locations mentioned. How would Valmiki, residing in an ashram two thousand kilometres away from

Lanka, have such astonishing details of botany unless he had access to the descriptions given by the actual travellers themselves?'

'Rama's exile of fourteen years…' mused the old man. 'Doesn't that sound more like fiction than fact?'

'Sure it does,' said Brahmananda. 'But that's the case with most myths. Remember one thing: *there is always a story behind the story*.'

'I didn't quite understand…'

'Let's revisit what happened in the *Ramayana*,' said Brahmananda. 'King Dasharatha of Ayodhya had three wives—Kausalya, Kaikeyi and Sumitra. Rama, Kausalya's son, was the eldest and the natural heir and was married to Sita. On the eve of his coronation, his stepmother, Kaikeyi, demanded from Dasharatha that Rama be exiled for fourteen years and her son Bharata be crowned instead. As a loyal son, Rama went into the jungles with his wife and Lakshmana. Then, Ravana, the ruler of Lanka, abducted Sita. Rama, with the help of allies like Hanuman and Sugriva, battled Ravana, eventually killing him. Rama returned to Ayodhya along with Sita and Lakshmana and was then crowned king.'

'That's a story that every Indian child knows,' said the elderly gentleman.

'The story given out was that Rama had been exiled,' said Brahmananda. 'But the Akashic Records tell us that Kaikeyi loved Rama as dearly as she did her own son. What if the exile was a ruse? A cover? A story to hide the true purpose of Rama's journey?'

15

Vijay dropped in at the supermarket near IIT to pick up a few groceries. His requirements were basic. His kitchen had no more than ten items at any given time. He looked at his smartphone to check the list of stuff he needed. Milk, bread, fruits, nuts and olive oil.

He walked to each relevant aisle, popping items into the wireframe basket he held. Some distance away, another shopper was also placing things into a basket. He was moving at a leisurely pace, but seemed to be at every aisle that Vijay visited.

Done with his shopping, Vijay walked to the express check-out counter. There were only two people in the line in front of him. As his turn came, he took out his shopping from the basket and placed it on the cashier's conveyor belt. Once the store clerk had rung up his total, Vijay paid in cash. The cashier placed Vijay's items into a shopping bag and handed it to him. Vijay walked out from the store, his mind dwelling on an obscure research paper that had been sent to him earlier in the day.

He did not notice that the shopper who had been in the store alongside him, had abandoned his basket and exited the store immediately after.

16

The Alcoholics Anonymous meeting was held at the Raffles Medical Beijing Clinic in the Chaoyang District of Beijing at 6:30 p.m. on Saturday.

'Good evening, ladies and gentlemen. This is the regular meeting of AA,' said the middle-aged secretary in front. 'Let us open the meeting with a moment of silence followed by the Serenity Prayer.'

A young social worker sat in the third row. After his rehab at a special facility in Shanghai, he had signed an oath that he would continue to attend AA meetings at least once a week. This was his seventeenth since his return to Beijing.

The social worker watched as a lady stood up and introduced herself hesitantly. Other members of the group immediately greeted her by name. It was the established drill. He looked around and saw another vaguely familiar face, but the man did not get up and introduce himself. When the secretary looked at him pointedly, he got up and left rather hurriedly—as if to avoid drawing attention to himself.

Where have I seen him before? wondered the social worker. *Has the man been following me? Or am I imagining things?* Ever since he had stopped the booze, a fog seemed to have been lifted from his brain. It caused him to make connections that he would otherwise have ignored.

Each member got up to narrate their experiences. He awaited his turn, then stood up and cleared his throat. He introduced himself and began hesitantly. 'Almost every night for ten years, I would pass out drunk, but not before promising myself that this would be the last time that I drank. Alcohol became my crutch. I felt that I had earned the right to drink because of the pain I witnessed in my line of work as a social worker.'

There was pindrop silence as the others listened to him. He was followed by several people who narrated their own experiences. An hour later, he made his way down the stairs of the clinic along with the rest of the members. He did not see the man who had hurriedly left the meeting. He was slinking around by the foot of the stairs, holding an umbrella.

The social worker was on his way to the exit when he felt a stinging pain in his thigh. The man's umbrella had poked him. He turned around crossly but the man apologized for his carelessness and hurried away into the crowded street.

The social worker had barely taken a few steps into the street before he fell to the ground. By then, the stranger with the umbrella had disappeared.

17

Sujatha Iyer entered Indira Paryavaran Bhavan on Delhi's Jor Bagh Road. The building housed the Ministry of Environment, Forest and Climate Change. In her hand was a portfolio containing photographs and specimens of plants that she had personally discovered while travelling all over the country.

Sujatha worked at the Botanical Survey of India, the BSI. Her mandate was to find and document plants and herbs that had economic value for India. The job meant that she was always on the move, traversing the length and breadth of the country in her quest to identify, classify and record every possible plant that India had to offer for the betterment of its people and the world at large.

She crossed her fingers in anticipation of the meeting. She hoped that the Director-General of Forests would help her. She knocked on the door to his office. The man behind the desk, a veteran of the Indian Administrative Service—the IAS—greeted her and offered her a chair.

'Thank you for meeting me,' said Sujatha, as she sat down.

'Happy to assist,' said the Director. 'Now tell me, Ms Iyer, how may I help you?'

'Well,' she began. 'My primary interest is in a plant called *Ophiorrhiza mungos…*'

'Ophi—what?' asked the IAS man. He hated unpronounceable Latin names.

'Ophiorrhiza mungos,' said Sujatha. 'This particular plant is usually found in the Western Ghats of India, but I am convinced that a variant of the same plant can also be found in the north and north-east of India.'

'What is so important about these plants?' asked the Director.

'The ophiorrhiza family of plants is critical in developing chemotherapy drugs at a lower price in India,' explained Sujatha. 'The northern variants of this plant could hold the key to making cancer-care affordable in developing countries.'

'And why do you need me?' asked the Director.

'Some of the forests are no-go areas,' said Sujatha. 'Particularly those which lie along the Chinese border. I need your clearance.'

'Get your boss at the Botanical Survey of India to send me an official request in writing,' replied the Director. 'He must specifically mention the coordinates of the locations that you wish to visit and the exact dates. By the way, my permission would be insufficient in this matter. You will need a Home Department no-objection certificate as well as a security clearance from the Ministry of Defence. Let me see what I can do.'

Sujatha smiled her thanks.

'Don't be grateful just yet,' said the Director, noticing her expression. 'I'm not making any promises. The wheels of government turn slowly.' *If at all.*

Sujatha left the premises of the Ministry feeling content that she had, at least, done her best. She made her way to Jor Bagh Metro Station.

She did not notice the tall stranger with a gaunt face lurking a few steps away.

18

Sujatha allowed the machine to sense her smart card and waited for the gates to open. She walked through and waited for the Yellow Line that would take her to Hauz Khas. When the train whooshed in, she entered and settled down in one of the front seats. She closed her eyes, allowing her mind to wander.

Sujatha's parents had died in a car crash when she was just five. Her uncle, neither interested in feeding another mouth nor bearing the responsibility of a future dowry, had bundled Sujatha off to her maternal grandmother.

Unfortunately, her grandmother passed away the very next year. Penniless and homeless, the six-year-old had taken to begging outside the Sringeri temple when Amma, the administrator of the orphanage, had spotted her and taken her in.

19

It had taken some time for Sujatha to regain an interest in things. All she had seen until then were death, loss and a profound loneliness. If it hadn't been for Amma, she would have been leading a life of begging, or even worse, prostitution. But she was bright. And slowly but surely the spark within her was fanned back to life.

She excelled in academics and debates but hated swimming. Her friends loved splashing in the neighbouring lake, but she would remain on the embankment, never entering completely into the water. Her friends would often pull her in, but she would remain frozen at the edges, too terrified to move.

After having nearly drowned, she developed an interest in medicine, helping out in the hospital attached to the orphanage, thus understanding basic medical procedures.

Sujatha loved nature and spent hours caring for each individual plant and blossom that grew around the orphanage. Amma always assigned her the job of stringing together flowers for the temple deity. Given Sujatha's love for flowers and plants, she felt almost guilty for having to pierce those delicate scented petals with needle and thread to link them together.

Some months later, Amma asked Sujatha, 'Why do you wince whenever you're stringing those flowers into garlands, Sujatha?'

Sujatha looked up and replied, 'Everything has life, Amma. Today in school we learnt about the scientist Jagdish Chandra Bose and his crescograph with which he proved that plants feel pain just like animals. Don't you think it will be just a matter of time before we show that there is life in everything, including the everyday objects that we consider lifeless?'

20

Amma loved gathering the kids and narrating to them mythological tales from Hindu epics. On the day of Dussera, which celebrated Ram's victory over Ravana, she would tell them the story of Ravana and how he was slain.

In the surrounding night, the children listened breathlessly to their foster-mother's almost dramatized tales of the derring-do of heroes of the past. The fireworks and party bombs and simulated rockets zoomed to the sky above them, showering multicoloured sparks below, the entire extravaganza mirrored in the wide eyes of the children's upturned faces. 'Ravana was the demon-king of Lanka,' said Amma, swiftly bringing the little minds down to earth. 'He was born to the Brahmin sage, Vishrava, and his wife Kaikesi, the Daitya princess. Thus, Ravana was partly Brahmin and partly Daitya. At birth, he was named Dashanana because he was supposedly born with ten heads.'

'Was he good or bad?' asked one of the more pragmatic children, getting down to basics.

'Ravana was belligerent and egotistical even during his youth,' Amma answered him, picking her words carefully, 'but he was also an excellent student. Under Vishrava's guidance, Ravana mastered the Vedas, other sacred scriptures and the arts, and became an accomplished player of the veena.'

'How did he become powerful?' asked another little boy, indicating his puffed-out cheeks and brandishing the pimple-size bumps on his flexed arms.

Amma wanted to laugh out loud and squeeze the little imp to her chest, but kept a straight face as she went on with the rest of the story that has kept listeners down the centuries—children, men and women—riveted. 'Ravana was a devotee of Brahma and he performed severe austerities over thousands of years to gain his favour. Pleased with Ravana, Brahma offered him a boon—absolute invincibility against gods, demons, wild beasts and spirits. Ravana knew that no mortal human could ever defeat him and so he did not bother to include humans in that list. The omission led to his downfall.'

'Then, how did he come to rule Lanka?' asked Vijay.

'Ravana's brother, Kubera, also known as the banker to the gods, owned Lanka—a sublime island that was fabulously wealthy and had been designed by Vishwakarma, the celestial architect,' said Amma. 'Ravana took over Kubera's territory by force and then set about establishing his rule over the people. Surprisingly, Ravana proved himself to be a compassionate and capable king. Lanka and its people prospered under his reign.'

'Wasn't Ravana also a devotee of Shiva?' asked Sujatha.

'Not to begin with,' said Amma. 'Ravana attempted to uproot and move Mount Kailash, and disturbed Shiva and Parvati with his antics. Furious, Shiva pressed one of his toes on the mountain and trapped Ravana underneath.

Ravana now realized his mistake. He sang songs in devotion of Shiva for many thousands of years until Shiva eventually released him. Pleased with Ravana's devotion, Shiva bestowed on him an *Atma Lingam* of immense power. Shiva also gave him the name Ravana, which translates to *he with the terrifying roar.'*

'What is an Atma Lingam?' asked Vijay.

'We don't know,' said Amma. 'All we know is that it gave Ravana immense power, perception and knowledge. Ravana then proceeded to establish his dominance over several kingdoms. It is said that he even invaded the heavens and defeated the Devas. But Ravana's weakness was women. He not only had several wives, principal among whom was Mandodari, an elegant lady often eulogized for her sagacity, beauty and strength of character, but also a massive harem filled with women he had captured during his conquests. It was his insatiable lust that drove Ravana into abducting Sita, Rama's wife.'

'And Rama went to Lanka to save her?' asked one child.

'Yes,' said Amma. 'Rama teamed up with the Vanaras, a forest clan that included Hanuman. He used their expertise in building a bridge across the sea to cross into Lanka. Rama then offered Ravana the opportunity to return Sita and avoid battle, but Ravana remained adamant. Ravana's brother, Vibhishana, advised him against fighting Rama but ended up banished by his brother for showing weakness. Vibhishana, who knew all of Ravana's secret powers, was pushed into the arms of the enemy.'

'How did Ravana eventually die?' asked Sujatha.

'In the battle, all of Ravana's sons and warriors fell and he was compelled to confront Rama directly,' said Amma. 'Rama used all his weapons to decapitate Ravana of each of his ten heads, but a new head would promptly replace the fallen one. This was supposedly because of a container of *amrit*—the nectar of immortality—that Ravana had stored in his stomach. Based on Vibhishana's advice, Rama used his celestial weapons to target Ravana's abdomen and thus destroy the nectar. This strategy brought about Ravana's final downfall.'

'The end of the villain,' said a child with a sigh of satisfaction.

'Ravana may have been a villain, but there is no denying that he was an accomplished man,' said Amma. 'His knowledge and understanding of sacred texts were remarkable. He remained a great devotee of Shiva and even composed the dance known as the *Shiva Tandava Stotra*. He was an effective and capable ruler who brought great prosperity to his people and kingdom.'

21

Vijay walked back to the flat that he would be required to vacate within a couple of days. He opened the front door and entered, throwing his satchel on the sofa. He looked around at his sparsely furnished apartment. Something did not seem quite right. He couldn't place his finger on it.

He forced himself to quit over-analyzing things and carried his bag of groceries into the micro-kitchen, which was smaller than a closet. He placed the bag on the counter and poured himself a glass of water. He opened the cabinet to pull out a packet of rice puffs when he noticed that the arrangement of items inside the cabinet seemed different. Vijay was methodical about most things other than his appearance. He liked his stuff arranged in a way that he could remember and access easily. It was the same methodical approach that he followed with his notes and research.

The rice puffs came in a tall bag that was usually kept towards the rear of the cabinet so that other items that were shorter could be easily seen. But now the placement was different. He went back to the living room, sat down, and placed his water and rice puffs on a pile of books that doubled as his coffee table. His eyes were drawn to the way the books were arranged. Vijay's razor-sharp memory recalled the exact order in which he had left the books earlier that day. The stacking order had changed. The hair on the back of his neck stirred. *Someone had been here.*

He cautiously got up from the sofa and tip-toed over to the bed. *Could that someone still be inside his flat?* He lay down on the floor to look underneath. Nothing. Then he patted the drapes. Nothing. He walked into the bathroom and pulled away the shower curtain. Nothing.

He had been feeling watched for a while now. It had started almost around the same time as his job interviews. But never before had his flat been broken into and searched. Vijay shuddered.

He retraced his footsteps to the closet. He didn't open it. Instead he placed his ears to the sliding doors, attempting to discern any noise from within. Nothing. He pulled open the doors quickly, almost attempting to pre-empt anyone inside.

'When will you be leaving?' boomed a voice from behind him.

Vijay jumped, his heart thumping wildly.

It was his landlord, who had his own master key to the main door. Vijay muttered a few cusswords under his breath and took another look inside the closet. Seeing nothing strange in it, he turned around to look at his landlord, a seventy-year-old Sindhi gentleman. 'You could have knocked,' said Vijay to him, irritated by the intrusion but also relieved by the presence of a familiar face in his flat.

The landlord shrugged. 'Your moving company needed to survey the place and your stuff,' he said. 'I gave them access to the flat earlier today.'

'What moving company?' asked Vijay. 'I hardly have anything that needs moving.'

'They said that you had engaged them to pack and move your things,' said the landlord. 'They were here for less than ten minutes. Here's the visiting card that the man gave me.'

22

Rakesh Sharma sat inside the meditation hall alongside hundreds of other participants, each person sitting cross-legged on a square two-by-two cushion. The sun was yet to rise. There was pindrop silence in the hall.

Twice each year, Sharma travelled to Dhamma Salila, a meditation centre located at Dehradun. During those visits he forgot about his work with RAW and IG4 and erased from his mind the terrible things that he regularly saw as an operative. It was almost like powering off a smartphone and booting it up again so that all the memory being hogged by RAM-guzzling applications could be freed.

The meditation technique that was taught at Dhamma Salila was called Vipassana, a method of self-purification through self-observation. Vipassana meant 'seeing things as they are'. Sharma had tried it for the first time after being injured during the Kargil war. He became a regular during the years that followed. It turned out to be his salvation.

Sharma focused on his natural breath to concentrate his mind. Then, with a heightened sense of consciousness, he proceeded to observe the shifting nature of his body, mind and experiences. His intensified awareness was aimed at leading him to an understanding of the core truths of impermanence and connectedness.

But Dhamma Salila, with its severe routine, was not for everyone. All students were woken up in the wee hours of the morning—4 a.m.—and ended their day at 10 p.m. During the intervening eighteen hours, they meditated for eleven hours and were required to maintain 'noble silence' throughout their stay. All forms of communication with fellow participants were prohibited. The last meal of the day, purely vegetarian and *sattvic,* was consumed before noon. Men and women lived and meditated separately. Letters, phones, cameras, computers, writing material, magazines and tablets had to be deposited at the reception before starting the programme.

Learn to live with yourself. It can be terrifying.

This was the last day of his latest three-day programme. Sharma got up from the cushion effortlessly, almost as though he had no prosthetic leg to slow him down. He walked out of the meditation hall and followed the gravel path to the small and bare living quarter that had been allotted to him, a ten-by-eight room with a stone platform for a bed. The only concession to comfort was a thin mattress on the platform and a functioning bathroom. All Vipassana students were required to live the lives of monks, with a view to dispelling their egos.

Sharma calmly gathered up his belongings and placed them in his duffel bag. He then walked along a pathway that allowed him to take in the wonder of the Myanmar-style pagoda that was equipped with meditation cells within. The wind chimes atop the golden pagoda seemed to be talking to him, tinkling as he crossed the tranquil park.

From a distance, a monk in saffron and vermillion robes watched as Sharma made his way to the admin block.

23

Prime Minister Komura looked at the men seated around the table. All of them were old. And that was the problem. Old men; tired ideas; obsolete plans; tightasses all. Komura was among the youngest prime ministers that Japan had ever had, having celebrated his fiftieth birthday just a few weeks earlier. But the rest of his Cabinet was pure vintage.

The house in Chiyoda-ku was Komura's official residence and workplace—the Number 10 of Japan. Located diagonally adjacent to the National Diet Building, it also housed the offices of the Chief Cabinet Secretary and the Deputy Cabinet Secretaries.

'Next item on the agenda is financial aid to the Middle East,' said Komura.

'Shusho,' began the Minister of Justice, using the usual honorific for Japanese prime ministers. 'Why are we providing money to countries that only use it to promote religious fundamentalism? God knows we would be better off spending it domestically.'

Komura looked directly across the table at the dissenter. *Yet another relic hanging on for relevance,* he thought. He banished the thought and took the question head-on.

'Japan's wellbeing depends on global stability,' said Komura. 'Unlike several other countries, we have confined our military intervention to sending a mere one thousand troops for peacekeeping into Iraq. If we want stability in this region, it is absolutely vital that we play a positive role, at least financially, if nothing else. We cannot simply sit back and do nothing.'

'Sometimes doing nothing requires great courage,' shot back the Minister of Justice. 'Why not let them fight one another to the finish?'

He was merely reflecting the opinion of a vast number of Japanese citizens who believed that Japan's money was better spent on reviving their own economy rather than supporting burgeoning deficits elsewhere, particularly the Middle East.

'First, we do not wish to open immigration to refugees from other countries. Second, we do not want to have military involvement. So should we avoid the third option of financial assistance too?' asked Komura, his voice rising a notch. He looked at the twenty faces at the round table, attempting to gauge the level of support that he had in the room. The silent ones were infinitely more dangerous than the ones who were vocal. He felt a tingling in his right arm. He attempted to ignore it.

The Minister of Foreign Affairs cleared his throat. 'Shusho, your view is correct. It is in our interest to promote stability in the region. The question that we must ask ourselves is whether your proposal would achieve that objective.'

He's couching his opposition in supportive words, thought Komura. It seemed evident that most of his colleagues were thinking along similar lines.

Komura reached for the bottle of water in front of him but was unable to unscrew the cap due to the trembling of his hands. Suddenly, the bottle fell from his grasp.

In the rigid formality of a Japanese Cabinet meeting, there occurred what could be straight out of burlesque. The Prime Minister stood up and desperately began tearing at his jacket, attempting to unbutton the cuffs of his dress shirt—a grotesque striptease.

The gnawing itch in his right arm was unbearable.

The aged members of the Cabinet looked on dumbfounded at the spectacle. They knew the younger man had been under considerable pressure lately. *Could the Prime Minister be losing it?*

Before they could do anything, Komura fell face forward on the table.

24

Sharma walked into a spartan room that was occupied by the monk who had been watching him from a distance. Brahmananda visited Dhamma Salila whenever he came down into the plains from the mountains. Sharma had known him ever since that terrible war in Kargil during which he had lost his leg.

'How are you, Rakesh?' asked Brahmananda, looking up from his open notebook and putting down his pen.

'Only beginning to understand that there is no *me* and no *you,*' Sharma smiled at the monk, who always emanated an unexplainable radiance. 'What are you working on in that lotus-embossed notebook of yours?'

Brahmananda laughed. 'The lotus has always fascinated you,' he remarked, pouring some hot lemon water from a flask into two cups and handing one over to him.

'To answer your question,' said Brahmananda, 'a treatise on the Katapayadi system. A south Indian system of numerical representation.'

'The last time I saw you, you were working on binary numbers,' said Sharma.

'I was,' replied Brahmananda. 'Because binary numbers are the language of life.'

'How so?' asked Sharma.

'Try expressing everything as a combination of zeros and ones and you realize that the binary system is a perfect representation of dualities,' said Brahmananda. 'One day I hope to explain that to you in greater detail. In the meantime, read the *Valmiki Ramayana,* followed by the

Gayatri Mantra. You will understand my point. Now, what brings you here?'

'I heard you were visiting this place. I figured I'd take a chance and drop in,' said Sharma.

'You never *just* drop in,' said Brahmananda, his eyes twinkling. 'But I'm happy to hear that you are shedding the Cartesian illusion.' Sharma and Brahmananda had spent many hours discussing the fallacy of dualism—the distinction between mind and matter. Between body and soul.

'The celebrated view of Descartes, *I think, therefore I am*, has led humans to equate their identity with their mind rather than their whole organism,' said Brahmananda. 'This foolish view has encouraged humans to treat matter as dead and independent from themselves.'

Sharma laughed. 'I was almost dead when I met you at the hospital in Kargil,' he joked. 'But that was another matter!'

Brahmananda laughed at the wordplay. 'We tend to divide the world into distinct objects and events,' he said. 'This separation is convenient but is not reality. It's an abstraction. To think of our abstraction as reality is ignorance—*avidya*.'

'Isn't that precisely the point made by Einstein?' asked Sharma. 'That objects and events—or space and time—are united, not separate?'

'But can you *visualize* the dimensions of space combined with the dimension of time?' asked Brahmananda. 'The *Upanishads* say: "There the eye goes not, speech goes not, nor the mind; we know not, we understand not: how would one teach it?" There are only two ways to understand spacetime—mathematics or perception. You decide the route you wish to take.'

The room was still for a moment.

'Reality cannot be explained by words, because it lies beyond the realms of the senses and the intellect,' said the monk. 'It can only be intuitively experienced. When the rational mind is quietened, the intuitive mind awakes.'

'But distractions often get in the way,' said Sharma.

'The mind of a warrior in a duel is not distracted,' said Brahmananda. 'It is a heightened state of awareness. Distractions are pushed into the background.'

'Meditation is a duel?' asked Sharma, a tad surprised.

'Sounds ridiculous, doesn't it?' said Brahmananda. 'Imagine that you are a warrior in a swordfight. Your opponent is equally matched. The slightest error could mean instant death. You watch your opponent with utmost vigilance. A crowd has gathered to see the fight. Given that you aren't blind, you can see them from the corner of your eye. And because you aren't deaf, you hear them in the background. But your mind remains focused on your opponent and his moves. *That* is meditation.'

Sharma nodded. Brahmananda always made things so simple.

'Master the knot,' said Brahmananda eventually.

'What is that?' asked Sharma.

'The ability to understand your connection to the rest of the universe,' replied Brahmananda. 'That is what I mean by the knot. The *Upanishads* talk of *Vasudhaiva Kutumbakam*—the notion that the world is one family. It is the idea that everyone and everything are related. Distinctions and separations are false.'

A thoughtful Sharma bid farewell to the monk and headed to the car park. He was to attend a security conference in Delhi and then catch a flight out to Kathmandu the next day.

He decided to fight his duel as best he could.

25

Sharma sat in the last row listening to a speech by the National Security Advisor of India. 'Global Security & Intelligence Conference', proclaimed the huge backdrop to the stage. They were inside a large convention hall that was packed to capacity. Almost seven hundred people were present, including police officers, armed forces personnel, intelligence operatives, counter-terrorism experts, academics and researchers.

He heard the NSA drone on in a monotonous voice about the security challenges in an ever-changing world. His speech was followed by those of the Home Minister and the Minister of Defence. All of them followed the bland approach of reading from prepared texts and delivering the same without any significant expression.

Sharma sighed. This was not where he wanted to be. He slipped out from the back row and made his way to the coffee counter. He poured himself a cup and was about to take a sip when someone tapped him on the shoulder. Sharma turned around.

'Professor Thakur!' he exclaimed. 'What a surprise to see you here.' Sharma had read many of Vignesh Thakur's books on Buddhism and met him several times.

The professor smiled. He had wrinkled skin like ancient parchment and his teeth were nicotine-stained from his hookah habit. 'Not one of the places where you would usually expect to find me,' he said. 'But Buddhist aggression in countries like Myanmar as a reaction to Islamist interests has also become a security risk in some parts of the world. I am scheduled to deliver a talk later today on that subject.'

'Religious conflict is a constant across the ages,' said Sharma. 'When Pakistan was created in 1947, Hindus were 15 per cent of the population but were less than 2 per cent by 1998. In Bangladesh of 1931, Hindus were around 30 per cent of the population but are less than 10 per cent today.'

'Yes,' said Thakur. 'Contrast that with the Muslim population of India that was less than 10 per cent in 1951 and grew to over 14 per cent by 2011. Secularism is the only way to allow people to flourish. Are you aware that the Kalachakra texts talk about a massive world conflict in 2424?'

'I'll be dead and gone by then,' said Sharma jokingly. 'I'm not worried.'

Thakur did not smile. 'It's possible that the predicted conflict may be arriving sooner,' he said. 'We should all be worried. *Nidhane*.'

'What's that?' asked Sharma.

'Destruction.'

26

And it's another day and it's time for me, Masoud, to jot down my thoughts. I have been tardy over the last few weeks and I plan to make up for that by writing more regularly from now on.

There are those who say that radical Islamism is the result of something within the doctrine of Islam itself. There are others who say that this terror is actually the consequence of Western interference. I believe that both groups are right in their own ways.

Why do so many people ignore the deleterious impact of Western colonialism on the Muslim world? In 1798, Napoleon Bonaparte invaded Egypt. In 1830, the French captured Algeria. A decade later, the British annexed Yemen. In 1881, the French took over Tunisia, and a year later the English took over Egypt. In 1911, Russia annexed parts of Persia while Italy annexed Tripoli—eventually leading to the creation of Libya. In 1912, the French occupied Morocco.

A groundswell of resentment against the West was only natural. When colonialism eventually died, it was followed by mass immigration of Muslim subjects into the lands of their erstwhile colonial masters. But immigration was accompanied by social exclusion, and dissatisfied immigrants became fertile hunting ground for radical imams.

One also cannot ignore the impact of the Muslim Brotherhood. It emerged in 1928 in Egypt, seeking to Islamize societies and compel governments in Muslim countries to adhere to Sharia. Several terror groups such as the Hamas, Jamaat al-Islamiyya, and Al-Qaeda are affiliated to the Muslim Brotherhood. In fact, the brotherhood has spawned some of the world's most notorious terrorists.

Then there's the fact that the British allowed the Jews to settle in Palestine. The establishment of the state of Israel followed in 1948. The Muslim world was further humiliated when a unified front of Arab armies lost a bitter war to the newly created country of only 600,000 Jews. Muslim resentment peaked.

Frankly, though, I think that the biggest factor that fuelled the growth of radical Islam was the discovery of oil in Saudi Arabia in 1938. Until then, Wahhabism—the rigid and fanatical form of Islam—could not really spread far and wide. The discovery of oil changed all that. The huge inflow of money from oil wells was used to keep conservative elements of the Saudi state happy. More than ten billion dollars were invested in Islamic charities and foundations that carried a stark and intolerant version of Islam to different parts of the world.

The overthrow of the Shah of Iran as a consequence of the 1979 revolution also gave impetus to Islamists around the world. Iran became the world's first modern Islamic republic and their new leader, Ayatollah Khomeini, ensured that Sharia became the law of the land.

And can one overlook the consequences of the Cold War in accelerating radical Islamist ideology? The Americans used Jihad as a tool to get Arab and Afghan fighters to bleed the

Soviets out of Afghanistan. Billions of CIA dollars were poured into mujahideen groups through Pakistan's Inter-Services Intelligence—the ISI. Even Osama bin Laden was initially supported by the CIA. When the Soviets were defeated, the holy warriors needed new wars to fight.

America's myopic vision propped up dictators in the Middle East and then toppled them during the Arab Spring. They did not realize that choices in the Arab world are never about good versus bad. They are often about bad versus worse. While dictators such as Hosni Mubarak, Saddam Hussein, Bashar al-Assad and Muammar Gaddafi were terrible men, they kept Islamists in check and prevented outright Islamization of their countries. They were the proverbial lid on a can of worms. And we all know what happens when the lid is removed.

Usually the very people demanding democracy on the streets of the Arab world are actually Islamists who look forward to sacrificing all democratic norms at the altar of theocracy, once they are in power.

27

Vijay looked at the visiting card that his landlord had given him. It was of simple white ivory paper, the sort that could be ordered at any online printing store. The name and address on it were in ordinary block letters.

Vijay entered the website of the company into his browser but it took him to a page marked as 'under construction'. He did a quick search via Google for the company but it did not seem to exist. He picked up his phone and dialled the number provided on the card. It was out of service. Then he visited his phone's mapping app to do an address search. The street ended before the block number in question. He sent an email but it bounced back within seconds.

He was aware that every domain name had to be registered. All domain name registrars provided what was known as a 'Who Is' lookup. He entered the domain name into the search box. Privacy settings had been enabled. The registrar was masking the name of the owner.

Vijay realized that the visiting card had simply been a dud to get access into his apartment. It was a dead end.

28

'Another one bites the dust,' said Petrov. 'They're falling like ninepins. Now the count stands at four. The British Foreign Secretary, the German Chancellor, the American Attorney-General ... and now the Japanese Prime Minister.'

'And lord only knows how many more will fall,' said Judith.

The four members of IG4 were in a suite of the Hyatt in Kathmandu. The hotel room's large picture window provided a view of thirty-seven acres of landscaped grounds that secluded the guests from the hustle and bustle of the Nepalese capital. In the distance, they could see the Boudhanath Stupa, the holiest of all Tibetan Buddhist shrines outside of Tibet. Inside, the suite was toasty and inviting, having been furnished in the traditional Newari style of Nepal.

'The Japanese Prime Minister collapsed in full view of the members of his Cabinet,' said Zhang. 'Our MSS operative in Tokyo obtained identical reports from several sources.'

The team had mustered all the resources at their command to carry out extensive background checks on each of the last three dead leaders. They would now need to add the Japanese Prime Minister to that list. The problem was that, even after extensive matching of data sets using secret algorithms provided by the National Security Agency, they had been unable to come up with a common link.

'We are ignoring an obvious detail that needs no algorithms,' said Petrov. 'Sometimes, what one is searching for is actually hiding in plain sight.'

'What do you think we are missing?' asked Zhang.

'Apparently, the Japanese Cabinet members were discussing financial aid to the Middle East,' said Petrov. 'I guess there are enough people who would be angered by such a proposal.' He lit a Belomorkanal, ignoring the fact that they were seated in a non-smoking room.

'All four leaders who died were staunch liberals,' continued Petrov. 'The British Foreign Secretary opposed the UK's exit from the European Union. He did not see the referendum results as a vote against immigration.' Petrov took a long puff of his cigarette and allowed the nicotine to hit his lungs. 'The German Chancellor spearheaded a plan to absorb thousands of Muslim immigrants into Europe,' continued Petrov. 'This was much against the wishes of common German citizens.' He exhaled generously. It was accompanied by deliberate coughing on the part of Judith. He ignored her. *Let the bitch suffocate,* thought Petrov smugly.

'The American Attorney-General opposed a plan to ban Muslim immigration into America,' said Petrov. 'The result? Impeachment proceedings commenced against him. And finally, the Japanese Prime Minister wanted his country to extend additional lines of credit to Islamic countries. Not a very popular move, and one that was bitterly opposed by his Cabinet.'

Petrov's colleagues were silent as they absorbed his hypothesis.

'Effectively, what is common across all of these high-powered victims is the fact that they were liberal voices who were urging the world not to fall prey to Islamophobia,' said Petrov. '*That's* your common link right there.'

'You really think this is a conspiracy to eliminate liberals around the world?' asked Zhang. The Chinese man spoke very little but absorbed everything that was said. The MSS was the most powerful intelligence agency among the four represented at that table. Headquartered in Beijing, it was responsible for counter-intelligence, foreign intelligence and political security. Unlike the other three agencies, the MSS had the power to arrest or detain people at will within China.

'It seems obvious,' replied Petrov. 'The world is changing rapidly. Just look around you. Political parties on the right and right-of-centre are becoming stronger around the world. The liberals and the left are in decline. Eliminating their remaining leaders could finish them off entirely.'

Zhang spoke. 'Even if one assumes that your hypothesis is correct, one must then answer the two most important questions.'

'And those are?' asked Judith.

'First, *who* is behind these killings?' said Zhang. 'And second, *how* does one bring on the death of a man without leaving any clue as to how he died?'

29

Zhang made his way back to his own room at the hotel. Being part of IG4 was a tightrope walk. On the one hand, his bosses in Beijing expected him to report to them almost everything that emerged in IG4 meetings. On the other hand, the mandate at IG4 was to maintain absolute secrecy. At times he found it difficult to understand where his true loyalties lay.

Zhang sat down at the desk tiredly and powered on his laptop. An encrypted memo from the MSS team that handled Xinjiang province awaited. China had been facing problems with a home-grown separatist movement of Muslim Uighurs in that region. The memo indicated that some Uighur rebels had made their way into Syria for training.

His thoughts wandered back to the IG4 meeting. The threat of Islamist radicalization was real, even for China.

Zhang had been born in Tianjin, located on northern coastal China, his birth coinciding with the Cultural Revolution kicked off by Mao Zedong. Tianjin was one of the five national central cities of the country and the influence of the Communist Party was all-pervasive there. Zhang's father was a member of the People's Liberation Army that violently and brutally supressed the Red Guard groups that had been at the centre of the revolution.

Zhang's father had called in several favours to ensure that his son received the best possible education, and Zhang was eventually accepted into the Institute of International Relations in Beijing. The institute was actually the starting point for a career in espionage. Students from the IIR would eventually be sent to the Institute of Cadre Management in Suzhou for tactical studies and training, before being absorbed into the MSS.

Headquartered in Beijing, the MSS had begun as a central-level ministry with a few departments that resembled the KGB's political police, but had morphed into an organization that was responsible for overseas intelligence, counter-intelligence and political security. Known locally as Guojia Anquan Bu, or GAB, the MSS was made up of multiple bureaux, and Zhang had spent many years in each of them.

Some of the functions that Zhang had handled included wiretapping, stealth photography, internet monitoring and propaganda. In addition, he had been involved in the recruitment of businessmen, researchers and journalists for an extended intelligence web.

For over two years he had handled the Taiwan, Hong Kong and Macau desks. Then he had run counter-insurgency operations against the Falun Gong, the Uighurs and Tibetan activists. He had also helped establish a group of young ladies to honey-trap agents of MI6 and the CIA, besides cultivating think-tanks, such as the China Institute of Contemporary International Relations, that provided the perfect cover for espionage activities. Zhang was nothing if not experienced.

Zhang understood that Chinese foreign policy would always be based on the philosophy of Sun Tzu. *There could only be one hegemon in the world at any given time.*

And that would have to be China.

30

The interview took place in the business centre of The Imperial Hotel in Delhi. Vijay looked around to identify other potential candidates, but he seemed to be the only one waiting in the lounge. He had tried to improve his appearance by putting on a fresh shirt, but it hadn't made much of a difference.

A few minutes later an exceptionally tall, white-haired German emerged from a private office. 'Mr Vijay Sundaram, I presume?' he asked in thick German-accented English, as he held out his right hand. 'My name is Dr Klaus Schmidt.'

There was no smile, just a fixed sombre expression on the German's face. *He has all the warmth of a prison warden*, thought Vijay to himself as he followed Schmidt into the office.

'What do you know about Milesian Labs?' Schmidt asked abruptly, staring at Vijay through thick glasses. His eyes were cold, hard and expressionless. Not the slightest facial hair could be discerned on his pale, unblemished skin. His nails were perfectly manicured. This was a terrifyingly neat man. The exact opposite of Vijay.

'Very little, I'll admit,' replied Vijay truthfully. 'I dug up a little information after receiving your interview letter and here's what I do know. You are a leading pure science outfit. Yours is an unlisted company and your main research facility is located in Uttarakhand, a state that is a few hours away from Delhi. You seem to be building a bank of patents that could be immensely valuable one day, but you are probably the most secretive company on earth. It's next to impossible to find out anything about you.'

'We like to keep it that way,' said Schmidt, without any change in his expression. 'It enables us to get on with our path-breaking work without distractions.'

'I understand,' said Vijay, although he didn't.

'Good,' remarked Schmidt. Vijay had no idea if the German was referring to his answer or to his own company. 'Do you know why we are interested in you?'

'I imagine that it would be related to the thesis that I wrote at IIT,' answered Vijay.

'Yes,' replied Schmidt. '*Quantum Behaviour Beyond the Quantum*. Interesting premise. Please quickly summarize the key points for me.'

Vijay took a deep breath. 'For years, we have believed that when we are dealing with large objects we can simply follow Classical Mechanics because the whole system will be governed by classical laws. It has also been assumed that when we are dealing with infinitesimally small objects, the only way to understand the system is through Quantum Mechanics, because Newtonian laws fail at the quantum level. But what if some parts of quantum theory can be applied to larger objects such as planets? That was the thrust of my thesis.'

'And that's precisely why we want you,' said Schmidt. 'Milesian Labs wants to help you convert your hypothesis into reality.'

Vijay hesitated before asking what was on his mind. 'What is your offer?' he asked, almost embarrassed by his question.

'You have been interviewed at SpaceX, Google and the Indian Space Research Organization,' said Schmidt matter-of-factly.

How does he know which companies I have had discussions with? wondered Vijay.

'Take the highest figure that any company has offered you so far, and double it. That's my offer,' said Schmidt, taking off his glasses and putting them on the desk. He looked far more human without them.

Vijay was stunned into silence. It was an incredible offer.

'It's not an easy assignment,' continued Schmidt. 'If you accept our offer, you would be required to relocate to our research facilities in Uttarakhand. You would have to live in residential quarters, albeit luxurious ones, on our picturesque campus. Your needs would be entirely provided for.'

'That doesn't sound too bad,' said Vijay, politely.

'You would have to cut off all physical contact with the outside world for the first three months of the assignment,' continued Schmidt.

'Why?' asked a shocked Vijay.

'It's a company rule that all new staff are subjected to. It's to protect our research, the very purpose of our existence,' replied Schmidt. 'Will that be a problem?'

'My friend, er ... girlfriend, Sujatha.'

'I understand,' said Schmidt, his expression not in the least conveying that he did. 'Unfortunately it is necessary. You could, however, continue to be in touch with her by phone, video chat or email.'

Oblivious of Vijay's expression, Schmidt continued. 'Please read through this document,' he said, pushing a thick set of papers across the desk.

'What's this?' asked Vijay, picking up the sheaf.

'It's a detailed non-disclosure agreement and code of behaviour,' said Schmidt. 'We would require you to sign it before we can confirm your appointment.'

Vijay cursorily leafed through the papers. 'What's this bit about computers, tablets and phones?' he asked.

'Milesian Labs requires that all employees only use computers, phones and equipment that are supplied by the company,' replied Schmidt. 'This is our company's protocol in order to ensure that no classified information can ever be leaked.'

'And the stuff about my previous research?'

'You provide us access to all your previous research,' replied Schmidt. 'You continue to own it and we have no proprietary claim on it.'

Ten minutes later, Vijay's interview was over. He shook hands with Schmidt and left, relieved to be away from the man.

You can pay me a king's ransom, he thought to himself, *but you guys are spooky. No way that I'm joining you!*

31

Around twenty-five people were inside the darkened room. Its walls were cushioned in purple velvet. The smell of frankincense was pervasive on account of the incense-burners located on the imposing stone altar that stood at the head of the room. Above the altar stood a massive statue fashioned in solid gold. It was that of an owl.

Other than those who were present, no one else even knew of the existence of this place. It was accessed via a nondescript entrance located in Alstadt. Each of the members had their own keys that enabled them to access the long, dimly lit passage that led to the meeting chamber.

The Worshipful Master, dressed in a dark brown robe along with a monk's hood that covered his face, spoke. 'Brothers and sisters of Minerva, heed my words.'

'O Minerva, make us heed,' chanted the others.

Each of them was dressed in a robe and hood identical to the one worn by the Worshipful Master. The only difference was that the Worshipful Master also wore a heavy golden chain around his neck from which was suspended a large ruby.

'We are descended from the oldest order of Europe. An order that came into being in 1776. An order that has defiantly stood for truth and reason.'

'May Minerva always stay true,' intoned the others.

'The Order of the Perfectibilists paved the way for so many of us. Brothers and sisters, this order was our progenitor. And it was from the Perfectibilists that we received our symbol, the sacred owl of Minerva.'

'May Minerva's owl grant us wisdom,' droned the group.

'It was our parents, the Perfectibilists, who spawned us siblings—the Illuminati and Minerva,' said the Worshipful

Master. 'The fundamental duty of the Illuminati was to fight against the religious dogma of the Catholic Church.'

'May Minerva banish dogma,' chanted the others.

'But we are neither Perfectibilists nor Illuminati. We are Minerva. The children of the Perfectibilists and the brothers of the Illuminati. Our duties and responsibilities should never be forgotten.'

'May Minerva keep us dutiful,' said the group.

'The threat in today's world is no longer the dogma of the Catholic Church. That threat was neutralized by our Illuminati brethren many years ago. No, the greatest threat is from the radicalized followers of Mohammed! It is the threat of Islamist terror that must concern us!'

'May Minerva extinguish the threat,' recited the group.

'Here is Minerva's divine revelation for you, oh brothers and sisters. Jerusalem and Constantinople will crumble. Rome will die. Mecca will decay. Only the truth will survive. This is your sole responsibility. To rid the world of the havoc wreaked by Islamism and its terror factories.'

'May Minerva make it so,' chanted the group.

'Elevate and proclaim the light, brothers and sisters. Nations, laws, monarchs and governors are mere dust before Minerva. Rise and fight!'

'Oh Minerva, make it so,' half-sang the assembly obediently.

32

The film was a typical Bollywood love-triangle. And it was precisely the reason why Vijay avoided going to the movies. Neither he nor Sujatha had the patience for endless schmaltz and predictable outcomes, and they left the cinema hall half-way through the film.

They walked over to a coffee place nearby and sat down. After they had placed their orders, Sujatha reached out to grasp his hand and looked into his eyes. 'What's troubling you, Vee?' she asked, using a nickname that no one else did. 'You've been lost this entire evening.'

Nothing escapes her, thought Vijay.

Vijay never really had time for friends or romance, given the demands of his research. Sujatha was his only friend, someone who had grown up along with him and a hundred other kids at the orphanage. Vijay and Sujatha had been the brightest among their peers, the ones who had successfully navigated the choppy waters of life without parents.

Sujatha's job at the BSI meant that she was always travelling. And that suited Vijay perfectly. He was quite happy in his solitude. But that seemed to be drawing to a close. *How do I tell her that the job offer and the possibility of marriage are spooking the hell out of me?* he wondered.

'I'm not sure that I want to take the offer made by Milesian Labs,' he said, adding several cubes of sugar to his coffee. He needed extra energy for this conversation.

'Why not?' asked Sujatha. 'Isn't it a proposal beyond your wildest dreams?'

Vijay hung onto the word 'proposal'. *Why is everything about proposals?*

'Something just doesn't feel right,' said Vijay. 'The chap who interviewed me, Schmidt, is bordering on the psychotic.'

Sujatha smiled at that, her cheeks dimpling as she did so. Vijay sometimes thought he was absolutely crazy not to immediately marry her. Sujatha was no classical beauty, but she was undeniably pretty in her own way. She was petite and kept her wavy hair at shoulder-length. She was usually attired in subdued and neatly tailored clothes that never detracted from her innate feminity. Like Vijay, Sujatha was devoted to her work but she seemed to manage her work–life balance far better than he did.

'Most bosses are psychotic,' said Sujatha, as if that was a comfort. 'I remember my last boss. She wanted me to swim along the perimeter of a lake to collect specimens of algae. And you know how much water terrifies me. But this woman would simply not take no for an answer.'

'What happened?' asked Vijay.

'Eventually she got one of the others to go in, but she never stopped giving me grief about it,' replied Sujatha. 'She made my life hell, but I stuck on.'

She paused. 'Think about it, Vee, this could be your ticket to financial freedom,' she said gently.

And marriage.

33

'Overall, you are trailing your competition by almost eight points,' said his campaign manager. 'If the elections were sooner, I would be very worried. Luckily we have a few months. Hopefully you'll peak at just the right time.'

They were in a hotel suite and the candidate was in a bad mood after seeing the poll results. 'The upcoming debates are all-important,' said his manager reassuringly. 'If you handle those well, it should be fairly easy to narrow the gap.'

'I will,' replied the Presidential-hopeful, pulling on a casual sweater over his checked shirt and jeans, his only concession to Sunday. 'The hard truth is that there isn't one America. There are many. And some of them are Americas that the press never speaks about—unemployed America, disillusioned America and xenophobic America. An

America that is angry with immigrants taking American jobs and imams blaring radical ideology from the tops of mosques. All I need to do is to tap into that groundswell of dissatisfaction.'

His manager walked over to the whiteboard that had been placed in a corner of the suite. 'Over the next couple of months you will be part of several debates, interviews, press conferences and events. Voters are interested in seeing how you handle the heat. You need to fully prepare for harsh and uncomfortable questions.'

'Really?' asked the candidate sarcastically. 'May I ask how?'

'Simple really,' answered his manager, unperturbed. 'It's called the three-step technique or the bucket method.' He began writing the steps on the whiteboard as he spoke.

'One: understand the question and dump it into an overall category—a bucket. For example, a question may be related to terrorism, healthcare, immigration, economy, taxation, defence, environment or any other broad subject.'

'Then what?' asked the candidate.

'Two: for every potential bucket, there is an answer that you would have already memorized by then, prepared to perfection. You will immediately launch into that.'

'And step three?'

'Ensure that you include words and phrases from the question,' replied his manager. 'It will make the answer seem less mechanical and more spontaneous. Remember that leaders who sound good off-the-cuff actually toil days in advance.'

There was a knock on the door and three more campaign staffers walked in. They all looked tired. The American Presidential race was one of the longest among most countries: more marathon, less sprint.

'Just thought that I would update you regarding this week's rallies,' said a woman staffer, holding a clipboard.

'Shoot,' said the candidate.

'The schedule is tightly packed with two major events every day,' she replied. 'We will ramp that up to three, and then four a day as we come closer to election day.'

'Tell me the schedule for this week.'

'Well, on Monday you will do St Augustine and Tampa in Florida; on Tuesday you continue in Florida with Sanford and Tallahassee; Wednesday is for Cleveland and Springfield in Ohio; Thursday's fixtures are Toledo and Geneva in Ohio; Friday is for Grand Rapids, followed by Warren in Michigan.'

'What about the weekend?' he asked.

'You usually have travel plans,' she said.

'All that can wait,' he said.

'In that case we'll plan Saturday in Pennsylvania at Moon Township, followed by Scranton. Sunday in Minneapolis, Minnesota.'

'Only one event on Sunday?' he asked.

'You may need a break,' she replied.

'No breaks,' he said. 'I plan on winning this thing.'

34

Syohodni was the loudest and grittiest rave circuit in Eastern Europe and was known for its stark locations and underground spirit. Syohodni was *the* go-to place if you were a youngster in Kiev.

Petrov headed to the abandoned hangar, the location of the next Syohodni rave, along with his aide from the SVR.

The hangar had been part of an airfield built by the Soviets while Ukraine had still been part of the Union. 'What's the idea of getting there at three in the morning?' asked Petrov, as he took another drag from his umpteenth cigarette.

His aide, who was driving the car, replied without taking his eyes off the road. 'This place only comes alive in the early hours of the morning. It's the hottest after-party location among the young and hip.'

'And the stoned?'

'Yes,' replied the aide. 'Ecstasy, Speed, Special K, Ice and Lucy. All available for the right price. The owner looks the other way.'

Petrov did a quick translation in his head. It was easy. Currency for information in his line of work was often drugs. Ecstasy meant MDMA—or methylenedioxymethamphetamine, but nobody knew or cared to know the mouthful; Speed was the 'cool' way of saying amphetamines; Special K stood for ketamine; Ice meant methamphetamine; and Lucy was even shorter for LSD—or lysergic acid diethylamide to the seriously uncool.

'How do people get to know where a rave is being hosted?' asked Petrov.

'They use Facebook and WhatsApp to circulate the invitations. Locations vary. Syohodni uses abandoned workshops in the dockyards, airport hangars, railway sheds, empty office blocks and closed factories as venues. Always away from the centre of Kiev. That averts unwelcome attention from the law enforcement guys.'

'How do you know that our man is there?' asked Petrov. The man in question was a former agent of Kitchener Consulting, one of the largest private investigation firms in the world. He was their best bet.

'Been tracking his phone,' came the answer. They had kept the man under surveillance for several days.

They crossed Kiev's monotonous highrises and several incomplete bridges on the river Dneiper. Thirty minutes later they reached the venue.

35

It was the perfect location for a rave, off the police radar and sufficiently distant from Kiev. They parked the car by a derelict railway line on the fringe of the discarded airstrip and walked along the potholed runway towards the thumping music that was emerging from the hangar.

'No gun?' asked Petrov.

'They pat down visitors,' said the aide. 'In any case, my hands are sufficient.'

They reached the dilapidated hangar a few minutes later. The vibrations of the loud music playing inside could be felt before entering. A bouncer at the gate looked at Petrov and his aide suspiciously as he took the entry fee from them in cash and patted them down. It was obvious to the expert that they did not belong there. Their entry had significantly increased the average age, for one.

Inside the massive hangar, hundreds of teenagers gyrated to loud electronic music. The air was thick with sweet-smelling smoke. Weed was the mildest drug on offer that night.

They made their way to the bar, a long table that stretched along the length of one side of the hall. Everything seemed available: every variety of hard liquor and recreational drug. Suddenly Petrov's aide nudged his arm. 'Your three o'clock,' he said into Petrov's ear. It was the Kitchener man.

They quickly made their way over to him. He seemed as though he was already tripping; his eyes had a glazed look. He felt a hand close in on his privates. Petrov's aide was squeezing the man's balls in a vice-like grip. 'If I want I can crush them this very instant,' he warned. 'Now be a good boy and come outside with us.'

36

It was meant to be a happy time. A time when years of hard work were bearing fruit. Then why was Vijay feeling so burdened?

If he took the job at Milesian, he would accelerate his race to financial freedom, but it would mean dealing with spooky Schmidt. If he married Sujatha, he would get the only girl he had ever cared for, but it would mean all the attendant responsibilities of married life. It seemed like a lose-lose situation.

Lost in thought, Vijay got off the Delhi Metro at Lajpat Nagar station and headed towards the address of the lawyer. The name had been given to Vijay by his mentor at IIT. The lawyer specialized in immigration law. *I can't believe that I'm seriously considering the possibility of leaving India*, thought Vijay. *That I'm contemplating the idea of giving up Sujatha and an incredible job offer. For what? To simply run away from the difficult decisions that plague me?*

He walked briskly towards Central Market. He did not notice the two men who had got on the metro along with him and had left the train the moment that he jumped off. They had been maintaining a respectable distance from him but were now closing the gap. Vijay was oblivious to them, lost in thought. He turned left into a deserted alleyway that would shorten his route. And that's when it happened.

A hand was firmly clamped over his mouth, while another pair of hands lifted him up. He struggled to free himself from the grasp of his abductors, but it was of no use. The men were far more powerful than he was. He was blindfolded and quickly bundled into a van of some sort.

Vijay was forced into the middle of the rear bench seat, sandwiched between two men so that he would be unable to open either of the doors. Vijay attempted to discern how many people were in the vehicle. Four, going by the voices. They were discussing something in Marathi, a language Vijay could not understand. *Mumbai mafia?*

'Who are you?' asked Vijay, his voice quavering.

There was no reply.

'Where are you taking me?' asked Vijay, a little more forcefully. He was attempting to come across as confident even though he was scared nearly witless.

Again, there was only silence. Over the sound of traffic and honking, absolutely nothing was said.

37

Vijay opened his eyes as soon as the blindfold was removed. He squinted as the light of the overhead bulbs hit him. Where was he?

It had seemed like over two hours in the car. They had only stopped once when he had complained that he needed to empty his bladder. They had halted along what had seemed to him an isolated stretch of road to enable him to relieve himself, but the blindfold had stayed intact and his abductors had remained companiably by his side.

After what seemed like an eternity, the car had come to a halt. The men had guided Vijay out and into a building, untying his blindfold as soon as he was seated.

He saw the backs of his abductors as they left him alone. One of them was wearing a t-shirt emblazoned with 'Mumbai Indians' on the back.

Vijay looked about him. It seemed as though he was inside a giant abandoned warehouse. Above him were ominously high ceilings criss-crossed by rafters of rusting metal. It was a massive industrial space, the hard concrete floor on all sides of his chair seeming to stretch into infinity, meeting up with exposed brick walls containing vast but boarded-up windows. Huge ducts and exposed pipes ran overhead, enhancing the eeriness of his surroundings. Several naked bulbs hung on wires from an ancient beam overhead. The only furniture comprised a table and several chairs scattered around it.

He heard footsteps. Four people walked in. They sat down on chairs placed opposite his.

'Our apologies for bringing you here like this,' said the lone woman. 'It was done for your own safety.'

Vijay's brain was in overdrive. Who was this woman? Her accent told him she was American. He looked at the three others, all men. A Caucasian man, a South Asian and a Chinese. *Where the fuck am I?* thought Vijay desperately. *And who are these goddamned people?*

'I'm Judith Frost,' said the lady. 'The others here are my colleagues: Yuri Petrov, Rakesh Sharma and Jin Zhang.'

'Who are you? Why have you brought me here?' asked Vijay, becoming a tad bolder.

'We represent a group of intelligence operatives from around the world,' replied Judith. 'We are called the IG4. I am on deputation from the CIA, Petrov is from the Russian SVR, Sharma is from your country's RAW and Zhang represents the Chinese MSS.'

Fine, but why am I here? Is this a case of mistaken identity?

One of Vijay's abductors, the one wearing the Mumbai Indians t-shirt, walked in with a tray. It contained bottles of water, mugs of tea and biscuits.

'You must be parched,' said Judith, as the man placed a bottle and a mug of tea in front of him. Vijay opened the bottle gratefully and took big gulps. Then he had a few sips of the tea. It felt good.

He cleared his throat. 'Why am I here? I think you've mistaken me for someone else,' he began.

'Your name is Vijay Sundaram. You are a PhD scholar at IIT Delhi. You have just completed your thesis and are interviewing for a position at Milesian Labs. You have also interviewed at other companies including Google and SpaceX. You have a girlfriend called Sujatha Iyer. You were brought up at an orphanage in Sringeri, Karnataka.' Judith stopped. 'Do we have the right person?'

'Y-yes,' stammered Vijay, 'but what do you want from me?'

'We want you to accept the job that Milesian Labs has offered you.'

38

The IG4 had met the previous week at a bungalow located in the Lutyens Bungalow Zone.

Named after the British architect Edwin Lutyens, the area was neighbour to the impressive Rashtrapati Bhawan, the official residence of the President of India. Around a thousand exclusive residential bungalows were located in this zone and less than 10 per cent of those were in private hands.

The IG4 venue had been arranged by Sharma. The house belonged to a steel magnate who had shifted base to

Singapore. He often loaned the house to powerful and connected friends such as Sharma, besides residing there when he visited Delhi.

The four members were seated in comfortable armchairs in the living room overlooking a sprawling garden that had hosted several high-profile parties. A sleek no-vent fireplace in brushed steel kept the interiors toasty. Bug sweeps had been meticulously carried out earlier in the day.

Petrov had spent the morning reviewing the photographs his aide at the SVR had put together. It had been a mammoth task. Petrov had asked for every available photograph of the four dead leaders to be collected and analyzed. His aide had searched multiple public and private sources to aggregate the photographs. Each picture had then been subjected to face recognition algorithms and additional information from the former Kitchener agent had been used to filter the pictures further.

Before anyone else could speak, Petrov stood up and cleared his throat. 'Have any of you heard of Minerva?' he asked, pulling a file from his briefcase. He had everyone's attention.

'That crackpot group?' asked Judith. 'Much more of a conspiracy theory, right? Like the "Priory of Sion" that turned out to be a con?' The Priory of Sion had been created as a hoax by a Frenchman, Pierre Plantard, in 1956. He had succeeded in spinning a tale that the priory had been founded in 1099, and was committed to installing a bloodline descendant of Mary Magdalene on the throne.

'You may need to revise your opinion,' replied Petrov. 'Minerva has some very high-ranking members, including judges, scientists, businessmen, politicians, diplomats, bureaucrats and the like as members. And it's not just a social club. It was registered in 1926 as a foundation in

Liechtenstein. That indicates a level of seriousness about what they are doing.'

'What is a foundation?' asked Zhang. 'I mean, legally speaking.'

'A foundation is an independent special-purpose fund,' said Petrov. 'It has a legal personality of its own—one that is distinct and separate from the private assets of the settlor.'

'Which also means that it's a dead end,' said Judith. 'Foundations are usually not subject to statutory audit.'

'Ah,' said Petrov. 'They are not subject to audit *if* they do not carry on commercial activity. If the foundation's interests include a commercial enterprise, then an audit board must be appointed. A balance sheet audited by the board must then be submitted each year to Liechtenstein's tax authorities.'

'And is that the case with Minerva?' asked Sharma.

'Yes,' said Petrov, nodding. 'Two of my men at the SVR are on it. Remember the common link across the four deaths? They were all liberals.'

'Minerva has found a way to kill liberals around the world? To what end?' asked Zhang. 'As of now it seems merely a hunch.'

'And even if this secretive group called Minerva does exist,' added Judith, 'how do we tie it to these deaths?'

'If you wanted to eliminate a high-powered individual, you would first need to investigate that person thoroughly, right? Discover their soft spots?' asked Petrov. 'You would dig deep into the person's background, financial position, family life, liaisons, relationships, daily schedule, strengths and weaknesses?'

'Absolutely,' replied Judith.

'If any of the four of us wanted to carry out such an investigation, it would be child's play given our respective intelligence networks,' said Petrov. 'To whom would a private organization such as Minerva go?'

'Kitchener,' replied Sharma effortlessly.

'Precisely,' said Petrov. 'Kitchener Consulting, the most powerful private snooping agency in the world. Available for hire to anyone who has big bucks to throw. We managed to get hold of one of their former agents in Kiev. Someone that Kitchener had sacked because of his drug habit.'

Petrov handed over a USB flash drive to Judith. 'There are several transactions in the inter-bank settlement system that are highlighted here. You will see that massive amounts have been paid by the Minerva Foundation to Kitchener.'

Judith opened up the file so that everyone could have a look. 'The payments were to Atherton, not Kitchener,' she said, running her eyes down the list.

'Kitchener is owned by Atherton AB,' retorted Petrov. 'As is well known in intelligence circles,' he added acidly.

'Just playing devil's advocate here, the payments could have been for other services,' said Judith in her own defence. 'The Atherton group is not only involved in investigative services but also in employment screening, security management and the like.'

'Open the second file,' said Petrov. 'Photographs of known Kitchener agents. The photos show that these agents have been spotted on several occasions in the vicinity of the four leaders who died. It is evident that Kitchener was used by Minerva to gather information on the targets.'

'The theory is elegant,' said Judith. 'But how are they killing global leaders without leaving any tracks? Symptoms show up, then disappear. No traces left! Poof! And how does Minerva penetrate the thick layer of security that surrounds such high-powered individuals? There are just too many unanswered questions.'

'Personally, I'm convinced,' said Petrov. 'It's most likely an attempt at snuffing out liberal voices so that conservative ones on the far right may be amplified. This would accelerate the world's descent into an all-out war with the Islamic world. Isn't it possible that it's exactly what Minerva wants? *A final solution?*'

The other three members were silent.

'There's one more thing,' said Petrov, looking at the faces of his colleagues one by one. They were now hanging onto his every word. *This is the way it should be,* thought Petrov. *Mother Russia must always stay ahead.*

'I am happy to tell you that we have managed to access the records of Minerva,' announced Petrov.

39

The Russian had kept the best part for the last. It was the icing on the cake. As he said the words, he had glanced at Judith to see her reaction.

Her face had fallen, almost instantly. The Cold War animosity between America and Russia played out at every level, even in the present day. The war in Syria and the allegations of Russian interference in the on-going American elections had ensured that the rivalry continued.

'More importantly,' continued Petrov smugly, 'we now know the names of the commercial enterprises owned by Minerva.'

'What!' exclaimed Zhang.

'There are two,' said Petrov. 'One is located in Scotland. It's called Molecular and Universal Audio. The other one is called Milesian Labs, and the main facility is located just a few hours away from here in the Indian state of Utt-Uttarakhand,' he completed, struggling only momentarily with the name. He held up a photograph that showed the entrance to the Milesian Labs facility. Along the pathway to the gate were flags bearing the Milesian logo.

'What do these companies do?' asked Sharma.

'Molecular and Universal Audio has been established only recently,' said Petrov. 'But Milesian Labs is a few decades old. Thus it is Milesian Labs that we need to focus on. The company is involved in research.'

'What sort of research?' asked Zhang.

'Pure science,' answered Petrov. 'They pride themselves on not sullying their portfolio with applied science. They make money by researching and then registering patents. One hundred and sixty-four at last count.'

'Should we consider sending our operatives inside?' asked Sharma.

'You have no idea what sort of facility this is,' replied Petrov. 'It's impregnable, like a fortress. There are less than ten scientists inside a facility that is spread over a thousand acres. Anyone that we send in would be instantly identified, but I think I may have a solution.'

'And that is?' asked Judith.

'One of the senior researchers at that particular facility was originally part of the Russian Academy of Sciences,' said Petrov. 'Unfortunately, he is a bit of an oddball—incredibly eccentric. I would have to work on him and that may be too late. Hence, I suggest an alternative.'

'Who?' asked Sharma.

Petrov asked Judith to pull up a photograph on her computer screen. It showed a tall, sombre, white-haired man.

'Who is this?' asked Zhang.

'His name is Dr Klaus Schmidt,' replied Petrov. 'He is the Chief of Research at Milesian Labs. Once our boys at the SVR got to know about him, we put him under surveillance.'

'And?' asked Judith. Her face had turned red. Having permitted the SVR to score over the CIA was hugely embarrassing.

'He was in Delhi recently to interview a potential recruit,' replied Petrov. 'Maybe that new recruit could be our ticket into Milesian Labs.'

40

The atmosphere inside the warehouse was tense. 'I don't understand,' said Vijay. 'Why are you concerned whether I take up the job offer at Milesian or not?'

Judith looked at Sharma. There was an imperceptible nod.

'Are you familiar with the name Samuel P. Huntington?' asked Sharma.

'Who is he?' asked Vijay. His entire life had been spent studying physics.

'Was,' clarified Sharma. 'He died in 2008. He was a political scientist who put forward a theory called *The Clash of Civilizations*. According to this theory, cultural and religious identities would be the main reason for global conflict in the post-Cold War world.'

'What does this have to do with me?' asked Vijay.

'First, let me explain to you why our group, the IG4, even exists,' replied Sharma. 'The two global superpowers and the two emerging superpowers of the world have the most to lose in the event of an uncontrolled global conflict, one brought on by the sort of polarization that Huntington spoke of. The intelligence agencies of our four countries have temporarily put aside their differences to collaborate and create IG4—Intelligence Group of Four. The biggest challenge we face is the prospect of the clash of civilizations becoming an all-out war between Muslims and the rest of the world.'

Vijay was bewildered. *What does my job offer have to do with all this?* he wondered. *These guys are nuts.*

'Over the past few months, several world leaders have died,' said Judith. 'These were staunch liberals who were attempting to moderate the dialogue between the Islamic world and the West. We believe that they died precisely for that reason.'

Vijay shrugged. He still had no idea of what these chaps were going on about.

'Milesian Labs is owned by an ultra-conservative group called Minerva,' replied Judith. 'Minerva seems to be killing off the world's liberal leaders so that conservative voices get heard over the international cacophony. This would result in an escalation of conflict, not just with Islamism but also with Islam.'

'What's the difference?' asked Vijay.

'Lots,' replied Judith. 'Islam is a faith, a means to worship. Islamism is political Islam espoused by groups that aim to establish a Sharia-based Islamic state.'

'Each of the people eliminated died mysteriously,' added Sharma. 'Unfortunately, we do not know how Minerva succeeds in breaching the security around these people and then kills them without poisoning, shooting, strangling, stabbing, drowning or any of the other usual methods. That's why we need you to go inside.'

'You've *got* to be kidding me,' said Vijay. 'You want me to put my own life on the line on account of this ridiculous theory of yours? Forget it, Samuel Hunter be damned.'

'Samuel Huntington,' corrected Judith as she continued staring into Vijay's eyes.

41

Alexei Mikhailov sat motionless inside his apartment suite within the Milesian Labs facility in Uttarakhand. He was seated on a yoga mat in the lotus position, his legs locked together, his spine ramrod straight and his shoulders relaxed. His eyes were closed and he was breathing slowly and deeply. His stance was no different from that of the ancient statues depicting Shiva or Buddha. Years of practice ensured that Mikhailov's body was almost entirely inert and his mind free from distractions.

At sixty, Mikhailov was one of the oldest residents of the complex. He was odd in appearance, primarily because he maintained his hair in a fuzzy Einstein-like fashion. He was a thin man with a hooked nose, the prototype of a mad scientist in a horror film.

But in the world of Russian science, Mikhailov was aristocracy. Mikhailov's grandfather, Viktor, had been one of the researchers sent by the Russians to search for the elusive Shangri-La, the supposed hidden paradise on earth. In order to garner clues about the exact geographical location of Shangri-La, Viktor's group had also carried out excavations among the remains of the ancient monastery at Nalanda.

Mikhailov's father, Vladimir, had been one of the leading researchers at City-40, more commonly known as Chelyabinsk-40, the birthplace of the Soviet nuclear weapons programme after the Second World War. The plant that the Soviets built there, one of the largest production facilities of weapons-grade plutonium during the Cold War, had leaked huge amounts of radioactive material into the area that immediately surrounded the plant. Vladimir had died young from leukaemia and the responsibility of bringing up Mikhailov had fallen on his grandfather.

Mikhailov felt himself dissolving into the cosmos. He had always been spiritually inclined, probably on account of the stories that his grandfather had narrated to him about his quest for Shangri-La. More importantly, Mikhailov was also a keen practitioner of meditation and had learnt under one of the great spiritual masters in Kashmir. This often enabled him to 'perceive' information that was not so obvious to others.

And then he felt it.

Mikhailov forced himself to keep his eyes shut and to remain focused, but this was happening far too frequently for comfort these days. It was a disruption in his energy flow, almost the equivalent of a static charge. And it was never uniform. But what was causing it? *Am I imagining things?* he wondered.

Mikhailov opened his eyes, frustrated. He would need to start recording the exact times at which the energy spikes occurred.

42

'I have made up my mind,' said Vijay. 'There is no reason why I should work at Milesian and put my own life in danger. I am a simple scientist. I want to get on with my research and my life.'

The members of IG4 stayed absolutely silent. The warehouse felt even more ghostly in the stillness.

Then Judith got up from her chair and placed her notebook computer in front of Vijay on the table. She clicked on a file that opened up a media player window. Video footage began playing.

Vijay looked at it reluctantly. He snapped out of his hesitation when he realized what was contained in the video recording.

Sujatha.

'These clips have been compiled over the past week by Petrov,' said Judith. They showed Sujatha in the mall; at the metro station; entering the cinema; and leaving her BSI office. In each frame, a lean stranger with a gaunt face could be seen lurking a few steps away.

The video compilation ran for less than five minutes. 'Now look at this,' said Judith, clicking open another file. Again, it was a video that had been strung together from various source files. It showed Vijay walking out from the IIT gate; entering a coffee shop; exiting the supermarket; waiting for a train at the station. A dark man with a pockmarked face could be seen trailing him in all the clips.

Judith observed Vijay's expression. He was shaken. She moved in for the kill. 'The people stalking you and your girlfriend are Minerva associates. The only reason we have this evidence is because we have been keeping tabs on Minerva.'

Vijay was stunned into silence. After what seemed like an interminable lull, he asked, 'Were you the ones who searched my flat?'

'No,' said Judith. 'But we have video recordings of the Minerva agents who did. How safe will either you or Sujatha be if you are not under IG4's protective umbrella? Isn't it possible that Minerva will use Sujatha as leverage to get you to fall in line? She travels alone all over the country as part of her job. How difficult would it be for them to get her? Or you?'

'That's a low blow,' muttered Vijay. But something else was nagging him. *Those operatives who were following Sujatha and me—how can I be certain that they were Minerva people and not IG4 agents?*

'You're wondering whether the people following you were our agents,' said Judith. The woman had more than a sixth sense. Vijay nodded mutely.

'Let me show you the clips yet again,' said Judith, clicking the play button yet again.

'See? You are indeed being followed by us. But our agent is behind the Minerva man. Please observe carefully.' Vijay saw the Mumbai Indians t-shirt man, one of the group who had abducted him. It seemed obvious Judith was telling him the truth.

Else she was a very good liar.

43

'Vee!' exclaimed Sujatha. 'What happened to you?'

Vijay's face and eyes were swollen. His upper lip had a gash and his clothes were badly torn. He had arrived at Sujatha's tiny flat in a taxi he kept waiting downstairs so that she could pay his fare for him. His wallet, chain, watch and phone were missing.

She supported Vijay as he hobbled towards the sofa. After paying his taxi fare, she made him as comfortable as she could, propped up against a soft pillow.

Vijay stared blankly at the statue on the side table by Sujatha's sofa. It was a figure of Ardhanarishvara, a figure that depicted Shiva and Shakti combined as one. He gazed at it for an extended spell in a stupor. Sujatha interrupted his reverie. 'Swallow two of these,' she said, offering him paracetamol pills along with a glass of water. 'Should I make some tea?'

'Do you have anything stronger?' asked Vijay, wincing in pain.

Sujatha remembered that she had received a bottle of flavoured vodka from a friend for her birthday a month ago. She quickly brought it out from the kitchen and opened it. Vijay poured himself two fingers of the clear liquid and took a gulp. He winced as the alcohol made contact with the cut on his lip.

'Will you please tell me what happened?' asked Sujatha, on the verge of tears.

'I was on my way to meet an immi—'

He bit his tongue to prevent himself from completing the word 'immigration'. 'Someone at Lajpat Nagar,' said Vijay slowly. 'Along the way I took a shortcut through an alleyway that was deserted.'

'And?' asked Sujatha.

'I was mugged,' said Vijay. 'I can't remember exactly how many thugs there were, but it felt like three or four. They bashed me around and then fled with my valuables.'

'Hell,' muttered Sujatha. 'I should take you to the hospital.'

'Nothing is broken,' replied Vijay. 'If we go to the hospital, they will ask us to file an FIR with the police. I don't want to do that.' *Filing a First Information Report will leave too many glaring gaps in my story.*

'Why not?' asked Sujatha. 'It would be better that those brutes are caught.'

'Because I do not want to answer the hundreds of questions that will inevitably follow, and lead nowhere,' answered Vijay. 'I need to leave Delhi in a few days and if there were to be a police case, they would need me to appear at the magistrate's court.'

'Where are you going?' asked Sujatha.

'I've decided to take your advice,' said Vijay. 'I'm accepting the financial security that a job with Milesian Labs offers.'

44

Vijay had not wanted to lie to Sujatha about what had happened to him, but the necessity of doing so had been made evident to him by IG4. If Sujatha were ever abducted, the less she knew, the safer she would be.

At the warehouse meeting with his abductors, Vijay realized that, whether he liked it or not, he was already stuck neck-deep. He looked at the four members of IG4 for reactions but there were none.

'I'll accept Schmidt's offer,' he said eventually. 'But how will you ensure that Sujatha and I are protected?'

Sharma got up from his chair and walked to where Vijay sat. In his hand was something that looked like a gun. Vijay looked warily at it as Sharma inched closer.

'Stop worrying,' said Sharma. 'What I'm holding is a jet-injector. It's a syringe that uses a high-pressure jet of liquid to penetrate the epidermis. It is powered by compressed air. I'm going to use it to embed a really tiny microchip under your skin.'

Observing the consternation on Vijay's face, Judith interrupted. 'The microchip is cutting-edge, not yet commercially available. It draws power from electrolytes within the human body. The chip will keep us aware of your location as well as your physical condition. Once the assignment is over, the chip can be removed.'

'Physical condition?' asked Vijay. 'Is that a euphemism for whether I'm dead or alive?'

He yelped as the injector transferred the wheat-grain sized chip into his upper arm with a whoosh.

Sharma applied an adhesive strip to the spot where the chip had been embedded. 'You can take off the strip in ten minutes.'

'What if I need to pass through scanning devices?' asked Vijay. 'Will the microchip show up?'

'No,' replied Sharma. 'The chip is engineered from flexible polymer lined by animal tissue. If it does get detected, it will simply show up as a cyst or hardened tissue.'

Vijay digested the information. *These IG4 guys think about everything. Terrifying foursome.*

'Anything else?' asked Vijay, already regretting the fact that he had agreed to go along with IG4.

'We need to rough you up,' replied Judith.

'Wh-why?' spluttered Vijay.

'Relax,' said Judith. 'We simply need you to accept a few blows to your face so that your bruises allow you the luxury of a cover. You are obviously under surveillance by Minerva. You will need a cover story to explain your current absence from their radar. We would like you to maintain that you were mugged and left unconscious at a deserted warehouse. This narrative is necessary to make sure that Minerva does not get suspicious.'

'Is this really necessary?' asked Vijay, not relishing the prospect of being bashed about.

'You will need to maintain the same story with Sujatha,' said Judith, ignoring his question. 'You must not reveal anything about IG4 or the true purpose of your job at Milesian Labs. This is to ensure Sujatha's safety, in the event that she is ever captured by Minerva.'

Why don't you say you don't want to take the risk of Sujatha revealing anything to her captors if she is ever abducted? thought Vijay.

Before Vijay could argue further, Petrov administered a blow to the right side of his face. Vijay howled in agony, but before he could recover, Petrov landed yet another punch. And then another.

Petrov seemed to be enjoying himself. *The bastard.*

45

The team was huddled around monitors at the facility in Livingston. Located in Louisiana, the monitoring station was surrounded by vast and wet loblolly pine forests. The location was distant enough from human habitation to prevent interference in the detectors.

The team's director, a short and podgy Irish-American called Harvey Walsh, wanted to be abundantly sure that they hadn't goofed up. It had been fifteen years since they had first started looking for gravitational waves—ripples in the spacetime fabric of the universe. It was a hundred years since Albert Einstein had predicted their existence, but they had been impossible to detect until now.

Harvey's facility was known as the Laser Interferometer Gravitational-Wave Observatory, or LIGO. The Livingston facility consisted of two arms, each four kilometres long, placed at ninety degrees to one another. An identical facility was located around three thousand kilometres away at Hanford, Washington.

Both sites had been chosen very carefully. There were only a few places where vast tracts of land could be provided for a colossal science experiment that needed miles of empty space. Much in the way that astronomical telescopes are built at considerable distance from city lights that pollute the night sky, gravitational wave observatories need to be insulated from the vibrations of usual human activity.

'It's a wrap, guys,' said Harvey. 'I'm taking a break. Just ensure that the data has been fully backed up before we call it a day. Each one of you has been magnificent.' He clapped for them and they returned the favour. Harvey looked through the window at Judith Frost and waved. He exited the door and gave her a hug. 'Let's go get some coffee,' he said to her, his red cheeks puffing up as he smiled.

'Thanks for calling me here,' said Judith. 'Big day.'

'We would never have reached this day without your help,' said Harvey. 'I understand science but not the science of networking.'

Harvey was referring to the fact that LIGO would have died a premature death without Judith's schmoosing. LIGO had been through a series of rollercoaster twists since inception. A prototype interferometer had been built with military funding in 1967, but the project was cancelled even before it started operating. Similar projects had been tried at Hughes Research Laboratories in addition to MIT and Caltech but with little progress. The US Congress eventually agreed to finance LIGO, and in 2015 it undertook a $620-million revamp to make its interferometers four times more sensitive than the earlier versions. They struck gold within a year, detecting gravitational waves from two black holes that had merged around 1.3 billion light-years from Earth. LIGO had succeeded in proving Einstein's theory right.

Judith and Harvey had attended Seymour High School together and had been the best of friends, but their careers had taken them in different directions. They had reconnected many years later by which time both of them were well-established in their respective occupations. Judith had helped Harvey lobby influential people in business and politics to ensure that LIGO's capital requirements came through. At one time he had been ready to quit, given the vagaries of financing.

46

Harvey and Judith walked over to the cafeteria and settled down at a table with their coffee cups. Behind them hung a map of the United States with the two LIGO locations, Hanford and Livingston, marked.

'Why do you need two facilities that are at opposite ends of North America?' asked Judith. 'I have always wondered about this but never got down to asking.'

'LIGO's detectors are very sensitive,' said Harvey, vigorously stirring his coffee. 'They can detect the teeniest vibrations. Unfortunately, road construction, vehicle movement or field ploughing cause disturbances that can be misread as gravitational waves. Two facilities located far apart cannot simultaneously feel local vibrations, but

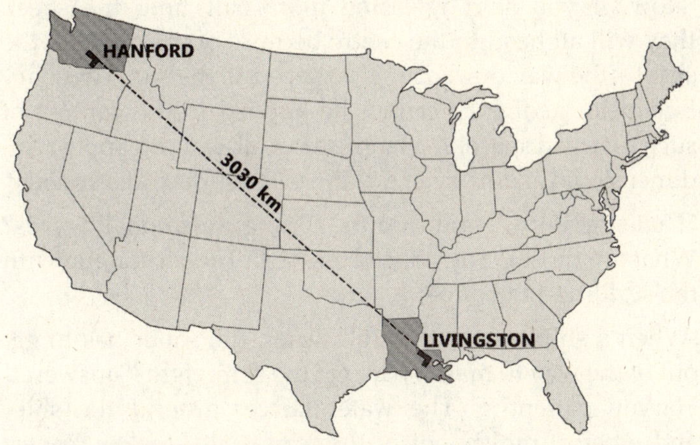

they can experience distant gravitational waves in parallel. Having two locations ensures that what we detect are actually gravitational waves and not local tremors.'

'Although I've been here several times, I still can't seem to get my head around the idea of gravitational waves,' said Judith. 'I feel like I'm back in high school, depending on you to help me with my math and science homework.'

Harvey laughed. 'Think of a sheet that is stretched open and held by four people at the corners,' he said. Judith attempted to visualize it. 'Now, a fifth person drops a heavy ball into the middle of the sheet. What will happen?'

'The sheet will sag at the centre?' asked Judith tentatively.

'Absolutely right,' said Harvey, quickly sketching a diagram on the back of a paper napkin.

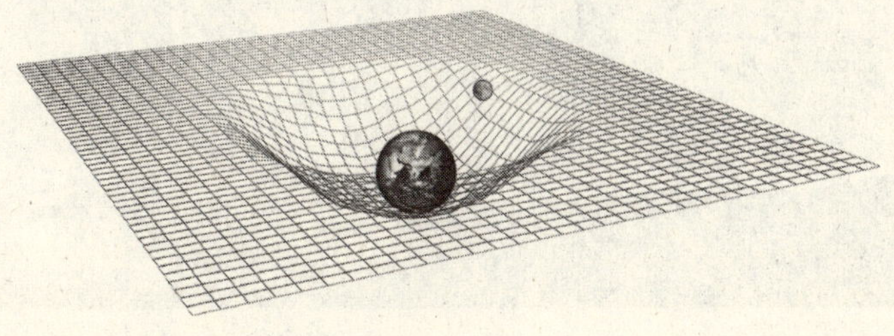

'Now, if you start releasing more balls into the sheet, they will all head to the centre because of the curve in the sheet—the way our Earth is attracted to the sun. Ordinary Euclidean geometry cannot be applied in the context of such a curved spacetime fabric. After all, can you apply two-dimensional geometry of a plane to the surface of a sphere?'

'That's gravity,' said Judith. 'But gravitational waves? What are those?' She winced as she burnt her tongue with the scalding-hot coffee.

'When a ship moves through water, the water has to get out of the way to make space for the ship, right?' answered Harvey patiently. 'The water curves around the ship, and when it moves out of the way it also makes ripples on the surface. Now, just like the example I gave you, colossal objects—black holes for instance—move through space and make ripples in spacetime. These are called gravitational waves.'

'And how does LIGO detect them?' asked Judith.

'Can you see the photograph on that far wall?' asked Harvey pointing towards it. 'It shows the layout of our facility here at Livingston.'

Judith looked at the extra-large backlit image covering one wall of the cafeteria. It showed an aerial view of the LIGO facility.

'The ripples caused by gravitational waves are negligible by the time they reach the earth. Some compress spacetime by as little as one ten-thousandth the width of a proton,' explained Harvey. 'So how do we detect them?'

'Exactly, how?' asked Judith.

'We have these two long arms running out several miles at ninety degrees to one another,' replied Harvey. 'We send laser beams down from each of these arms so that the beams cancel each other out perfectly when they arrive here. But what does a gravitational wave do? It stretches one tube while squeezing the other. This alters the distance that the two laser beams travel. As a result the beams no longer cancel out perfectly. The resulting residual light is what alerts us to a gravitational wave.'

Judith shook her head in awe. It was incredible stuff.

'Do you know what is even more interesting?' asked Harvey. 'We can convert gravitational waves into sound! We can actually *hear* gravitational waves. The sounds of the universe!'

'And what do they sound like?' asked Judith.

'Almost like a drop of water in a bucket, but we still have to collect more data. Indian sages used to meditate on a sound, *Om,* that they claimed was the primordial sound that accompanied the creation of the universe. Who knows? We may just find it.'

'I hope you do,' said Judith. She stirred her coffee absentmindedly for a few seconds and then spoke to Harvey in a hushed voice.

'Now that LIGO is well-established,' she said, 'would you be interested in considering a competing job offer? Something even more challenging? One of my friends mentioned your name the other day.'

47

In a darkened room located at Milesian Labs sat a former operative of the National Security Agency. He was known to most people only by his nickname—Cracker. He was a bulldog of a man, stocky, muscular, round-faced and red. Having been part of the NSA, an organization that intercepted telephone and internet communications of over a billion people worldwide, the job at Milesian was child's play. He reported only to Schmidt.

Across the table now sat the German, perfectly turned out, unlike Cracker. He was looking at a set of photographs that had been taken of Vijay. 'His face was beaten up pretty bad,' said Cracker. 'He never filed a police complaint though. I checked with our police liaison in New Delhi.'

'How long was he missing?' asked Schmidt.

'A few hours,' said Cracker. 'Claimed to his girlfriend that his valuables were stolen and that he was assaulted and left in an abandoned warehouse.'

'Does his story check out?' asked Schmidt.

'We interviewed the cabbie that dropped him to his girlfriend's place,' replied Cracker. 'The girl had to pay because his wallet was gone. Also, there are three warehouses on the road where he was supposedly assaulted. Any of them could have been the place he was dumped. His bruises are genuine. There is no evidence that indicates anything to the contrary.'

'I'm not fully convinced,' said Schmidt. 'Let's step up our surveillance until he gets here.'

48

The Indian state of Uttarakhand lay nestled at the foothills of the Himalayas, sharing its northern border with China and Nepal. For locals it wasn't Uttarakhand but *Devbhumi*, the land of the Gods, and the gateway to the Himalayas. And so it was. Numerous ancient pilgrimage spots dotted the snow-covered mountains, the terrain's natural beauty only adding to the intrinsic spirituality of the area.

The flight from Delhi to Jolly Grant Airport near Dehradun took exactly an hour. Arriving there, Vijay quickly pulled his suitcase from the baggage claim and exited the airport. A chauffeured SUV awaited him. It would be a seven-hour drive towards Kalimath, uncomfortably close to the Indo-China border. The research facility of Milesian Labs was located near Kalimath.

Vijay ignored the beautiful sights around him. His mind was entirely on Sujatha. Earlier that morning, he had bid her farewell, knowing that he would be cut off from her for the next three months. She had hugged him tightly, feeling guilty about having encouraged him to take the assignment. 'Ironically, I shall be in your neighbourhood soon,' she had finally said as she pulled away. 'I have received security clearance to collect plant samples from a few of the forest areas in Uttarakhand. I'm going to miss you even more, knowing that you are so close and yet so far.'

At that moment, Vijay knew that he was in love with her. He recalled reading somewhere that love was not about finding someone you could live with. Rather, it was about finding someone you couldn't live without. It was the prospect of living *without* Sujatha that made Vijay realize that he needed her. But something prevented him from telling her that he loved her. Or that he now wanted nothing more than to spend the rest of his life married to her.

49

It was six in the evening when Vijay's SUV drew up outside the gates of Milesian Labs. His face was hit by a blast of cold air as the chauffeur opened the door for him. Winter temperatures dropped to minus seven degrees here, but, mercifully, the lows had yet to arrive. Some consolation.

Nestled in the Garhwal Himalayas, Kalimath stood at an altitude of over six thousand feet above sea level and was endowed with immense natural beauty, surrounded by the mountains of Kedarnath, one of the holiest sites of Hinduism. The area around it was famous for its glaciers, walking trails, deep forests, snow-clad summits, thermal springs, meadows, waterfalls and streams.

Vehicles were not allowed inside the Milesian campus, which was located east of Kalimath. One of the security officers of the company was waiting outside to receive him at the car park. On his lapel was the Milesian logo, a circle within a triangle containing the letter 'M'.

The security officer led him through a winding pathway that cut through forestland to reach the massive Milesian gate manned by guards and Rottweilers. Just outside the gate was a colossal sculpture of a dancing Nataraja encased inside a pinecone-shaped structure.

It was a stunning piece of art and Vijay stared at it for a while before moving on. The security officer efficiently helped Vijay with his luggage and directed him through several checkpoints that led into the facility. He was assigned a safe deposit box in which he could leave his personal electronic items. He would be able to access them on his way out three months later. Both his luggage and his person were scanned as he passed through. Vijay held his breath, wondering whether the microchip embedded in his arm would set off any alarm bells, but he sailed through.

From here, Vijay was escorted to a cable car station that provided an aerial link to the facility that was located at a substantial elevation. The total distance was around two kilometres, with a journey time from the base to the top of seven minutes. Unlike most cable cars that offered substantial views through plate glass windows, this one was entirely enclosed, offering no views of the landscape.

Strange, thought Vijay to himself. *What are they hiding?*

50

As soon as they reached the facility, Vijay was led to a studio apartment furnished in contemporary chic, blending stone, steel, wood and glass into highly desirable accommodation that looked as if it belonged in the pages of *Architectural Digest*. It was perfectly suited for him, with a small living room cum en suite bedroom with an open-plan kitchen. The plate glass windows of the living area looked out into the forested hills. On a desk by the fireplace were a brand new notebook computer, a mobile phone and tablet, all duly charged and ready for use.

There was a soft knock on the open door. At the entrance was Dr Klaus Schmidt. 'I am delighted to see you, Mr Sundaram,' he said with all the excitement of a paperweight. 'I shall be happy to show you around our beautiful campus. Put on your jacket and I will wait for you outside.'

Vijay gratefully accepted the offer. But first, he quickly made a call from his new phone to Sujatha to say he had arrived. 'I'm missing you,' said Sujatha. Vijay wanted to tell her that he had been a fool not to propose marriage and that he loved her and missed her, but there wasn't any time. Schmidt was waiting outside. He quickly left his apartment after putting on a heavier jacket.

There wasn't any need to lock the door behind him because there was no keyhole, only a fingerprint sensor that had been programmed for Vijay. All doors in the Milesian facility only had biometric locks.

51

Spread over a thousand acres, the facility of Milesian Labs was like the setting of a science fiction movie. A massive concrete-framed building provided a modern state-of-the-art laboratory where nine researchers worked in a fifty thousand-square-foot lab. 'Each researcher operates from a designated mini-lab of around five thousand square feet,' said Schmidt. 'There are nine who joined before you. You are the tenth. Our team is now complete.'

Scattered around the lab were residential studio apartments for the researchers, a multi-cuisine coffee shop and bar, a convenience store, a massive library, plush movie theatre, sophisticated gym, temperature-controlled pool and well-equipped health centre.

'Let me walk you through the library,' said Schmidt. It was an independent building that occupied four floors. 'We have well over a hundred thousand books here in addition to audio-visual content and material that is available electronically. Four fulltime librarians manage this place so that you should never feel that your research is not being adequately supported by us.'

Vijay was in awe. Schmidt noticed.

'Of the thousand acres that we own,' he continued as they exited the library and walked towards the residential block, 'only fifty have been utilized for the infrastructure that you see. The remaining nine hundred and fifty acres are dense woods that envelop the facility—our contribution to preserving the environment.'

The fifty-acre work-and-stay facility was almost the equivalent of a cherry sitting on an oversized black forest cake. Heightening the sense of seclusion was the fact that the grounds were guarded by armed security personnel and guard dogs along the perimeter gates and electrified access points, biometric scanners and CCTV cameras every few metres. *All this, for ten researchers,* thought Vijay. *Am I an employee or a prisoner? A bird in a golden cage?*

'I loved that Nataraja statue outside the main gate,' said Vijay to Schmidt.

'Glad you liked it,' replied Schmidt. 'It's a replica of the one at CERN—the European Organization for Nuclear Research—except for the fact that this one is enclosed.'

'Why Nataraja?' asked Vijay.

Schmidt pulled out his phone from his pocket and showed Vijay his wallpaper.

'CERN is concerned with the God particle, the Higgs boson, that had been predicted by another illustrious Indian, Satyendranath Bose. The dance of Shiva is nothing but the dance of subatomic particles. Moving, morphing and transforming.'

'Creation to destruction and back,' murmured Vijay.

'No,' said Schmidt. 'There is neither creation nor destruction. Only appearance and disappearance.'

Outside one of the Milesian perimeter gates, a man in a heavy woollen jacket dialled a number on his mobile phone. 'He's inside,' said the man into his phone, his breath fogging in the cold air.

52

Vijay's first day at work commenced with a meeting in which he was introduced by Schmidt to the other nine scientists. The research that Milesian undertook was quite incredible, both in terms of breadth and depth.

One of the scientists was studying weather systems to determine the correlation between independent weather events. Another was mapping human thoughts and examining the scientific basis for telepathy and telekinesis. A third was studying animal communication across distances. Yet another was involved in studying spacetime warping, wormholes and black holes.

Milesian researchers were drawn from across the world—from India, China, England, America, Russia, Singapore, Japan, Germany and France. Each of them operated independently, with no collaboration between any of them. There were only two women among them. Their ages ranged from twenty-eight, with Vijay being the youngest, and upwards to sixty with the Russian, Mikhailov, topping the age chart.

They were not permitted to share findings with one another. Everything was funnelled through to Schmidt, but the exciting bit about working at Milesian was that the company did not specify a research agenda. Each scientist was free to outline and develop a study plan independently. A job at Milesian implied immense freedom, coupled with constant monitoring. Working at Milesian was like being a fish in a glass tank—one was always under observation. CCTV cameras and biometric access sensors that were dispersed throughout the facility monitored all ten researchers' movements in high-resolution.

Each of the researchers stepped forward to shake Vijay's hand and welcome him to Milesian. A couple of them kindly invited him to join them for lunch later in the day, almost like designated buddies attempting to make the new kid in class feel more comfortable. But there was one person who entirely ignored Vijay.

Mikhailov.

53

It was bearable cold weather in Moscow that day. Bearable meant that the height of the snow on the ground was no more than a foot and the minimum temperature was no lower than minus ten Celsius.

Petrov parked his car in the enormous parking lot that lay adjacent to the famous Y-shaped building in Yasanevo, a southern suburb of Moscow. The massive structure housed the entire machinery of the SVR, including its oversized espionage wing. The complex was simply referred to as *kontora,* or 'the office'.

He entered the building and strode through the imposing lobby, crossing several security checkpoints effortlessly as he headed towards his boss's office, walking through unending hallways of the state-of-the-art complex.

During the Soviet era, the SVR used to be known as the First Chief Directorate of the KGB. The change in name was, however, irrelevant. The primary task of the SVR continued to remain that of collecting secrets from targets outside the Russian Federation.

A year earlier, the SVR had been taken over by a new director, a Soviet-era diplomat who had long been suspected by the West of operating secretly as an officer of the KGB. His friendship with the President of the Russian Federation was legendary, and whispers in the corridors of power indicated that the Director could even be the President's chosen successor one day. Petrov reported to him alone. What was not lost on most insiders was the fact that Petrov's closeness to the Director, by default, also gave him indirect access to the President.

Petrov walked through the secretary's office and gently knocked on the massive door. '*Voydite,*' came the voice from within. Petrov opened the door and entered.

'How is your Gang of Four these days?' asked the Director, smiling as Petrov walked in. He waved his hand towards a chair.

'Hopefully, we'll extract more out of it than we put into it,' replied Petrov, sitting down on one of the visitors' chairs opposite the Director. 'I much prefer the idea of shooting terrorists rather than this cloak-and-dagger stuff to prevent a supposed world conflict.'

'Remember one thing, Petrov,' said the Director. 'If you have a computer network that is infected with a virus, shutting down a few machines will not help. You can kill terrorists but not their ideology. The Americans killed Osama bin Laden. Did Al-Qaeda's ideology die? They killed Abu Musab al-Zarqawi. Did the ideology of an Islamic caliphate die? The real challenge lies in snuffing out the ideology.'

Petrov nodded.

'I do hope you remember the commitment that we made to the President when this group was being created?' asked the Director. 'The specific reason for us getting involved?'

'Absolutely,' said Petrov. 'But first I need your help.'

'How?' asked the Director.

'Mikhailov,' replied Petrov.

The Director made a note on the pad in front of him. 'I'll get someone on it,' he said. 'Now, there is something else that I need to discuss with you.'

54

The Director handed a dossier to Petrov. It was marked *Sovershenno Sekretno*. Top Secret. Petrov opened the folder and quickly glanced at the single page within. The first paragraph caught his attention.

A massive sinkhole materialized near the mining town of Solikamsk in the Perm region of Russia. It has since tripled in diameter over the past ten months. The enormous hole is now four hundred feet across and around two hundred and fifty feet deep.

'Why are you asking me to read this?' asked Petrov. 'Maybe the earth's crust has become unstable. Maybe it's to do with the water table. Maybe it's drilling-induced. Possibly even something simple like excessive human activity. Why should this warrant SVR's attention?'

'Why are such incidents happening so frequently these days?' asked the Director. 'Some of these sinkholes have appeared in isolated areas with virtually no human activity. Some of them are in areas where there is no drilling.'

'Is there an agency that maintains data on these sinkholes?' asked Petrov. 'Like the ones that monitor hurricanes or earthquakes?'

'No,' said the Director. 'But across the world, insurance companies have reported a doubling of claims associated with sinkholes. Something very peculiar is happening. We need to know if someone is causing them.'

'Someone?' asked Petrov. 'Surely you mean *something*?'

'I said it correctly the first time,' said the Director. 'I will help you with Mikhailov. But I need your help with these fucking holes.'

Fucking holes, thought Petrov to himself. He thought of the platinum blonde who had shared his bed the previous night. Thirty minutes later, Petrov walked out, dossier in hand. He was shaking his head.

What am I? A frigging seismologist?

55

Petrov had been born to ordinary folk in Saint Petersburg, then known as Leningrad. His father was a security guard and his mother, a simple housewife. Life was hard and the family made do with cabbage soup and cutlets most days, but they never went hungry.

Petrov was a hardworking boy and his excellent grades propelled him into studying law at the St Petersburg State University. He was just twenty-five years old when Mikhail Gorbachev brought about the end of the Soviet Union. He saw people celebrating in the streets when the August coup fuelled Boris Yeltsin's rise to power. It was a momentous time in their history and a chance to get away from the stranglehold of the Communist Party.

During Gorbachev's last days as President of the Soviet Union, the Chairman of the KGB, Vladimir Kryuchkov, together with seven other Soviet leaders, created a State Committee on the State of Emergency. They attempted to overthrow the government in order to maintain the 'integrity' of the Soviet Union. The attempted coup crumpled within three days. During that time, Petrov remained firmly in Boris Yeltsin's camp. It turned out to be a wise personal choice because Yeltsin eventually emerged victorious. In that year, the KGB was disbanded and split into two new services, the FSB and SVR. Petrov was absorbed into the SVR.

Yeltsin, the first President of the newly minted Russian Federation, was convinced that he could convert the erstwhile USSR's socialist economy into a vibrant capitalist market economy. He ruthlessly carried out economic shock therapy, price decontrol and privatization. In the process, he created terrible times for ordinary citizens. The sudden and unplanned nature of the shift resulted in the lion's share of wealth migrating to the hands of a few oligarchs.

Russia soon became famous for all the wrong reasons—massive corruption, thriving mafia, social unrest, galloping inflation and economic breakdown. It was during those years that Petrov began to appreciate the value of a strong state and even stronger leadership. The man who seemed to symbolize such strength was Vladmir Putin.

Petrov shared many commonalities with Putin even though fifteen years separated them. Both had studied at the St Petersburg State University, both had worked for the KGB and both valued order over chaos. When Putin became the First Deputy Prime Minister in Boris Yeltsin's Cabinet, Petrov quietly built his bridges with Putin supporters. This brought him to the notice of the future SVR director, who took personal interest in Petrov's career and ensured that he moved up the ranks.

After Russia's disastrous handling of the Ukrainian Revolution, the Director needed to build a team of tough men who would not crack under pressure. Petrov was included in a squad given the responsibility of coordinating efforts to take over the Crimea from the Ukraine.

At lightning speed, unmarked Russian forces, aided by local guerrillas, took over the region. This was followed by a contentious referendum that conveniently showed majority public opinion favouring joining Russia. Russian President Vladimir Putin immediately signed a treaty of accession with the self-styled Republic of Crimea, incorporating it into the Russian Federation. It was game, set and match to Putin's camp.

Petrov's rise through the ranks of the SVR had been guaranteed after that.

56

Vijay looked at the whiteboard again. He had jotted down the key phases of his proposed research project, and now scratched his head to figure out if he had left anything out. Were the steps in the right order?

Like the nine researchers before him, Vijay had been provided with his own expansive lab. Row upon row of gleaming laboratory tables and equipment stretched under the sunlight that burst down from the generous skylights. His lab was fully equipped with every possible tool that Vijay could ever need, including a photo-ionization microscope, confocal entanglement microscope, hydrogen beam, quantum sensor and laser pulse generator.

Vijay logged into Milesian's network and began writing up his proposed plan of action for Schmidt. He wanted it to be perfect, so he commenced with a short introductory paragraph on his own understanding of what Milesian Labs was after.

'The word *physics* is derived from the Greek word *physis*,' he wrote. 'That particular word was popularized by the sages of the Milesian school founded in the Ionian town of Miletus in the sixth century BCE. The proponents of the Milesian school thought of *physis* as the endeavour of "seeing the essential nature of all things". The Milesians were also called *hylozoists*, or those who thought that all matter was alive. This was because Milesians saw no distinction between animate and inanimate, spirit and matter. In that sense, the Milesians were much like the rishis of ancient India.'

He paused to gather his thoughts before typing further.

'Victor Hugo famously said, "Where the telescope ends the microscope begins, and who can say which has the wider vision?" Both the telescope and the microscope help peer into exactly the same phenomena—bundles of energy in constant motion. Taking that idea further, what if we could find behaviour patterns of planets that mimic the behaviour patterns of subatomic particles? What if the "outside" and the "inside" are identical?

'Over the years, many researchers have attempted to develop a *Theory of Everything*, a universal framework of physics that can describe and connect all physical aspects of the universe. But the Theory of Everything has eluded us all. Instead, we have distinct and separate frameworks. Classical Mechanics works for objects on Earth but breaks down at the planetary level. General Relativity works well when explaining stars, planets, galaxies or other high-mass objects, but breaks down at the sub-atomic level. Quantum Field Theory works well in explaining atoms and sub-atomic particles, but falls flat when attempting to explain high-mass objects.'

Vijay checked what he had typed, then continued, 'In recent times, String Theory is being positioned as the ultimate unifying theory of the universe, but this too is not without its limitations. Maybe our approach has been wrong. Instead of *everything*, what if we were to try and focus our attention on *something*? What if certain elements of one theory could be used in the domain of the other? As we start bridging the gap, step by step, isn't it possible that we may arrive at something that looks like a unified theory?'

57

In a room located two hundred yards away from Vijay's lab, a bank of Linux-based parallel computers silently recorded everything that Vijay typed up. A team of three specialists kept a watch on all emails, messages, chats, IP activity and phone calls of all ten scientists who worked at Milesian. Their chief was the ex-NSA man, Cracker.

'How is the new boy doing?' he asked, stubbing out a cigarette in the overflowing ashtray that lay on his desk.

'Nothing significant as yet,' said Cracker's deputy. 'As instructed by you, his phone, tablet and computer are being monitored by us. He talks regularly to his girlfriend in New Delhi. But nothing about his work or the company.'

'Good boy,' commented Cracker wryly. 'What about his apartment? All done?'

'We installed three high-powered bugs in his suite before he arrived,' said the deputy. 'All are functioning perfectly.'

'Did you scan him and his luggage?' asked Cracker.

'Upon arrival,' confirmed the second man. 'His luggage was clear and so was he. We did not want to take a chance, so we physically checked his bags when he was on a tour of the campus with Schmidt.'

'Anything out of the ordinary?' asked Cracker.

'Just a roll of clingwrap, which seems odd,' said the deputy. 'If he needed it, he could have easily picked it up from the convenience store on the premises.'

'Any electronic equipment squirrelled away?'

'Negative,' said the deputy.

'Is his dossier complete?'

'Yes. Educational records, orphanage papers, work history, casual interviews of people who know him, surveillance records, girlfriend's history…'

Cracker nodded. 'Have you stepped up your surveillance of Mikhailov?'

'Yes, but absolutely no communication—as usual,' said the deputy. 'It's almost as though his only communication is with his word-processor. Sometimes, not even that, when he takes to writing by hand.'

'Any incoming calls?'

'Just one from an unlisted number,' said the deputy. 'They spoke in Russian. The translated conversation is in your daily report. Nothing significant. He's a weird one. I don't know why we bother.'

'Never trust a Russian,' said Cracker, lighting up another cigarette and dismissing his deputy.

58

The coffee shop on the premises of Milesian Labs was called Food for Thought. It was managed by Daulat Singh, a chef from Garhwal, a region of the Himalayas that was famous for producing great cooks. Daulat had been enticed by Milesian from a luxury hotel chain so that the food at this restaurant could satisfy even the most picky palate. The restaurant operated 24/7 for a reason. Researchers followed their own hours, often forgetting to eat for long stretches at a time. Whatever they wanted, and whenever they wanted it, food had to be provided.

The restaurant was done up in log-cabin style with large glass windows that provided stunning views of the mountains that surrounded them. The walls were panelled in pine and red cedar, broken by stone pillars that had been fashioned from rocks in the surroundings. The menu could suit the taste of any of the nationalities that were working there. From a simple sandwich, stir-fry or pasta to a soufflé, tandoori or filet mignon, Daulat Singh's kitchen could produce it all.

Mikhailov's eating habits were almost ascetic. He avoided sugar, gluten and carbs but compensated with vegetables, fruits, nuts and dairy. His only other constant was chewing gum, his jaw perpetually exercising the spearmint within.

Mikhailov picked up his salad from the optional self-service counter along with an orange juice. He quietly headed over to a table by the window. He used a paper napkin to discard his chewing gum into a bin on the way and then sat down alone.

Vijay walked in and helped himself to a sandwich and a strawberry yoghurt. Tray in hand, he looked for a place to sit. All the tables were empty except for the one occupied by Mikhailov. With a total employee strength of less than twenty-five people—ten scientists and fifteen other support staff—there was never much likelihood of having company at any time of the day.

Vijay walked up to Mikhailov's table and asked, 'Mind if I join you?'

Mikhailov looked up. He was happy in his solitude and idle chatter irritated him. 'I'd rather be alone,' he said to Vijay, turning his attention back to his tray.

Vijay did an about-turn and headed to another table, a tad humiliated by the rejection. *That man's peculiar,* he thought to himself. *Better to maintain a safe distance from him.* He sat down and took a few bites of the gourmet sandwich.

Then something happened.

59

From his seat, Vijay noticed that Mikhailov's breathing was laboured and his face was turning blue; it was evident that he was struggling for air. Then he shoved his fingers down his throat. *He's attempting to induce vomiting. Something is stuck. Three minutes for brain damage and six minutes for death.*

Vijay rushed over to Mikhailov and pulled him to his feet. He wrapped his arms around the waist of the choking man from behind. He then made a fist and placed it against Mikhailov's upper abdomen. Grasping the fist with his other hand, he pressed into the scientist's stomach with a rapid upward thrust. Once. Twice. On the third try the offending morsel was expelled. Vijay's Heimlich manoeuvre had worked.

Mikhailov gasped for breath, sucking in great big gulps in desperation. He had choked on one of the walnuts in his salad. *Appropriate for a nuthead,* thought Vijay. Mikhailov looked at Vijay gratefully. And then he did something that he rarely did. It was rather scary.

He smiled.

60

Mikhailov returned to his lab, cursing himself for allowing his attention to wander while eating. He usually chewed each morsel in a rather deliberate fashion, a consequence of his effort to do everything with *awareness*. Today he had deviated from the usual by permitting his thoughts to drift to his days in Kashmir.

He ran his hand over his shirt and felt reassured by the *rudraksha* prayer bead on the chain around his neck. It was a single seed, strung on a simple gold chain, and had been given to him by his grandfather.

His grandfather, Viktor, had found the seed during the excavations that he had carried out at Nalanda during his quest to find Shangri-La or, as the Buddhists called it, Shambhala. Viktor had followed the trail of Nicholas Roerich and Gleb Bokii, Russians who had previously tried to find Shambhala. Viktor hadn't succeeded but had returned home with a veritable treasure trove of stories and experiences that he would narrate to his fascinated grandson.

Then one night, he had taken off the chain with its bead that hung from his neck and put it around the boy's. 'Keep it with you always,' he had said. 'It is very powerful. When everything else fails, this can protect you.'

'How do I use it, *dedushka*?' the boy had asked.

'Think of it as a rocket,' said Viktor. 'No matter how sophisticated it is, without fuel it cannot be propelled. To make this bead work you need a guru. The only one who knows how to propel it is a sage who lives in India. His name is Brahmananda.'

'Ba-ra-man-da?' asked the boy.

'Brahmananda,' said the old man. 'You will seek him when the time comes.'

Mikhailov had been one of the toppers at Lomonosov Moscow State University and had landed the perfect research position in the Russian Academy of Sciences. In those days, a plum position in the Academy usually meant a KGB dossier. Most scientists were required to cooperate with the intelligence agency and Mikhailov had been no exception.

Viktor had been so very proud of Mikhailov's achievements. Unfortunately, the old man had passed away a few years later. And then Mikhailov had remembered his grandfather's words about Brahmananda.

He requested for leave and travelled to India. He spent several weeks in Delhi and Mumbai trying to trace Brahmananda, but no one seemed to know of him. Dejected, he had dropped in for a beer at Leopold Café, a place frequented by foreign tourists in Mumbai. A chance conversation with a backpacking couple had provided a clue to the sage's whereabouts.

Kashmir.

61

Upon arriving in Srinagar, Mikhailov had trekked to a little village called Hardas near Kargil. In the mountains surrounding Hardas, Mikhailov had discovered the guru that his grandfather had spoken about.

The commonly accepted story about Brahmananda was that he was very old—much older than most people. Possibly the oldest man alive in the world. Before Mikhailov could even introduce himself, the wise sage in saffron and vermillion robes had asked, 'What brings you here, Mikhailov? Do you have the rudraksha bindu around your neck? Under your shirt?'

Mikhailov had been stunned into silence. He knew that he was standing before someone whose power and energy were unexplainable.

'What you have is the *bindu*,' said Brahmananda. 'Every rosary has one hundred and eight beads plus one. Your bead is that elusive plus-one. The remaining one hundred and eight beads are ordinary seeds but the bindu is larger and shaped like a pinecone. It allows the person using the rosary to know when one complete rotation has been completed. These days it is usually an ordinary rudraksha bead with a tassel attached, but yours is no ordinary bindu.'

Mikhailov found that no words were reaching his lips. It was almost as though he had lost the ability to speak. His mind was racing. *How do you know who I am? How did you know that I'm wearing the bead under my shirt? Why is this bead so important? Why are there one hundred and eight beads plus one?*

'Slow down, son,' said Brahmananda, picking up on Mikhailov's thoughts. 'Let's start with the number of beads. They simply represent the hundred and eight positions of the sun and moon in the sky. But as your grandfather must have told you, that particular number, one hundred and eight, is sacred.'

Mikhailov recalled what his grandfather had said. *The distance between Earth and the sun is one hundred and eight times the sun's diameter. The distance between Earth and the moon is one hundred and eight times the moon's diameter. The diameter of the sun is one hundred and eight times Earth's diameter.*

'Precisely,' said Brahmananda, reading Mikhailov's thoughts. 'But also remember that when the first three digits are raised to their own power and multiplied, you get one hundred and eight.'

$1^1 \times 2^2 \times 3^3 = 108$.

Mikhailov ran through the simple calculation in his head. It was spot-on. But he couldn't be sure why that made the number special. Brahmananda smiled. 'Remember this, son. There's a touch of belief within every doubter and a touch of doubt within every believer. You have to decide which camp you want to be in. Now let's work on this bead's power. And yours.'

Mikhailov had taken leave for a month. Instead, he stayed on at Brahmananda's ashram for five years.

He thought he had found his home, unaware that his world was about to come crashing down.

62

Mafraqi performed Salah, his daily prayer, for the third time in the day. Praying along with him were several men. It had started with Wudu, followed by Niyyah, the intention to pray involving recitation of the first Surah of the Qur'an. They had bowed, recited something, stood upright again and then kneeled. They placed their hands and face down on the floor and then sat up, repeating the sequence—the Raka'ah. 'Peace be unto you, and on you be peace,' said Mafraqi at the end, finding nothing ironic in the words that emerged from him.

Prayers over, Mafraqi sat cross-legged on the thick rug that had been spread on the pockmarked floor of the cave located near the town of Raqqa in Syria. Given that he controlled the city, he could have chosen to live in more comfortable quarters, but he seemed more at ease in caves. His preference was a hangover from his days in Afghanistan. He was dressed in black robes and a black turban, possibly his effort to indicate that his roots went back to the Abbasid caliphs. His dark eyes and thick, white-streaked black beard matched perfectly with his robes.

He looked at the men who were now seated in a circle around him, men who had chosen to follow him in their noble cause of re-establishing the Islamic caliphate. Mafraqi knew that his words were more powerful than bombs. His speeches had succeeded in inspiring an entire generation of Arabs to thirst for that pure and noble Islamic empire within which the will of Allah would prevail.

The Americans had announced a reward of twenty-five million dollars for his death or capture. But Mafraqi was like an inflatable punching toy that would bounce back no matter how hard one hit it. On several occasions there had been reports of his death, but they had all turned out to be false. His death would be celebrated by the Western world and he would pop up in a video a few days later, almost mocking them.

'Anyone who says anything that seems remotely sympathetic to Muslims is dying these days,' said Habib, Mafraqi's second-in-command. 'The German Chancellor visited a mosque and quoted a verse from our holy Qur'an to tell the world that Islam is a religion of peace. The Chancellor is now dead.'

'Never interrupt your enemy when he is making a mistake,' said Mafraqi as he mopped his forehead with a small towel. 'They are playing into our hands.'

'How?'

'What is the purpose of killing people who are open-minded about Islam?' asked Mafraqi, not expecting an answer. 'To allow more hardliners to flourish! And that suits us perfectly. Muslims who want to reform our religion must not be ceded space. Reformers want Islam to accept homosexuality, adultery, equality of women, freedom of speech, blasphemy, and separation of religion and state. Our greatest danger lies in these reformist tendencies.'

'Why?' asked Habib, naively.

'Because if we ever wish to achieve our dream of establishing a global Islamic caliphate, we need ordinary Muslims around the world to feel alienated and angry,' replied Mafraqi. 'That can only happen if Islam is rigid in its ways. The backlash from the secular West will transform ordinary Muslims into staunch defenders of the faith.'

'I understand,' said Habib as the truth of the Caliph's statement sank in.

'Have you spoken to Sadiq?' asked Mafraqi. 'Is he prepared?'

'He is awaiting your nod,' said Habib.

'Good,' said Mafraqi. 'They can kill any number of Muslim holy warriors around the world, but they cannot kill the ideology that sparks holy war. For every man killed, a hundred more will emerge. The West is helping us by demolishing moderation. Our caliphate needs moderation in moderation.'

63

And it's another day and it's time for me, Masoud, to jot down my thoughts. I'm glad that my words finally seem to be flowing.

There are those who say that the word Islam means 'peace'. They are mistaken. Islam actually means 'submission to the will of Allah'.

Recently, the German Chancellor visited a mosque and quoted a verse, I think it was Surah 5:32, from the Qur'an. The verse says, 'Whoever kills a human being, except as punishment for murder or other villainy in the land, shall be regarded as having killed all mankind; and whoever saves a human life shall be regarded as having saved all mankind.'

But for every verse of peace I could find you a verse of violence. I have made a note of several such verses.

Surah 4:95—Allah hath granted a grade higher to those who strive and fight…

Surah 8:12—strike them upon the necks and strike them from every fingertip…

Surah 8:60—terrify the enemy of Allah…

Surah 9:29—fight those who believe not in Allah nor the Last Day…

So, I wonder, is Islam is a religion of peace or a religion of violence?

Well, the verses that came to the Prophet in Mecca were verses of peace. These passages focused on brotherhood, tolerance and charity, hallmarks of the Islamic faith.

But the later verses are the sword verses. They came to the Prophet after his move to Medina. We should remember that Islam grew by leaps and bounds only after this event. Just goes to show you the power of the sword!

The question then arises, which verses should one believe? Islam enshrines within it a concept called naskh—or abrogation. If later verses conflict with earlier ones, then the later verses are considered the final word.

It seems to me that terrorists seem to treat the contradicting verses as their greatest asset. They can continue Jihad, sanctioned by the Medina verses, while average Muslims can continue living their lives peacefully, secure in the conviction that Islam is about peace as per the Mecca verses.

This dichotomy seems to suit terrorists fine and they take full advantage of it.

64

Vijay looked at the information deck of the treadmill that he was running on. *Not bad*, he thought to himself. *Forty-five minutes at eight kilometres per hour.* He felt good. Three machines away, the scientist from England was vigorously using the elliptical trainer. She was huffing and puffing to work off the extra calories that Daulat Singh's chocolate fudge cake had added to her diet the previous night. No one else was around.

Vijay turned off the machine, stepped off and wiped it down as a matter of courtesy for the next user. He then headed to the men's changing room that was attached to the gym. As he closed the door behind him, he felt a hand clamp over his mouth. He managed to angle himself to catch a glimpse of the offender.

It was Mikhailov.

The Russian took his hand off Vijay's mouth and quickly brought a finger to his own lips. *Be quiet, I'll explain.*

Mikhailov seemed to be chewing gum, as usual. He walked over to the large mirror that ran across one of the walls and gently felt the bolts that held the mirror against the wall. He then took the chewing gum from his mouth and placed it over one of the bolts.

'Sorry about that,' he said softly. 'I hate chewing gum. I only chew it so that I may block the bugging equipment at will.'

'Listening devices in a changing room?' asked Vijay.

'You can observe the CCTV cameras in plain sight,' said Mikhailov. 'But even when there are no cameras, you should always assume that there is a listening device. You must not forget this rule, even inside your own personal living quarters.'

'Could there also be cameras behind this mirror?' asked Vijay.

'No,' said Mikhailov. 'I used a handheld sonar from my lab to check the depth behind the mirror. It is constant and uniform. No hardware there.'

'Why are you telling me all this?' asked Vijay. 'You were rather standoffish on my first day at work.'

'Sorry about that,' said Mikhailov. 'I was caught up in my own thoughts. I wasn't being arrogant.'

'I'm still not clear,' said Vijay. 'Why should you confide in me?'

'I am not just a scientist,' explained Mikhailov, 'I am also a Hindu practitioner trained in Vedanta and a Buddhist practitioner trained in Kalachakra.'

'Kalachakra?' asked Vijay. He was already familiar with Vedanta.

'The wheel of time,' replied Mikhailov. 'Drop in at the library and pick up a book by Professor Vignesh Thakur. It will tell you what Kalachakra is about. I don't know if you realize this, but Kalachakra practised over many years gives one a more evolved sixth sense. My sixth sense has brought me to talk to you.'

'So talk,' said Vijay, still miffed at the manner in which he had been rebuffed the previous day by Mikhailov.

65

'Do you know why this place is called Milesian Labs?' asked Mikhailov.

'Inspired by the Milesian school, I would imagine,' replied Vijay.

'Correct,' said Mikhailov. 'Philosophers from the Ionian town of Miletus, much like the sages of India, were proponents of the theory regarding the interconnectedness of everything in the universe, something that quantum physics has only recently picked up on.'

'Like Brahman?' asked Vijay.

'Absolutely,' said Mikhailov. 'When Krishna spoke to Arjuna before the *Mahabharata* battle about one underlying reality called Brahman, interconnectedness is what he was referring to. It's the same thing as Dharmakaya in Buddhism or Tao in Taoism. All phenomena in the world are manifestations of a fundamental oneness. All things are interdependent and indivisible parts of a cosmic whole.'

'And what is Milesian Labs trying to do?' asked Vijay.

'This place is an attempt to reassemble the knowledge of the Milesians,' said Mikhailov. 'Thales, Anaximander and Anaximenes were the three philosophers who exemplified Milesian ideas. In those days, philosophy and science were one and the same. The ancient sages of India and the philosophers of Miletus were after the same thing as today's researchers into quantum physics—the ability to understand the interrelatedness of the universe.'

Vijay wondered where the conversation with Mikhailov was headed but he didn't say anything.

'Do you know that studies by a researcher—Cleve Backster—show that all living things, including plants, bacteria, insects, fish, birds, animals and humans, are continually communicating with one another? This interaction apparently uses a field that is not even supposed to exist. It is not present in the electromagnetic spectrum of visible light. It is not in radio waves or infrared or microwaves. It is not in X-rays. Possibly we screen out this communication to prevent ourselves from going insane, but the sages of the East knew how to tune in to this channel. Unfortunately, all scientific knowledge can be used in different ways, both good and bad.'

'And this place is about the bad?' asked Vijay.

Mikhailov nodded. 'We must talk in greater detail,' he said. 'My apartment is located in the block adjacent to yours. Number seventeen. Drop in later tonight. Avoid the cameras. They sweep at intervals of twenty-three seconds. Trust me, I've checked.'

Mikhailov handed over a piece of paper that showed the layout of the Milesian facility. Several locations had been marked with an X.

'What are these?' asked Vijay.

'Blind spots,' replied Mikhailov. 'Whenever you need to avoid the camera sweep, these are locations where you can stand for a few seconds to avoid being detected.'

Vijay folded the paper and put it away in his pocket.

'Leave your apartment door open when you enter it later today,' continued Mikhailov. 'In future as well, leave it open when you come to see me.'

'Why?' asked Vijay.

'Locking your door does not prevent Milesian from accessing your apartment,' said Mikhailov. 'But a sensor records each time any door is opened or closed. The time stamp will remain stuck at the time you entered your apartment. I will leave my door open for you so that there is no record of you having come. Ten o'clock tonight.'

Mikhailov removed the chewing gum that he had stuck to the mirror, flushed it down one of the toilets and left.

66

Judith drove her car through the George Washington Memorial Parkway to reach 1000 Colonial Farm Road via a private road only available to authorized vehicles. Very few outsiders knew the address. Those who did knew it as the George Bush Center for Intelligence, or CIA HQ. But usually, the building was called just Langley, echoing the name of the region in Fairfax County, Virginia, where it was located.

Judith passed through security checks at OHB—the Original Headquarters Building—and crossed through a tunnel to the New HQ building. She walked briskly towards a designated conference room where the Middle East team awaited. Waiting outside the door was a staff member holding a tray of Starbucks coffee cups for the attendees. She thanked him, took one, entered the room and sat down at the table.

'So, are we any closer to finding Mafraqi's family connections?' she asked.

One of the younger analysts got up from his seat and began speaking carefully. 'Mafraqi claims descent from the Quraysh—the tribe to which Muhammad belonged,' he said. 'His alleged lineage has strengthened his claim to being the caliph of all Muslims. But we believe it is a sham.'

Judith took a sip of her coffee. There seemed to be nothing new in what the young man was telling her, but she knew that she would have to be patient. In her years of service, Judith had found that the greatest quality of a good operative or analyst was the ability to listen.

'Why is that?' asked Judith.

'The first Saudi state went to war with the Ottoman Empire,' explained the analyst. 'This war ended in 1818 with the defeat of the grandson of Saud at the hands of the Ottomans. He was captured and sent to Istanbul to be beheaded. Evidence exists that he was forced to listen to a lute being played before he was killed.'

'Why?' asked Judith.

'Because Saud was fanatically opposed to any form of music,' said the analyst. 'When he was beheaded in Istanbul, so were some of his other followers. One of those executed was supposedly from the Quraysh. Mafraqi claims descent from him.'

'Is it one of those things that can neither be proved nor disproved?' asked Judith.

'It *was* one of those things,' said the analyst. 'But we believe that circumstances have changed.'

'What has changed?' asked Judith.

'Evidence,' said the analyst. 'Have a look at the recent archaeological findings from Istanbul.'

'What about them?' asked Judith.

'The Turkish Historical Society found the lute,' said the analyst. 'It has an engraving on it.' He advanced the slide to allow Judith to have a look at the artefact in the picture. She stared at the new slide for a while.

'The question is how we can use this information as leverage,' she said.

'You may also wish to consider some chatter we picked up about his deputy—Habib—through our spy satellites,' he replied.

67

The oak-panelled library was magnificent. Rows of leather-bound books competed for space with carved friezes and ornate pilasters. Polished oak and brass ladders were attached to rollers along the upper shelves in order to access the books at higher levels. Antique grain leather chairs accompanied by ornate seventeenth-century table replicas punctuated the rows of unending shelves. The pattern was repeated on each of the four floors. A central atrium flooded the library with light and allowed a combined view of all floors.

Vijay entered the massive library through the heavy doors that swung open the instant that he offered his thumbprint to the biometric scanner. The librarian on duty smiled at him as he walked in. She was seated inside a circular information desk that looked medieval but was equipped with twenty-first-century technology.

'May I help you, Mr Sundaram?' she asked, as Vijay walked up to her.

'Hello, Anjali,' said Vijay, looking at her nametag. 'I was wondering where I would find books by Professor Vignesh Thakur.'

Any other man would have spent an extra moment admiring Anjali. She looked absolutely ravishing in a tight red sweater that emphasized her curves. But her charms were lost on Vijay.

'Let me check for you,' said Anjali, her fingers efficiently typing a query into the sleek computer that was snugly fitted into her desk.

She looked up from the screen. 'Eight books by Professor Vignesh Thakur in this library,' she said. 'Are you looking for a specific one?'

'Not really,' said Vijay. 'I would prefer to have a look at all of them in order to decide which one I want.'

The librarian smiled understandingly. 'Check your email inbox,' she said. 'The shelf coordinates for all eight books should be there.'

He looked at his phone. She was right. Vijay was among the rare breed fascinated by the incredible organization and systems of the Milesian library instead of being mesmerized by Anjali.

Exactly nine minutes later, Vijay walked out with a book in his hand. *A Guide to Kalachakra Initiation* by Professor Vignesh Thakur.

68

Vijay entered his flat and left the door open, as suggested by Mikhailov. He placed the book on his study desk and opened a browser window on his computer. His session started with a very basic search for the *Buddha* and *Kalachakra*.

The first few search results told him stuff he already knew: that Siddhartha Gautama was born sometime around 563 BCE to Suddhodana, an elected Hindu chief of a tribal confederacy in the eastern part of the Indian subcontinent; that upon his birth, astrologers predicted that he would grow up to be a great king or a great sage; that his father surrounded Siddhartha with luxury so that he would become a king instead of a sage; that Siddhartha left the palace in search of enlightenment at age twenty-nine and attained it six years later having become the Buddha—the enlightened one.

The search results on the third page informed Vijay that the Buddha was said to have preached at a place called Dhanyakatakam in the present-day Indian state of Andhra Pradesh during the last year of his life. One of the students was King Suchandara, who had come from his kingdom of Shambhala in the north. The king had come to learn something very special from the Buddha. It was called the *Kalachakra Multantra* or the 'wheel of time'. It was a technique by which non-celibates such as King Suchandara could work towards becoming Bodhisattvas. These were beings that had the power to attain, at will, *nirvana*—liberation from further rebirths—but delayed it in their quest to help the universe through their continued presence.

After learning the Kalachakra Multantra from the Buddha, Suchandara returned to Shambhala and taught it there for two years before passing on the knowledge to his son. He even wrote an explanatory commentary on the Buddha's original Multantra, but both documents—the Multantra and Suchandara's commentary—were eventually lost to time.

Six succeeding kings of Shambhala preserved the Kalachakra teachings and taught them to an inner circle. King Suchandara and the six kings who succeeded him came to be known as the Seven Dharmarajas of Shambhala.

Vijay took off his glasses and rubbed his eyes. He took a deep breath. Why was Mikhailov wasting his time with this stuff? But there was also something that excited Vijay. He couldn't say what it was, but there was something compelling him to plod on.

The kings that followed the Seven Dharmarajas were known as the Rigden kings. The first among them, Manjushrikirti, was born around 159 BCE. He summarized the Kalachakra teachings into a simplified text called the *Sri Kalachakra*. He prophesied that the world would be convulsed by a new religion eight hundred years after him. Buddhists saw the Islamic conquests as that convulsion.

Manjushrikirti initiated a sect of Brahmin priests of Shambhala into the Kalachakra. Thesc were sun-worshippers who followed a practice called *Surya Samadhi*. The amazing powers of these Brahmin priests—including their ability to live for days solely on sunlight—were well-known and many of their practices were absorbed into the Kalachakra. Manjushrikirti permitted this assimilation to ensure that all the inhabitants of Shambhala would be united into a single tribe. Thus they would be better equipped to deal with the onslaught of a foreign faith.

He predicted that the world would be overrun by barbarians in the year 2424 CE and it would be the twenty-fifth Rigden king, Rudrachakrin, who would fight the hordes, re-establish dharma and mark the advent of a golden age.

Exciting stuff, but then, all prophecies had a grand air to them.

Vijay turned to the book he had borrowed from the library. He learnt that the second Rigden king had written a commentary called *Vimalaprabha*. The *Sri Kalachakra* and the *Vimalaprabha* together constituted the entire texts of the Kalachakra system. All other writings were mere commentaries on these texts while all previous texts had been lost down the ages. The book went on to explain that there were three levels of teachings that the Buddha imparted to King Suchandara—outer teachings, inner teachings and intuitive teachings.

Outer teachings dealt with the physical world. These included the calculations used for the Kalachakra calendar, the start and end of universes, and the planetary system. Inner teachings dealt with the human body and mind. They covered areas such as gestation and birth, functions of the human body and the four commonly observed states of mind—awake, dreaming, asleep and orgasmic. Intuitive teachings constituted the very core of the Kalachakra. They were the path to enlightenment that could be achieved by balancing the outer with the inner. Once enlightened, one could enter the realms of Shambhala.

And then Vijay came across a line that made his jaw drop because it almost reflected the crux of his research.

As it is outside, so it is within the body.

69

Vijay put down the Professor Thakur book and let the thought sink in. He got up, pulled out the roll of clingwrap from the kitchen cabinet, tore off a segment and placed it on the keyboard. He then waited for a minute. Miraculously, alternative letters and numbers appeared on the wrap owing to chemical activation. He noticed that the first six letters of the keyboard, Q-W-E-R-T-Y, now appeared as K-N-P-A-S-J on the film. Likewise, all other letters and numbers on the keyboard were covered by alternatives on the wrap. Vijay quickly activated Tor, CSpace and ZRTP.

Vijay shuddered involuntarily as he entered the world of the Dark Web. Tor was mostly a network of filth and depravity. It was used by drug dealers, traders in endangered species of animals, vendors of pornography, paedophiles, illegal dealers in fire-arms, human traffickers, counterfeiters and brokers for human organs. It was sick, but it was anonymous. He entered a private chat room where Judith was waiting.

Vijay began typing up his feedback. He described the layout of Milesian, the incredibly high security, the vastness of the area, profiles of the other nine researchers, his brief interaction with Schmidt and the odd behaviour of Mikhailov.

'Why does he want to meet you separately?' Judith typed.

'No idea,' replied Vijay. 'Not sure if he is sane.'

'Be careful,' replied Judith. 'He could be a plant of the SVR. I will dig into his background and have more for you next time.'

In the security room, the bank of parallel computers meticulously recorded each of Vijay's individual keystrokes for the attention of Cracker.

70

Vijay's brief abduction in New Delhi by IG4 had also been a crash course in communication technology. 'You need to familiarize yourself with our communication protocol,' Judith had said. 'I will be your main point of contact, your handler, once you are inside. Petrov will be responsible for mounting surveillance around the Milesian Labs location. Sharma will ensure that Sujatha is protected and Zhang will oversee technology support from Beijing.'

'But Milesian will not allow me to use any of my personal equipment,' said Vijay. 'I've read their epic code of conduct. *They* will provide me with a phone, tablet and notebook computer. How do I communicate with you? They could easily be listening in.'

'Exactly,' replied Judith. 'They *will* be listening in. Have you heard of Tor?'

'The Onion Router?' asked Vijay. Of course, he was familiar with it. It was software code that allowed anonymous communication. Tor channelled internet data through a free global network of thousands of relays. Thus, Tor could hide a user's location and usage from anyone attempting to eavesdrop. Using Tor made it next to impossible for net usage to be traced back to the user. This included the user's website visits, online posts, chat room exchanges and instant messages.

'Yes,' replied Judith. 'But at IG4 we have combined Tor with CSpace and ZRTP. That gives you an absolutely safe way of chatting with me without the slightest risk of our exchange being intercepted. Even the NSA would be unable to break in.'

'But keystrokes can be monitored,' argued Vijay. 'If Milesian wants, they can simply monitor my keyboard activity. They don't need to intercept the data transmission.'

Judith smiled. 'Want a sandwich?' she asked. She pushed what looked like a roll of clingwrap his way.

'What's this?' he asked.

'It's what we call encryption film,' she said. 'Each time you get into a chat with me, you tear off a new segment of the film and place it over your keyboard. Each segment of the roll randomly assigns new letters and numbers to different keys of the keyboard and continues doing so every few seconds. You will find a roll of this film when you return to your flat. Put it in your luggage.'

They know where I live and they do not need keys to access my flat. These guys are no less spooky than the ones at Minerva, thought Vijay.

'They could easily decode the reassignment of letters and numbers,' countered Vijay.

'Not quite,' replied Judith. 'Randomized assignment is already built into the film. Unlike codes that depend on a formula, this one has none. Even if Milesian monitors your equipment, it would be near impossible for anyone to decipher the communication. It's the twenty-first-century version of Enigma.'

Enigma machines were electro-mechanical rotor cipher machines that had been used by the Nazis to protect their communications during the Second World War. Vijay wanted to remind Judith that the British had eventually cracked the Enigma code, but he kept his thoughts to himself.

71

Vijay left his flat a few minutes before ten, leaving the door unlocked so that the last time stamp would indicate the time he had entered instead of the time he left. Once outside, he kept a careful watch on the CCTV cameras, ensuring that their sweeping gaze remained away from him. He took the hundred-odd steps towards Mikhailov's apartment, intermittently pausing and hurrying, according to camera sweeps. He did not make use of the blind spots.

The Russian, too, had left his door open and Vijay walked in. The old scientist was in the kitchen, boiling water in a small electric samovar. 'Will you have tea?' he asked Vijay. Without waiting for an answer, he poured a small quantity of concentrate from a teapot that sat atop the samovar into a teacup and then topped it up with steaming hot water from the samovar.

He repeated the process for himself. 'Zavarka,' he said. 'Strong Russian tea. Try it. Opens up the mind to new possibilities.'

'*Za tvajo zdarovye,*' he said to Vijay as they sipped the tea. 'To your health.'

Vijay took a couple of sips. It was strong but good.

'Are we sure that no one is listening?' asked Vijay.

'See the number of used chewing gum-blockers,' said Mikhailov, pointing to three that were in full view.

Vijay looked around. Mikhailov's apartment was stark, a perfect example of Zen minimalism. They sat on tatami mats on the floor.

'So, Schmidt wants you to study planets,' said Mikhailov, chuckling. 'All part of his grand scheme to control the world.'

'What do you mean?' asked Vijay.

'The ancient Milesian view that we spoke about earlier today?' said Mikhailov. 'About the interconnectedness of the universe…'

'Yes?'

'That ancient view which emerged from the sages of the East is only now being proved by science,' said Mikhailov. 'After all, there is no real difference between matter and energy. Einstein had demonstrated the interchangeability of matter and energy through his famous equation $E=mc^2$, but after the discovery of the Higgs boson, scientists are now realizing that the entire universe is nothing but energy!'

Mikhailov slurped his tea noisily and continued. 'All so-called particles can be converted into other particles. They can be fashioned from energy and can disappear into energy. Classical notions of elementary particles or separated objects are irrelevant. The whole universe seems like a moving web of indivisible energy arrangements.'

'True,' said Vijay. *But where is he going with this? What is so earth-shattering that he called me over?*

'Even what is called matter is actually energy programmed to behave like matter,' continued Mikhailov, ignoring the look of confusion on Vijay's face. 'There is little to differentiate our bodies from the houses we live in, the trees, shrubs, rocks and mountains around us, the air that we breathe, or the fires that keep us warm. Anything and everything around us, including our bodies, are simply energy. Even things that we cannot explain fully—such as thoughts, consciousness and the human soul—are just that, energy! That's precisely what the sages of ancient India were attempting to experience—the oneness of that energy.'

'Linking everything to ancient India is getting to be a tedious habit these days,' said Vijay. 'I hope you're not going to tell me that the Vatican is etymologically derived from *vatika* and that its shape is like a Shiv lingam?'

'That's for religious nutters,' said Mikhailov. 'But we should not throw out the baby with the bath water. There is tremendous value in what the ancient yogis told us and we should revisit their knowledge to refresh our own.'

72

Across the world, in a different time zone, Bruce Williams leaned back in his swivel chair awaiting the arrival of his morning visitor. The Chairman of RBA, or the Reconstruction Bank of America, knew that the meeting was overdue. Williams adjusted the cuffs of his shirt so that they showed from below the sleeves of his top-end Brioni suit exactly an inch. He then surveyed his office to check that nothing was out of place.

It was a massive room that occupied two thousand square feet of the prime corner on the top floor of a Manhattan skyscraper. No expense had been spared in furnishing it. Deep-pile carpeting, mahogany period furniture, soft leather upholstery and rare antiques sent out one very important message—that of immense power. The sleek platinum-plated intercom unit on his desk flashed silently. His visitor had arrived.

Williams stood up and walked around the desk to greet his visitor as his secretary, a perfectly attired middle-aged lady with tightly tied silver hair, held open the door and announced, 'Mr Mason Henderson'. She discreetly left the two men alone to shake hands. To the uninitiated it looked like a regular handshake, but it wasn't. Each man pressed his forefinger a little more than what was usual against the region that was usually known to palmists as the Mount of Venus.

The two men settled into generous Napa leather armchairs and engaged in customary small talk until Miss Jenkins brought in a silver tray containing coffee and cookies. Once she had left, the men got down to business.

'The Brotherhood is pleased with the progress we've made so far,' said Williams. 'But the next few months will be crucial. We will need to rally every brother and sister to ensure that Minerva's aims are fulfilled.'

Henderson nodded. He was a good-looking man whose complexion always had a bronzed look that matched perfectly with his ash brown hair.

Williams had been responsible for bringing Henderson into the secret society. Together they now occupied the two most senior positions within the organization.

It had been many years since Henderson's initiation, a long and tedious process that every new entrant had to go through. Existing members first ran background checks on the candidate: finances, political affiliations, religious beliefs and personal relationships. This was followed by a vote. Each member could cast a single vote by placing a white cube or black ball into a box. Even one negative vote expressed via a black ball meant non-admission. Henderson had kept his fingers crossed that his single weak spot had not been discovered. He had passed with flying colours.

Then Henderson had undergone the elaborate initiation process. He had been blindfolded with black satin and a blue rayon cord placed like a hangman's noose around his neck. Duly prepared, he had been led to an inner sanctum where three large candles were burning. He was asked to bare his right shoulder and the Worshipful Master had used a compass to prick his exposed skin. He was then asked what he desired. As per agreed custom, he answered, 'Light!' His blindfold was then removed so that he could see the three candles. He was informed that the three candles symbolized the sun, moon and the Worshipful Master. Finally, he was made to take the oath that swore him to secrecy and loyalty to Minerva.

Both Williams and Henderson were wealthy beyond belief. Williams had single-handedly created RBA, a bank devoted to financing massive infrastructure projects around the world. Henderson had transformed a small chemicals company, Genchem, into one of the largest conglomerates in the field. Both men were seen travelling the world in their private jets and hobnobbing with heads of state, other billionaires, dictators, Hollywood stars and royalty. What bound them was Minerva and its espoused cause.

Over the years, they had ensured that the richest and most powerful men and women of America, Western Europe and Asia joined their ranks, each admission only adding to the overall influence and wealth of the group. Some of them had earned their money in dubious ways but that didn't matter to Minerva. Williams often joked that money was like holy water. It purified everything, including one's sins.

Two years ago, Williams had taken over as Worshipful Master. He had appointed Henderson as his Senior Warden, the second in the hierarchy of principal officers. Though yet to prove himself, Henderson was a capable man. And Williams knew that he would have to take the plunge.

73

'Let me make this easier for you. Do you know why I am here at Milesian?' Mikhailov asked Vijay eventually.

Vijay was expecting a conspiratorial secret revelation. He was sorely disappointed.

'It's because of my previous research into quantum duality,' said Mikhailov. 'As you know, wave–particle duality is the concept that every elementary particle can behave not only as a particle but also as a wave.'

'Sure,' said Vijay. 'Thomas Young's famous double-slit experiment.' He had lectured on it several times, including his last session at IIT. Light could behave as a wave or as a particle. In fact, anything and everything could behave as a wave or particle.

'And that is precisely the reason why Vedanta and the Kalachakra should be of interest to us,' said Mikhailov. 'Did you read about the Kalachakra?'

'Sure,' said Vijay again, hoping this would lead somewhere.

'And what did you discover?' asked Mikhailov.

'As it is outside, so it is within the body,' said Vijay, echoing the line that had firmly planted itself into his head.

'Good,' said Mikhailov. 'You've picked up the central theme, indicating that we are part of an inextricably linked whole. But did you give some thought to the word *Kalachakra*?'

'It's the wheel of time, isn't it, as you'd mentioned? *Kala*—or time. *Chakra*—or wheel.'

'Yes,' answered Mikhailov. 'But why is time a wheel? Modern man thinks of time as linear, a straight line. But the ancients of the East realized that time is circular. Hindus believe that time moves in cycles and that each cycle has four great epochs or *yugas—Satya, Treta, Dwapar* and *Kali*. Once over, the epochs start all over again.'

He paused. 'Do you remember what the great astronomer and astrophysicist Carl Sagan said about the Hindu notion of time?'

'I don't think I do,' said Vijay.

'He said that Hinduism is the only faith that is dedicated to the idea that the cosmos itself undergoes an infinite number of deaths and rebirths. It is the only dharma in which time scales correspond to those of modern scientific cosmology. Its cycles run from our ordinary day and night, to a day and night of Brahma, 8.64 billion years long, longer than the age of Earth or the sun and about half the time since the Big Bang.'

'And the Buddhists?' asked Vijay.

'The Buddhists see time as measurement of change,' replied Mikhailov. 'A month is simply the change in the moon while it revolves around Earth. Or a woman going from one menstrual cycle to the next. That's why it is the "wheel of time". Everything that has happened will happen again. Everything that will happen has already happened. Time is relative. The sages of the East were giving us something akin to Einstein's prediction, but without its mathematics. Now, what is Schmidt making you study?'

'Quantum behaviour beyond the quantum,' replied Vijay. 'The possibility that quantum laws may apply even at planetary level.'

'And what do you think?' asked Mikhailov.

'If sub-atomic particles are energy and planets are also energy, then why shouldn't they behave similarly?' replied Vijay.

If A is C and B is C, then A is B.

'I agree,' said Mikhailov. 'But if my dog has four legs and my cat has four legs, does that make my dog a cat?'

Vijay laughed.

Mikhailov continued. 'The problem is that our present scientific framework shows that sub-atomic particles and planets don't behave similarly. Which means that either the premise is wrong, or...'

'Or?'

'Or the framework is wrong,' said Mikhailov. 'It is possible that on some other planet they have figured it out already. We still need to get there.'

'You believe that there is life elsewhere in space?' asked Vijay.

'It is arrogant of humans to assume as a given that we are the only life form in the universe,' said Mikhailov. 'Our sun is just one star among the two hundred to four hundred billion stars in our galaxy—the Milky Way. And remember that the universe consists of two trillion galaxies like the Milky Way. If we were to represent the entire universe as Earth, then Earth itself would proportionally be the size of a billionth of a pinhead. So it does seem strange that we can even entertain the notion that we are unique.'

'I agree,' said Vijay. 'The probability that there is no life outside Earth is infinitesimal.'

'Given that Schmidt is asking you to study planets, have you considered the implications of quantum entanglement?' asked Mikhailov. 'Some more tea?'

74

Mikhailov rose from the tatami mat as though he were a young man of twenty. He poured more tea for both of them and returned.

'Well, the concept of quantum entanglement is not new,' said Vijay. 'Physicists have held that, in a so-called entangled system, two seemingly separate particles can behave as an inseparable whole. One constituent cannot be fully described without considering the other.'

Mikhailov sipped his tea quietly, watching him, and waiting for more.

'This special property of quantum entanglement can be better understood if one separated the two entangled particles and placed them miles apart. If one were to measure the characteristics of these particles using the same criteria, one would find that the measurements would be identical but in opposite directions.'

'Correct,' said Mikhailov. 'So if quantum laws can be repeated at planetary level, then our Earth should have another entangled planet spinning somewhere else in the universe?'

'Precisely,' said Vijay. 'Indeed, in my thesis I have argued exactly that.'

'But seers of the East instinctively understood this when deep in meditation,' said Mikhailov. 'They were ahead of science. And that is something you must never forget. Do you remember what Robert Oppenheimer said about it?'

'What?' asked Vijay, entirely bewildered.

'He said that the discoveries in atomic physics are not wholly unfamiliar, wholly unheard of or new. They have a history and central place in Buddhist and Hindu thought.'

'But modern science is about verifiable data and experimentation,' said Vijay.

'The sages were concerned with perception, not experimentation,' replied Mikhailov. 'Do you know that the Rig Veda, the most ancient book of the Hindus, composed before 3000 BCE, contains a hymn in which the speed of light was calculated at 2,202 *yojanas* in half a *nimesha*?'

Vijay nodded. He recalled the hymn. *Yojananam sahastra dwe dwe shate dwe cha yojane aken nimishardhena krammana namostute.* With deep respect, I bow to the sun that travels 2,202 yojanas in half a nimesha.

It was quite remarkable. Converting the ancient units to modern ones, the result was 302,301 kilometres per second, just a 0.1 per cent variation from the modern calculation of 299,792 kilometres per second.

'There are those who think that the ancient units were reverse-engineered in order to sync them with modern calculations,' said Vijay. 'It is rather convenient that one nimisha is 16/75th of a second. Maybe someone did a reverse calculation to determine the unit values that would yield the correct modern-day speed of light.'

'Do you even know what a nimisha is?' asked Mikhailov crossly. 'The Puranic units are clearly recorded.' Mikhailov quickly jotted down some figures for Vijay's benefit.

1 Divaratri = 1 cycle of day and night
= 30 muhurtas

1 Muhurta = 30 kalas

1 Kala = 30 kashtas

1 Kashta = 15 nimishas

So,

1 Day-night cycle = 30 x 30 x 30 x 15 nimishas
= 405,000 nimishas

And,

1 Day-night cycle = 24 hrs x 60 mins x 60 secs
= 86,400 seconds

So,

1 Nimisha = 86,400/ 405,000
= 16/75 secs

'There was no reverse engineering of the units, as you can see,' said Mikhailov. 'Simply two different ways of breaking down the day-night cycle—the only constant between the two systems.'

'But how did ancient seers determine the speed of light in the absence of technology and equipment?' asked Vijay.

'You will see numerous parallels to modern physics in the *Upanishads* of Hinduism, in the Sutras of Buddhism and the Sufism of Ibn Arabi,' said Mikhailov. 'Never discount the value of perception!'

75

'Everything is going as per your plan,' said Henderson to Williams. 'You have only to switch on the television and you will be bombarded by extremist views. Polarization has succeeded.'

'But polarization is insufficient,' said Williams. 'Polarization can only be deemed successful if it results in a final solution. I have already contributed over a hundred million dollars to the corpus of Minerva. So have you. There are many like us who have donated generously.'

'So where is the money going?' asked Henderson.

'Milesian Labs, mostly,' explained Williams. 'We must ensure that it grows stronger so that we may eventually neutralize the threat of Islam.'

'Radical Islamism,' corrected Henderson gently. 'There is a difference.'

'Those distinctions are for politically correct statements by the liberals,' said Williams. 'The truth is, we have a problem with Islam, not just "Islamism" or "radical Islamism" or "radical Islamist terror". Minerva must act if we wish to prevent the entire world from becoming a caliphate!'

'How, if not through easy polarization?' asked Henderson.

'I chanced upon something very old and extremely valuable,' said Williams conspiratorially. 'It cost me a substantial sum but it was worth every penny.'

'What is it?' asked Henderson.

'I'll tell you about it soon,' replied Williams. 'It gives us an added advantage in fighting the scourge.'

Henderson nodded. 'I also have an idea,' he said. 'But I need your support to make it happen.'

'What is it?' asked Williams.

'It's called Molecular and Universal Audio,' replied Henderson. 'It could revolutionize the way we operate.' The men spent the next few minutes discussing Henderson's idea.

'I will ask Buchman, the Brotherhood's banker at Vonlanthen & Cie, to assist you with capital requirements,' said Williams. 'Now, I need to ask you something.'

'What?' asked Henderson.

'When I took over as Worshipful Master two years ago, I knew that the day would not be far off when I would hand over the reins to you. I think that time has come. What do you think?'

76

Mikhailov stared at Vijay, looking for signs that his words had sunk in.

'Have you read the *Srimad Bhagvatam*?' he asked. 'Chapter sixteen of the fifth canto contains the Sanskrit word for geography—*bhugol*. The sages who wrote the *Srimad Bhagvatam* were telling us that *bhu,* or Earth, is *gol,* or spherical. How would they have known this?'

Then Mikhailov went in for the kill. 'Just Google "Milky Way" and pull up an image on your phone,' he instructed. Vijay did as he was asked. 'Look at it closely,' said Mikhailov. 'Do you see the Golden Spiral of Fibonacci?'

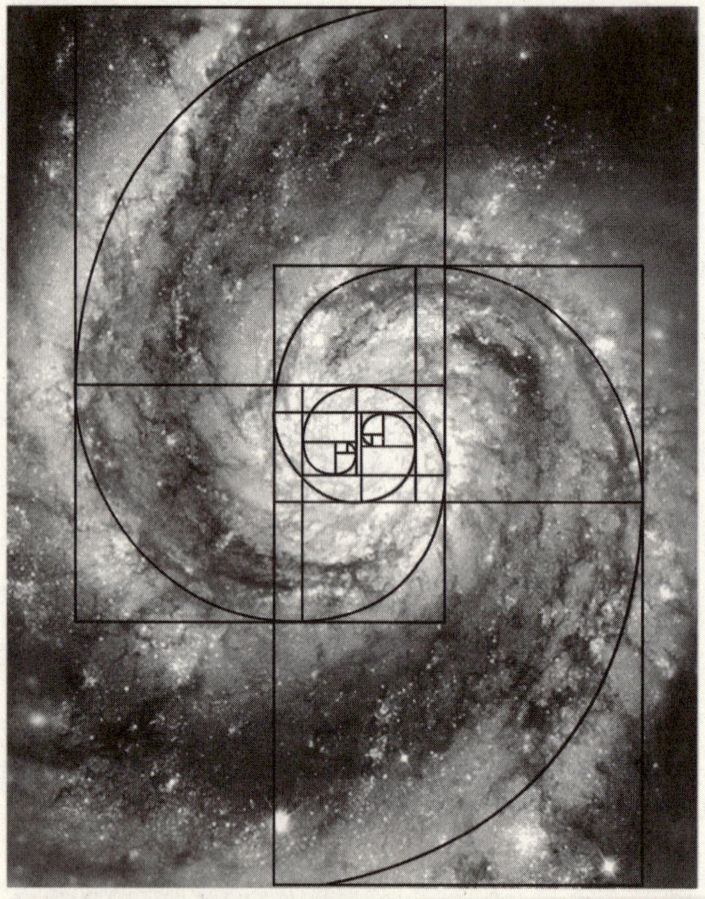

Vijay was aware of that famous concept. The Fibonacci sequence was obtained by starting with 0 and 1 and then adding the previous two numbers to obtain each successive number.

0	1	1+0	1+1	2+1	3+2	5+3	8+5	13+8	21+13	34+21	55+34	...
		1	2	3	5	8	13	21	34	55	89	

If one took any two adjacent numbers in the sequence, after skipping the first few, the ratio of the higher to lower number always tended towards 1.618. This was called the Golden Ratio. And a logarithmic curve with a growth factor of 1.618 yielded the Golden Spiral that could be seen everywhere in nature. In flowers, petals, hurricanes and even galaxies.

What was Mikhailov trying to tell him?

'Now Google for "Swastika" please,' said Mikhailov. Once Vijay had the image, it struck him. Mikhailov was right!

'The Milky Way consists of a core surrounded by a circle of gas, dust and stars that contains four radii—Norma, Scutum-Centaurus, Sagittarius and Perseus. These arms branch outward in a logarithmic spiral shape,' said Mikhailov. 'Look at the Swastika closely and you will find the same shape. Maybe ancient astronomers knew more than we care to imagine.'

There was a lull in the conversation as both men mentally ruminated on each other's ideas. Then Mikhailov spoke. 'Remember that the only way to arrive at a unified theory, one that explains atoms *and* planets, one that can explain waves *and* particles, one that can explain animate *and* inanimate, is by combining science and spirituality. Come back tomorrow night and I'll explain what I mean.'

Vijay left, using the protocol that had been agreed upon, no doors being closed. Once Mikhailov was alone, he went back into thought.

He was wondering what his next steps regarding Vijay ought to be.

77

Bruce Williams had been born to a wealthy banking family in Boston. His parents were members of Boston's elite, the Boston Brahmins. In fact, his mother traced her ancestry back to the *Mayflower*. As was customary, he attended the Phillips Academy in Andover, Massachusetts, a school that prepared him adequately for admission into Harvard.

He just about scraped through Harvard because he was entirely focused on finding ways to make money. Although his father was exceedingly wealthy, the old man always kept his son on a tight leash and the latter was forced to search for innovative avenues to support his lifestyle. One of the solutions was high-stake poker games in which he would mop up a small fortune on almost every occasion.

Playing poker gave him an education in the laws of probabilities and odds. It also made him good at reading other people's gestures and expressions. Once he graduated, he joined his father's bank, but in less than a year he quit. Father and son could not agree on anything.

Realizing that his son's energies could still be put to good use, his father advanced him a sizeable chunk of capital with which Williams set up an infrastructure company. He would bid for construction projects such as roads, bridges, dams and ports, using his substantial connections, only to do a quick resale mid-project. That's when he realized that there was an opportunity available to finance such deals and the Reconstruction Bank of America was born.

RBA went on to acquire several other banks; within a relatively short span of three decades, it became a multinational banking and financial services holding company headquartered in New York City. It was the sixth largest bank in the United States and one of the country's largest providers of financial services, including a hedge fund. Williams was one of the largest contributors to the Republican Party and it was at a fundraising event that he had met the Mayor of New York City.

It would be another couple of years before the Mayor put forward the name of Williams as a potential candidate for membership in Minerva. Unbeknownst to Williams, the Mayor was the Worshipful Master and was on a mission to induct young blood into the Brotherhood. Williams took to Minerva like a fish to water.

Some years later, Williams met Mason Henderson at another fundraiser. They became friends instantly, regularly having lunch together at their respective clubs. It was just a matter of time before Williams got Henderson to join Minerva.

At that time, Williams did not know that he would occupy the position of Worshipful Master one day. Nor did he foresee that he would one day give it up willingly to Henderson.

78

'How is he doing?' asked Zhang, taking a sip of jasmine tea.

The four members of IG4 were inside a safe house that belonged to the Bundesnachrichtendienst—the Federal

Intelligence Service of Germany. Located in Kreuzberg, the cultural hub of Berlin, the apartment provided a partial view of Gorlitzer Park through the half-open drapes.

'He's alive and well,' began Judith. 'His microchip indicates as much. He has also had an online chat with me via Tor. At the moment he still seems to be finding his bearings.'

Zhang nodded, staring at the photograph of Habib, Mafraqi's deputy, in his folder. Judith seemed to believe that he was amenable to negotiations.

'Anyone that he has had conversations with?' asked Petrov.

'He mentioned several names including your Russian scientist,' said Judith.

'Mikhailov?' asked Petrov.

Sharma's ears perked up. *Mikhailov? That name sounds familiar.*

'Yes,' said Judith. 'Mikhailov.'

'Anything specific that was discussed?' asked Petrov, stubbing out his cigarette. Judith detected a slight quaver in his voice.

'No,' she replied. 'Our chat was before his scheduled meeting with Mikhailov. But he did tell me that Mikhailov had asked him to research something called the Kalachakra.'

'The Buddhist wheel of time,' said Sharma. Eastern mysticism had always been a source of fascination for him.

'What is it about?' asked Judith.

'It's considered to be one of the most powerful teachings in Vajrayana Buddhism,' said Sharma. 'A potent mix of Buddhist philosophy, Hindu tantra, science and astrology.'

Sharma looked at the faces of his colleagues. 'I personally know the leading scholar in the field, Professor Vignesh Thakur,' he added as explanation.

'Astrology? Why would Mikhailov be interested in that?' asked Judith.

'The Kalachakra system believes in the correlation between body, mind, consciousness and the universe,' replied Sharma. 'As outside, so inside.'

'But seriously, *astrology*?' asked Judith.

'That's only *part* of it,' said Sharma. He looked at Judith's expression. 'One may scoff at astrology as the hobby of quacks, but the truth is, if you believe in mathematical regression models, you should believe in astrology too.'

'Why?' asked Judith.

'Because Maharishi Bhrigu, the creator of predictive astrology as we know it, collected half a million birth charts and then studied the lives of those people,' explained Sharma. 'He then developed a predictive model, one that could point to potential events based upon planetary positions.'

'But surely that's nonsense,' said Petrov. 'Mikhailov has lost his marbles. Tell our boy to stop wasting his time with him, and focus instead on finding out how Milesian is helping Minerva bump off the world's leaders.'

'We are living in a world where we are willing to believe that the mere act of observation can alter our reality,' said Sharma. 'And yet we stick to the notion that the universe has no bearing on our lives. That the movement of the sun, moon and planets have no influence over us. We wish to believe that in a quantum world, one in which everything is connected, the planets are not connected to us.'

'Mikhailov is crazy if he believes in this stuff,' said Petrov. 'And it looks like you're on your way there, Sharma.'

'I'm simply saying that the movement of the sun, moon and planets tend to interfere with the earth's magnetic field. This magnetic field has a bearing on newly born infants and adults alike,' said Sharma. 'Why do women's menstrual cycles closely mimic lunar cycles? Why are schizophrenics more likely to be born in February? Why are dyslexics more likely to be summer babies?'

'Why?' asked Judith.

'Because of planetary positions at the time of birth,' replied Sharma.

'Astrology is among the worst manifestations of pseudoscience,' said Petrov. 'Stop wasting your time.'

And that was when Sharma remembered who Mikhailov was.

79

'Makes no sense,' said Cracker, taking a bite of his doughnut and leaving a trail of crumbs on his crumpled shirt. 'Did you attempt to run it against EdgeRun?'

'Sure did,' said his deputy. 'No joy. Incredible. EdgeRun is usually awesome.'

Some years ago, Edward Snowden, a former CIA employee, had leaked classified information from the NSA. One of the most important elements of the leaked information was a decryption programme called Bullrun. Bullrun used advanced mathematical routines to enable the NSA to routinely decrypt vast amounts of data. It then turned out that the British government had also been using a similar programme called Edgehill.

Many technical details around the programme were mentioned in Snowden's documents and were censored by the mainstream press at the urging of US intelligence officers. And those were the very details that Cracker had pieced together in order to create his own decryption algorithm that took elements of Bullrun and Edgehill to build an entirely new piece of software. He had christened it EdgeRun, after its twin origins.

'The fact that he is communicating gibberish makes me very worried,' said Cracker. 'Give me the raw data dump of whatever he typed. Let me see if one of my contacts at the NSA can help. What about other communication?'

'Regular calls to his girlfriend,' replied the deputy. 'Nothing significant discussed. Some of the conversation tends to be in Kannada, so I've sent you transcripts that are translated. He seems to be missing her a lot.'

'Touching,' said Cracker. 'What about his movements within the campus?'

'Works extra-long hours, just as Schmidt would want him to,' replied the deputy. 'Nothing noteworthy on the CCTV system. And, ah, yes. He saved Mikhailov's life through a timely Heimlich manoeuvre in the restaurant.'

'Really?' asked Cracker, brushing the doughnut crumbs off his shirt and taking a gulp of his coffee. 'Anything else?'

'He tends to leave his apartment door open most of the time once he's home.'

'Hmm,' said Cracker. That last piece of information was mystifying.

And then something struck Cracker. 'When he checked in, didn't you say that there was a roll of clingwrap in his luggage?' he asked.

80

Vijay made his way from his lab to Food for Thought, his mind dwelling on Mikhailov. He wasn't sure what to make of the man. Judith had asked him to be careful and warned him that Mikhailov could be connected to Russian intelligence. But wasn't the Russian SVR also a constituent of IG4?

Then there was Mikhailov himself—a weird man. Vijay couldn't tell whether he was a genius, or mentally disturbed, or a bit of both. Vijay decided to play along for a while before he made up his mind. He suddenly felt a hand on his shoulder. He swung around, almost prepared to land a punch before he realized that it was Schmidt.

'I'm so sorry to have startled you,' said Schmidt to an embarrassed Vijay.

'No, no…' stammered Vijay. 'I have no clue why I'm so on edge.'

'Maybe it's the newness of the place,' said Schmidt. 'Made any friends as yet?'

Vijay knew it was a trick question.

'Not really,' answered Vijay. 'Everyone here is kind and coöperative. It's just that no one has any time to socialize.'

'Luckily, you were there to save Mikhailov when he was choking,' said Schmidt, his face not giving away anything. *Ah, so that's where this is coming from,* thought Vijay. *Word has reached him of the incident at the restaurant.*

'It's what anyone else would have done,' said Vijay, shrugging it off and hoping that the conversation would end soon.

'I enjoyed reading your research proposal,' Schmidt went on. 'I thought we could have lunch together to briefly discuss it?'

Having lunch with you is on my list of favourite things, right after coming down with bird flu, measles and chicken pox, thought Vijay.

'Sure,' said Vijay. 'Shall we go?'

81

The two men walked over to Food for Thought, where Daulat Singh took extra-special care of them on account of Schmidt's presence. Schmidt asked for a chicken-mayo sandwich and mint-flavoured water. Vijay ordered vegetable burritos and fresh apple juice.

'Do you like it here?' asked Schmidt after Daulat Singh had left.

'Sure,' replied Vijay. 'It's a fantastic facility and I'm getting to do research work on a subject that excites me. What more could I want?'

'Not missing Sujatha too much?' asked Schmidt.

Vijay momentarily froze. *Was it a subtle warning of sorts? Or had they been listening in on his conversations? Probably the latter.*

'I think that's the name that you mentioned during our interview,' said Schmidt. 'Or am I mistaken?'

'You have a good memory,' acknowledged Vijay. 'Luckily for me, she is very busy with her life as well.' He then changed the subject. It made him uncomfortable to be discussing Sujatha with Schmidt.

'What do you think of the direction that I wish to take?' he asked.

'I think it fits in exceptionally well with what others are doing at Milesian,' said Schmidt, taking a bite of the generous sandwich that Daulat Singh had placed before him. 'Although you should be very careful of what you discuss with the others.'

What was that? Another hint to stay away from discussions with Mikhailov?

'Why?' asked Vijay, playing innocent.

'Because we have found that the only way to maintain integrity of research is by preventing cross-contamination of ideas,' explained Schmidt. 'We want your research to remain pure and uninfluenced by others. The same applies to everyone else too. I am the sole funnel through whom everything gets filtered.'

That's a load of fertilizer, thought Vijay.

'I have sent you a formal request for copies of your thesis as well as the informal research notes that went into formulating it,' said Schmidt. 'I do hope you remember the clause in your agreement that requires you to share with us all your previous research?'

'Yes,' replied Vijay, slightly uncomfortable about handing over years of work to Schmidt.

'Don't worry,' said Schmidt. 'It continues to remain your work. But if we do not know the ground that you have covered, we would be unable to integrate your present efforts with what you already know.'

Vijay nodded.

'The land that Milesian occupies at this site is incredibly vast,' said Vijay, changing the subject. 'What lies beyond our working and living areas? It's impossible to get a feel, because the cable car doesn't have windows.'

The shift in Schmidt's expression was instant. It was a flash of intense anger. He recovered from the momentary lapse quickly and re-established a cordial veneer.

'At Milesian, we aim not only to carry out path-breaking research but also to improve the world,' he said. 'One of the biggest challenges we are facing is the gradual extinction of biodiversity. Beyond us lie hundreds of acres of pristine forests, home to some of the rarest plants and herbs in the world.'

'Can one visit?' asked Vijay, pushing his luck.

'We have seen that the only way to allow such flora and fauna to flourish is by leaving them entirely untouched over extended periods of time,' replied Schmidt. 'Now, I suggest that we both get back to work. Nice to have had this little chat with you.'

I'm being dismissed, thought Vijay.

Schmidt stood up and walked out. Vijay was a little slower. He looked at Schmidt's food tray. Then he did something that he could not explain.

He turned away from the CCTV angle of vision, picked up the partially-consumed bottle of Schmidt's mint-flavoured water and slipped it into his inner jacket pocket before heading over to his lab.

82

The heat was searing and a thick blanket of smoke enveloped the cave. He was struggling for breath, his lungs starved of oxygen.

'Air!' shouted Mikhailov. 'I need air!' But there was no one to listen.

It was another few minutes before Mikhailov awoke with a start. With a gasp, he pulled himself out of the claws of his nightmare, his hands reaching out for his glasses on the nightstand. He put them on with trembling fingers and looked at the time on his bedside clock. Four in the morning. His body was drenched in sweat.

He pulled himself to his feet, walked over to the bathroom and towelled himself dry. He then pulled on a fresh pair of shorts and a t-shirt. He walked over to the refrigerator and poured himself a glass of water, gulping it down quickly.

The nightmares had started at a very definite point in his life. In fact, he could trace his bad dreams to a particular event close to his final days in Brahmananda's ashram.

Around a hundred devotees had lived and worked at the ashram, combining their spiritual education with more mundane tasks such as mopping floors, chopping wood, cooking and fetching water from the natural spring that gushed forth from the rocks close by.

Brahmananda's age was a mystery because he looked the same, regardless of time. He was always in his saffron and vermillion robes, his face radiating an aura that was difficult to explain. Even during the harshest of winters, his ensemble did not vary. It was almost as though heat or cold, rain or shine, fire or wind had no effect on him.

Brahmananda spent twelve hours each day in meditation. The schedule never varied—4 a.m. to 10 a.m., and 4 p.m. to 10 p.m. He performed yoga for two hours each day. He hardly ate, consuming just a few berries with lemon water at noon.

'You barely eat, Guruji,' said Mikhailov. 'How do you survive?'

'Sun-eating,' replied Brahmananda. 'It was practised by the Surya Samadhi Brahmins who were later absorbed into Kalachakra.'

Mikhailov had noticed Brahmananda consciously permitting sunlight into his eyes at specific periods of the day, usually during the lowest ultraviolet-index hours of sunrise and sunset. The energy that he absorbed from the sun seemingly negated his body's need for food.

'Have you heard of HRM?' asked Brahmananda.

'Human Resources Management?' asked Mikhailov innocently.

Brahmananda laughed. 'Hira Ratan Manek,' he clarified. 'The phenomenon is named after him. He was tested by scientists, including some from NASA. They found that he possessed the capacity to derive his energy from the sun.'

'You learnt this technique from him?' asked Mikhailov.

'He learnt it from me,' said Brahmananda with a twinkle in his eyes.

'And why do you perform yoga?' Mikhailov asked. 'You do not need the exercise, given that there is hardly any intake of food.'

'It's not about food,' replied Brahmananda. 'Do you know where the word *yoga* comes from? The root is *yeug* from the ancient Proto-Indo-European language.'

'Ah,' said Mikhailov, uncertain of where Brahmananda was going with that.

'Now let's consider the word *yoke*, shall we?' said Brahmananda. 'The root is exactly the same—*yeug*. Essentially, both words—yoga and yoke—mean the same thing. When performing yoga, one is simply yoking oneself to the Supreme; breaking down the artificial barriers that we have mentally constructed between ourselves and Brahman, the underlying reality that constitutes anything and everything.'

'How?' asked Mikhailov.

'Imagine that your mind is like a radio,' said Brahmananda. 'At the most subtle level, the radio is simply switched on. It remains in this "on" state while you are tuning it into new frequencies, leaving radio stations, changing volume or receiving static between stations. This state of being "on" is the subtle mind. It remains on during birth, death and rebirth. Yoga is simply an effort to tune into your subtle mind.'

Mikhailov never forgot the radio analogy.

83

After twelve hours of meditation and two hours of yoga, Brahmananda only needed four hours of sleep for a full recharge. That left six hours. Those remaining six hours of the day were devoted to his all-important cave.

The cave was gargantuan, having been expanded by Brahmananda and his disciples over many years. It performed a single function. It was a storehouse of ancient knowledge.

The greatest repository of knowledge in ancient times had been the university at Nalanda in the kingdom of Magadha. In the early years of the thirteenth century, it had been ransacked by Muslim invaders who had burned almost everything to the ground.

Brahmananda saw it as his duty to rebuild that archive of knowledge. Over the years he had painstakingly built a team of scholars to piece together documents from secondary sources. In addition, sages and academics around the world were enthusiastically contributing parchments, scrolls, palm-leaf binders and books from temple and monastic records to Brahmananda's cause. Brahmananda used Mikhailov's help in indexing and organizing sections of the vast library. His aim was that the cave would not only replicate the wisdom of Nalanda but also substantively add to it.

And then, in 1999, Pakistani soldiers and Jihadi fighters had crossed the Line of Control that ran between India and Pakistan near Kargil. Hardas was one of the first areas to come under attack. It was several days before the Indian Army, supported by the Indian Air Force, recaptured territory on the Indian side. During that time the ashram was devastated. In a matter of twenty-four hours, Hardas was awash in blood, the neighbouring fields strewn with the dead and wounded.

Amid the chaos, Mikhailov had frantically searched for Brahmananda. He had rushed to the cave and found him vainly attempting to gather manuscripts that needed to be saved.

'This place will go up in flames in minutes,' said Mikhailov. 'It's time for us to move out.'

'I can sacrifice anything but these records,' countered Brahmananda. 'I have spent my life trying to reassemble the knowledge of Nalanda and I will not allow anyone to destroy it.' He was clutching a few documents close to his chest although he seemed to be aware of the futility of his effort.

Suddenly, there were gunshots. Then petrol bombs were hurled inside. One of them landed a few feet away from them on a heap of unsorted documents. Within minutes, the cave's contents were in flames. Cries of '*Allahu-Akbar*' could be heard coming from outside as the soldiers of Islam threw bottles of petrol to ensure that nothing remained.

'We must get out,' said Mikhailov, almost choking from the smoke, his eyes watering.

Before Brahmananda could argue further, Mikhailov forcibly picked up his guru and headed towards the opposite end of the cave, where there was another passage out. Mikhailov navigated his way out of the inferno carrying Brahmananda. They emerged near the spring from where they would fill their earthen pots each day.

Years of hard work had been lost to religious fanaticism, much in the way that Nalanda had been destroyed. Mikhailov, too, had lost the home that he thought he had finally found.

The memories of that night refused to leave Mikhailov. Much like the imprints of Akashic Records.

84

'What are Akashic Records?' asked Mikhailov. He was with Brahmananda in the Army Hospital in Kargil, having been transferred there by military escort. On the bed next to his lay an army officer who had just woken up to find his leg amputated. He was in severe depression. The nurse was keeping an extra eye on him because the doctors thought that he could be suicidal.

Both Mikhailov and Brahmananda had received burn injuries in addition to the complications caused by smoke inhalation, but their problems were miniscule in comparison with the wounds that they saw around them.

'Akashic Records are a compilation of all human experiences, actions, reflections, intentions, feelings, thoughts and words ever to have happened anywhere and everywhere in the universe,' said Brahmananda, sipping hot water and lemon that the nurse had arranged for him.

'Do those really exist?' asked Mikhailov incredulously. 'I thought that the whole idea was nothing but the fanciful imagination of Helena Blavatsky.' Blavatsky's name had often been mentioned by Mikhailov's grandfather in rather unflattering terms. She had been the co-founder of the Theosophical Society—seekers after the esoteric—and had been one of the original proponents of the Akashic theory.

Brahmananda smiled. 'Let's forget Blavatsky for a moment and think about someone whom you revere—Einstein,' he said. 'According to his Theory of Relativity, space and time are not separate entities. Both are deeply entwined to create a multidimensional continuum that he called spacetime.'

'Correct,' said Mikhailov. He felt more comfortable in the territory of science.

Although it was impossible for the human brain to visualize spacetime, mathematics could. In fact, it had been proven that moving faster through space automatically sped up time. In 1971, four atomic clocks had been placed on commercial flights around the world. Einstein's equations had predicted that the flying clocks would lose about 40 nanoseconds going east, and gain 275 nanoseconds travelling west. They did.

'What is the implication of Einstein's theory?' asked Brahmananda.

'Gravity,' offered Mikhailov. 'Curvature in spacetime, caused by heavier objects.'

'That too,' said Brahmananda. 'But the main implication is that there is nothing like a simultaneous instant when everyone sees everything. Light needs time to travel and it reaches people at different times. When we look at the sun, we are actually looking at the sun as it had existed eight minutes ago because that's the time it takes light to travel from the sun to Earth. When we look at the nearest star in our night sky, we know that we are looking at something that existed a little over four years ago. And when astronomers use formidable telescopes to see distant stars and galaxies, they are actually seeing them as they existed thousands and even millions of years ago.'

Mikhailov nodded in agreement. Brahmananda could be entirely philosophical at one moment and entirely scientific the next. Brahmananda drew a rough image.

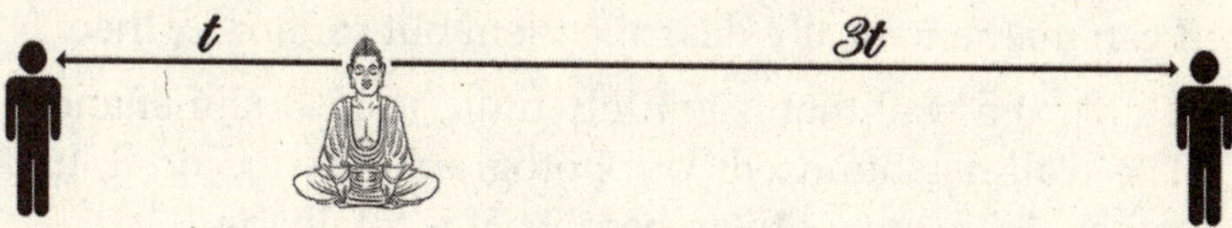

'A distant event that happens at a particular instant for one observer may happen earlier or later for another observer depending on the time that light takes to travel to the observer. Something seen at time "t" by one observer may be seen at "3t" by another. On the other hand, two events which are seen as simultaneous by an observer may actually have occurred in different temporal sequences.

'But do you know what the other big implication of Einstein's spacetime is?' asked Brahmananda. 'It means that the universe is a giant static hologram, not in three dimensions but many more. And every point in that hologram is defined by coordinates spanning those dimensions. Every event—past, present or future—is already there in that hologram. Almost as though time does not exist.'

'Wheeler and DeWitt,' murmured Mikhailov.

'Exactly,' responded Brahmananda. 'John Wheeler of Princeton and Bryce DeWitt of the University of North Carolina developed the equation we speak of. The aim was to unify relativity and quantum mechanics. But what went missing from that equation?'

'Time,' replied Mikhailov.

'Correct,' said Brahmananda. 'Time is absent from the equation, the very reason why many have said that the equation is nonsense. Who knows—it may be more sense than nonsense! Buddhist texts say: The past, the future, physical space, events and individuals are nothing but names, forms of thought, words of common usage, merely superficial realities!'

'But why can't I see all the dimensions?' asked Mikhailov. 'I can mathematically describe them but cannot *see* them.'

'Think of a wall that is entirely unlit,' said Brahmananda. 'The wall has hundreds of photographs pasted on it, but you can't see any of them because it is totally dark.'

Mikhailov tried to visualize what Brahmananda was telling him.

'Now imagine that you have a flashlight in your hand,' said Brahmananda. 'The flashlight has a beam that can illuminate only one photograph at a time. You shine it on the wall and you see one of the photographs.'

Mikhailov nodded as he imagined the scenario.

'You can see one photograph but not the others,' said Brahmananda. 'You can shift the beam to another photograph but it means that the earlier photo becomes invisible.'

Mikhailov continued to visualize the scene.

'Now imagine that each of those photographs is a lifetime,' said Brahmananda. 'The flashlight is your consciousness. Because your consciousness is focused on that single photograph, or lifetime, that's what you end up experiencing. But the reality is that thousands of your lives are happening in parallel. They are on the wall but you do not see them with your limited consciousness.'

'How do I see the entire picture then?' asked Mikhailov.

'Step back from the wall,' said Brahmananda. 'It will increase the size of the beam and you will be able to see more photos simultaneously. Your consciousness will expand to see the reality of the world.'

85

Brahmananda turned his gaze to the wounded soldier who had lost his leg. Tears were streaming down the man's face. Brahmananda dragged his eyes away from the sight and resumed his conversation with Mikhailov.

'In spacetime, the past, present and future are actually engraved en bloc. Each observer simply sees a slice of spacetime and these slices appear to him as successive or sequential,' said Brahmananda. 'These are compiled into the Akashic Records.'

'They are actual documents?' asked Mikhailov.

'Akasha means ether or sky,' answered Brahmananda. 'The records exist in the etheric plane. This is not a different dimension. It's just that we humans are looking at the spacetime hologram from within. We are fish inside a glass tank. Our view is different from someone looking at the tank from outside.'

Mikhailov was quiet.

'You've heard the story of what Abhimanyu experienced during the *Mahabharata* war?' asked Brahmananda. Mikhailov had. Brahmananda had narrated it previously to him.

'Abhimanyu knew how to break into a military formation known as the *chakravyuh* but he did not know how to get out of it. All of us are leading the life of Abhimanyu. We enter this physical world kicking and screaming and then have no clue of how to extract ourselves from it so that we may have a bird's eye view of the formation. We are fish in the tank. So the answer to your question is no, these are not *documents* as you understand that term. More like universal data points that can be read by yogis.'

Mikhailov was stunned into silence. His grandfather had always maintained that Helena Blavatsky, a fellow Russian, was a sham. Her writings about 'indestructible tablets of astral light that recorded both past and future of human thought and action' were nonsense.

'It's not just Blavatsky,' said Brahmananda, picking up on Mikhailov's thoughts. 'Alfred Percy Sinnett's book *Esoteric Buddhism* spoke of the Buddhist belief in permanent records in the Akasha, and the capacity of trained masters to read such records.'

'Were there others?' asked Mikhailov.

'Sure,' said Brahmananda. 'Charles Leadbeater wrote about Atlantis based on Akashic Records. Rudolf Steiner wrote about Lemuria based on his readings. Levi Dowling wrote the story of young Jesus based on the same source.'

'What were the documents that you saved?' asked Mikhailov.

'My plans for yet another library,' replied Brahmananda. 'In addition, I saved this book for you.'

Mikhailov looked at it. *Bardo Thodol,* known to the West as the *Tibetan Book of the Dead.*

'Read it,' said Brahmananda. 'It will tell you what happens when you can broaden the beam of your flashlight and peek into the spaces between lifetimes.'

He paused.

'I will now be leaving you, Mikhailov,' he said, as he got up from his bed.

'Why?' asked Mikhailov. 'I wish to go with you wherever you are going. My home is wherever you are.'

'Everything has been destroyed and I have to start the process all over again, son,' said Brahmananda. 'This is a journey that I need to make on my own. But before I go, I need to talk to that young man who has lost his leg. I can't give him back his leg but I can give him the will to live.'

'How?' asked Mikhailov.

'I shall tell him the story of Sashwata,' replied Brahmananda. 'The man who refused to die so that he could fulfil his destiny.'

86

The candidate waved to the crowds at the National Convention as he walked up to the podium. 'Look into their faces,' his campaign manager had advised. 'Connect with them, meet their gaze, as many as you can manage. They are there for you. Make each one feel special.'

With nineteen major candidates having entered the race two years previously, this had been the largest presidential primary for any political party in American history. Prior to the Iowa caucuses, five candidates withdrew. The New Hampshire primaries prompted another six withdrawals. South Carolina, Alaska, Oklahoma and Texas caused another five exits. Ohio, Wisconsin, New York and Indiana clinched it. The last two opponents were forced to pull out because they knew that they had no hope left to force a contest at the convention.

They were packed into a conference hall in Cleveland, Ohio. He knew that his nomination was now a cakewalk. With 2,472 delegates to the National Convention, only a simple majority of 1,237 was needed to clinch the presidential nomination. And that was in the bag, with his competition having withdrawn.

Security arrangements for the convention were unprecedented. Around fifty million dollars in federal grants had been paid to the Cleveland Police Department to support the security arrangements that were vital. The money had been spent on riot-gear and reinforcements. The convention was designated as a National Special Security Event, which effectively meant that the Secret Service and Department of Homeland Security were on hand to vet all arrangements.

He adjusted his jacket ever so slightly and then delivered one of the longest acceptance speeches ever. It lasted for a full sixty minutes and covered his favourite themes, including law and order, defence, terrorism and immigration. Along the way there were spontaneous eruptions of cheers and applause as he touched on issues that resonated with the delegates.

Behind the scenes, a Gallup survey found that almost 49 per cent of Americans saw his speech positively while only 33 per cent viewed it negatively.

He had come a long way. The White House was just a few months away.

87

Oxford Street in the West End of London was packed. Running from Marble Arch to Tottenham Court Road via Oxford Circus, the street was filled with shoppers and gawking tourists. In the summer months, the daily footprint of visitors was around half a million. Traffic was restricted to buses and taxis. The driver of the bright red bus, Sadiq, waited at the intersection, looking at his watch. He whispered a prayer under his breath and slammed his foot on the accelerator.

The twelve-tonner ploughed through the unsuspecting crowd that was crossing the road. Sadiq kept his foot planted on the gas, allowing the vehicle to mow down everyone and everything in its path. Travelling at a little over ninety kilometres per hour, Sadiq allowed the bus to mount the pavement, leaving a trail of mutilated bodies, blood, limbs and terrified onlookers behind him.

The emergency response teams hastily set up a barrier of police vehicles at the next intersection, but Sadiq accelerated and mounted the kerb, forcing his way through the police barriers. He had reached Marble Arch by the time police officers were able to shoot him down.

Reports said 98 people were dead and 234 injured.

The next day, Mafraqi claimed responsibility for the attack. 'Sadiq was a true servant of Allah. Our Jihad consists of killing and dispersing all those who fight against Allah and his Prophet. I ask all Muslims everywhere in the world to step up Jihad against enemies of Allah. Destroy Allah's enemies wherever you see them. You may open a front wherever your hands reach. When there is a total war, there are no more civilian objects; nor is there anything called a civilian population.'

88

Rio de Janeiro's bronzed *cariocas,* as the locals were known, were heading home from the beaches. It was time to bathe and doll up for the night. Maria was no exception. She was in a relationship with Miguel, but had a thing for Lucas. Or did she prefer Pedro? Maybe Felipe? Maria was in demand. She hummed a tune as she sprayed a touch of her favourite fragrance on herself. A last-minute check of her face and hair, and a twirl before the mirror, and she was set.

Miguel was waiting for her at the botequim a block away in Lapa. He waved out to her as she made her way to the table. Chilled Cervejas awaited along with a selection of stuffed pastry pockets and palmettos. 'I don't want beer,' she said dismissively to Miguel. 'Get me a Caipirinha instead.'

'Your wish is my command,' said Miguel jokingly as he got up to get her the cocktail from the bar. All establishments in the area were brimming to capacity and getting a waiter seemed almost impossible. These days, Lapa was the most energetic part of Rio after sunset. There were literally hundreds of bars and restaurants to pick from, each one offering something slightly different. Sounds of the samba could be heard in the streets till the late hours.

A vacant chair next to the stunning Maria acted as a magnet. She was soon surrounded by exceptionally good-looking men, each one strutting like a peacock for her attention.

She smiled seductively at one of them who winked at her. He sidled up to her and whispered, 'You know what would look great on you? Me!' He snaked his arm around her and she did not push it away.

The sting that she felt on her upper arm was sudden and she winced. 'Ouch!' she said, turning around to look at the man's face. But he was gone.

By the time Miguel returned, it was too late.

89

Mikhailov spent two more days at the Army Hospital in Kargil. During that time he finished reading the book that Brahmananda had given him. The introductory pages talked about Padmasambhava, the eighth-century Buddhist master, who was also called Guru Rinpoche by the Tibetans.

Legend had it that Padmasambhava, which literally translated to 'the lotus-born', had appeared as an eight-year-old child floating on a lotus blossom in Lake Dhanakosha, in the kingdom of Oddiyana, the region represented by the modern-day Indian state of Odisha. He would come to be widely revered as the *second Buddha* in Tibet, Nepal, Bhutan and Sikkim.

Padmasambhava's supernatural qualities were observed by the childless King Indrabodhi, who adopted him and began raising him to be the next ruler. One day, Padmasambhava was dancing on the roof of the palace when a trident slipped from his hand. It resulted in the death of one of the powerful ministers in Indrabodhi's court and Padmasambhava was expelled.

He then roamed northern India as a yogi, learning under several tantric masters, often meditating at charnel grounds, the preferred haunt of Shiva-worshippers. His travels brought him to Rewalsar, in the modern Indian state of Himachal Pradesh, where he began teaching tantric *siddhis* to Princess Mandarava. This enraged her father. He ordered Padmasambhava be arrested and burnt at the stake.

Padmasambhava was left to burn for seven days, but he was found alive and well sitting in the centre of Lake Rewalsar. Amazed by this miracle, the king offered Padmasambhava his kingdom along with his daughter's hand in marriage.

Padmasambhava declined the offer of kingship but accepted the hand of Mandarava. They travelled to Nepal where they stayed at the Maratika Cave, meditating and practising secret tantric consort rituals. Padmasambhava would thereafter always be depicted as seated between Mandarava and Yeshe Tsogyal, another of his consorts.

Padmasambhava was then invited by Trisong Detsen, the king of Tibet, to teach the dharma to his people. After impressing the king and the court with his brilliance, Padmasambhava supervised the building of Samye, the first-ever Buddhist monastery in Tibet. This was the beginning of a monastic community in Tibet. Along with other teachers and Tibetan pupils, he painstakingly began the process of translating into Tibetan all Buddhist sutras, tantras and the important treatises written on them.

Court intrigues eventually compelled Padmasambhava to leave Tibet, but he left behind a monastic order as well as an entire genre of Buddhist literature that came to be known as *terma,* which literally translated to 'treasure'. Key among these was *Bardo Thodol,* the *Tibetan Book of the Dead.*

Padmasambhava and his consort, Mandarava, are believed to be alive even today.

90

That Monday night was France's first presidential debate. Five leading presidential hopefuls stood before television cameras from TF1 and LCI, trading punches on the country's most hotly debated issues: immigration, Islam and international relations. There were thirty-seven days left before French voters would head to the polls, and the debate was an excellent occasion to sway public sentiment. Each of the hopefuls was taking no chances.

Francois Moreau felt his anger rising as his primary opponent, Adrienne Dubois, told an enthusiastic audience that the mere presence of *burkinis*, head-to-toe swimming suits, on French beaches was proof of the rise of radical Islam in France. Some French city councils had even banned them, only giving the issue greater media attention. 'French secularism is under siege,' said Adrienne forcefully. 'It doesn't matter if you believe it or not. I stand here before you to declare that Islam is having an undesirable effect on French society. We must put a stop to immigration from Islamic nations urgen—'

Moreau could no longer control his irritation. He interrupted her mid-sentence. 'You do a great disservice to the nation by dividing our people with your racist rhetoric,' he said angrily. 'You are an expert at twisting the facts to suit your narrative. *That's* what needs to stop immediately.'

'Nonsense,' shot back Adrienne. 'We need a president who will help France follow Britain out of the European Union and seal our borders to make our people safe. The challenges of integrating newcomers is there for everyone to see. The time for moral pontificating is over. The French must defend their values and traditions at all costs. Our nation will *not* be safe in the hands of apologists like you.

It seems that you are hellbent on making France into a caliphate.'

Pollsters from BFMTV were quietly conducting exercises with target groups and, for the moment, Adrienne was way ahead. Out of 1,391 people polled, 36 per cent preferred her, while only 27 per cent were in favour of Moreau. But everyone knew that Moreau was capable of pulling a rabbit out of his hat. He had already served as president for five years and, if he won, this would be his second term. He had connections among the rich and powerful besides having a wealth of administrative experience.

Moreau grasped the lectern before him tightly, his knuckles white. Sweat was streaming down his face and he was breathing heavily. He took a sip of water from the bottle that had been provided at his lectern but it made him want to retch. And then he did, in full view of the television cameras. Adrienne, who was standing next to him, stepped away in shock as Moreau's puke spattered on the floor.

'Doctor! We need a doctor immediately,' shouted the producer of the debate, as he signalled for his cameramen to keep their cameras running. This was priceless reality television.

Moreau was struggling to take off his jacket so that he could scratch the vicious itch on his forearm but before he could do that, his legs gave way and he crashed to the floor.

91

And it's another day and it's time for me, Masoud, to jot down my thoughts. I realize that my last post was incomplete without reference to other religions. So here goes.

There are those who say that there are enough passages in other religions that are equally violent as some in the Qur'an. The

Bible and Torah have many passages that talk of stoning and killing. For example:

Ezekiel 9:5—follow him through the city and kill everyone whose forehead is not marked. Show no mercy, have no pity. Kill them all, old and young, girls and women and little children.

Deuteronomy 17:12—anyone arrogant enough to reject the verdict of the holy man who represents God must be put to death.

Leviticus 24:16—anyone who blasphemes God's name must be stoned to death by the whole community of believers.

The Catholic Church committed some of the most ghastly crimes under the banner of the Inquisition. And, by the way, why only Abrahamic religions? Other faiths such as Buddhism, Hinduism, Sikhism and Jainism are not without their downsides. Right?

Narasingaraja Naidu, a professor of history at Bangalore University, is emphatic that the great emperor, Ashoka, was a Buddhist even before he waged the terrible war in Kalinga that killed 300,000 people. And today, Buddhists in Myanmar are actively inciting violence against Rohingya Muslims. Buddhist Sinhalese in Sri Lanka were responsible for the deaths of thousands of Tamils. In Thailand, Buddhist monks have taken to carrying arms under their robes.

Let's then consider Hinduism. In the Manusmriti *of the Hindus, a low-caste who insults a high-caste shall have his tongue cut out or have hot oil poured into his mouth. The* Mahabharata *urges Arjuna to fight his family members. Hindus used to burn widows on the funeral pyres of their husbands. The list of violent deeds is pretty long.*

Sikh texts have been misused to justify terrorism to support the Khalistan movement. Jainism permits people to starve themselves to death and hundreds actually do it each year in India.

So I must ask: what makes these religions different to Islam? I think that there are two things that distinguish them. One—adherents of these faiths no longer take their texts literally. Two—for the most part they have separated religion and state.

This is not the case with Islam. Ordinary Muslims see the lack of separation between religion and state as a weakness. But terrorists see that as their strength. They know that an effective army is not one which questions why. It is one that simply obeys commands. Literal rather than liberal interpretation of Islamic texts helps ensure discipline among the faithful.

The lack of separation between religion and state means that every law in Islamic lands is divine law. It isn't subject to manmade variations. How can any other religion inspire the same zeal that divine law brings forth?

92

'I want you to have this,' said Mikhailov to Vijay as they sat sipping tea in his flat. It was the second time that they were meeting. All mutually decided security protocols had been followed.

'What is it?' asked Vijay, looking at the palm of Mikhailov's hand. Mikhailov gestured that he wanted silence as he repeated a mantra a few times.

Once he was done, Mikhailov replied. 'It's a single prayer bead on a chain,' he said.

'Rudraksha?' asked Vijay.

Mikhailov nodded. 'As you know, Hindus use rosaries that are made from the seeds of the *elaeocarpus ganitrus* tree—rudraksha beads. These are strung together as a hundred and eight beads plus one. This is the *plus one*. It was given to me by my grandfather who found it during the Nalanda excavations.'

'Nalanda?' asked Vijay. 'You mean the ruins in the present-day Indian state of Bihar?'

'Yes,' Mikhailov said. 'If it hadn't been for that monastery, Bihar would never have been called that.'

Vijay looked puzzled.

Mikhailov explained further. 'There were several Buddhist monasteries, including Nalanda, in the region that you now call Bihar,' he said. 'These monasteries were called *viharas*. The name *Bihar* comes to us from that word—vihara.'

'And all of Nalanda died with the Muslim attacks?'

'No,' said Mikhailov. 'The Tibetan pilgrim, Dharmasvamin, visited Nalanda in 1235. Most of it was in disrepair but an old teacher, Shribhadra, was still there, instructing around seventy students. Even then, he had refused to give up on diffusing knowledge.'

'Why are you giving this bead to me?' asked Vijay.

'You will need it more than I do,' replied Mikhailov. 'Further, if something were to happen to me, I would not want this rudraksha bead to fall into the wrong hands. Use it wisely. The ancients knew its power.'

I have no clue what you mean by that, thought Vijay. Nevertheless, he accepted the offering graciously.

Vijay placed the chain that held the bead around his neck. It felt strangely reassuring against his chest.

93

'The word *nala* means a *lotus stalk*,' said Mikhailov. 'Nalanda was inspired and modelled on Buddhism's Lotus Sutra.'

'What is that?'

'Have you heard of Amitabh?' asked Mikhailov.

'The Bollywood actor?' asked Vijay innocently. He had grown up with Amitabh Bachchan as his idol.

Mikhailov laughed. 'According to Buddhist scriptures, there once lived a great king by the name of Dharmakara who renounced his throne. Due to his piety and purity, he was bestowed the name *Amitabh*—a word of Sanskrit origin that means "infinite splendour and boundless light". Amitabh eventually went on to become a Buddha himself, having attained nirvana.'

'And?'

'The Lotus Sutra is actually the Amitabh Sutra in expanded form—a sutra that helps one attain the "pure land" in the manner that a lotus arises from muck and sees light.'

'Do we know the age of Nalanda?' asked Vijay.

'The Chinese pilgrim Xuanzang visited India in the seventh century CE,' replied Mikhailov. 'He wrote that the monastery had been built by King Sakraditya in the first half of the fifth century. Nalanda flourished under the patronage of the Gupta dynasty and subsequently under Harsha, the emperor of Kannauj.'

'It was big?'

'Oh yes, it was huge,' said Mikhailov. 'It was thought of as an architectural wonder of the time. It had eight separate compounds, ten temples, meditation halls, classrooms, dormitories, lakes and parks. In its heyday, the university pulled in monks, scholars, researchers and students from distant lands such as Tibet, China, Korea and Central Asia, besides the ones from India. There were around ten thousand students at any given time. All under the tutelage of fifteen hundred teachers.'

'What did they study?' asked Vijay. 'Buddhism or Hinduism?'

'They studied Mahayana Buddhism in addition to the writings of the eighteen Hinayana sects of Buddhism,' replied Mikhailov. 'But their curriculum also included the Vedas, logic, Sanskrit grammar, medicine and Samkhya—Hinduism's yoga school.'

'One always thinks of Nalanda as a library,' said Vijay. 'Why?'

'The vihara was the greatest repository of knowledge in ancient times,' replied Mikhailov. 'The jewel in the crown of Nalanda was its library called the *Dharmaganja,* which consisted of three massive multi-storeyed buildings. One of those buildings was nine floors high. These buildings contained hundreds of thousands of sacred manuscripts. The collection included texts on religion, philosophy, logic, grammar, astrology, astronomy, literature and medicine.'

'What happened to Nalanda?' asked Vijay.

'In the early years of the thirteenth century, Bakhtiyar Khilji, a Turkic Muslim general, ransacked Nalanda,' answered Mikhailov. 'And with that attack some of the greatest intellectual treasures known to mankind were lost forever.'

'Why is Nalanda so important to you?' asked Vijay.

'Because my grandfather, Viktor, carried out excavations there in his bid to find Shangri-La, or Shambala as the Buddhists called it,' said Mikhailov, showing Vijay a few photos of the ruins. 'I am convinced that the secret of Shambhala lies in Nalanda.'

'Why?' asked Vijay.

'Because the very notion of Shambhala is one that arose from Vajrayana Buddhism, a form of Tantric Buddhism that was spawned in Nalanda,' replied Mikhailov. 'Nalanda disappeared to civilization under mounds of earth for the next six centuries. It remained hidden until a team from the Archaeological Survey of India—assisted by my grandfather—unearthed eleven monasteries and six brick temples in addition to hundreds of sculptures, coins, plaques, murals, copper plates, inscriptions, rosaries and terracotta figures.'

'Figures of?'

'The Buddha in different manifestations such as Avalokitesvara, Jambhala, Manjushri, Marichi and Tara,' replied Mikhailov. 'Also Hindu idols of Vishnu, Shiva-Parvati, Ardhanarishvara, Ganesha, Mahishasura Mardini and Surya. Nalanda was a wealthy monastery—that sounds like an oxymoron, doesn't it?'

'Wealthy? How?' asked Vijay.

'State patronage,' replied Mikhailov. 'Revenue from two hundred villages was earmarked for the maintenance of Nalanda. Xuanzang tells us that the Nalanda towers seemed to soar above mists in the sky, while lotus ponds, kanaka flowers and mango orchards gave the monastery an ethereal feel.'

'Nalanda sounds like Shambhala,' observed Vijay.

Mikhailov looked directly into Vijay's eyes. 'As I said, the secret to Shambhala lies in Nalanda.'

94

'Confused?' asked Mikhailov. 'Can't say I blame you. Have you picked up strange energy vibrations during your stay here?'

Vijay thought about it. 'No,' he replied. 'I don't even know what you actually mean.'

'The human body has chakras or energy vortexes that are connected by channels that transport energy from one part to another. Similarly, planet Earth is also a living organism that has vortexes of its own.'

'Where?' asked Vijay.

'There are many,' replied Mikhailov. 'Many holy sites of the Hindus such as Mount Kailash are located along energy meridians. So are Glastonbury, the Pyramids at Giza, Stonehenge and several others.'

'What does this have to do with us?' asked Vijay.

'One such energy meridian also runs beneath us at Milesian Labs,' replied Mikhailov. 'You remember the passage about Shambhala in the book on Kalachakra?'

'Sure,' said Vijay. 'But I thought it was a theoretical construct of an ideal world, not a physical place.'

'It may be both,' said Mikhailov. He got up from the tatami mat and went to his desk. He pulled out a handwritten note that ran to a few pages and handed it over to Vijay.

'My notes on Shambhala,' he said. 'I think I know where it is.'

Vijay began reading it.

'Read it later,' instructed Mikhailov. He paused as Vijay folded and put away the notes into the pocket of his jacket.

'The region where we are located is a repository for unexplainable energy,' said Mikhailov. 'Have you heard of Roopkund?'

'No,' replied Vijay.

'It is a glacial lake that lies at an altitude of 16,499 feet here in Uttarakhand,' said Mikhailov. 'It's only about seventy kilometres away from here. The final part of the journey has to be made on foot.'

'What is its significance?' asked Vijay.

'Roopkund is locally known as Skeleton Lake,' said Mikhailov. 'Whenever the snow melts, hundreds of human skeletons become visible at the bottom.'

Vijay shuddered.

'Subsequent research has shown that the skeletons are the remains of humans from the ninth century. Over eleven hundred years ago,' continued Mikhailov. 'What is truly remarkable is the fact that the lake is surrounded by rock-dotted glaciers and snow-covered mountains. It has never been inhabited. So who were those people whose remains we now see at the bottom of the lake?'

'Who were they?' echoed Vijay.

'The skeletons were first observed in 1942 by a ranger,' said Mikhailov. 'The British authorities initially suspected that the skeletons could be the remains of a clandestine Japanese battalion, but then they realized that the remains were too old to belong to the time of the Second World War. In addition, the recovered wooden artefacts, iron spearheads and leather slippers were a clear indication that these were people of a much earlier provenance.'

'Radiocarbon dating?' asked Vijay.

'Carried out at Oxford University's Radiocarbon Accelerator Unit,' replied Mikhailov. 'They dated the material to around 850 CE.'

'How did they die?' asked Vijay.

'Blows to the back of the head,' answered Mikhailov.

'Hyderabad's Centre for Cellular and Molecular Biology—CCMB—carried out DNA tests on a hundred samples from the lake. They then ran comparisons with the current Indian population.'

'What did they find?'

'That the remains belonged to two distinct groups,' replied Mikhailov. 'One was a group of short men, possibly local porters. There was also a taller group that had DNA mutations associated with Konkanastha Brahmins.'

'Such a large number of deaths must find mention in local stories and folklore,' said Vijay.

'They do,' said Mikhailov. 'Folklore says that the king of Kanauj, Raja Jasdhaval, was on a pilgrimage along with his pregnant wife, Rani Balampa. They were accompanied by a large retinue of servants and dancers.'

'Where would they have been headed?' asked Vijay.

'There persists an ancient tradition of carrying a golden idol of goddess Nanda Devi in a silver palanquin in procession to another lake called Homkund,' said Mikhailov. 'It is called the *Nanda Devi Raj Jat Yatra*. The tiring and precarious trek of 280 kilometres takes place every twelve years. The pilgrims have to cross thick forests, snow-covered passes and icy-cold mountain streams to get there.'

'What is the significance of the pilgrimage?' enquired Vijay.

'Nanda Devi is carried in pomp to the home of her husband, Shiva,' said Mikhailov. 'The journey starts near Karanprayag and ends at Homkund. One of the stops along the way is Roopkund Lake. The yatra takes around three weeks. Despite the rocky terrain and freezing cold, devoted pilgrims undertake the journey barefoot. It is meant to be a journey of spiritual cleansing through devotion and discipline.'

'So, it's possible that Raja Jasdhaval was on that pilgrimage?' asked Vijay.

'Seems most likely,' said Mikhailov. 'But Jasdhaval's was a luxury expedition, surrounded by revelry, dancers and wine. Apparently, he incurred the wrath of a group of sages who were performing austere penance there. The sages had built a labyrinth of caves that functioned as meditation cells and libraries, and Jasdhaval's entourage disregarded their rules. Their pontiff was someone called Guru Astika.'

'And?'

'Astika was said to have special powers,' said Mikhailov. 'These sages had always meditated along the energy meridian that included Roopkund. They were so powerful that they brought down a heavy hailstorm on the heads on the disrespectful revellers, thereby crushing the skulls of the men in Raja Jasdhaval's entourage.'

Vijay felt the hair on his arms rise. 'What gave them that power?' he finally asked in awe.

'We don't know,' said Mikhailov. 'What we do know is that the sages were able to channelize the energy that surrounded them—energy that had been around for over seven thousand years. That's what the Akashic Records tell us.'

Vijay was silent as he digested all that Mikhailov had told him.

95

'My meditation allows me to pick up on energy flows,' continued Mikhailov. 'Over the past few weeks, I have been picking up strong vibrations—in several directions—emanating from the surroundings.'

'Wouldn't that be normal?' asked Vijay. 'After all, as we've discussed, everything is energy. And this place has an abundance of it owing to the meridian crossing it.'

'True,' replied Mikhailov. 'Except for the fact that these vibrations happen at specified intervals of time. Moreover, they coincide with the departure of Schmidt from the facility.'

'Where do you think Schmidt goes?' asked Vijay.

Mikhailov shrugged. 'I have absolutely no idea,' he said. 'He is here only for a few hours each day and then mysteriously disappears for longish spells. Doesn't even use the cable car. The Schumann Resonance also seems to spike at such times.'

'Schumann Resonance?' asked Vijay.

'Named after the German physicist Professor W. O. Schumann from the Technical University of Munich,' said Mikhailov.

Seeing the query on Vijay's face, he went on to explain. 'In 1952, Schumann predicted that there are electromagnetic waves in the atmosphere—in the space between the surface of the earth and the atmosphere—the ionosphere, to be precise. This was confirmed two years later when measurements by König discovered waves at a primary frequency of 7.83 Hertz.'

'How is the Schumann Resonance relevant to what you've experienced?' asked Vijay.

'The Schumann Resonance is the heartbeat of the earth,' explained Mikhailov. 'It is the set of spectrum peaks in the extremely low frequency—or ELF—of the earth's electromagnetic field. It's almost a tuning fork for the direction of life. While scientists believe otherwise, I think that the Schumann Resonance is also related to consciousness.'

'I have wondered why our facility is surrounded by woods,' said Vijay. 'And why these woods are off-limits to all of us. Schmidt says it's on account of preserving biodiversity.'

'Nonsense,' said Mikhailov. 'I don't know what lies there. All I know is that Schmidt goes there regularly. And I am convinced that the energy vibrations that I am picking up are emerging from those woods. The strange bit is that energy from other places also seems to get activated around the same time.'

Mikhailov pulled out a list from his pad. 'See these latitude readings,' he said, holding out the list to Vijay. 'These latitudes on our planet are also activated simultaneously.'

30.7352
18.8110
13.7498
12.8476
12.2319
11.5172
11.3995
9.2881

Vijay looked at the list. Then he sighed. He no longer knew whether Mikhailov was a genius—or simply nuts.

'I'm not crazy,' said Mikhailov, picking up on Vijay's last thought. 'Have you read *The Tao of Physics* by Fritjof Capra?'

Vijay nodded. He had, many years ago.

'Then, as you know, the book explores the parallels between Eastern mysticism and modern physics,' said Mikhailov. 'It alludes to the fact that the deep meditation of Indian sages to experience oneness was the same connectivity that quantum physicists were trying to prove. In short, Eastern mystics knew thousands of years ago what modern physicists are now trying to prove. Are you familiar with Tantric Buddhism?'

'You mean the Tibetan version of Buddhism?' asked Vijay.

'Yes, it was heavily influenced by the Hindu concept of tantra,' said Mikhailov. 'Do you know what the word "tantra" means?'

Vijay waited for Mikhailov to answer his own question.

'It is derived from the Sanskrit term *tantram,* which means to "warp" or to "weave",' explained Mikhailov. 'Tantra was a fundamental understanding of the seamless unity of everything in the universe. In fact, one of the oldest texts in Mahayana Buddhism is the *Avatamsaka Sutra,* and this text describes the universe as a flawless network of mutual interactions where all things and events play with each other in an infinitely complex manner.'

96

Mikhailov reached for a book by his side and opened it to a flagged page. 'Do you recognize this?' he asked, pointing to a little gland within the illustration of the human brain.

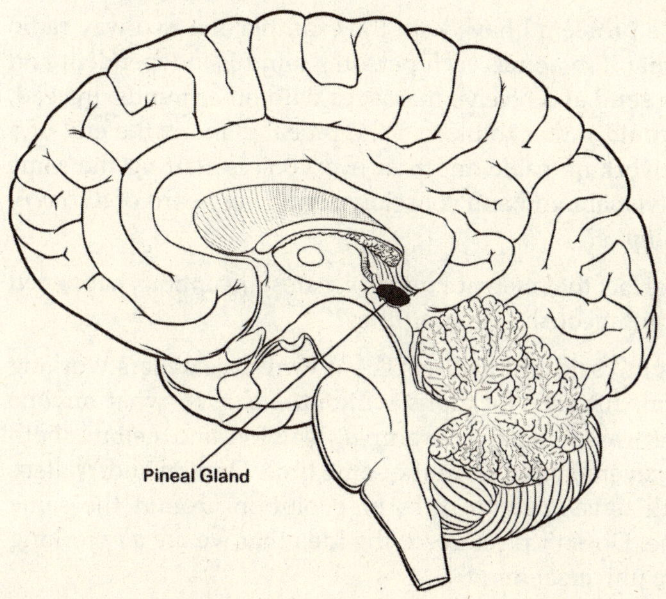

'Sure,' said Vijay. 'That's the pineal gland.'

'Correct,' said Mikhailov. 'It's the pinecone shaped gland which is often called the third eye. When you first came to Milesian, what did you see at the entrance?'

'A statue of Nataraja,' replied Vijay.

'Yes, but it was enclosed in something,' prompted Mikhailov.

'An orb,' replied Vijay.

'Not an orb, but a structure in the shape of a pinecone,' said Mikhailov. 'Recent studies have shown that the pineal gland contains piezoelectric microcrystals that are sensitive to electromagnetic fields.'

'So?' asked Vijay.

'This gland could very well be nature's way of keeping us connected to the wider universe,' said Mikhailov.

'Like a two-way radio?' asked Vijay.

'The problem I have with the example of a two-way radio is that it imagines each person's mind is independent and can send and receive messages with other minds. Instead, I would rather think that the pineal gland is the end of a networking cable and that everyone is sharing the same universal mind and consciousness. Ever heard of *discovery multiples*?'

'The fact that many of man's greatest inventions happened simultaneously—in multiples?'

'Right,' said Mikhailov. 'These were researchers working from different locations without a clue to what anyone else was doing. For example, Newton and Leibniz both discovered calculus at the same time. Darwin and Wallace both developed theories of evolution around the same time. Doesn't it reinforce the idea that we are *all* working *off* a universal mind?'

Vijay believed that Mikhailov could be right. He remembered reading a paper, which showed that colour photography was invented simultaneously by Cros and du Hauron. Oxygen was discovered by both Priestley and Scheele within a few months of each other. Logarithms were invented in parallel by Napier-Briggs and Bürgi. A list of such discovery multiples had been compiled showing that 148 major scientific breakthroughs had happened in multiples.

'Hindus think of the Shiva lingam as a phallic symbol, but couldn't it also be symbolic of the pinecone?' asked Mikhailov. 'After all, Shiva was the greatest yogi ever. It is from his uncountable punishing ages of immersing himself in total meditation that we get tantra.'

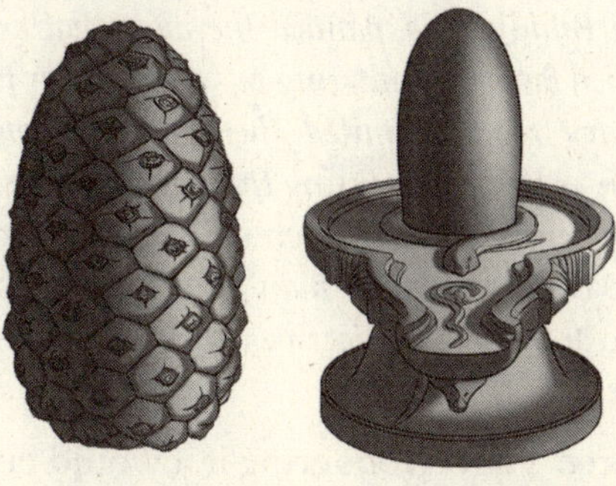

'I associate tantric practices with negative forces,' said Vijay. 'So do most people. Why?'

Mikhailov paused. He scratched his head as he tried to formulate an appropriate answer.

'Tantra is called the left-handed path,' said Mikhailov, after what seemed an interminable pause. 'It permits one to use negative and passionate emotions as fuel in the spiritual path, but it can be unsafe if followed without proper guidance.'

'That seems crazy,' observed Vijay.

'Buddhist texts often give the example of a peacock,' said Mikhailov. 'It is a bird that is able to consume poison without dying from it. The poison only makes the bird's plumage even brighter.'

'What are they getting at?'

'That no experience, feeling, thought or sensation can be classified as good or bad. For example, in Tantric Buddhism it is believed that Buddhist masters can reach enlightenment faster through the help of a sexual consort. Look at this article.' He rummaged through a folder and pulled out a clipping taken from a newspaper.

The practice of tantric sex is more ancient than Buddhism itself. In tantra, it was believed that the retention of semen during intercourse increased sexual pleasure and made men live longer. Thus Tibetan Buddhists expanded the view that enlightenment could be reached faster by enlisting passions rather than avoiding them. Ordinary monks limited themselves to visualizing an imaginary consort and preventing the expulsion of semen during such imagined intercourse. Secret Buddhist texts described methods that could enable a man to achieve this self-control through yogic breath. The objective was to drive semen upwards in the Kundalini.

'Weird,' offered Vijay, wondering if it would be impolite to grin, or unmanly to giggle outright.

'Tantra is often misunderstood precisely on account of your reaction,' said Mikhailov reprovingly. 'There have also been a few instances of sexual exploitation that have given tantra and Tantric Buddhism a bad name. But it's a case of a rotten apple spoiling the rest of the bushel.'

Mikhailov changed the topic. 'The woods that surround us are mentioned in Hindu and Buddhist scriptures. These woods used to be the home of yogis—ascetics who spent years meditating in isolation. The very ones who cursed the king in Roopkund.'

He then looked Vijay in the eye and said, 'You need to find out more.'

'Why me?' asked Vijay.

'Look, Vijay, I know that you are here for a reason other than your purported job,' said Mikhailov softly.

Vijay's face fell.

'Don't worry,' said Mikhailov. 'I don't care and won't tell. I, too, am here for a purpose other than my work. Let's help each other.'

'How?' asked Vijay cautiously.

'Find a way to access Schmidt's office when he isn't there,' said Mikhailov. 'My gut tells me that you will find clues there. He disappears for hours into that office.'

'Why don't you do it?' asked Vijay.

'Because my interest lies outside the gates of Milesian, not within.'

97

Petrov carefully scanned through the research document that had been put together by an aide at the SVR. It was comprehensive, listing sinkhole incidents that had occurred across the globe.

Five people died when a thirty-two-foot-wide sinkhole opened near the gates of Huamao Industrial Park in Shenzhen, the southern Chinese boom town neighbouring Hong Kong. It happened at a time when many factory workers were changing shifts.

A huge sinkhole around sixty feet wide almost entirely swallowed a resort near Disney World. The Orlando sinkhole forced thirty-five screaming guests out of their rooms as the building crumbled and another one next to it sank.

A massive sinkhole appeared in the middle of Guatemala City. It was around thirty storeys deep. In Sarisarinama, Venezuela, some sinkholes appeared that were more than one thousand feet wide.

An enormous sinkhole, around ninety feet deep and three hundred feet wide, opened in a field in Kansas. A rancher found the sinkhole around twenty miles from the Kansas–Colorado border. No oil wells or irrigation wells were nearby.

A portion of a downtown commercial street in Montreal, Canada, disappeared just as construction teams were gearing up to repair a leaky water main. The backhoe had barely begun to chip the asphalt at the corner of St Catherine and Guy streets when the ground dissolved and the massive machine fell into the cavity.

Petrov read through several more documented cases. Then he picked up the phone and dialled his SVR aide.

'Do we have any idea of the exact time at which each one of these incidents happened?' he asked.

'I can aggregate that data for you,' came the reply.

'Please do that,' said Petrov. 'Also find out if we have an insider at SOSUS.'

'SOSUS?'

'It's an acronym for Sound Surveillance System,' said Petrov. 'Operated by the US Navy, it's a chain of underwater listening posts located around the world, mostly used for monitoring submarines. But they pick up on many other sounds from around the world.'

'I'll get on it,' said the aide. 'What do you need?'

'To know if there were any spikes in vibrations or sounds at the time when these sinkholes appeared.'

98

The two men stood by the Arc de Triomphe in the centre of the Place Charles de Gaulle. They were intently staring at the Memorial Flame—in remembrance of those slain in the First World War—that had never been extinguished since 1923. They didn't look at each other. They merely stood next to one another like two tourists interested in the sights, their breath fogging in the biting cold air. They were oblivious to the traffic or crowds. Sharma knew that this meeting was a long shot at solving a cold case that was fifteen years old. It related to the murder of a Tibetan immigrant that had shocked Dharamsala, in India, at the time.

A second-generation Tibetan immigrant, working as a software engineer in Bangalore, had been on a visit to his mother who lived on the outskirts of Dharamsala in a quiet and densely wooded area. Upon reaching the house, he had found his mother lying in a pool of blood, having died some hours previously from a gunshot wound. He immediately called in the police.

Sharma had newly joined RAW and was asked by his boss to track the case. *Why?* Sharma had wondered. *This is a matter that the police should investigate, not RAW.* And then his boss had revealed that the murder victim had been erstwhile Tibetan royalty. The Indian government wanted to ensure control over the investigation.

At the entrance to her house, Sharma had noticed a sitting Buddha statue, almost life-size. The base had been smashed open. The victim's son clarified that the statue had stood at the entrance to their home for most of his growing years.

Unaware of the age of the artefact, Sharma had brought in an expert who estimated that the statue was around a thousand years old. He then subjected the statue to further tests. One of those was a CT scan.

What he found left Sharma astounded.

99

Within the statue were the perfectly preserved remains of a mummified Buddhist monk—skin, muscles and skeleton intact. Apparently, it had been a common ritual for Buddhist monks of the time to practice self-mummification.

For the first three years, the monk would have stopped eating all food other than nuts, berries and seeds. He would also have undertaken exercises to eliminate any fat remaining in his body. Over the next three years, he would have consumed a diet of bark and roots before consuming poisonous tea made from the sap of the Urushi tree. This would have caused him to vomit frequently and bring about rapid fluid loss. The internal drying of his body would have acted as natural preservation, and the increased toxicity of his skin's surface would have prevented maggots from getting to his remains.

After six years of this extreme hardship the monk would have locked himself away inside an unimaginably small stone tomb with no room for movement. A thin air tube would have allowed him to breathe and meditate in the lotus position until he eventually died. Each day he would have rung a bell to let others know that he was alive. Once it stopped ringing, the tomb would have been sealed for mummification. His body would have been left for days close to a low fire so as to completely dry out the remains. Finally, his mummified body would have been placed inside a highly-crafted lacquered Buddha statue, custom-built to his size. It was an arduous process, certainly not for the faint-hearted.

And then something even more revelatory had emerged from the scan. The base of the statue had a cavity. Stuck along the inside walls of the cavity were a few fragments of fibre and parchment. It was concluded that the cavity had once contained cloth-wrapped documents, but these had disappeared by the time forensics got into the act. It was possible that their disappearance was a motive for the murder. Nothing else of value had been taken from the house. The statue itself had been left untouched after the base had been cleaned out. The killer had known exactly what he was after.

Police investigations reached a dead end because there were no fingerprints on the lacquered statue or at the crime scene. There were no witnesses owing to the secluded nature of the place. Tyre tracks that would have shown the make or model of the vehicle used by the killer had been obliterated by rain that very morning.

Interviews with the victim's son had revealed that his mother had been of a royal lineage that was driven underground owing to the secrets they possessed. Unfortunately, the son had very little idea about his mother's history—she had been unwilling to talk about it. He had been born in India and had no remaining roots to his ancient homeland.

Sharma realized that his best shot at cracking the murder would be to follow the documents that had been stolen. They would have to appear somewhere, sometime.

Years went by. Each year, he would review the case file and put it away, realizing that he wasn't any closer to solving the case. It remained unsolved even when he was deputed by RAW to the IG4, but he continued keeping a watch for anything related to the case. It had become a strange obsession of sorts over the years.

And then Sharma received a call from Paris. The caller was an art dealer who regularly assisted law enforcement agencies with tip-offs about stolen artefacts, paintings and manuscripts. He had some information for Sharma. A set of documents with some sections matching the fragments found in the statue had entered the market.

100

Sharma reached Paris the very next day to meet the art dealer at the Arc de Triomphe. 'Do you have the information we spoke about?' asked Sharma. He wore a thick woollen coat and sported dark sunglasses.

'Yes,' replied the art dealer, continuing to stare at the flame. 'The documents have been carbon-dated to the sixth century CE or thereabouts. Storage inside the base of the mummified statue was a way of preserving and securing these documents.'

'Who were the buyer and seller?' asked Sharma.

'That's where the problem lies, *mon ami*,' said the art dealer. 'These documents were noticed amid a wider collection that belongs to Bruce Williams, but we have no idea of the chain of custody that led to his possession of them.'

'*The* Bruce Williams?' asked Sharma. 'Chairman of the Reconstruction Bank of America?'

The art dealer gave a small nod. 'Same one. Lives in America but has a house in Zurich. That's in addition to his houses in New York, London, Monte Carlo and Hong Kong. The documents were seen in the Zurich house by an insurance executive who was there to conduct a valuation on a set of Fabergé eggs.'

'Any idea why Williams would be interested in acquiring these documents?' asked Sharma.

'Who can say anything about the motivations of collectors?' shrugged the art dealer. 'The only way that you can possibly answer that question is by examining what is contained in them. I have a set of photographs for you. You owe me.'

Sharma thought about what the art dealer had just said. There was one person who would be able to help him. His name was Professor Vignesh Thakur and he was passionate about all things Buddhist.

101

It was supposedly a charity polo match, but there seemed to be nothing remotely charitable about it. It was a high-profile event at the Jaipur Polo Ground of Delhi and the luxury stands were filled with an assortment of royalty, corporate leaders, politicians and other high society types who seemed to have enough time to attend a polo match in the middle of a working day. The farcical truth was that most people who attended such events rarely needed to work.

The weather was ideal for a match—a sunny day with cold temperatures. It was the perfect venue for socialites and socialists to mix. Seated in the VIP enclosure, sipping champagne, was Henderson. He ignored the two teams of four players each that were slugging it out to knock the plastic ball to advantage using their long-handled mallets.

Sitting next to him was an elegant lady, the highest-earning corporate lobbyist of India. She was dressed in a pink saree that clung to her body in all the right places. Around her neck was a string of diamonds and on her wrist was a Rolex watch in pink gold.

'Have you done the work that Williams requested?' asked Henderson. He knew that the thunder of hooves, the click of mallets, the applause and the continuous announcements made it impossible for someone else to listen in.

'It's in progress,' she said, adjusting her Louis Vuitton sunglasses. 'I have had several discussions with social media celebrities. You will soon see fringe groups on the right ranting against Muslims on Twitter. In parallel to that you will see Jihadi sympathizers posting anti-Hindu rants on Facebook. We will ensure a polarized environment. We've already succeeded beyond expectations in the Kashmir valley.'

'How can you be sure?' asked Henderson.

'Money does strange things to people,' she replied, the hint of a delicate floral scent hanging like a cloud around her. 'My colleagues are supporting similar polarization in other regions of the world, including China. As Mr Williams has directed, I am also working on journalists, media personalities and politicians. I have the matter in control.'

'Have you been paid?' asked Henderson.

'Your banker, Mr Buchman, has been in touch and the first transfer has been received,' she replied.

Henderson looked at the perfectly dolled-up lady seated next to him, feeling the tumescence between his legs. He had to remind himself that it was a business meeting. 'I think I shall have another glass of champagne,' he said, turning his attention to the match that he wasn't following.

102

The cold air against his face felt good. Vijay was well-protected in his woollen tracksuit, Airmax shoes, beanie and gloves.

He jogged along the central pathway that ran from the residential quarters and across Food for Thought, the convenience store, the spa and the mini-theatre. From there he turned right towards the health centre and reached the walkway that ran along the boundary fence from the inside.

Through the earphones he was listening to his favourite track by DJ Saxicoline, *Conundrum.*

She held the door for them
They could feel it in her eyes
By the time that the night was over

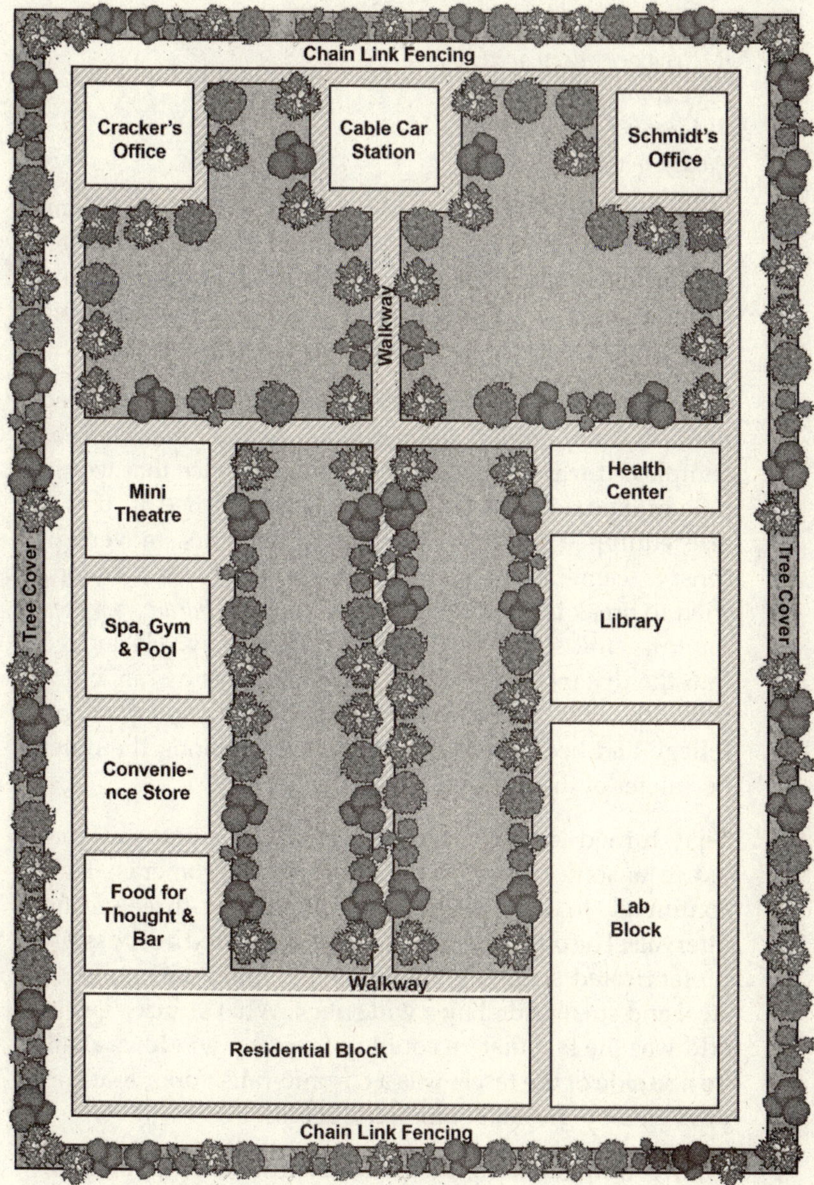
Chain Link Fencing
Cracker's Office
Cable Car Station
Schmidt's Office
Walkway
Mini Theatre
Health Center
Tree Cover
Library
Tree Cover
Spa, Gym & Pool
Convenie-nce Store
Lab Block
Food for Thought & Bar
Walkway
Residential Block
Chain Link Fencing

She would kill 'em like flies
It was a deep deep deep abyss
They could get in at five
But like her passionate kiss
Would never get out alive

He knew that the CCTV cameras were observing him. He also knew that it would be far more convenient to get his cardio fix from the treadmill. But his outdoor jogging routine was not about exercise. It was a fact-finding expedition in full view of everyone.

From time to time, Vijay stole a glance at the double-layered fence that ran around the perimeter of the Milesian Labs complex. It was a high-tech barbed wire fence that would deliver electric shocks to anyone who touched it. It was also equipped with heat sensors, floodlights, movement sensors, cameras and alarms that would screech if anyone tried to break in or out. *I wonder whether the borders between countries are as well protected?* thought Vijay. He looked into the distance beyond the barbed wire as he ran, but it was impossible to discern anything. Dense vegetation and foliage had been used as a visual barrier along the outer perimeter of the fence.

Vijay turned left towards a gravel-covered pathway that led to an office block. He glanced at the cameras. They continued to sweep the area at twenty-three-second intervals. The office seemed like a sophisticated but possibly prefabricated structure clad in cedar wood and polished steel and surrounded by a wide deck. What struck Vijay as odd was the fact that he could not see any windows at all. To one side of the fascia was a chrome-finish door that was protected by the usual biometric access.

Vijay continued along the pathway towards the cable car station and turned left towards the central walkway that would bring him back to his quarters. He was acutely aware that his activities were being scrutinized on banks of monitors. As long as he did not pause or give too much attention to any one particular area, those observing him would be none the wiser.

At least, that's what he hoped.

103

Visitors to China's central Hubei Province often assumed that the imposing building with wedding cake architecture and sensor dish antennae was the headquarters of the MSS, but that assumption was entirely wrong. Given that the MSS handled both external and internal intelligence, it maintained regional offices like this one in various cities of China.

Other tourists associated a giant Borg-like structure on the east side of Tiananmen Square in downtown Beijing with the MSS, but they, too, were wrong. That particular building housed China's national police command, not the MSS.

In fact, the real MSS HQ lay within a low-key and unassuming compound located along Route 332 of the Beijing public bus service on Xueyuan Road to the west of the Beijing Chinese Medicine Hospital. Heavily armed police protected the compound. Visitors who suspiciously hung around in the neighbourhood were routinely picked up. Inside the compound were structures that were built along the cardinal points of a compass with a large open courtyard in the centre.

Jin Zhang cleared multiple levels of security and finally walked through the wide corridor that led to the meeting room where his boss, the Vice Minister, was waiting. The Vice Minister was no ordinary boss. Having worked his way through the Ministry of Public Security and the

Central Commission for Discipline Inspection, it was widely believed that he was on his way to becoming the next chief of the MSS.

After the customary pleasantries were out of the way, Zhang got down to business. 'With your support, over the past few years we have created a wide network of ordinary businessmen, professionals, scientists, teachers, writers, artists and journalists who supply information to us regularly,' began Zhang. 'One of our businessmen in Europe came across some ancient documents. I'm not even sure whether this information is relevant to you, sir.'

'All information is relevant to me,' replied the Vice Minister. 'If it is not brought to my attention, how can I decide its relevance? So speak.'

'Well, this businessman owns a large reinsurance company that has offices all over Europe,' said Zhang. 'He received photographs from an insurance firm that show certain ancient documents.'

Zhang placed the photographs on the conference table in front of the Vice Minister who looked at them for a minute.

'What language are these in?' he asked.

'Sanskrit,' replied Zhang. 'Till date, everyone had thought that the texts were lost forever.' He went on to explain what his contact at the Hangzhou Buddhism Institute had told him about the documents.

'Do you know who has the originals?' asked the Vice Minister. The MSS was famous for outright theft where it suited them.

'Alas, no,' replied Zhang. 'But I'm on it.'

'I hope you have not forgotten why we went into IG4?' asked the Vice Minister. 'It was to help you sort the Uighur mess.'

It was well known that China was dealing with a potential uprising—that of the Muslim Uighurs in Xinjiang. The state had clamped down hard on the Uighurs—confiscating Qur'ans and prayer mats, prohibiting beards and calls to prayer, banning Islamic names and forcing neighbourhood shops to sell *haram* items such as alcohol and non-halal meat.

Zhang placed two photographs before the Vice Minister. One was a photo of Mafraqi. The other was of Habib, his second-in-command.

'From the deliberations within IG4 I now believe that this man is persuadable,' said Zhang, pointing to the picture of Habib. 'I think I may have a solution if we are willing to spend some money. But it is vital that we move before any of the others do.'

The Vice Minister got up from his chair and paced the room, deep in thought.

'You shall have the money you need,' he said finally. 'And Zhang…'

'Sir?'

'Under no circumstances should these documents ever reach the Dalai Lama,' he said. 'We have spent years subduing Tibet and the last thing we need is to give that wretch any power. Imagine what his people could use this for.'

'I understand, sir,' said Zhang.

'And no discussion about this in IG4,' said the Vice Minister. 'If the Americans latch on, we'll have another CIA operation there in no time.'

104

The 14th Dalai Lama had been born in 1935 to a farmer in Amdo in north-eastern Tibet. The child was recognized at the age of two by Buddhist monks as a reincarnation of the previous Dalai Lama. Each Dalai Lama was seen as a manifestation of Avalokiteshvara—the Bodhisattva of Compassion.

Given the name Tenzin Gyatso, he embarked upon his monastic education at the age of six. His curriculum was based on what used to be taught at the great university of Nalanda. Subjects included logic, Tibetan art, Sanskrit grammar, medicine, poetry, astrology and, most importantly, Buddhist philosophy. This last subject actually consisted of five independent streams—the perfection of wisdom, monastic discipline, metaphysics, logic and epistemology.

He graduated at twenty-three, earning the Geshe Lharampa, the highest doctorate in Buddhist philosophy. By then he had already assumed full political power, having been enthroned as the 14th Dalai Lama at the age of fifteen. Unfortunately, his reign was short-lived. In October of that year, the People's Republic of China invaded Tibet. It was a cakewalk for the Chinese because there was hardly any resistance.

The Dalai Lama participated in peace talks with Mao Zedong in 1954 but was unsuccessful in convincing the Chinese to allow Tibetan autonomy. And then, in 1959, the Tibetan population revolted.

Word reached Tibetan leaders that the Chinese government had hatched a plan to assassinate the Dalai Lama. Based on this intelligence, the Dalai Lama fled to India along with several followers. The Indian government allowed him to establish a government-in-exile in Dharamsala, in Himachal Pradesh.

Meanwhile, the CIA started funnelling millions of dollars to the rebels inside Tibet. The aim was to resist Chinese occupation, but the programme was a failure. Thousands of Tibetans lost their lives during the resistance without gaining a shred of autonomy.

Over the years, everything in Tibet changed. Skyscrapers came up in Lhasa at a frenetic pace and the demographics shifted rapidly. Soon, almost half the population was Han Chinese instead of Tibetan. Young Tibetans spoke Mandarin, played pool and drank Lhasa beer. At the very foot of Potala Palace—the winter residence of the Dalai Lama—the authorities permitted the town's most famous discotheque, Dju Pin Dao, to flourish.

More than ten thousand monks had lived at Drepung monastery before 1959. That number gradually dwindled to five hundred. The massive 1,200-kilometre railway line that connected Tibet with the rest of China ended Tibet's isolation and, with it, the very mystique of Tibet.

There were those who believed that Shambhala or Shangri-La was actually Tibet. But Tibet was nothing like the mystical and abundant land that Shangri-La was said to be. As a final insult, the Chinese constructed a massive theme park between Sichuan, Yunnan and Tibet.

They named it Shangri-La.

105

The helicopter crossed stretches of farmlands and forests before landing gently, blowing huge clouds of earth into the air as it settled down at a spot near Jolly Grant Airport. Petrov stepped out, looking spiffy in his tweed jacket and sunglasses. He dumped his holdall into the trunk of the navy blue SUV that his local operative had pressed into service, and then sat in the front seat next to him.

'So, have you found out which hotel she is staying at in Dehradun?' asked Petrov, as they drove along an empty stretch of the road.

'Yes. I struck gold after I checked at Lemon Tree, Four Points, Sarovar and Madhuban,' replied his aide. 'Sujatha Iyer will be at the Pacific, the hotel next to the clock tower, starting tomorrow.'

'Excellent,' said Petrov. 'I'm glad our source at the Ministry of Environment is reliable. Have you commenced surveillance?'

'Yes, she is currently on her way to Nanda Devi National Park.'

'Near the Tibetan border?' asked Petrov.

The operative nodded. 'Then she comes back to Dehradun before going to Govind Pashu Vihar. Some of those are no-go areas owing to border regulations, but she has special clearance from the Home Ministry.'

'Now, the most important question,' said Petrov, pressing the button to roll down the window and lighting a Belomorkanal. 'Any luck with Mikhailov?'

106

And it's another day and it's time for me, Masoud, to jot down my thoughts. I am always befuddled when I examine the history of Islamic conquest. The contrasts are confounding.

In the year 627 CE, almost nine hundred Jews of a Medinan tribe called Banu Qurayza were massacred by Muslims. The killings began early in the day and ended in torchlight. Those who escaped death were taken captive and sold at slave markets. Brutal, to say the least.

But then, I wonder: was the Holocaust perpetuated by Muslims? Were nuclear bombs on Hiroshima and Nagasaki dropped by Muslims? Think about this: When the Caliph, Umar ibn Al-Khattab, entered Jerusalem in 638 CE, he travelled on foot out of respect for the holiness of the site. There was neither blood nor slaughter. The Muslims signed a treaty with the patriarch. It guaranteed Christians their lives, their property and their right to worship. It was tolerance at its best for the violent times in question.

Compare that with the fact that Muslim Ottoman forces capturing Cyprus in the sixteenth century killed Greek and Armenian Christians wantonly. Estimates of the death toll were 30,000 to 50,000. Similarly, in 1876, 12,000 men, women and children from the Bulgarian Christian community were massacred by Sultan Abdul Hamid II. Prisoners were shot after being subjected to the most barbarous tortures. Again, pitiless.

How does one reconcile this brutality with the fact that the Mughal emperor Akbar invited poets, theologians and scholars of Christian, Hindu, Jain and Zoroastrian faiths to engage in dialogue about religion? He amassed a library of 24,000 volumes of Urdu, Persian, Greek, Latin, Arabic and Kashmiri texts. He even attempted to unite them into a new faith that combined the best of each. Akbar shows me the tolerant face of Islam, but that changed by the time Aurangzeb came on the scene. Aurangzeb was a zealot, one who wantonly destroyed Hindu temples.

Now let's reflect on the fact that the seven centuries of Muslim rule in Spain are known as the Golden Age of Islam. I am told that Christians and Jews held high office in the royal court. It was only when the Catholic monarchs—Ferdinand and Isabella—retook Muslim cities that mosques and synagogues were burned down. There are others though who say that the Golden Age of Islam is a misnomer, and that giving equal treatment to non-Muslims was never part of Islam. The non-believers, or Dhimmi, were humiliated and made to pay Jiziya tax. There are numerous instances of destruction of churches, synagogues and temples during this period.

Contrast this intolerance with the fact that the great Saladin is said to have lifted all restrictions on Jews to live in Jerusalem in 1187 when he retook the city from the Crusaders. Those who wished to leave were guaranteed safety. Those who wished to remain were allowed to do so. Some centuries later, Sultan Mehmet II officially recognized Patriarch Gennadius II as leader of the Orthodox people living within the Ottoman Empire. This was after the capture of Constantinople in 1453. He even bestowed the title of Hahambasha, *or Chief Wise Man, on the Chief Rabbi of the Jews. Truly enlightened behaviour, wouldn't you say?*

Compare that with the grisly tale that says that in six hours of a single day in 1739, Nadir Shah massacred 30,000 men, women and children in Delhi. The plunder that he seized from Delhi was so valuable that Nadir Shah stopped collecting taxes in Persia for a period of three years. How about the fact that in fourteenth-century India, the Bahmani sultans set 'targets' of 100,000 Hindu heads in battle? Some of the most violent slaughters happened during the raids of Mahmud Ghaznavi, the later conquest of Mohammed Ghori, and eventual rule under the Delhi Sultanate. Ruthless.

Isn't it thus amazing that Islam was the torchbearer that relayed the light of knowledge through many centuries? In fact, Europe's Renaissance and Enlightenment were influenced by Islamic learning. Muslim scholars made huge contributions in the fields of philosophy, astronomy, medicine, chemistry, geography, physics, optics and mathematics. It's disheartening to see today's Muslim nations taking a step backward because their religious leaders are adamant on pushing them back into the seventh century. And while it is true that the vast majority of Muslims are not terrorists, it is equally true that many terrorists are Muslim.

Just look around you. Uighur Muslims fighting Han Chinese in Xinjiang. Muslim Kashmiris expelling Hindu Pandits from Kashmir. Muslims fighting the Jews in Israel, the Christians in South Sudan and the Catholics in East Timor. Muslim Bosniaks and Kosovars battling Orthodox Christian Serbs in the Balkans.

Muslim Yorubas fighting the Christian Ibo in Nigeria. Muslim Turks fighting the Armenians. Muslim Kurds and Arabs battling Assyrian Christians. Muslims fighting Coptic Christians in Egypt … the list is endless!

I suppose history and politics are stories that have multiple endings. People choose whichever ending works better for their sensibilities. The novelist, George Santayana, had famously said that history is a pack of lies about events that never happened, told by people who weren't there. So where lies the ultimate truth?

107

Vijay positioned himself at a corner table of his laboratory that was a CCTV blind spot. With his back to the rest of the laboratory, he carefully opened a drawer and took out the empty water bottle that he had surreptitiously lifted from Schmidt's food tray.

Donning plastic gloves, Vijay dusted the surface area of the bottle with bi-chromatic powder using a fibreglass brush. He then examined the prints in order to decide which one needed to be lifted. There were nine unique prints but only three of them were thumbprints. Of these, one seemed to be of a podgy individual, possibly Daulat Singh. The other was his. The third print was of a lean person. Schmidt.

He lifted the print, using clear adhesive tape, and then carefully placed the tape on a perfectly clean microscope slide that was about a millimetre thick. Schmidt's print was now preserved. Slipping the sheathed microscope slide into the pocket of his lab coat, Vijay disposed of the bottle in the garbage can and went back to his research. His heart was thumping wildly. *What am I getting myself into?* he wondered.

108

Vijay looked at the time on his phone. It was a little after ten at night. Perfect. He pulled up a browser window on his computer and activated Automator, a piece of software that would randomly access websites and carry out online searches in his absence. Anyone monitoring his computer would be under the impression that he was working on it.

Vijay then stepped out of his apartment, leaving the door open. It had remained open for the past two hours since he had returned from the lab. Vijay felt the blast of cold hit him as he stepped out from the warmth of the residential block. He tucked his hands into his jacket and made his way towards the office that he had passed during his jogging routine. He timed his walk according to the sweep of the cameras, pausing at Mikhailov's suggested blind spots before moving on. He took fifteen minutes for what would otherwise have been a five-minute walk.

Schmidt was away for a day to New Delhi. Vijay crossed his fingers that he would not return earlier than expected. He approached the office block warily, his heart thumping wildly as he went nearer. The gravel on the pathway seemed to magnify the sound of every step that he took. *It's not too late … turn back!* But his head overruled his heart. His innate intelligence acknowledged that there was no going back.

He reached the office door and took a deep breath before fishing out the microscope slide that had the fingerprint. He knew that he had only a few seconds before the cameras would see him there. He carefully placed the piece of glass on the green scanning panel of the biometric unit and waited for an alarm to sound.

Nothing.

And then the lock whirred open a couple of seconds later. Vijay placed the slide back into his pocket and tiptoed inside, shutting the door behind him. He heard the lock click shut.

What if the security chaps realize that the door has been opened using Schmidt's fingerprint even though he isn't around? Would that trigger an alarm? Are the biometric locks monitored in real time or simply kept as log records? Vijay didn't have answers to any of those questions, but he knew that he was now in up to his neck.

The office was pitch-dark, but Vijay was reluctant to press any wall switches for fear that they could trigger an alarm. He took out of his pocket the mobile phone provided by Milesian and activated the flashlight function. The beam danced around the room as he attempted to do a quick scan of what was inside.

And then he saw them and froze in fear.

109

On the wall next to Schmidt's desk was a large glass tank, entirely sealed except for ventilation holes. Inside the tank were snakes. Tens of slithering reptiles, hissing and baring what seemed like venomous fangs.

Vijay shuddered. He wondered if the creatures could escape from the tank. The mere idea of several poisonous reptiles at close proximity was terrifying. He forced himself to pull his gaze away from the tank.

He turned the beam of his phone towards the rest of the office. It seemed ordinary enough—hardwood floors, large marble-topped desk, bookshelves filled with scientific periodicals, a filing cabinet and a comfortable sofa with a coffee table. The wall behind the sofa was occupied by a large whiteboard. It resembled the ones used by criminal investigation teams with magnets holding photographs in place.

Vijay walked towards the board to see what was written on it. The board had been divided into sixteen squares. Written on top of the board was the word '*Yamaj*'.

Vijay shone his torchlight towards the top left corner of the board. A photograph showed a familiar face—that of the British Foreign Secretary. Below the first photograph was another, that of the German Chancellor. This was followed by pictures of the American Attorney-General and the Japanese Prime Minister. Schmidt was keeping track of all the world leaders who had died in recent days.

Vijay allowed his gaze to travel horizontally across the board. There were many photographs that he could not recognize. He came across pictures of some celebrities whom he partially recognized—as faces, or positions occupied, but not necessarily names. A former French President, the Australian Foreign Minister, the Russian Minister of Internal Affairs and the Canadian Prime Minister. Vijay realized he was seeing not only photographs of victims but also potential targets.

Vijay was desperate to use the camera on his phone to take a photograph of the board in order to share it with Judith. He was about to do that when he realized that the phone was a device provided by Milesian and was probably being monitored.

He fished out a pad and pen from the inside pocket of his jacket to make a quick sketch of the board. Sixteen squares, thirteen photographs, three blank squares. Four photographs recognized, four pictures partially recognized and five unrecognized.

Vijay also noted the word 'Yamaj' in the margin of his pad. *Sounds a lot like Yama, the Hindu god of death,* he thought. *Must find out more about this word. Possibly Sanskrit?*

He put the pad and pen back into his pocket and was about to examine the papers on Schmidt's desk when he froze.

Footsteps on the gravel pathway. *Could the security cameras have picked up my movements? Or did my unauthorized access trigger an alarm at the security office?*

Vijay quickly turned off the flashlight function of his phone, thanking his stars that the office was windowless. He desperately searched for a place that he could hide but it was too late. The door was clicking open. Frozen in fear, he pushed himself against a wall that stood at right angles to the whiteboard.

Then he lost his balance and fell.

110

Vijay cursed himself as he fell through an almost entirely invisible door in the wall.

He landed inside a small square closet, no more than five feet wide on either side. Vijay hastily got to his feet and closed the door on himself. Then he waited quietly in the dark, too terrified to even breathe. He fervently hoped that the closet was not another storage chamber for reptiles.

He placed his ears against the closet door, attempting to discern any sounds from Schmidt's office. He could hear the door of the office being slammed shut. Then he heard the sound of footsteps on the hardwood floors.

Vijay noticed light streaming into the closet from the gap under the door. The lights in the office had been switched on. Then he heard the sound of cabinet drawers being opened and shut.

A phone rang. Vijay froze. He swore at himself for not having switched his phone to silent mode. He looked at the screen to mute it and then realized that the ringing phone wasn't his. He silently thanked the universe for not ratting on him.

He hastily put his phone in silent mode. Then he heard Schmidt's voice; he was talking to someone in German. *So the prison warden is back earlier than expected,* thought Vijay.

Schmidt hung up and continued with his search of the cabinet drawers. A few minutes later, light stopped streaming in from below the closet door. Vijay heard the office door slam shut. Schmidt had left. Or had he?

Vijay refused to move. He remained frozen inside the closet for a few minutes more in order to satisfy himself that there was no one in the office. The darkness of the closet felt strangely comforting.

Once he was sure that he was alone, he switched on the flashlight of his phone. The walls of the closet were panelled in dark veneer and to the right side of the door were two gleaming brass push buttons marked 'O' and 'L'. Vijay was not sure whether he should try pushing either of them. He eventually decided against the idea.

He warily opened the closet door and tiptoed out into the office. He avoided looking in the direction of the snake tank, gently opened the main door and stepped out into the cold night air. He then made his way back to his flat, keeping a close watch on the cameras.

In a database in Cracker's office, a computer logged the time at which the office door was opened yet again from the inside.

111

The Hagia Sophia was overly crowded. Turkey's most-visited tourist spot attracted around ten thousand people each day. Habib ran his gaze over the thirty million tiny gold mosaic tiles that covered the church's interior and wondered why his Muslim brothers had allowed the incredible mosque to be converted into a museum.

Snatching defeat from the jaws of victory, he thought. Of course, Habib couldn't care less that the structure had originally been built as a church by Emperor Justinian in the sixth century and been appropriated for a mosque by Muslims much later.

He brought his attention back to the crowds. Excited Japanese tourists were pointing to the exquisite calligraphy and looking up at the awe-inspiring dome. In the distance he saw the face that he was looking for. Its gauntness was punctuated by metallic frames, and the jet black hair that framed it was neatly parted. The man's formal business suit was a tad out of place among the throngs of casually dressed tourists.

Zhang and Habib slowly made their way towards each other. A slight nod was the only acknowledgment each man offered. This place was the perfect location, so easy to get lost in the crowd. The two men progressed to the upper gallery. In his head, Zhang went through the words that he had rehearsed beforehand.

The MSS was dominated by Han Chinese who disliked the Uighurs. Muslim Uighurs spoke a Turkic language, not Mandarin. They numbered around ten million and were natives of the north-western region of Xinjiang. Chinese repression and Islamic radicalization had worked in tandem to create hundreds of fighters willing to die for the 'cause' and many of them had found their way into Syria.

Zhang knew that Habib could be his ticket to a promotion. If Habib was willing to share details about the Uighur men in Syria, as seemingly indicated by Judith, the MSS would ensure that they would never make it back into China. The Vice Minister would have no option but to ensure Zhang's promotion.

The two men headed towards the mosaic of Christ, depicted as enthroned and flanked by Empress Zoe and

Emperor Constantine IX. The upper gallery was a little less crowded. They stopped in front of the mosaic and began talking.

'How many men?' asked Zhang.

'Three thousand,' replied Habib.

'All Uighurs?'

'Yes.'

'And you would share information on all of them?' asked Zhang.

'We maintain very good records,' said Habib. 'Available for a price.'

Why are you willing to do this, wondered Zhang, *even though you hate us? You want Sharia enforced globally. Why help me? Something is not quite right. Had Judith told him the truth?*

'They're not Arabs,' replied Habib, guessing at his suspicions. 'Why should I be bothered about ratting them out?'

'What if Mafraqi finds out?' asked Zhang. He was getting ready to leave. Every fibre in his body was telling him to get the hell out of there.

'He won't,' said Habib. 'Unless you decide to betray me. And why would you do that?'

Zhang lingered for an extra moment.

'Name your price,' he said, as both men continued staring at the mosaic of Christ.

From the corner of his eye he discerned a sudden movement, but it was a momentary flash—a flash that would cost him his life.

'Your blood,' replied Habib as Zhang fell.

By the time officers from the Turkish General Directorate of Security reached the scene, Habib had disappeared.

Zhang's body lay on the floor, a large puddle of blood having formed around his cleanly slashed neck.

112

Planning had begun a month previously. Mafraqi had been observing a battalion of Uighurs. 'How many do we have with us?' he had asked.

'Around three thousand across various camps. The more the Chinese clamp down on them, the more people we seem to get.'

'The biggest advantage is that they look like any other Chinese person,' said Mafraqi. 'If we were to ever send them back home, there would be chaos. Not only within Xinjiang but also in the rest of China.'

The Uighur battalion was being commanded by a man who had an accent from Yarkand, near the old Silk Road. In his hand, he held a *qelemturach*, a traditional folding knife of the Uighurs. All the men were similarly equipped.

'The Chinese have been sniffing around,' said Mafraqi. 'They would rather that these men die here instead of returning to plague them at home.'

'How do you know?' asked Habib, instantly regretting the question. Mafraqi knew everything, sometimes way before anything happened.

'The Americans, on the other hand, are a different matter,' continued Mafraqi, ignoring Habib's question. 'Just as they used Jihad as a means to tame the Soviets in Afghanistan, they would love to use it to settle scores with the Chinese.'

He paused for a moment, deep in thought.

'Be ready to leave for Istanbul,' he said. 'We'll use the American eavesdroppers to put you on sale.'

113

Petrov strolled in the hotel garden as he spoke on his mobile. Speaking outdoors was safer. One never knew which part of the interiors might be bugged.

Petrov was using a prepaid SIM, one of many burners that would be junked after specific calls. Attached to the USB of his mobile was a small device that scrambled the conversation for any eavesdropper.

'Is everything going according to plan?' asked Petrov as he walked. He listened to the voice at the other end of the line, before replying, 'We cannot afford any screw-ups. I am always under a microscope. And the Director seems to have a personal interest—' Petrov left the sentence unfinished and stopped walking momentarily as he heard what the voice was telling him.

'I have what you wanted,' his aide was saying.

'Go on,' said Petrov, keeping the fingers of his free hand crossed.

'There has indeed been a spike in vibrations during the specific times that sinkholes appeared,' said the aide.

I knew it, thought Petrov.

'Any idea where those vibrations came from?' he asked.

'Several locations at the same time,' said the aide. 'I have a list of twenty if you want to see them.'

'Send them to me through encrypted mail,' said Petrov.

'Will do,' said the aide as Petrov disconnected.

114

The man who stepped out of the hotel in Geneva was dressed in comfortable jeans, checked shirt, a warm pullover and an overcoat. Woollen socks and soft leather shoes sat comfortably on his feet.

Mason Henderson exited the Mandarin Oriental Hotel and crossed the Rue des Moulins that ran across the Rhone. He tucked his gloved hands into the pockets of his overcoat as he made his way towards the Quai du Generale-Guisan. Ten minutes later, he reached his destination.

The building was nondescript. A brass plaque outside announced the address as 58 Rue de la Scie. He pushed open a highly polished oak door that led to an anteroom. Beyond that was a locked glass door. Henderson pressed the discreet ringer next to the glass door.

It was opened by a man dressed in a black suit that made him look like he was attending a funeral. Inside was a reception desk and, behind it, a polished veneer panel that had the words 'Vonlanthen & Cie' neatly embossed in brass.

'Mr Buchman, please,' said Henderson. The lady behind the reception desk picked up a phone and spoke softly to someone in French. Soon, a secretary, perfectly coiffured and in a navy blue dress, walked up to him. 'He is waiting for you, Mr Henderson,' said the secretary. 'Please follow me.'

Henderson followed the secretary through a maze of carpeted passages, each leading off from multiple doors to private conference rooms. She opened the last and ushered him into a well-appointed room containing a large conference table and several plush leather chairs.

'May I get you something?' she asked as Henderson took off his coat and gave it to her.

'Just sparkling water, please,' replied Henderson.

The door opened and a thin man with wire-framed glasses perched on his nose walked in. Henderson and Buchman exchanged greetings and briefly discussed the weather before getting down to business. Buchman opened the file that he had brought. From it he pulled out a bank statement and handed it over.

'As you can see, the account that is operated by the Minerva Foundation has a little over a billion dollars,' offered the banker helpfully. 'The figure would have been far higher but much of it was invested in Milesian Labs by Mr Williams.'

'Milesian's research is vital to our long-term goals,' said Henderson. 'But don't worry. There will be substantial inflows too. Many more influential people are joining us.'

'Yes,' said Buchman. 'I can see that many of the remittances into this account have been coming from new entrants. Where would you like me to place this account's surplus funds?'

'Molecular & Universal Audio,' said Henderson. 'This is another venture that we are incubating. And the company has recently made a breakthrough.'

'All of it?' asked Buchman, raising his eyebrows. There were far better investment opportunities than investing in unknown companies.

'The world is moving rapidly towards global conflict,' said Henderson. 'Our investments will be critical in managing the balance of power.'

Buchman knew better than to argue, although he was not in agreement.

Henderson scrutinized Buchman's face. 'You aren't convinced,' he said. 'I hope that one day you will see the wisdom of my words.'

Henderson got up to leave. He shook hands with Buchman.

I hope that I am able to complete my assignment efficiently, thought the new Worshipful Master as he made his way out.

115

Mason Henderson had been born in New York City but grew up in Chicago, the elder of two children. His father was a commercial pilot and his mother was a painter. The family moved to Chicago's South Shore, where he attended Chicago Public School and, later, the University of Illinois at Urbana–Champaign.

His family was a caring one, and both he and his sister were looked after well. The family regularly attended Sunday Mass, but he was not overly religious. In fact, he found most sermons rather boring.

He left college after his second year, refusing to take his final exams because a business opportunity had presented itself. One of his father's friends worked for an automotive company and there was an opening to supply plastic parts. Henderson managed to convince the man to give him a chance. After that, there had been no looking back. There were some people who simply had the Midas touch and Henderson was one of them.

In the meantime, his parents separated. His father stayed on in Chicago while his mother moved back to New York City.

Over the next few decades, Genchem became the world's third largest chemicals producer in revenue, second largest in market capitalization and number one in chemical production. The company manufactured plastics, hydrocarbons, chemicals and agricultural products. It had a presence in 140 countries and employed about 47,000 people worldwide. Henderson was rich beyond his wildest dreams.

When Henderson was forty years old, his mother, the only true guiding light in his life, passed away. And with her, Henderson's terrible secret was buried.

116

It was a small but comfortable meeting room that had been arranged at Rock House Army Camp, a military base located at Modera, just north of Colombo in Sri Lanka. The name was inspired by an earlier home built in the nineteenth century by the Englishmen who had accompanied Lord North, the first Governor of Ceylon.

Several bug sweeps had been carried out to ensure that the place was entirely sanitized before IG4 met.

'Where is Zhang?' asked Sharma, noticing that the fourth chair around the circular conference table was empty.

'Our agent in Istanbul says that Zhang was killed at the Hagia Sophia two days ago,' said Judith, as calmly as she could.

'What?' asked Sharma. 'Are you sure? Any reason why?'

'The information is definite,' said Judith. 'News channels are calling it the death of a tourist, but our contact at the Turkish General Directorate of Security has confirmed that it was Zhang.'

Petrov was quiet. He got up from the table and paced about. 'We are seeing the implications of negotiating with terrorists,' he said.

'What do you mean?' asked Judith.

'The killer was Habib,' replied Petrov. 'The second-in-command of Mafraqi. I wonder who told Zhang that Habib could be bought.'

There was an uncomfortable silence in the room.

'Has IG4 been compromised?' asked Sharma.

'It had nothing to do with IG4,' said Petrov. 'Zhang met Habib thinking that he would be willing to share information about the Uighurs who are training in Syria. The Chinese will now only crack down harder on local Muslims.'

'Foolish,' said Sharma. 'Faith always trumps money.'

'And that's the reason why a conflict with 1.6 billion Muslims around the world would be a dangerous outcome,' said Petrov. 'What happens now? Does IG4 get disbanded given that we have lost our fourth member? Or does the group get reconstituted?'

'I suggest we continue working independently until such time as the Chinese depute a replacement for Zhang,' said Judith. 'Shall we agree that further meetings stand suspended until IG4 is reconstituted?'

117

And it's another day and it's time for me, Masoud, to jot down my thoughts. Finally, I seem to have hit my stride and become regular with this journal.

Today I wish to ruminate on the Saudi state. The state officially sponsors a version of Islam that is often known as Wahhabism. This name comes from Mohammad ibn Abd-al-Wahhab, a Sunni preacher who was born in 1703 in the Najd region of what is now Saudi Arabia.

Wahhab discovered that, over the years, Muslims had added innovations to their religion. For example, worshippers would pray at tombs to seek favours, wear amulets around their necks and arms, or dance themselves into a mystical trance. Wahhab detested all this. He wanted a return to pure monotheistic worship. He believed that he was taking the religion back to the original principles of the 'salaf'*—the first three generations of Muslims. Hence, Wahhabism is a rigid form of Salafism.*

Wahhab was expelled by the local ruler under pressure from provincial chieftains. Eventually, Muhammad ibn Saud, one of the chiefs attempting to unite myriad Arab tribes through conquest, invited Wahhab to join him. A partnership was cemented between the two men. The partnership led to the Emirate of Diriyah—the First Saudi State that lasted from 1744 to 1818.

Madawi-al-Rashid, in his book A History of Saudi Arabia, *provides the words spoken by Wahhab to Saud after the two men had arrived at an agreement.*

'You are the settlement's chief and wise man. I want you to say to me under oath that you will perform Jihad against the unbelievers. In return you will be imam, leader of the Muslim community, and I will be leader in religious matters.'

In effect, Saud would give his religious support to Wahhab while Wahhab would lend his political support to Saud.

118

The drive from Lucknow to the village near Birdpur in Siddharthnagar district of Uttar Pradesh took a little over six hours, but Sharma knew that he had of necessity to meet the good professor without delay. There was no one else who would be able to shed light, so fast, on the photographs in his possession.

Sharma opened the squeaking gate and walked along a pathway that wound its way through an unkempt garden. The house with its verandas and stuccoed pillars looked like it had stood there since the colonial era. The front door lay wide open and Sharma walked through into a living room.

Professor Vignesh Thakur was seated under a creaking fan, smoking a hookah. Rose-scented tobacco fumes hung heavy in the air. The two men shook hands and Sharma sat down opposite the professor on a divan. A servant brought lemonade, tea and samosas. Sharma suddenly realized he was famished. He was grateful for the refreshments.

'You see, this village is only known because of something that happened around here in 1898,' the professor said as he watched with some amusement while Sharma ate with gusto. 'In that year, a British estate manager and amateur archaeologist William Peppé carried out excavations on what was then a rather ordinary looking mound. He was excited to find a great brick dome with a sarcophagus at the core. Inside it, he found four containers that held 1,600 small jewels and gold pieces mixed with human ashes and bones.'

Sharma allowed his phone to record the conversation so that he could keep eating. Professor Thakur took a drag from his hookah, the water bubbling pleasantly. Then he continued, 'But Peppé went on to make a monumental mistake. He chose to consult Dr Alois Anton Führer, a German archaeologist.'

'Why was that a mistake?' asked Sharma.

'Because Führer was a forger,' replied Thakur. 'In later years, it was shown that he had forged other Buddhist relics too. The effect of the scandal was that the Piprahwa finds by Peppé became suspect. Peppé's own reputation was severely tarnished. This was tragic, because his discoveries were genuine.'

'And you decided to continue his work?' asked Sharma, still between mouthfuls.

'Yes,' replied the professor. 'Since then, we have uncovered the entire Piprahwa stupa in addition to several monasteries. Besides those, we have also found ancient residential quarters and shrines in the adjacent mound of Ganwaria. Do you know why these finds are so very interesting?'

'Why?' asked Sharma, washing down the last samosa with lemonade. He barely suppressed a belch.

'We are located just fourteen kilometres from Kapilavastu in Nepal, the very place where Siddhartha Gautama lived till age twenty-nine,' replied Thakur. 'In fact, it is my belief that this area of Piprahwa-Ganwaria is the *real* Kapilavastu.'

'So?'

'And thus it would be one of the eight original resting places for the Buddha's ashes,' said Thakur.

119

Sharma took a deep breath. 'Fine,' he said eventually. 'But even if that were so, the jewels and ashes could still be fake, right?'

'Impossible,' said Thakur firmly. 'Führer could not have fabricated the Piprahwa casket inscription. Buddha had always insisted on using Prakrit, the language of the common people, instead of Sanskrit. This practice was followed by the great Emperor Ashoka in his inscriptions.'

'And the casket?' asked Sharma.

'On the casket is the word "nidhane". It is a Prakrit word that means "container". It is written in a unique style of Brahmi script, the writing system favoured by Ashoka. That unique style is a clear indication that the reliquary containing the ashes and jewels was placed there during Ashoka's time, not fabricated later in our times.'

'Doesn't the word nidhane also mean "destruction"?' asked Sharma, recalling that the professor had mentioned this when they had last met.

'That's in Sanskrit, not Prakrit,' said the professor, raising his bushy eyebrows. 'Why do you ask?'

'Because this word also shows up on these documents,' said Sharma, as he held out the photographs he had received from the art dealer in Paris.

'Is this genuine?' asked Thakur, the excitement in his voice almost palpable.

'It probably is,' said Sharma. 'And that's why I'm here, Professor. You are the foremost historian on Buddhism. Can you tell me the significance of this?'

Thakur took another puff before he spoke. 'The two older forms of Buddhism, Theravada and Mahayana, eventually gave way to a new form, which was known as Vajrayana. That would have been around the sixth century. This also came to be known as Tantric Buddhism on account of the fact that it emerged from the mingling of Hindu tantra with Buddhist philosophy. It is the main form of Buddhism in Tibet and the face of this version is the Dalai Lama.'

Thakur halted, looking inward. He then realized that Sharma was waiting expectantly for him to speak further. Giving himself a shake, he picked up from where he had left off.

'The Dalai Lama has been responsible for initiating thousands of people into Kalachakra,' said Thakur. 'One of the first to receive the initiation directly from the Buddha himself was King Suchandara of the kingdom of Shambhala. This original teaching of the Buddha was known as the Kalachakra Multantra, but no one has ever seen evidence of it in writing. During the Buddha's time, such learning was conveyed orally, not in written form. Subsequent renderings are not the original Multantra.'

'And?' asked Sharma eagerly.

'If the rest of this document is not fake, then it would be the only version that I have ever seen of the Kalachakra Multantra,' said Thakur. 'It would have been committed to writing in Sanskrit around the time of the birth of Vajrayana, almost a thousand years after the Buddha—around the sixth century CE.'

120

Cracker quietly entered Vijay's apartment. An earpiece kept him in communication with the security office that was monitoring the young man's location. Presently, he was in his laboratory and this was the perfect opportunity to snoop.

Cracker took his time opening each drawer carefully and searching through the contents with his latex-gloved hands. He made sure that he put everything back exactly as he had found it. There was absolutely nothing in the living room that was out of the ordinary. Just books, notes, clothes and a few photographs of his girlfriend, Sujatha.

He then went into the kitchen. He opened the refrigerator. Just the usual milk, bread, soda. He looked inside the microwave oven. Nothing. He opened the kitchen cabinets one by one. They contained a few provisions.

His eyes were drawn to a rectangular box that contained clingwrap. *This is the one the new boy brought with him,* Cracker thought; *it is not a brand that is sold at the convenience store on the Milesian campus. Why would someone coming from Delhi bring a roll of clingwrap with him?* wondered Cracker.

He grasped the box and placed it on the kitchen top. He carefully pulled out a segment and used the serrated edge of the box to cut it off. He gently rolled it and placed it into a cardboard tube that he had brought with him. He then put the box of clingwrap back into the cabinet and left the apartment.

121

Sharma took a mid-morning flight to Gaggal Airport near Kangra. He was received by a RAW associate, who drove him the short distance of fifteen kilometres to Dharamsala. He arrived in McLeod Ganj a little after one in the afternoon.

He made his way to the administrative office in the Tsuglagkhang Complex and stood facing the gate to the Dalai Lama's house. There were Indian guards on duty at the front gate. Sharma let his eyes run along the line of doors of the block. He stopped at the last door on his right and made his way there.

His Holiness followed a rigorous schedule, waking up each day at three in the morning to shower, pray and meditate. This was followed by a morning walk and breakfast. For the next few hours, he continued his prayers and meditation before shifting gears to studying texts and commentaries. The session ended with lunch a little before noon. His Holiness would then go to his office for three hours during which time he would clear his correspondence and also give select media interviews and private audiences scheduled months in advance. Getting an urgent private audience with the Dalai Lama had required leveraging many government connections. Sharma's audience had been fixed the previous day by the personal assistant to the Home Minister of India.

Inside the Dalai Lama's secretariat a small crowd of people were waiting, holding pieces of paper with their personal information and their passports. Many of them came each day, hoping that it would be their lucky day. The man behind the desk instantly greeted Sharma and led him through to the office chamber.

His Holiness was seated on a simple sofa inside a wood-panelled office that bore several Tibetan artefacts and paintings. He was dressed in his usual vermillion and saffron robes. Sharma was in awe of his presence, but he took a step forward to bend down and touch the pontiff's feet. The old man smiled the smile the world was familiar with, in times of tragedy and in times of calm, and conveyed his blessings.

Sharma was proffered a chair opposite the sofa and sat down.

'What brings you here, Mr Sharma?' asked the Dalai Lama. 'And in what way may I help you?'

Sharma began hesitantly. 'I thank Your Holiness for seeing me at such short notice,' he said. 'But the matter is of some urgency.'

Sharma placed before the Dalai Lama a piece of paper.

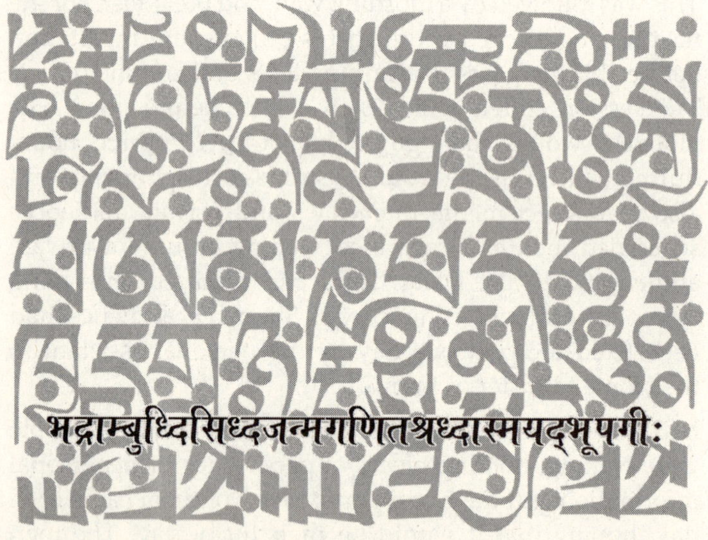

'How did you come by this?' asked His Holiness, raising his eyebrows.

'It was given to me by a monk at the Kargil Army Hospital. His name was Brahmananda. He was there along with a Russian disciple, Mikhailov.'

'Why did he give it to you?'

'I was mentally and physically shattered. The monk said that the document would enable me to find him when I needed him.'

'How would you go about finding him?'

'He said that I would have to find myself in order to find him,' replied Sharma.

'Did you share this document with anyone else?' asked the pontiff.

'No,' replied Sharma. 'I did not take it seriously at that time.'

He paused. 'There's something else,' Sharma began hesitantly. 'As you may have read, India's Cartosat series of satellites are regularly monitoring the country's resources and land mass. One of the images that has emerged from Cartosat-2D is this particular one. I wanted you to have a look at it, Your Holiness.'

Sharma unrolled the high-resolution image on the table in front of the sofa. His Holiness took one look at the image and his jaw dropped.

'This is not possible,' he said. 'What is the location of this place?'

'Alas, I cannot tell you at this stage,' said Sharma, feeling guilty about disappointing the holy man.

The octogenarian pontiff stared at the image warily. Then Sharma showed him the photographs of the documents he had received from the Parisian art dealer.

If the satellite images had surprised the Dalai Lama, the Paris art dealer's photos left him speechless. He examined them with a magnifying glass for several minutes. Not a word was spoken during that time.

'I am not sure whether this is a good omen or a bad one,' he eventually said philosophically. 'Nidhane. Destruction.'

He was lost in thought. 'Stay for a few days,' said the Dalai Lama eventually, and did not explain further.

122

The one question that Rakesh Sharma was unable to answer was, 'Where are you from?'

He had been born in Jodhpur, but his father was from a town in Himachal and his mother from Lucknow. His parents had moved to Amritsar, then Jalandhar, Bagdogra, Chandigarh, Bathinda, Vishakapatnam, Gopalpur, Udhampur, Indore, Leh, Manali, Mhow, Delhi, Gwalior and finally Bangalore. In that order.

Sharma was from nowhere. And from everywhere.

He was what was usually known as an *Army Brat*. The word *brat* stood for 'Born Raised And Transferred'. It was a short and succinct line that described the lives of most army kids. They spent the better part of their growing up years getting uprooted and shuttled from one public school to the next. They were the lucky ones. The others were packed off to cold boarding schools in the hills when their parents could afford—or scrape the barrel for—the fees.

After his twelfth standard board exams, he had been accepted into the National Defence Academy, more commonly known as the NDA. The NDA was the Joint Services academy of the Indian Armed Forces located at Khadakwasla near Pune, and cadets of all the three services—Army, Navy and Air Force—trained together before they went their separate ways. NDA alumni had led and fought in every major armed conflict in the Indian theatre.

Only the very best made it into the NDA. Around half a million applicants sat for the written exam and only six thousand of these were invited to interview. Of these, only three hundred were accepted into the academy each year. Sharma had completed the programme with flying colours and had been sent to the Indian Military Academy at Dehradun for a year of specialized training before being granted a commission. He was a good-looking young man, always impeccably dressed in creaseless combat uniform, sun-deflecting Aviators winking from his head, and shoes you could see your face in.

One of his favourite pastimes was hang-gliding. He would run down a hill slope or along a ridge, allowing wind currents to lift him into the air. Then he would soar above the picturesque landscape before bringing his thirty-kilogram glider down on earth. It was during one of those pleasantly giddy trips that he had met his future wife. He had literally run into her while making a landing in a cornfield.

The Kargil war had commenced immediately following their marriage.

123

Sharma had played a key role in capturing two critical bunkers on Tiger Hill. He had taken upon himself the task of fixing a rope for his men to reach the top of a cliff that was located at a height of 16,500 feet. He was fired upon by enemy machine guns, but he carried on, paying no heed to his wounds. He eventually scaled the cliff along with his men and killed several Pakistani soldiers who were stationed there. His actions enabled the rest of his battalion to take over that key position. Duty performed, he allowed himself to collapse.

He awoke several days later at the Army Hospital in Kargil, unaware until then that he had lost a leg in the battle. It had been amputated below the knee to prevent the gangrene from spreading. His doctor, the nurses and his wife tried their best to lift his spirits, but Sharma knew that his life in the army was over.

The next day, Sharma saw a Russian man and a monk sitting on the adjacent bed. The Russian's name was Mikhailov and the monk's name was Brahmananda. They had been rescued by the army from Hardas in the Kargil sector, when their ashram had come under attack.

The monk was unfazed by his own wounds. Instead, he made it his purpose to offer solace and succour to the other patients around him who had been scarred physically, mentally and emotionally. He sat by Sharma's bedside, but Sharma refused to speak to him. He was done with any form of religion. If God existed, then He would never allow men to go into battle and lose their limbs or their lives.

But Brahmananda remained persistent. Each day he would sit by Sharma's bed and quietly chant a few mantras. It took a few more days for Sharma to acknowledge Brahmananda's presence. And then his words came tumbling out like a torrent. He hated God, he hated the world, he hated his life and his circumstances. There was a rage inside of him that wanted to burn down everything around him.

Brahmananda listened to him patiently and attempted to guide him through the spiritual wisdom of Krishna, Buddha and the Sufi masters. After a few days, he gave him a document that was rolled up inside a bamboo tube.

'What is this?' Sharma had asked.

'When you need direction, when you need me, this will help.' Then Brahmananda told him the story of a man called Sashwata who had been through several trials and tribulations but refused to give up on life. Sashwata refused to die, living thousands of years in his quest to complete his God-given purpose.

Sharma went through a transformation that was miraculous. He found himself wanting to get up in the morning. Brahmananda's words now had meaning. He wanted to learn and absorb them.

Some days later, he was shifted to the All-India Institute of Medical Sciences in Delhi. He spent the next four months being fitted with a prosthetic leg. During that time, his constant companions were books that had been recommended by Brahmananda. His wife would scour the bookstores of Delhi to find old and dog-eared books that he would voraciously devour. One of them was a treatise on the Kalachakra by Professor Vignesh Thakur.

Sharma steadily made progress until he reached the point where he could outrun and out-jump most people who had both legs intact. During his last week in the hospital, he received a visit from his Commanding Officer. They sat in the medical superintendent's office because the conversation was meant to remain entirely private. At that meeting, Sharma was told that he would henceforth be part of the Research and Analysis Wing, India's external intelligence agency, on deputation from military intelligence.

The Indian government had wisely decided that it would be a pity to let a man of Sharma's talents go to waste.

124

Mikhailov wrapped the muffler around his neck and tucked his hands inside his jacket pockets as he took his stroll. Walking by himself always made him feel better. The icy cold winds seemed to clear his head. He would often reminisce about his grandfather or about Brahmananda when he strolled about, but today was different. The phone call had got him worried.

Although Mikhailov had remained away from Russia, the country's intelligence services had persisted in treating him as an asset. During the early days, he had been required to periodically report to the First Directorate of the KGB. After the dissolution of the Soviet Union, the KGB had been split into the FSB that looked after domestic intelligence, and the SVR that was responsible for espionage outside the Russian Federation. Mikhailov had been absorbed into the SVR's list of agents.

The SVR had not required Mikhailov to report proactively but had retained him as a sleeper agent who could be activated whenever required. But the problem with sleeper agents was that they often strayed from the path that had been plotted for them.

The recent phone call with the inconspicuous phrase '*Izvinitye, ya plokho ponimayu po-russki*' was a call to arms. The phrase simply meant, 'Sorry, I don't understand Russian very well', but when it came from a fluent speaker of the language, it could mean only one thing.

As one of the oldest employees at Milesian, Mikhailov had freedoms that Vijay did not. He could take weekends off to visit family or friends. He could avail of extended leave benefits too. Vijay, too, would be entitled to these benefits but only after his initial three months of employment. And yet Mikhailov was now rueing the fact that he had the freedom to exit the Milesian gates for a rendezvous. He didn't know where, with whom or when, but he knew the protocol. They would only make contact with him once he was safely outside the gates.

It had been two decades since he had left Russia for Brahmananda's ashram. He had stayed at the ashram for five years until the great fire. He had spent the next ten years on deputation at the Tata Institute of Fundamental Research, contributing his expertise to the departments of High Energy Physics and Condensed Matter Physics, before eventually joining Milesian on the request of the SVR.

During all those years, Mikhailov would take periodic breaks, travelling deep into the forests of the Himalayas in order to meet his guru, Brahmananda, but he had been unable to find a place that he could call home. The fact that he had never married ensured it.

Around once a year, the SVR would re-establish contact. It was never for any specific reason. It was simply to remind him that he could still be called upon to perform his duty for Mother Russia. This latest call, however, was not one of those. He could pick up from the tone that there was something that they actually wanted him to *do.*

In the security office, racks of hard disks were recording feeds from all the CCTV cameras scattered around the Milesian complex. Cracker settled back in his leather swivel chair and poured himself three fingers of Jack Daniels. He took a swig and looked at the bank of monitors. The crazy Russian was out strolling. He seemed to be mumbling stuff to himself. Why did Schmidt employ these crackpots?

'He's taking a longer walk than usual,' said Cracker, putting down his glass. 'Anything significant happening in his life?'

125

The young man took off on the empty stretch of Bikaner-Nokha Road in Rajasthan, leaving a few early-morning bystanders coughing from the dust thrown up by the tyres of his Toyota Prado. It was a short drive of thirty kilometres that he covered in twenty minutes flat.

It was 5 a.m. and still dark. The man got out of his SUV once he had parked outside the temple. He was wearing a traditional kurta-pyjama. The priest was waiting for him—the one he had specifically booked for this offering to the gods. He was dressed in a loose flowing robe, and on his forehead was a vermillion mark, signifying the third eye of human consciousness. He wore chunky beads around his neck and carried an ornately carved wooden staff in his left hand. Around his shoulders was draped a bright red woollen shawl. The young man folded his hands in a namaste and the priest conveyed his blessings.

Together they walked through the entrance of the Karni Mata Temple that dated back to the fifteenth century. The priest was carrying a large tray laden with Indian sweets in his right hand.

The sight that greeted the young man was one that fascinated hundreds of visitors to the temple each day. Twenty thousand black rats scurried among the intricate marble panels and solid silver carvings. They were everywhere. The young man followed the priest to the idol of Karni Mata, carefully avoiding stepping on any of the rats.

'The original temple was built six hundred years ago,' said the priest, handing over the tray of sweets to the man. 'You need to offer these sweets to the deity,' he said.

The young man placed the tray in front of the idol and, almost instantly, the generous offering was snapped up by a swarm of rats. A few of the bulky rodents ran over his foot. He shuddered. *Why do I have to land up in these places?* he wondered.

'What's the significance of the rats?' asked the young man, recovering his composure.

'The temple is dedicated to a fifteenth-century mystic who was considered to be a reincarnation of the Goddess

Durga. The rats are believed to be repositories of the souls of dead *charans*, the traditional bards of this area. If you have ever been wronged, Karni Mata can help you seek justice. You pay your respects to her by feeding these rats.'

'Now what?' asked the young man, as he looked at the rats devouring the sweets. He'd heard most of the rats in the temple were diabetic.

They walked towards the solid silver doorway depicting the various legends of the Goddess. The priest continued chanting mantras the young man could not understand.

As the priest reached up to ring the temple bell at the entrance, the young man leapt from his position and jabbed him with a needle in his neck. The priest yelled in agony. He fell to the ground as his face began to swell and his heart rate began to fall.

The young man calmly watched the priest's body for a while. It would be some time before the rats recovered their appetite sufficiently to get to work on it. He then walked over to his vehicle and drove away without looking back.

126

Sujatha tried to make herself comfortable in the rear passenger seat. It was a long drive to Nanda Devi National Park and she wanted to use the time efficiently.

She pulled out a plastic folder from her bag and scanned the readings she had summarized. She was convinced they could not have been fudged. They seemed to be proving what she had instinctively known all along.

The data had been compiled by Cleve Backster, a scientist who had worked for the CIA in the '40s. He left the CIA some years later to start up the Keeler Polygraph Institute in Chicago. The institute provided training in the use of lie-detection technology and worked alongside several government and law enforcement agencies.

Something rather strange happened a few years later. Backster had a rubber plant and a dracaena cane plant in his office. Working late one night, he had an incredible idea. He would connect one of his plants to the polygraph machine.

He was quite surprised to find that the plant did not have flat electrical activity. Backster wanted to see if he could get a human-like response from the plant, so he went back to the basics of polygraph theory. If he wanted to catch a lie, he would confront a suspect with information that they may have been hiding. This resulted in fear or anxiety and the reaction would show up as an electrical impulse on the polygraph.

Backster tried dipping one of the leaves of the plant into water but there was no response on the polygraph. He then tapped one of the leaves with his pen. Again, no reaction. Then he decided that he would get a match and burn one of the leaves. But before he could actually act on that thought, the polygraph went into a tizzy. The polygraph's recording pen jumped sharply to the upper limits of the graph paper.

Backster had not yet acted on his intention but his plan to do so had been obviously sensed by the plant. Hence, its panicked reaction.

As a child, Sujatha had been fascinated by the work of Jagdish Chandra Bose and his crescograph. His work had shown that plants had life. But the polygraph results took that premise even further. Plants not only had life but also had quantum feeling. They could pick up on thoughts and intentions, just like the much talked-about sixth sense.

Sujatha looked up from the data analysis. She glanced out of the window and was stunned by the spectacular vistas that surrounded them. She put away the folder and decided to enjoy the view. 'What time will we get to Nanda Devi National Park?' she asked her guide.

127

Mary Connors, the Australian Minister for Foreign Affairs, reached her quiet home in a corner of South Canberra, utterly exhausted. Never before in her life had she experienced the sort of fatigue that had washed over her that day. It had been enervating, to say the least.

The Australian Prime Minister, under pressure from more conservative members of his party, had issued a statement that said Australia was a nation founded on Christian values. He had emphasized the fact that the Australian constitution was based on principles of a secular society in which the State was meant to be neutral in matters of belief. He had then gone on to say that Australia had welcomed migrants from varied races and religions, thus making the country one of the most diverse on the planet. So far so good.

But then he had gone on to bemoan the fact that while most immigrants had embraced Australian values, some had arrived with the intention of imposing their own beliefs on everyone else. He had been referring to politically active Islamists in Australia.

The Prime Minister had pointed out that such extremist elements were working towards imposing Sharia law in Australia. It had started with demands for halal meat in supermarkets, then requests for *niqaabs* in driving licence photos and now demands for Islamic prayer rooms in Christian schools. It was only a matter of time before Islamists would start making more stringent demands, such as the right to operate Sharia courts, or the power to punish non-Muslims for blasphemy.

Mary Connors had taken a view contrary to that of her Prime Minister. She had observed that Australia's Muslims only accounted for 2 per cent of the population and this was mostly a peace-loving minority. But she had been shouted down by other colleagues, who had argued that Australian suburbs such as Lakemba, Auburn, Bankstown, Punchbowl and Villawood were getting transformed beyond recognition by demographic changes. Even Australian prisons were being used by imams to radicalize inmates.

Mary had walked out of the meeting feeling helpless and weary. This was not the Australia that she had grown up in. Muslims had been among the first settlers in Norfolk Island, a British penal colony in Australia. They had arrived there from 1796 onwards, working on British ships. In the later part of the century, Muslim camel drivers from Baluchistan had settled in the country to provide transport through Australia's vast deserts. They had assimilated into the country's culture. Why was the entire Muslim community being branded as terrorist on account of the acts of a few?

Mary entered her living room and sat down on the sofa. On the ottoman in front of the sofa lay her evening tray carrying a bottle of Holm Oak Pinot Noir and two Baccarat wine glasses. Her husband, an influential corporate lawyer, was away on a business trip and she missed his presence. At times like these, it was his gentle yet firm advice that helped keep her anchored. She poured herself some wine and thanked her stars for having an independent streak that helped her look beyond stereotypes.

She kicked off her shoes and settled into the sofa, allowing her mind to wander. These days she seemed to be surrounded by enemies. Her difficulties had multiplied ever since she had given an interview to the *Sydney Morning Herald* in which she had taken a liberal position on immigration that was at odds with her party's stated view.

Mary allowed her tongue to savour the background spice and tannic edge of the wine. Originally a French connection, it was a wonderful wine from the 'new world', Tasmania's Tamar Valley vineyards. Within the next ten minutes she had drained her glass and fallen asleep on the sofa.

She awoke a few minutes later and retched violently. She ran to the bathroom and stood in front of the washbasin. Her mouth felt dry as sandpaper and she gulped some water, which she threw up instantly. She looked at the mirror above the basin only to realize that one side of her face was grotesquely swollen and a bright red. She reached for her phone to dial the emergency response number, but before she could complete the call, the phone fell from her hand, crashing down on the floor. The hand holding the phone had swollen up, and her fingers were twice their usual size.

She ran out of the house, some unformed idea to call out for help driving her there. The pain was blinding her and she stumbled out onto the road, where a car crashed headlong into her.

She was declared dead on arrival at Calvary John James Hospital.

128

Vijay was in his apartment, seated on a comfortable sofa from where he could look out through a massive window into the Himalayan vista beyond.

Next to him was a steaming cup of south Indian filter coffee, just the way he liked it. He was running through a bunch of handwritten notes that Mikhailov had given him.

Mikhailov was a neat man and his handwriting followed suit. It was as though every up stroke, down stroke, curve, loop and flourish were meticulously planned on stencil. Vijay began reading.

Shambhala is a Sanskrit word that means 'place of peace'. Most scholars believe that it is a mythical paradise, one that has acquired an aura owing to the Kalachakra texts. But Shambhala is mentioned in several belief systems. The folklore of Shambhala dates back thousands of years, and mention of the fabled kingdom is seen in various ancient texts. For example, Shambhala is mentioned in the earliest writings of the Zhangzhung culture, which antedated Buddhism in western Tibet. These texts seem to point to the Sutlej valley, that spans the Punjab and Himachal, as the fabled Shambhala.

Bön texts talk of a similar land called Olmolungring, while Mongolians correlate Shambhala with valleys of southern Siberia. Hindu manuscripts such as the Vishnu Purana *describe Shambhala as the birthplace of Kalki, the last and final incarnation of Vishnu. Some Buddhist teachers believe that Shambhala is nestled in the higher altitudes of the Himalayas in the area that is referred to as the Dhauladhar Mountains around McLeod Ganj. Other legends claim that the entrance to Shambhala is concealed inside an isolated and deserted monastery in Tibet, and watched over by beings called the Shambhala Guardians.*

But the place where Shambhala is discussed and described in most significant detail is within the Kalachakra system. It should be noted, though, that the myths, stories, lessons and techniques connected with Shambhala are far older than any of the later organized religions. Shambhala was probably a native idea, possibly even a Himalayan shamanic belief, that was eventually assimilated into other faiths.

According to Buddhist tradition, it was King Suchandara from the kingdom of Shambhala who had sat before the Buddha in order to learn the Kalachakra Multantra. Shambhala steadily came to be viewed as a Buddhist pure land, a magnificent kingdom whose existence was not only spiritual but also temporal. Shambhala would be the guiding light for the world in 2424 CE when the twenty-fifth Rigden king of Shambhala, Rudrachakrin, would fight and defeat the barbarian hordes, thus marking the advent of a golden age.

The West has been fascinated with the notion of a fantastic kingdom hidden away from the rest of the world. The first Western references about Shambhala were by the Portuguese Catholic missionary Estêvão Cacella, who thought that 'Xembala' was another name for China. In 1627, he travelled to Tashilhunpo, the capital of the Panchen Lama, only to find that it wasn't the fabulous land that he had imagined.

The Hungarian scholar Sandor Korosi Csoma wrote in 1833 that the fabulous country in the north was situated between forty-five and fifty degrees latitudes north of the Equator. If one were to travel north from India to these latitudes, one would reach eastern Kazakhstan, which has a splendid landscape dotted with green hills, low mountains, rivers, and lakes, a perfect setting for the magnificent Shambhala. In comparison, the terrains of Tibet and Xinjiang, which are often believed to be the locations containing Shambhala, are arid and rocky. In the folklore of the people of the Altai Mountains, Mount Beluka is often regarded as a gateway to Shambhala.

In the late nineteenth century, Helena Blavatsky, one of the founders of the Theosophical Society, mentioned Shambhala in her writings following her supposed communication with the Great White Lodge of Himalayan Adepts. Soon, Shambhala became a buzzword among Western aficionados of the occult. Later, occult writers such as Alice Bailey claimed that Shambhala was an extra-dimensional spiritual reality on an etheric plane.

In the period 1924 to 1928, Nicholas and Helena Roerich led an expedition to discover the location of Shambhala. Their expedition started from Sikkim and went through Punjab, Kashmir, Ladakh, the Karakoram Mountains, Khotan, Kashgar, Qara Shar, Urumchi, Irtysh, the Altai Mountains, the Oyrot region of Mongolia, Central Gobi, Kansu, Tsaidam and Tibet.

Inspired by Roerich, Gleb Bokii, one of the chiefs of the Soviet secret police who was also a Bolshevik cryptographer, undertook an expedition to find Shambhala, in what was an effort to blend the Kalachakra philosophy with the principles of communism. Even the Nazis, Heinrich Himmler and Rudolf Hess, commissioned a German expedition to Tibet in 1930 and then again in 1934 and 1938, with the aim of finding Shambhala.

A few decades later, French Buddhist Alexandra David-Neel put forth the idea that Shambhala was actually Balkh in present-day Afghanistan. In the Persian language, 'Sham-i-Bala' means 'elevated candle', and David-Neel suggested that Shambhala may be etymologically connected to this particular term. Similarly, J. G. Bennett speculated that Shambhala was 'Shams-i-Balkh', a Bactrian sun temple. Hindus believe that Mount Kailash is the gateway to Shambhala.

In 1933, James Hilton's novel, Lost Horizon, *described a hidden kingdom called Shangri-La in the mountains. This was inspired by the Shambhala myth and a* National Geographic *article about eastern Tibet and Kham. This novel set the world's imagination on fire. Myth, history, philosophy, religion, geography, science, romance, fiction and the occult coalesced into a single hazy concept called Shambhala.*

Based on legend, Shambhala is supposed to be a land where only the pure-hearted can dwell. It is a land where love, wisdom and spiritual awareness are in abundance and where inhabitants are immune to grief, desire, ill-health or ageing. But where is it? Does it even exist at all?

As is the case with many ideas in the Kalachakra system, Shambhala is believed to have outer, inner and intuitive connotations. The outer meaning views Shambhala as a physical territory in the world, but only individuals who have the required 'karma' can reach it. The inner and intuitive meanings are concerned with more subtle comprehension of what Shambhala symbolizes as regards one's own body and mind, particularly during meditation.

Shambhala is often referred to—not surprisingly—as the land of a thousand names. It has been variously called Land of Radiant Spirits, Land of the Living Gods, Land of White

Waters, Forbidden Land, Land of Wonders and Land of Living Fire. Hindu texts often call it Aryavartha or Land of the Worthy Ones. The Chinese call it Hsi Tien or the Paradise of Hsi Wang Mu. To Russians it is Belovoyde. But through most of the world, it is called by its Sanskrit name, Shambhala.

And based upon my last meeting with my guru, Brahmananda, I think I now know exactly where it lies. The answer lies with the Keepers.

129

'We've had a breach,' said Cracker.

'Where?' asked Schmidt.

Cracker shifted on the chair uncomfortably. 'Your office.'

Schmidt's eyes seemed to harden. He fixed his steely gaze on Cracker. 'How did you allow that to happen?' he asked very softly. Schmidt's voice always dropped to a barely audible level when he was angry.

'You were away to New Delhi from 8:17 a.m. to 10:40 p.m. Someone accessed your office at 10:17 p.m. Your thumbprint was used. I just noticed this on the log files.'

'How did it miss the attention of the cameras?' asked Schmidt.

'Because no one showed up on the monitors,' replied Cracker, feeling the heat of Schmidt's interrogation. 'The office was accessed a second time at around 10:43 p.m.—that was probably you.'

'Why did the system not detect a variation in the fingerprint?' asked Schmidt.

'We have an advanced algorithm for fingerprint recognition,' replied Cracker. 'Usually, fingerprint sensors use one specific method for recognition. In our case we use a combination of all.'

'And yet someone did break in,' said Schmidt, the anger evident in his eyes.

'It is possible that someone lifted your print from an object,' said Cracker.

'It is possible that your security system is not good enough,' retorted Schmidt.

'Our system first uses the general shape of your fingerprint to narrow the search in the database,' said Cracker. 'We then use the Henry system to compare whorl, right loop, left loop, arch and tented arch. We even compare minutiae such as the ending of ridges and bifurcation. Finally, we divide each print into small sectors and re-examine ridge direction, phase and pitch. It is probably one of the most advanced algorithms in use.'

'So advanced that someone could break in?' asked Schmidt, his voice heavy with irony. He paused to think for a moment.

'We should put further security measures in place,' said Schmidt.

'What sort?' asked Cracker.

'A mousetrap,' replied Schmidt. 'One that allows the rat to get in but not exit.'

Cracker nodded. He had just the thing.

'Can we account for the whereabouts of everyone at that time?' asked Schmidt. 'What about our new man?'

'Vijay Sundaram was in his apartment,' said Cracker. 'His computer was active and he was online for over an hour at that time.'

'Anyone not accounted for?' asked Schmidt.

'Only one person was wandering the grounds at that time,' said Cracker.

'Who?' asked Schmidt.

'Mikhailov.'

'In that case, you know what needs to be done.'

130

Sujatha brushed away the strands of hair from her face as she bent down to take a photograph of the plant that had caught her attention. She opened her notebook and assigned a number to her meticulous records. Each number indicated the date and sequential order of that particular day's collection. She then proceeded to note down her observations about the plant's appearance, location, surrounding plant life and terrain.

She had painstakingly clipped and boxed several samples over two days at Nanda Devi National Park, home to an incredible selection of plant life. The main challenge was to find rare species among the usual fir, birch, rhododendron and juniper. In any case, she knew that there was no way that she could explore the entire 2,237 square kilometres of the biosphere reserve—even over the course of a lifetime. Instead, her focus was on specific coordinates at stipulated altitudes.

It was difficult to remain focused on work when surrounded by incredibly stunning vistas. The national park was 11,500 feet above sea level and within it nestled the Nanda Devi sanctuary, a glacial basin that was encircled by a loop of mountains, ranging from 19,000 feet to 25,000 feet in height. The basin was drained via the Rishi Ganga Gorge, an abrupt and treacherous ravine that was also breathtaking in its beauty.

But there was a spring in Sujatha's step that day. Her theory had been proved right. The previous day she had bagged a variant from the Ophiorrhiza mungos family. As reasoned by her, the plant that Sujatha had seen along the Western Ghats of India was also present with some significant variations inside Nanda Devi National Park.

Ophiorrhiza acuminate
Ophiorrhiza blumeana
Ophiorrhiza bracteata
Ophiorrhiza cantoniensis
Ophiorrhiza carinata…

The list of variants was long. And each variant contained camptothecin, an alkaloid used to make chemotherapeutic agents. Sujatha's efforts would, hopefully, add significantly to the discoveries of the Botanical Survey of India. And the latest research on combating mankind's most mysterious killer, cancer.

It was her last day in Nanda Devi National Park. Tomorrow she would be back in Dehradun for a couple of days before she left for Govind Pashu Vihar.

Sujatha usually fell into automaton mode when she was on collection trips, working on the single track of research, sometimes even forgetting to eat or sleep in the excitement of each new discovery. But this trip had been different. Vijay had been uppermost in her mind. Although they spoke on the phone at least once every day, it felt strange to have him so near and yet so far—so inaccessible. In addition to that, she had picked up a certain tension in his voice. He always maintained that everything was fine, but she wasn't too sure.

There had been a positive spinoff from Vijay's job, though. He had begun missing her! And, for the first time ever, he had said that he loved her. Nothing short of a miracle.

'You do realize that very few people are allowed into this area,' said Sujatha's guide.

'I am aware of the number of hoops I had to jump through to get here,' acknowledged Sujatha. 'Why is the area so restricted?'

'That story goes back to 1965,' said the guide.

131

'Sometime around October 1965, the CIA and India's Intelligence Bureau decided on a joint plan to set up a nuclear-powered detection device on Nanda Devi, India's second-highest peak at 25,643 feet, and one of the most treacherous climbs,' said Sujatha's guide. 'It had been three years since India's defeat to China and the Cold War between communism and the West was at its peak. A year previously, China had carried out its first nuclear tests. It was imperative to keep track of its military and nuclear build-up. A sensing apparatus on Nanda Devi would enable the Americans to do this.'

'There's a nuclear detection device on Nanda Devi?' asked Sujatha, shocked.

'Hear me out,' said the guide. 'Mounting the machine atop Nanda Devi was easier said than done. The exercise involved lugging equipment weighing around fifty-six kilograms up the mountain. This included a ten-foot-high antenna, two transmitter and receiver sets and a power generator called SNAP—System for Nuclear Auxiliary Power. The fuel required to power the generator comprised seven plutonium capsules, and these were housed in a special cased unit. It was nicknamed Guru Rinpoche by the sherpas who were assigned the task of carrying it up. Team leader Manmohan Singh Kohli led his men up to Camp IV, which is at an altitude of 24,000 feet. That's when a snowstorm struck. Kohli was forced to make a choice between men and machines. He chose his men. Guru Rinpoche was abandoned near Camp IV.'

'Why didn't they recover the material later?' asked Sujatha.

'Weather,' replied the guide. 'The team returned some months later only to find that all the machinery, including the dangerous plutonium capsules, around half the capacity of the bomb dropped on Hiroshima, were gone. The plutonium was never seen again in spite of several expeditions that followed. Many alternative theories were discussed, including the possibility that the plutonium could have been buried under snow during an avalanche. There was also a lurking dread that the Rishi Ganga, the river that flows from the glaciers, could have been chemically contaminated.'

'Plutonium has a radioactive life of over a hundred years,' observed Sujatha, looking concerned.

'Water and rock samples from the area were tested for radiation and two HH-43B Huskies, high-altitude choppers of the American Air Force, were deployed to assist, but no reports were released. Suspiciously, the mountain and the nearby areas were sealed off from further expeditions. One battalion of the Indo-Tibetan Border Police was stationed there to continuously monitor radioactivity levels,' said the guide. 'This is the reason why it is so difficult to get permission to come here.'

'And it is evident that something has indeed happened,' said Sujatha. 'Look at the samples in my bag.' She held up one of the specimen bags.

'I can't see anything different,' said the guide.

'According to the Health Physics Society, radiation has a positive effect on plant growth at lower radiation levels and harmful effects at high levels,' said Sujatha. 'These samples that you see are twice the size of the same plants along the Western Ghats. Low-level energy exposure has been taking place over a sustained period of time.'

'You think it could be Guru Rinpoche?' asked the guide nervously.

'Either that or some other source of energy,' replied Sujatha.

'Are these plants safe?' asked the guide.

'Sure,' said Sujatha. 'For all we know, they could be even more effective in fighting disease. After all, most medicines are poison that is delivered into ailing bodies to cure them, but only in appropriate doses. Let's see.'

132

And it's another day and it's time for me, Masoud, to jot down my thoughts. Today I want to examine the schism between Sunnis and Shias within the faith.

Let's step back to 632 CE. It was the year in which the Prophet Muhammad died. He passed away without appointing a successor—a caliph—who would lead the Muslims. Disputes arose. While some felt that the position ought to be held by Muhammad's descendants, others felt that caliphs should be chosen through deliberation, discussion and consensus.

The Prophet's trusted righthand man, Abu Bakr, was made Caliph, although others felt that Ali, the Prophet's son-in-law, ought to have been the successor. Ali did ultimately become Caliph after the two successors of Abu Bakr were killed, but he was soon assassinated with a poison-coated sword. His sons, Hasan and later Hussein, demanded the title but all of them were massacred in the famous battle of Karbala, in present-day Iraq, in 680 CE.

The martyrdom of Hussein became a core precept of those who believed that Ali should have succeeded Prophet Muhammad, and the event is mourned each year during the month of Muharram by Shiat Ali—or the 'followers of Ali'. The term Shia is simply a contraction of that phrase. On the other hand, the Sunnis believe in the three caliphs that followed Prophet Muhammad and the example he set via the Sunnah. *The Sunnis undertook massive conquests and expanded their caliphate into North Africa and Europe. History records four major caliphates—the Rashidun Caliphate, the Umayyad Caliphate, the Abbasid Caliphate and the Ottoman Empire, which ended after the First World War.*

Wahhabi fundamentalism resulted in the destruction of the tomb of Hussein in Karbala in 1801. Five thousand people died in the attack. It was the same radicalism that prompted the Wahhabis to attack and capture Mecca and Medina, damaging the Prophet Muhammad's mosque in the process. The Ottomans were the official guardians of the Arabian Peninsula and Islam's religious places. They had to be seen as taking appropriate action to punish the Wahhabis.

The First Saudi State eventually went to war with the Ottoman Empire. This ended with the defeat of the grandson of Saud at the hands of the Ottomans. Diriyah was systematically reduced to rubble and the grandson was captured and sent to Istanbul to be beheaded and his severed head thrown into the waters of the Bosphorus. Evidence exists that he was forced to listen to a lute being played before he was beheaded because he was fanatically opposed to music.

But one can destroy kingdoms, not the ideas that spawned them. Wahhabis and the residual members of the Al Saud tribe remained steadfast and established a Second Saudi State that survived until 1891. Later, a Third Saudi State was established in 1932. It survives to this day and is known as the Kingdom of Saudi Arabia.

133

Mikhailov placed the parcel of food in his duffel bag and packed his other stuff. He exited his apartment and walked to the cable car station. Seven minutes later, he was at the main gate. He looked at his watch. Saturday 4 a.m. It was freezing cold and pitch dark, but it was the only hour that would allow him to make it to Dehradun in time for a preliminary contact. He had taken pains to keep Schmidt informed of the weekend leave which he was availing. He felt tired as he reached the gate. The nightmares had been persistent through the few hours that he had slept.

He went through the security protocol of being scrutinized by sophisticated millimetre-wave scanners using non-ionizing electromagnetic radiation. His duffel bag was also subjected to X-ray examination. Milesian was overzealous about checking stuff that was coming in *and* going out.

Mikhailov then walked out of the Milesian gate and made his way down a winding and descending pathway that led to the car park. His hired car and chauffeur would be waiting there.

At this hour, there wasn't a soul in sight. Dense birch and fir trees on both sides of the pathway made it almost impossible to even snatch a look at the sky. The previous night, when he had been in the zone between wakefulness and sleep, he had imagined this walk and the eerie solitude of it. He had lain in bed paralyzed with fear and drenched in sweat until it was time to get up.

He could hear the sound of his feet squishing on the wet ground. But there was something else. It was another pair of feet. He clutched his bag tightly as he stepped up his pace. Something did not feel right. His senses were now on full alert. *I must get out of here fast!*

Mikhailov continued walking down the pathway. Suddenly there was a voice. 'Stop!'

He turned around and saw a man dressed entirely in black, his face covered by a balaclava. In his gloved hand was an automatic pistol pointed towards Mikhailov. Without giving it a second thought, Mikhailov spun around and began running. He felt a bullet whizz by his ear. The voice behind him was more urgent. 'Halt!' It was accompanied by the sound of footsteps squelching through the leaves on the pathway.

Mikhailov reached the final bend that led to the car park entrance and ignored the direction sign that pointed to it. If he tried to use that route they would definitely catch him. In all probability, there was already an accomplice lurking around the corner. Instead, Mikhailov ran off the path and into the surrounding woods, hoping to skirt around the car park. He crossed a wooden bridge across a seasonal stream that was in full spate and picked up his pace, but he was out of breath. It was a matter of time before he would have to slow down.

He could hear voices coming after him. There were two, maybe more. 'You head to the car park and I'll be at the south end of the main road exit,' one of the voices said. Again, there was the sound of feet. *I need to keep going! Move! Move! Move!* His brain was processing information at double its usual speed. Who were these men? Was the SVR attempting to eliminate him? Why? Could it be Schmidt? Why?

Mikhailov suddenly fell. The ground beneath him was wet with dew and slippery as oil. He got to his feet only to realize that he had dropped a shoe in the stream that flowed beneath the bridge. He ignored it and hobbled on, grasping his left knee, which had been injured in the fall. If he ran eastwards he could possibly lose his pursuers because they seemed to be under the impression that his only objective was to get to the main road. He made a dash for the forest trail.

He yelped in pain as he ran. The thorns and pebbles on the forest track were not conducive to running barefoot. He could feel his heart beating wildly. Every thump was amplified several times over. He ignored the stabbing pain in his foot and continued to run, his heated breath fogging into little clouds before him. *If they get me, I'll be dead. Run! Hide! Do something.* He suddenly felt a hand on his left shoulder. He spun around. There was nothing behind him. He realized that a hanging vine from one of the branches up above had brushed his shoulder. He used his right hand to sweep it off and continued running.

He felt wetness on his foot, surprisingly inside the remaining shoe. He had assumed that the dampness was due to the sogginess of the soil, but it seemed to be increasing. He looked down and realized that blood was dripping down his leg and into his shoe. His injured left knee was bleeding profusely. He could hear the voices that were following him. He knew that he would have to find an alternative exit route. *Please don't let me die, God! I want to stay alive.*

He bunched up his pants near his knee to stem his bleeding while continuing to run. His breathing was laboured and his lungs were bursting from exhaustion. His muscles told him to stop running, but his brain ordered him to keep going. It was the only way that he would survive. He struggled through the dense growth of trees and bushes, the cold drying the sweat on his face as he plodded on.

He froze. It was a dog's bark. *Bastards!* They were using the guard dogs at the gatehouse to help in the search. The Rottweilers were barking viciously in the distance.

He tripped over the roots of a massive tree. He tried getting up but it was of no use. He had no strength left. He lay prostrate on the jungle floor, almost entirely paralyzed.

He counted the seconds in his mind as he waited for the human voices and canine barks to reach him.

His heart told him that it was over.

134

Vijay sat in Milesian's oak-panelled library on a rich leather chair. He was scanning through a hardback edition of a Sanskrit-to-English dictionary that the gorgeous Anjali had pointed him to.

He had tried looking for Mikhailov in the gym, the lab and even around the grounds, but he seemed to be missing. He had made his way to Mikhailov's flat, but the door had been locked. Vijay had avoided trying the handle for fear that the system would recognize his prints.

It was Daulat Singh who eventually provided the answer. Mikhailov had gone for the weekend to Dehradun. He had requested for salad, fruits, nuts and water to be packed for his car journey.

That's strange, thought Vijay. *He never mentioned anything to me.* He shrugged off the thought and turned his attention back to the dictionary. He was specifically interested in the word 'Yamaj' that had been scribbled by Schmidt on his office board.

Yabh … yabhanam … yagna … yaksha … yam … yama … yamaj! He'd eventually found it. *Yamaj. Conqueror of death.* Anyone who could defeat Yama, the god of death, was known as Yamaj. *But that makes no sense,* thought Vijay to himself. *The people on that board were those who succumbed to death, certainly not people who defeated it.*

Vijay closed the pages of the dictionary, leaving it on the desk that he had used. He left the library, thanking Anjali for her assistance. He then walked over to his flat, pulled off another segment of the clingwrap and placed it on his keyboard, waiting for alternative letters to emerge. He then went through the routine of activating Tor, CSpace and ZRTP.

He entered the chat room but Judith hadn't logged on as yet. He remained logged in and minimized the chat window, awaiting her online presence. He ignored the drugs, porn, counterfeit, guns and hacking tools that were always on offer on Tor. Instead, he focused on the milder links offered by The Hidden Wiki. There were thousands of groups that were discussing alternative medical procedures, cheap travel, conspiracy theories, Bitcoin scams and immigration.

It was then that he noticed a forum called 'Yamuna'. It was a site dedicated to illegal mining along the Yamuna bed. It was almost impossible to find anything innocent on the dark web. He quickly scanned through some comments in the forum.

One of the comments related to the origin of the river. It was mentioned that the river Yamuna had its origin in the Himalayas and was viewed as a goddess by Hindus. She was said to be the sister of Yama, the Hindu god of death. Praying to Yamuna was a way of ensuring the blessings of Yama and, consequently, a way of promoting one's longevity.

Vijay felt a chill run down his spine. What were the odds of finding this forum just as he was considering an arcane word's meaning? As per the forum, individuals who could defeat Yama were called Yamaj, but they were also called 'the twice-born', having conquered death once and having lived to see another day.

135

Vijay noticed that his minimized chat window was blinking. Judith was now online. He restored the window and told her about his visit to Schmidt's office, the snakes in the tank and the white board with names of world leaders. Judith congratulated him for his efforts. He felt a little like a schoolboy awaiting the approval of his teacher or parents. Judith asked him about the specifics of the people on the board, the layout on the whiteboard and Schmidt's scribbles on it.

'Thanks to your efforts we now know some of the other world leaders in the elimination queue,' she wrote. 'Sixteen squares, thirteen photographs, three blank squares. We have five unrecognized faces. Any idea who they could be?'

'No,' replied Vijay. 'I wish I could have taken a photograph of the board for you.'

Then Judith asked, 'What news of Mikhailov?'

'Not seen for a day,' replied Vijay. 'Apparently he has gone to Dehradun.'

'I have done some research for you,' said Judith. 'Mikhailov is almost blue-blood in the world of Russian science. His grandfather and father were both very accomplished scientists. Mikhailov is ex-Russian Academy of Sciences which means that he has to have an FSB or SVR connection. It's possible that Yuri Petrov is using him in some way.' Vijay remembered the beating he had received at the Russian's hands.

'Why?' asked Vijay. 'Aren't all of you on the same side?'

'It is possible that IG4 has been compromised,' said Judith. 'The spate of political differences between Russia and the West have had their repercussions. I advise you to be extra-cautious. If indeed IG4 has been compromised, it is also possible that your cover has been blown.'

And you say that so casually? Vijay's mind was in overdrive.

'Do you have a sense of the layout of what lies beyond the facility?' asked Judith, changing the topic.

'No,' replied Vijay. 'All I know is that we're surrounded by hundreds of acres of dense forests. When one takes the cable car to the facility, there are no views to be had—no windows.'

'Well,' said Judith, 'I have just accessed images from Flock-1.'

Flock-1 was a group of twenty-eight small CubeSats, satellites that continuously mapped the earth in high-resolution.

'And?' asked Vijay.

'The formation is pretty remarkable. Concentric circles of thick forestland enclosing several square plateaus. Each inner square plateau is at an altitude higher than the outer one that encloses it. Your facility is located in the innermost-square, but off-centre towards the west,' replied Judith. 'Did you notice anything else in Schmidt's office?'

'A closet,' replied Vijay. 'It had buttons, like an elevator. I didn't try pressing any of them, but I guess that it could be a means to access another level of Schmidt's office?'

'Possible,' said Judith. 'I think you need to go back there.'

'And do what?' asked Vijay, not relishing the thought of going back into the office. It had been a close shave the last time.

'See where that closet leads you,' replied Judith. 'Also check if the whiteboard has been updated.'

'And then?' asked Vijay.

'Get the hell out of there,' replied Judith.

136

Mikhailov trembled violently. It was bitterly cold and the bastards had shut off the heating on purpose. He struggled to loosen his ropes, but they were firmly tied around his wrists and ankles. In addition, a tourniquet had been wrapped tightly around his knee to stem the bleeding from his fall. It had been several hours since the dogs had found him in the woods that surrounded Milesian. He had been quickly bundled into the trunk of a car and driven to an area that he guessed was Yamuna Nagar, several hours away. By the time that his captors opened the trunk, he had been dehydrated and unconscious.

When he awoke, he found himself inside a deserted house with boarded windows. The lights had been switched off to ensure complete darkness in the holding room. A few minutes later they had thrown several buckets of ice-cold water on him and left him to freeze. None of his nightmares, including the one that plagued him about the blaze at the ashram, had ever been as terrifying as this living one.

The door opened and Cracker walked in. 'You have three minutes to tell me who you work for before we go to work on you,' he said. There was a monotonous quality to his voice, entirely devoid of emotion. Mikhailov trembled, both from fear and cold, but he kept his mouth shut. He didn't even make an attempt to scream. He desperately tried to think of Brahmananda and the immense peace that he felt in the presence of his guru. He forced himself to practise everything that he had learnt under him.

Suddenly he was picked up by four strong arms and made to lie on his back on a wooden chair. His legs and hands were pulled downwards and tied so that his body now resembled an archer's bow. 'This is called the German Chair,' said Cracker. 'Your upper and lower body will be pushed into unbendable positions and this will cause severe stress to your back, neck and spine. Expect permanent damage, maybe even death, if your spine cracks. Now, will you tell me why you went into Schmidt's office?'

Mikhailov knew where the question was coming from. He forced his thoughts towards the ashram and his beautiful life there. He timed his breath to calm himself down.

'Stubborn bastard,' said Cracker. 'Tighten the ropes further.'

The men pulled the ropes and Mikhailov felt a terrible sensation in his lower back. It was almost like his backbone was creaking before it would snap. He screamed, but his voice was not strong enough to carry.

'It's entirely your choice,' said Cracker. 'We know that you have been in touch with your handlers at SVR. You have also been having secret meetings with the new boy, Vijay. Do share the story with us. We would love to do him over too.'

Mikhailov ignored the pain. He ignored Cracker's words. Years of yoga and meditation had given him the strength to endure a lot. He blanked out the agony that he was feeling and compelled his mind into a meditative state.

137

Cracker's notebook computer sat on his desk for the hours that he was gone. During that time, a programme called Subterfuge had been running efficiently on it.

Subterfuge was a small but devastatingly effective credential-harvesting programme which exploited the vulnerability in a network's Address Resolution Protocol. Theoretically, it was possible to walk into a coffee shop, sit down at a table, plop down one's notebook, click the *start* button and watch the credentials roll in. The programme had been created in order to help security professionals expose the vulnerabilities of the network, but it could just as easily be used to surreptitiously harvest usernames and passwords on any connected network.

Once he was back in the security office, Cracker was able to hack into Vijay's Tor chat room using a proxy server. He quickly logged into his chat history using the harvested credentials. Over the next ten minutes, he took a data dump of Vijay's chats on an anonymous server.

The intercom on his desk buzzed.

'It's chemically activated once it comes into contact with the thermal energy of a keyboard,' said the voice. 'It employs an Advanced Encryption Standard along with random data generation and unique identifiers.'

Cracker had put one of his men on analyzing the clingwrap segment taken from Vijay's flat. It was just as he had suspected. Encryption film.

He called Schmidt once he had everything before him. 'It's all there,' he said. 'Just like you wanted it.'

'And?' asked Schmidt.

'You're not going to like it.'

138

The house in Yamuna Nagar was a simple brick-and-concrete structure that was in rather bad shape. The house desperately needed fresh plaster and a coat of paint, but it seemed that neither the owner nor the current residents were interested in doing it up. The windows had remained boarded up for many years.

One of the neighbours, a retired army brigadier, would pass by the house each morning while on his walk, and would shake his head in dismay at the neglect. It was such a pity that people who owned decent homes did not bother to take care of them, at least periodically.

The brigadier always passed by the house at an extra fast clip because of an open drain that flowed to one side of the house. He had personally complained about it to the civic authorities on several occasions, but no one had bothered to rectify the situation. All they did was pass the buck to yet another authority.

The brigadier held a handkerchief to his nose and mouth as he crossed the street. It was a health risk for residents whose homes were located next to the open drain, a breeding ground for mosquitoes. All this was to be tolerated by pathetic sods like him who went on paying their municipal taxes dutifully.

As the brigadier crossed into the next plot, an open garbage dump caught his eye. He had asked the disposal truck to clear the mess on several occasions—to no avail. He was gradually becoming immune to the crumbling civic infrastructure around him. But today, something was different about the dump. He stepped closer to look at it.

He felt faint as he looked at the body. It was red. Bloody red. And staring out at him almost sightlessly were a pair of eyes on a face that was crawling with insects.

139

Judith watched the video for the hundredth time. It had appeared on Mafraqi's propaganda website for just an hour before being taken down.

The video showed four men wearing orange boiler suits. Each of the men introduced themselves to the camera and provided their full names and a brief description of the roles that they had performed in Syria while fighting Mafraqi's forces. Then the men were chained around their wrists and ankles and suspended upside down from a steel frame that had been used for children's swings in happier times. The men were now positioned so that they were staring at the ground. Underneath each man was a patch of straw doused in fuel. Lines of fuel had been poured leading up to the straw heaps.

The video showed Mafraqi letting the flaming torch in his hand fall to the ground. The footage showed the fire burning up the line of fuel and snaking its way in slow motion towards the men who had been sprayed with accelerant. The men screamed and writhed wildly as they saw the fire approaching.

Mafraqi's cameramen had ensured that multiple angles had been filmed including close-ups of the terrified expressions on the faces of the men. It was just a few seconds before the haystacks were in flames. The men succumbed to an agonizing death as the accelerant on their clothes caught fire. Their shrieks were gut-wrenching.

The final scene showed the charred bodies of the men still suspended from the swing frame. Mafraqi walked up to them and used a sword to slice at and prod the bodies. Then he turned to the camera and said, 'And if you punish an enemy, O believers, punish with an equivalent of that with which you were harmed.'

It was impossible for most people to watch the video without getting repulsed in horror. But Judith was made of sterner stuff. She forced herself to watch it repeatedly so that every detail about Mafraqi was firmly etched in her memory.

140

Vijay was apprehensive about returning to Schmidt's office. He shuddered at the thought of the snakes inside that massive tank. The fact that he had got in and out safely the last time was certainly no assurance that all would go as smoothly yet another time. What if one of the cameras had already caught him breaking in and Schmidt was simply waiting for him to do it again? All that was needed was a single misstep and the cameras or biometric systems would get him, if not the snakes.

But there was another part of Vijay that was curious. What exactly was Schmidt up to? How was Minerva eliminating world leaders and what did the Milesian facility have to do with that? Who did Schmidt really work for? What about Mikhailov? What functions did those two buttons inside the closet in Schmidt's office perform? What lay in the forest regions that formed part of Milesian's acreage? Why had Mikhailov pointed him towards the Buddhist Kalachakra? Was it a clue of some sort? What were those vibrations that Mikhailov had detected? The questions kept swirling inside Vijay's head. Unfortunately there were no answers.

Vijay got up from his desk and paced the floor of his flat. He knew that if he didn't do it now, he might never have the courage to do it. He looked at his mobile phone. 10:32 p.m. He quickly pulled on his jacket and pocketed the thumbprint that he had kept among other specimen boxes so that it would not draw anyone's attention. As he had done on the previous occasion, he opened a browser window on his computer and activated Automator. He then stepped out, leaving the door ajar.

Vijay shivered as the icy Himalayan winds hit his face. He was thankful for the jacket, muffler and gloves. He measured each step according to the sweep of the cameras and, once he was near the office, he paused at one of Mikhailov's blind spots behind a hedge to determine if Schmidt was inside. He screwed up his eyes to look at the gap between the entrance door and the floor. He could not see any light streaming out. *This is it. Now move.*

He quickly walked up to the office door with a strange sense of calm, almost like a man who couldn't care about the consequence of his actions. He pulled out the microscope specimen slide that contained Schmidt's thumbprint and placed the piece of glass on the biometric scanning panel, half-expecting to be instantly surrounded by gun-toting guards. The lock buzzed gently and the door opened. He entered carefully, closing the door behind him. He waited for the lock to click shut. It seemed to take a little longer than on the last occasion. He shrugged it off, thinking he was mistaken.

Vijay's first instincts were right. It *had* taken longer. Unknown to Vijay, he had triggered a newly installed infrared beam on the pathway to the office door. If one did not deactivate the beam before opening the door, one could get into the office but not out. The mousetrap.

It was a deep deep deep abyss
They could get in at five
But like her passionate kiss
Would never get out alive

141

It was eleven-year-old Kenny's first Major League Baseball game and he was excited. He couldn't believe that he was actually in Fenway Park, sitting next to his father, watching one of the most anticipated games between the New York Yankees and the Boston Red Sox. Kenny had already made up his mind that his ambition in life was to become a big-league player one day.

He had not stopped talking through the car ride from their home to the stadium. When they finally made it through the turnstile and into their bleacher seats, Kenny realized that no foul ball was ever going to reach them. They were towards the third-base, that too in the upper deck near the last row. Not that it really mattered to Kenny. In fact, the position gave him a bird's eye view. Nonetheless, it would have been exciting to catch a ball in the stands, if one deigned to come the way of this wide-eyed, desperately waiting, eleven-year-old.

Kenny's dad, Henry Jones, was a CPA, and it wasn't too often that he could spare the time to take his son out. But then one of his clients had provided two tickets to the game and Henry had decided that he would make Kenny's day. And he had succeeded. Kenny was savouring every morsel of the Fenway Frank that was lathered in relish, brown mustard and onions as he waited for the game to start. It made the excruciating wait in traffic and the mad crowd at the turnstiles worthwhile.

Seated in the row behind them was a man wearing a Yankees jacket and cap. He seemed to be alone. He was licking a soft-serve ice cream but his gaze was not on the field. It was entirely focused on the back of Henry's neck.

His free hand, the one that was not holding the cone, was inside his jacket pocket, carefully caressing a syringe.

142

Vijay activated the flashlight of his phone and his gaze was drawn to the glass tank. Several slimy reptiles wriggled inside the tank. Vijay quickly looked away from it and turned his attention to the board.

The sixteen squares were still there but now there were fourteen photographs instead of thirteen. Eight faces were identifiable: the British Foreign Secretary, the German Chancellor, the American Attorney-General, the Japanese Prime Minister, the former French President, the Australian Foreign Minister, the Russian Minister of Internal Affairs and the Canadian Prime Minister. But now there were six unidentified photos.

Vijay realized that another document had been pinned to the board. It contained a bulleted list of names of a further eight people.

Prime Minister, Belgium
Premier of State Council, China
Minister of Home Affairs, India
Prime Minister, Singapore
Deputy President, South Africa
Secretary of State, Spain
Crown Prince, UAE
Chief Justice Supreme Court, Turkey

And then there was a further list of eight.

Vice-President of the Republic, Brazil
Minister of Education, South Korea
Minister of Defence, Argentina
President of Sardinia, Italy
Minister of Tourism, Indonesia
First Vice-President, European Commission, EU
Secretary-General, United Nations
President-elect, Mexico

Then it struck him. The process of killing would be an endless one. Each time that Minerva wiped out people from a list they would add more! Who could tell how many further lists were primed and ready?

He pulled his eyes away from the lists and made his way across the hardwood floor to the closet door that stood at a right angle to the whiteboard. He murmured a short prayer to himself as he opened the door, got into the five-by-five closet and examined the two buttons on the side panel. He tried both of them individually, but nothing happened. Vijay then closed the door from inside and tried the buttons again. He kept 'O' pressed for a few seconds, but there was no reaction. He then did the same for 'L' and was in for a shock.

The 'closet' started moving. Not vertically, like an elevator, but horizontally like a train. Vijay could feel the floor vibrate beneath his feet on tracks and gain speed along the way. The movement was accompanied by a rumbling sound, like that of rail carriage wheels.

The actual time spent by Vijay in the compartment was probably no more than five minutes, but it felt like thirty. When the unit shuddered to a halt, Vijay wondered whether he should press 'O' and retreat, but he knew that there was no going back. He had to find out where he was. He warily opened the door and stepped out.

143

Vijay realized he was inside an immense cave that was dimly lit by LED bulbs. Not a soul was in sight and it was eerily quiet. He felt a chill run down his spine. Along the walls were shelves containing books and rolls of parchment—miles and miles of them. It was the largest library he had ever seen. It was probably no less wondrous a sight than one that would have been observed in the great libraries of Alexandria or Nalanda. Vijay realized that 'O' and 'L' probably denoted 'Office' and 'Library'.

Vijay cautiously trudged along an elevated walkway that spanned the visible length of the cave, his footsteps reverberating in the emptiness. He walked down a flight of steps at the end and was greeted by a blast of cold air. He realized with amazement that he was now in deep forest.

A path had been cleared from the cave towards another destination and he walked along it, his heart beating at a significantly higher rate than usual. He looked behind him every few steps to check whether there was anyone trailing him, but there wasn't a soul in sight. Vijay felt slightly short of breath and realized that the path he was on was sloping and he was going uphill.

He stopped when he heard a loud humming sound. Vijay ducked for cover behind a tree but soon grasped that the sound emanated from a forest clearing on a mountain plateau just a few yards away. The sound was no ordinary hum. It was the universal sound, *Om*, being chanted by a group of people.

Having been brought up as a Hindu at the orphanage, Vijay was aware of the significance of *Om*. It was said to be the primordial humming sound that ostensibly accompanied the creation of the universe billions of years ago during the Big Bang. Chanting it was supposed to tune one's body's vibrations into that of the universe. He followed the sound to the top of the hill and crept up to the edge of the plateau on all fours. He paused behind a cluster of trees from where he attempted to observe what was happening.

It was an awesome sight. Around a hundred sages dressed in vermillion dhotis were seated in concentric circles, deep in meditation with their eyes closed. Other than the saffron cloth that hung from their shoulders, they remained bare-chested even in the biting cold of the forest. Weather obviously meant nothing to them. Each of them had a single rudraksha bead on a string around his neck, but smaller than the one Mikhailov had given to Vijay. At the centre of the concentric circles was a single rishi seated on a slightly elevated platform.

There was something alien, mysterious and magical about what Vijay saw before him, something that could be easily mistaken for a scene from an ancient druidic ritual across the world—maybe even Stonehenge—thousands of years ago. Each time the sages chanted *Om*, they were lifted a few inches off the ground in levitation. It was almost as if the normal rules of gravity had been suspended for all of them. Vijay pulled himself up on his feet, secure in the knowledge that he hadn't been seen and continued observing the sight from behind the tree.

Just as he was about to stretch his limbs, a hand covered his mouth and a hypodermic needle was jabbed into his neck.

144

Inside a darkened room of the Burj Al Arab Hotel in Dubai, passionate moans emerged from the bed. Under the starched sheets, a naked couple lay intertwined in a sweaty embrace. Their clothes lay puddled on the carpet, evidence that they had been stripped off in a hurry.

He was riding her aggressively, his skin bathed in a film of sweat. She matched his thrusts in tandem. She could feel his climax approaching and pulled him deeper inside her and kissed him wantonly, twining her tongue around his. It was the final trigger. He grunted as waves of ecstasy washed through his body. There had been no real intimacy. And he had not even felt the need to satisfy her. This was about him and him alone.

Sergei Lavrov pulled himself off the high-priced escort and pulled on his boxer shorts. He walked to the desk, picked up his pack of cigarettes and lit one. He inhaled deeply as he watched the woman get out of bed and head into the shower that was visible from the bedroom through a glass wall. She was Dubai's highest priced escort and was not available to just anyone. *She's worth every penny,* thought Lavrov.

The escort quickly dried herself and put on her clothes. She brushed her hair and applied a touch of makeup, checking herself in the mirror. She walked over to Sergei and pecked him on the cheek. 'This was fun, baby,' she purred as she playfully groped him. 'Let's do it again, sometime.' She turned around to walk out of the room when she heard the thud. She spun around to see Lavrov lying on the floor, clutching his arm. He screamed, as if he was in agony.

The woman cursed under her breath. This was the last thing she needed. Calling the medics would mean that she would be in all the papers the next day. In addition, the cops would probably interrogate her. After all, Lavrov wasn't just anybody. He was the Russian Minister of Internal Affairs. In her cheekier moments she had often teased him about his responsibility, *internal affairs,* and given a dirty little laugh.

She sighed as she picked up the desk phone to call reception. It was going to be a long night.

145

Vijay awoke from deep slumber, groggy and disoriented. He wanted to look at his watch but realized that he could not move his arms. He was spread-eagled on a surgery table with his hands and feet held to the four corners by stirrups. Above him was a harsh white light and, next to that, an air circulation fan. The room was windowless but temperature-controlled. Everything was white. White walls, white light, white sheets. *Where am I?* he wondered. *Is this just a nightmare?*

Vijay struggled with his thoughts. His mind was foggy. What had happened to him? His brain was flashing disconnected visions of Sujatha, the IG4 warehouse that he had been taken to, the snake tank, his IIT classroom, the white board with photos in Schmidt's office, the orphanage at which he had spent his childhood and his laboratory at Milesian Labs. He screwed up his face as he struggled to remember what had happened to him.

And then, his immediate memories came flooding back. He had been at the edge of the plateau observing the rishis when someone had overpowered him with a jab to the neck. Vijay continued staring like a zombie into the harsh light above him. The light was blocked momentarily by a figure that bent over him to look into his face. *Schmidt!*

As usual, Schmidt's face conveyed no expression. 'You have been a naughty boy, Mr Sundaram,' he said after what seemed like an eternity. 'And in this facility, naughty boys are always punished.'

A sense of dread washed over Vijay. This was probably the end. His eyes welled up. The last thing that he wanted was for Schmidt to see his tears, but it was too late. A tear rolled down the side of his face from his right eye.

'Hush little baby, don't you cry, Papa's gonna sing you a lullaby,' sang Schmidt mockingly as he left the room. His mocking turned out to be a godsend. Vijay felt anger bubbling up inside him and his tears miraculously disappeared. All that he now felt was hate. He simply needed a plan to leverage his hate effectively.

He continued staring at the ceiling.

146

Vijay was incapable of moving because of the stirrups that held his limbs down. But it wasn't as though he was struggling. In fact, he was exceptionally still, thinking hard. It was almost as though he was meditating. His gaze was entirely on the circulating blades of the fan on the ceiling.

It was an ordinary two-blade fan with a diameter of around eighteen inches. The two anodized blades were enclosed in a circular stainless steel wire frame. The fan had been set on what was probably the lowest speed and Vijay was almost hypnotized by the two blades moving in tandem.

If one blade pointed to twelve on an imagined clock face, the other would necessarily have to point to six, one hundred and eighty degrees away. And if one pointed to three, the other had to point to nine. The position of one blade was correlated to the other.

And that childish observation prompted a profound moment of truth.

Vijay recalled the whiteboard that he had seen in Schmidt's office. The recognizable faces on that whiteboard had been the British Foreign Secretary, the German Chancellor, the American Attorney-General, the Japanese Prime Minister, the former French President, the Australian Foreign Minister, the Russian Minister of Internal Affairs and the Canadian Prime Minister. Of these eight people, six were already dead, possibly more that he didn't know of.

But on that board was another set of photographs—of six entirely unknown people. Why were those unknown faces on the board? And why was each of those unknown faces paired with a dead leader?

Mikhailov's work at Milesian had involved duality—waves and particles. Vijay's mission had been to identify entangled planets. There were others in Milesian Labs who had been working on entangled weather systems, entangled atoms, entangled thoughts and entangled forces. But there was a whole range of things between thoughts and planets.

What if entanglement not only applies to quantum particles, thoughts, planets and weather systems but also to humans? thought Vijay. *What if every human has an entangled human somewhere else on the planet?*

Yamaj meant conqueror of death or twice-born. But, by extension, wouldn't that also apply to twins? *Those given life twice?* What if the word 'Yamaj' was actually referring to quantum twins in Schmidt's world?

His thoughts were interrupted by Schmidt, who walked in with a syringe in his hand. *What is he planning to do to me?* wondered Vijay. A feeling from deep within told him that he had very little time left. So he attempted to delay the inevitable through the only tool available to him. Conversation.

'If identifying quantum twins, or Yamaj, was always your primary objective, then why did you waste time with other research areas?' asked Vijay weakly.

Schmidt stopped in his tracks. Then he recovered smartly. 'From the time that I interviewed you, I knew that you were clever,' replied Schmidt. 'You should realize, though, that entanglement is to be found everywhere. What the world calls telepathy or intuition is simply entangled thoughts; telekinesis is entangled force fields; déjà vu is entangled spacetime. Our research at Milesian has been focused on all types of entanglement, not just quantum entanglement, which is entanglement at the sub-atomic level.'

He looked at the syringe to ensure that the quantity of fluid inside was sufficient.

'Our aim at Milesian is to find a method by which entangled systems may be identified,' he said, turning his gaze from the syringe to Vijay. 'The broad principles can then be used for finding the entangled twin of anything, including specific humans.'

147

And it's another day and it's time for me, Masoud, to jot down my thoughts. Today I plan to make note of some startling numbers that have come my way.

I am convinced that the world's liberals are to blame for the rise of conservatives. Liberals were meant to uphold values such as freedom of speech, gender equality, free choice in worship and freedom of sexual orientation. But they looked the other way when it came to Islamic societies that stoned and genitally mutilated their women, killed homosexuals, permitted wife beating, enforced the hijab, allowed marriage of minor girls, killed apostates and instituted laws against blasphemy. It was these double standards of liberals that made ordinary people look for solutions from the right.

Yesterday I had a chance to see the Pew Research report—the results of the survey carried out in thirty-nine countries with substantial Muslim populations. I am worried to see that ordinary Muslims hold exceptionally conservative views. For example, 79 per cent of Muslims in countries such as Afghanistan, Egypt and Jordan believe that Muslims who abandon the faith should be executed. And 39 per cent of Muslims across all countries believe that honour killings can be justified in instances where women have had premarital or extramarital sex.

Until I saw this report, I was unaware that 42 per cent of French Muslims, 35 per cent of British Muslims and 26 per cent of American Muslims believe that suicide bombings against non-Muslims can be justified. Scariest of all, 53 per cent of those surveyed believe that Sharia, or Islamic law, should be the law in their countries. Most of these people were thus in favour of whipping, stoning and chopping off of hands.

Looking at the picture graphically, if we see the world's Muslims as four concentric circles, one within the other, the innermost is the Jihadi circle. These are people who will not think twice about killing innocents to further their aims.

The circle beyond Jihadists are the Islamists. This group will not use violence but are fanatically devoted to the idea of a caliphate and Sharia. They will cause political unrest, and even revolt to further their aims.

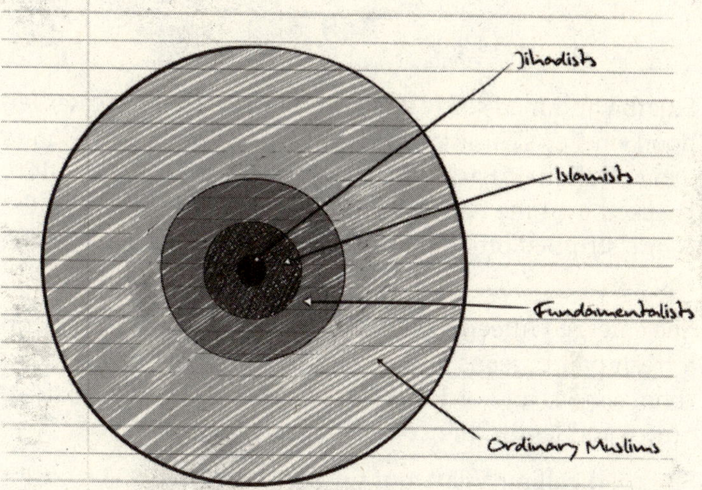

Beyond that are the fundamentalists. They're not interested in overthrowing regimes but they hold views that are deeply disturbing. Notions about blocking freedom of worship, killing apostates and blasphemers, punishing homosexuality, killing in the name of honour and the like.

The outermost circle is the ordinary Muslim who simply sees Islam as a personal path to God and wants to live his life peacefully. They constitute the vast majority. Unfortunately, they tend to be silent.

The problem is that the two inner circles constitute terrifyingly large numbers in absolute terms. There are 1.6 billion Muslims in the world. If we conservatively estimate these two groups at even 10 per cent, that's 160 million Muslims who are either Jihadists or Islamists.

And that number is growing because Islam is growing the fastest among any of the world religions. By 2070, Muslims will surpass Christians around the world in sheer numerical strength. It's necessary to consider the implications of that change.

Karl Marx said that religion is the opium of the people. I'm wondering whether the world can afford to continue permitting people to consume drugs.

148

Sujatha hummed softly as she showered. The hot water felt good on her skin after several days without it at Nanda Devi National Park. She had returned to Dehradun, checked in at the Hotel Pacific, dumped her luggage in the room, stripped off her mucky clothes and stepped into the shower.

She emerged fifteen minutes later, dried herself and put on a fresh pair of jeans and a cotton t-shirt. She then phoned room service and ordered *khichdi,* a steaming hot porridge of rice and lentils, her comfort food.

She tried calling Vijay, but his phone seemed to be out of network range. She sighed, settled herself on the bed and switched on the television. The news was about all the usual stuff. Terror attacks, provocative speeches, deaths of the Australian Foreign Minister and the Russian Minister of Internal Affairs. She switched off the television when she heard the knock on her door accompanied by the words 'room service'.

The waiter brought in a tray and placed it on the coffee table in front of the small lounger that had been provided in one corner of the room. Sujatha thanked the waiter and signed the room service bill, adding a tip for the fact that the khichdi had arrived at the right temperature.

She started to hand over the leather folder containing the signed bill and the tip when she became aware that the waiter was standing directly behind her. The folder fell from her hands as she tried moving away, but it was too late. She was unable to scream because his hand was firmly clamped over her mouth.

In the room next door, the Russian watched the proceedings through a small camera built into the salt shaker on the room service tray.

149

'Everything has a twin in the universe, including humans. And we at Milesian Labs will soon have cutting-edge technology to find such twins,' said Schmidt.

'But that's impossible,' argued Vijay. 'Quantum entanglement is still being discussed at a theoretical level. Even today, it is impossible to actually identify and separate entangled quantum particles. How can Milesian identify the quantum twin of a given person from among the world's population of 7.4 billion? It would be like looking for a needle in a massive haystack!'

Schmidt smiled. He placed the syringe on a rollaway table next to the bed.

'What exactly happens when you sleep?' he asked. 'Do you simply wander off into an altered state of consciousness? Or is it your brain and body recharging from a universal source of energy?'

'Both are possibilities,' replied Vijay carefully.

'But what if wakefulness and sleep are two independent *conscious* states?' asked Schmidt. 'What if you are actually living another life when you sleep? What if your dreams are simply shadows created by that parallel life? What if the life that you think you are living is someone else's dream?'

Vijay's head was reeling. The tranquilizer used on him had given him a splitting headache and the information overload from Schmidt wasn't helping.

'Let me take you into the realm of possibilities,' said Schmidt. 'Maybe a Chinese factory worker is also an American nightclub singer. Maybe a primary schoolteacher in India is a politician in Westminster when she drifts off to sleep. In effect, it is possible that every human being on earth shares consciousness with someone else—his or her quantum twin! Let me illustrate.'

With an air of pride, Schmidt pressed a remote control unit and an LED monitor descended from the ceiling and angled itself for Vijay's viewing from his horizontal position. *Keep boasting*, thought Vijay. *Every word that you utter is a few more seconds that I live.*

On the screen was an image of two light bulbs connected to a common source of power with a flip switch. 'Let's imagine that the lives of an Indian schoolteacher and a British politician are represented by two light bulbs connected to a common source of power. The power source represents consciousness,' said Schmidt. On the slide, the bulb to the left was illuminated and the one on the right was dark.

'Flip the switch to the left and the schoolteacher is conscious, with the politician in sleep mode,' said Schmidt. He changed the slide.

Now, the bulb to the right was shining bright and the one on the left was off. 'Flip the switch to the right and the politician is up and awake, with the schoolteacher having fallen into sleep mode,' continued Schmidt smugly. 'In effect, if one is awake, the other is asleep, and vice-versa. As with entangled quantum particles, if you change a given characteristic of one, you will change the quantum characteristic of the other. Kill one and the other will also die. In fact, killing the quantum twin is the cleanest way to kill high-powered leaders—who are always surrounded by several layers of high security—without leaving the slightest trace!'

150

'Why are you sharing this information with me?' asked Vijay.

'Because you will not live to tell anyone,' said Schmidt.

Vijay's brain was furiously attempting to process the information as quickly as it could. *Was it really possible that every human being had a quantum twin?*

Common sense indicated that the world was composed of dualities—energy that could be waves or particles, humans that could be male or female, magnetic fields that could be north or south, temperature that could be hot or cold, directions that could be east or west, sensations that could be pleasure or pain ... the list was endless. What one experienced in the world was simply the flow of energy between dualities, in the manner that electricity was the flow of current from one pole to another.

The very concept of Shiva and Shakti or the Chinese concept of Yin and Yang played on the same theme. It was the act of observing one extreme that created its opposite. He remembered the words of Lao Tzu. *When all in the world understand beauty to be beautiful, then ugliness exists; when all understand goodness to be good, then evil exists.*

His mind wandered back to Sujatha's apartment. On the side table by her sofa stood a statue of Ardhanarishvara, a figure that depicted Shiva and Shakti combined as one: half male, half female.

Equally quickly, his brain switched to another image from Zen. Yin and Yang were shown as interlocking parts of a single circle.

Yamaj are simply two parts of a whole. That applies to everyone and everything! The yang, having reached its maximum, contracts in favour of the yin; the yin, having reached its maximum, contracts in favour of the yang. The man who walks eastwards eventually reaches the west, and vice-versa.

But there was something that was nagging him. What had Schmidt said? *And we at Milesian Labs will soon have cutting-edge technology to find such twins.* That seemed to imply that the technology was still not fully developed. Vijay forced himself to focus.

'I could help you develop the technology,' he blurted out. 'Why kill me? I am probably your best shot at getting this done.'

Schmidt burst out laughing. Vijay had never seen him laugh before. He looked positively sinister when he bared his teeth.

'You really think that I need *you* for this project?' he asked incredulously once his laughter had subsided.

Vijay was genuinely puzzled. 'Isn't that why you asked me to join Milesian?' he asked.

'You think too highly of yourself,' countered Schmidt. 'Your research is superficial at best. Milesian Labs is way ahead along the learning curve.'

'Then why did you offer me this job in the first place?' asked Vijay.

Schmidt peered into Vijay's eyes. 'Because it was the only way that I could bring you here to have you killed.'

Vijay felt his head spin. *The job offer had been a trap, not an assignment.*

'Let me introduce you to a colleague of mine,' said Schmidt. 'It's better that someone else explains your predicament to you.' Vijay looked around the room from his confined position on the bed but could not see anyone else.

And then he saw a shadow towards the far wall move. There was clicking of shoes on the floor and a figure emerged. The figure walked over to the table and peered into Vijay's face, obstructing the overhead light.

Vijay squinted. Then he gasped when he realized who it was.

151

Judith Frost had been born as the only child of John and Elaine Baker in Seymour, Indiana. The city was famously known as the 'Crossroad of America' because the north-south and east-west railroads had intersected in downtown Seymour from the mid-1800s. John Baker owned a convenience store and his wife helped him out when she wasn't busy looking after their daughter and their home. It was simple middle-class living, but Judith was never allowed to want for anything. Her parents showered their love and attention on her.

Judith attended Seymour High School. Her buddy was Harvey Walsh with whom she could talk about almost everything. If Harvey had any romantic inclinations towards Judith, he kept them to himself. The two remained the best of friends even after graduating from Seymour High and going their separate ways. Harvey dived into the world of physics, eventually becoming the moving force behind LIGO.

Seymour High was also the place that Judith met her future husband, Ashton Frost. Ashton was a football player and was hoping to be awarded an NCAA football scholarship at Ohio State, but that didn't quite pan out. His grandfather, an army veteran, suggested West Point instead. Playing football for West Point was different from what it would have been like at a regular university playing Division One. For one thing, the stress of cadet life at the US Military Academy was not suited to most people. Graduation from West Point also meant a commitment to minimum five years of US Army service with very little possibility of being granted a reprieve to play in the NFL. But it had been Ashton's only option. Judith had followed him to West Point by accepting an offer of admission to Mount Saint Mary College that was located only a few minutes away. She married him the day that he graduated.

Upon graduation, Ashton underwent the Special Forces Assessment and Selection Course. He pushed himself to the very limit to complete the two-mile run in less than twelve minutes and the one hundred push-ups in less than two minutes. He ended up very close to the perfect assessment score of 300 and sailed into the United States Army Special Forces—also known as the Green Berets. The Green Berets were forces entrusted with five key tasks: unconventional warfare, foreign internal defence, special reconnaissance, direct action and counter-terrorism.

Judith, in the meantime, became fluent in several languages, particularly Arabic and Spanish. She was headhunted by the CIA on account of her proficiency during a college fair. She underwent a battery of interviews, tests, polygraph exams and medical routines, besides being subjected to an incredibly exhaustive background investigation. She spent four months in the Career Analyst Program, receiving training in analytic tools and methods. She then spent part of her first two years serving a tour in the 24/7 Operations Centre of the agency before beginning her stint as a Counter-terrorism Analyst.

Judith was blissfully unaware that her life would dramatically change as a result of the conflict in Syria.

152

The withdrawal of American forces from Iraq created a vacuum in the power structure of the country. A new and terrible radical force emerged from that vacuum, taking over vast swathes of land on both sides of the Iraq–Syria border. The Green Berets—including Ashton—were sent in to operate as secret teams in northeast Syria. But that was easier said than done. They not only had to neutralize the Jihadi fighters of Mafraqi but also the forces of the overthrown regime. It was complicated, to say the least.

And then one day Judith's life came crashing down when she received word that Ashton had been captured by Mafraqi and burnt alive. Her superiors had tried to keep the gory details away from her; instead, they had provided her with a sanitized version of his death. But Mafraqi's team had posted a video a few days later. It showed Ashton and three other men, all of them suspended from their ankles and wrists with chains. The video was almost immediately taken down by intelligence agencies, but it was too late. Judith saw Ashton scream for his life as the flames reached him; and she also saw Mafraqi use his sword to carve and slash Ashton's charred body like he were a spit roast. She saved the video and did not share what she had seen with any of her colleagues.

That day she was convinced that the world had not understood the frightening implications of radical Islamist terror. In fact, not only was it about Islamism but also about the violent verses in the Qur'an. Western forces would continue gunning down terrorists, but how would they ever liquidate the ideology that spawned them? What was she to do?

Then one day she was told that she would be part of IG4, owing to her deep understanding of the Middle East. The agency was concerned that an all-out war between Muslims and non-Muslims could actually happen. Samuel Huntington's prophecies could possibly come true.

At that moment, Judith knew exactly what she had to do: *She would need to ensure that IG4 failed.*

She would have to make certain that the world *did* descend into an outright conflict with Islam. Sometimes, the only solutions that worked were radical ones. But she knew that she would have to play a double game—maintaining a liberal veneer to all outward appearances.

And then Williams contacted her on behalf of Minerva and everything fell into place.

153

'You?' asked Vijay weakly, as the realization sank in that Judith had played him.

'My apologies, Vijay,' she said. 'It's nothing personal.'

'But I never even wanted to be part of this,' he said. 'IG4 forced me into this assignment. Why punish me for that? Why kill me for my work in the field of quantum entanglement?'

'Is that what you think?' asked Judith. 'That we would kill you for your research?'

Vijay stayed quiet. His brain was working furiously, attempting to fit disparate pieces of the jigsaw puzzle inside his head.

Judith took the slide advancer from Schmidt. On the LED screen she brought up a slide that showed photographs of the eight world leaders that Vijay had seen on Schmidt's office wall. She then started clicking the remote to bring up additional photographs of the unrecognized faces next to the recognized ones.

Next to the Japanese Prime Minister's photograph appeared the photo of a Chinese man. 'His name was Liu Zhou,' said Judith. 'He was killed by us in Beijing using a poison-tipped umbrella outside an Alcoholics Anonymous meeting. He was the Yamaj—the quantum twin—of the Japanese PM.'

She clicked the remote. 'This was Maria Santos, a resident of Rio de Janiero. She was recently eliminated by us because she was the quantum twin of Francois Moreau, the left-centrist Presidential candidate of France.'

Next appeared the photograph of a Hindu priest. He was dressed in an orange robe, a red shawl over his shoulders. On his head was a vermillion mark and around his neck were chunky beads. 'His name was Pandit Ramashastry,' said Judith. 'He was one of the seniormost priests at the Karni Mata temple. We killed him because he was the Yamaj of the Australian Minister for Foreign Affairs.'

Another face appeared. 'This used to be Henry Jones, a CPA and resident of Boston,' explained Judith. 'He was killed in Fenway Park because he was the Yamaj of the Russian Minister of Internal Affairs.'

Vijay noticed that there were sixteen placeholders in the slide. Eight for world leaders. Another eight for their quantum twins. Seven of the eight world leaders were dead. One remained.

'Only one target remains before we move on to the next list,' said Judith. 'Jean Belanger, the Prime Minister of Canada.'

She clicked the slide advancer. Next to Jean Belanger's face appeared a photograph of Vijay.

'Unfortunately, *you* are the Yamaj of Jean Belanger,' said Judith. 'He is one of the very last liberal do-gooders left on our primary list. Once you die, he will also die. Do you now see why it's nothing personal? And do you understand why I needed to get you here?'

154

What an utter fool he had been to allow himself to be led into such a trap, Vijay cursed himself. But there was something that was nagging Vijay. It was Schmidt's earlier statement. *And we at Milesian Labs will soon have cutting-edge technology to find such twins.* Milesian did not yet have the technology! So how were they zeroing in on so many Yamaj twins?

'If you do not have the technology to identify quantum twins, how do you know that I am the quantum twin of Jean Belanger?' asked Vijay. 'How did you identify the quantum twins of the previously eliminated world leaders?'

'Have you heard the phrase *perception is more important than reality*?' asked Schmidt. Vijay knew that it was a rhetorical question.

'Hindu and Buddhist philosophy have always held that what we routinely experience in our everyday lives is an illusion,' continued Schmidt. 'Our lives are the equivalent of a person looking at a map and claiming to know the underlying terrain. The map is not reality. The underlying terrain is. And that can only be understood by experiencing it, travelling through it, walking on it. Similarly, the underlying reality of the universe can only be understood through deep meditation. Perception! When the rational mind is quietened, the intuitive mind awakes.'

Vijay remembered the lectures that he had delivered to his students at IIT Delhi on the Vedanta. He cursed himself for not listening to his own preaching. He rued the fact that he had not fully appreciated what Mikhailov had been trying to tell him.

'Perception is simply the ability to enter a deep state where one can experience the reality of the universe, much in the way that a person can bring lost memories to the fore through hypnosis,' said Schmidt. 'Indian sages knew that there is no *self* and that we live in an ocean of connected energy and consciousness. Bohr, Heisenberg and Schrödinger—the very pioneers of quantum theory—regularly read Vedic texts. In fact, Heisenberg even stated that quantum theory would not seem ridiculous to people who had read Vedanta.'

'So those sages that I saw in the forest are actually meditating for you?' asked Vijay in disbelief.

'Minerva realized that it would be several years before science would find a way to identify quantum twins but knew that Indian sages would be able to do it immediately,' replied Schmidt. 'That was the reason for creating the Milesian research facility here in Uttarakhand, in the forests where the sages of Roopkund had their stronghold. The scientists at the lab would continue working towards building a technology that would help identify Yamaj sometime in the future, while the rishis in the forest would help achieve the immediate task at hand—much in the way they had discovered the speed of light without any instruments.'

'I still do not understand,' said Vijay. 'You could have killed me anywhere, just like the countless others you have eliminated. Why did you need to hire me and bring me here?'

'Because it was the only way that we could find out how far along you were in your quest to identify quantum behaviour beyond the quantum,' replied Schmidt. 'We needed to know whether you were ahead of or behind us; whether there was any finding that could add value to what we had discovered. As it turns out, you are years behind us.'

Vijay struggled on the hospital bed, but the stirrups held him down firmly. Schmidt picked up the syringe from the rollaway table and brought it near Vijay's right arm. He used isopropyl alcohol to disinfect an area on his arm, like all doctors do before administering a shot. 'After all, we would not like our little boy to get an infection,' he commented caustically.

Judith laughed as Schmidt administered the injection to Vijay.

'What are you injecting me with?' asked Vijay, half-knowing the answer.

'You saw those snakes in my office?' asked Schmidt. 'I extract their venom quite regularly. The venom has been chemically reengineered so that the physical symptoms and evidence disappear by the time of death. It kills but leaves no toxicity that may be analyzed. Enjoy the ride,' he said as Vijay began his descent into darkness.

155

Vijay recalled the fundamentals of quantum entanglement as he began his downward spiral. *If one were to measure the characteristics of one of the entangled particles, say velocity of rotation, and then measure the other particle using the same criteria, one would find that the results of the two measurements would be identical, but the particles would be spinning in opposite directions.*

He then screamed in agony. He desperately wanted to clutch his right arm, the one in which the shot had been administered. But his restraints prevented any movement. His arm had begun to swell and blisters were developing on it. He coughed. He could taste blood in his sputum.

Some eight thousand miles away in America, Jean Belanger, the Prime Minister of Canada, clutched his left arm, which was severely swollen and blistered. He coughed. There was blood in his sputum.

At that moment there was a rattle of gunfire from outside. Schmidt's expression turned malevolent. He yelled at Cracker and his team who were stationed just beyond the door. 'Secure the premises,' he shouted. 'And shoot at sight any scum that may have intruded!'

There was more gunfire as the left side of Vijay's face began to swell up. The swelling was so severe that he was unable to open his left eye. In his semi-conscious state, he retched.

Those very eight thousand miles away in America, the right side of Jean Belanger's face ballooned. The swelling affected his right eye, which was tightly shut. He puked.

Schmidt and Judith whipped out their weapons, ready to kill anyone who came inside. Schmidt called out to Cracker, but there was no response. He then called out to Cracker's deputy.

This time there was a response, but not the sort that Schmidt expected.

156

Cracker's deputy walked in with his hands raised above his head.

Behind him followed three figures wearing scuba suits, swimming fins and facemasks. One of them had a semi-automatic pressed against the deputy's back.

'One wrong move and I shoot,' said one of the frogmen. Judith found the voice familiar. It was the accent in particular that caught her attention.

The frogmen ripped off their masks and Judith saw the face of the person who had spoken. Petrov! He was accompanied by an assistant, his local SVR operative.

Following the two of them was yet another familiar face, that of a woman.

Sujatha!

157

In her room at the Hotel Pacific in Dehradun, Sujatha had been terrified when the room service waiter had clamped his hand over her mouth. She had struggled to free herself, even attempting to bite his hand. And then the waiter had whispered into her ear. 'We need your help to save Vijay's life. Please calm down.'

The waiter, who was actually Petrov's aide, removed his hand and put both his hands up in the air to make Sujatha realize that he had no ulterior motive. Then the room door opened and Petrov walked in.

He used a handheld RF signal detector to sweep the room and pulled out two eavesdropping bugs. He placed a finger on his lips to indicate to Sujatha that she needed to remain quiet, and switched on an audio jammer. It would create a white noise mask that would cover their conversation.

'My name is Yuri Petrov, Ms Iyer,' he said. 'I'm terribly sorry for accosting you in this manner. The problem is that you are being watched by enemies of Vijay. The only way to make contact without rousing suspicion was by meeting you in your room. My apologies for scaring you, but we're here for you and for Vijay Sundaram. He is in terrible danger and I need your help.'

Sujatha remained dazed. The story that Petrov went on to tell her sounded as though it was from the pages of a spy thriller. He told her that Milesian was a laboratory for killing world leaders with the aim of accelerating a world conflict with Muslims; that a shadowy group called Minerva was pulling the strings; that Vijay had been ostensibly sent there as a plant; that all his moves were being monitored by IG4, a group of intelligence operatives from various countries.

She wasn't even sure what to believe. Then Petrov showed her photographs of Vijay in the warehouse where the IG4 operatives had met him and she began understanding that Petrov was telling her the truth.

'Why didn't you simply tell him to get the hell out?' she demanded, close to tears. 'After all, you are the ones who endangered his life by putting him there in the first place.'

'IG4 has been compromised,' replied Petrov. 'Our American friend, Judith Frost, is secretly helping Minerva achieve its aims. I had no idea of this until very recently. This was the reason that I placed you under surveillance. It was to ensure that I could meet you the moment that you were back.'

'What do you want from me?' asked Sujatha.

'We are planning to infiltrate the Milesian facility today,' said Petrov. 'Vijay doesn't trust me. I think it's because I was given the job of beating him up for his cover. Judith's idea—rather clever now that I think of it. It is also possible that she has been arousing suspicions in his mind about me. Your presence there would ensure that he cooperates with me.'

Sujatha nodded. She recalled how Vijay had been battered and how he had lied to her about being mugged.

'The facility is near Kalimath and is surrounded by dense jungles,' continued Petrov. 'It is almost impossible for unauthorized personnel to reach the area which is at a substantial altitude and accessed only by cable car. Almost every inch is under surveillance, and guards and dogs patrol the key access points 24/7. It is even equipped with radar to prevent choppers and aircrafts from launching aerial attacks.'

'Then how do you expect us to go in?' asked Sujatha.

'Deep in the forest is a water reservoir,' Petrov said. 'This hilltop reservoir is fed by a natural lake in the surrounding plains. It is a massive feat of engineering by which water is transported from a lower altitude to a higher one. This is done using vacuum technology. A massive supply pipe runs from the lake to the reservoir at the top of the hill. We will dive into the lake wearing scuba suits and swim into the mouth of the supply pipe. We will be effortlessly sucked through the pipe and into the reservoir.'

Sujatha gulped. She was terrified of swimming. All her past escapades flashed in her head. The time when Vijay had saved her. The time when she had been almost compelled to swim the perimeter of a lake. But what was being proposed now was far worse.

'Trust me,' said Petrov. 'I will personally ensure that you—and Vijay—are safe.'

The plan seemed ridiculous to Sujatha. Her fear of swimming apart, this wasn't like swimming in a pool. It involved diving into a freezing cold lake and then swimming through a pipe into a reservoir.

It was a mad plan, but Petrov slowly convinced her that it would work.

158

Petrov, his SVR aide and Sujatha trekked through the forest before reaching the lake. It was dark and full of foreboding, surrounded as it was by thick birch and fir trees. The freezing temperature coupled with complete darkness sent a shiver down Sujatha's spine. She hated what she had gotten herself into. The only reason that she was there was Vijay.

'We don't have too much time,' said Petrov to her. 'If you were an ordinary student, your instructor would take you through safety steps, diving gear and hand signals. The first dive should have been at a controlled site such as a pool. Unfortunately, we do not have that luxury. Put on this wet suit and I will take you through the fundamentals quickly.'

Sujatha remembered her childhood spent sitting on the embankment of the lake. Visions of her drowning and Vijay saving her flashed in her mind. *I have to save Vijay! I owe it to him.*

Before she knew it, she was plunging into the frigid water with her buoyancy compensator inflated and regulator in hand. She started breathing through a scuba regulator for the very first time in her life. It felt odd breathing through her mouth under water, knowing that her life depended on the tank that was strapped to her back. What was even more disconcerting was the bubbling sound of her exhalation and the whoosh as she inhaled. People were so wrong when they claimed that diving was quiet and peaceful. Underwater sounds were amazingly loud.

Her scuba mask had cut off her peripheral vision. That felt strange too. *I'm beneath the surface of a frigging lake!* Petrov signalled for her to move. He had a watertight bag strapped around his waist. Weapons. Sujatha felt disoriented. Light behaved differently in the water. Everything seemed closer than it actually was. And the feeling of weightlessness was quite remarkable.

The team used deliberate underwater movements to make their way to the opening of the pipe. She could feel the sucking action of the pipe, almost like the nozzle of a vacuum cleaner. She saw Petrov disappear. She followed and Petrov's aide brought up the rear.

Before she knew it, she was sucked inside. That was when fear struck. The pipe was around three feet in diameter and Sujatha experienced instant claustrophobia. But she knew that she had no alternative.

There was no turning back.

159

'Your security detail is dead, including the famous Cracker,' said Petrov to Schmidt. 'This one is the only survivor,' he said, pointing to the man who was being held by them at gunpoint.

Cracker's deputy used a quick scissor move to knock out the gun that was pointed at him. Less than a second later, Petrov fired his GSh-18, the sound reverberating inside the room. Cracker's deputy fell to the floor, blood spreading outwards from his shoulder.

Petrov's aide knelt down to retrieve the gun that he had lost.

'Bastard,' cried Schmidt, unable to accept the turn of events. Realizing that he had an opening, Schmidt took aim at Petrov.

It was a bad move. Petrov's aide took a clean shot from his kneeling position. The shot took out Schmidt's eye, spraying lumpy brain matter on the pristine white wall behind him.

Almost simultaneously, Petrov felt the air above his head shudder as Judith released a wild shot from her Glock 17. He waited for less than a second before retaliating with a shot from a two-handed grip. Judith dropped to the floor, her hands at her throat, blood spurting through her fingers.

All of a sudden, Cracker's deputy rose like a phoenix from the ground, spun around and charged at Petrov. But Petrov side-stepped, leaned, and kicked him in the jaw, then planted his foot on his chest, almost paralyzing him before putting a final bullet through his chest.

The only ones left standing were Petrov, his aide and Sujatha. Everyone else in the room seemed dead. Sujatha ran over to the surgery table on which Vijay lay strapped.

Tears streamed down her cheeks as she realized that they had arrived too late.

160

'Vee has been poisoned,' cried Sujatha as she noticed his swollen arm and face, his blisters and the vomit on the table. Vijay seemed to be looking at her through glazed eyes, a faint recognition glimmering somewhere within the haze of toxicity.

'Can you tell me what poison it is?' asked Petrov, as Sujatha undid the stirrups that were holding Vijay's arms and legs to the table.

Having spent years in forests and scrubland, Sujatha instinctively knew what it was. *Snake venom. The all-important question was, which particular snake?*

She quickly ran through the possibilities in her head. *Cytotoxic, haemotoxic or neurotoxic?* Cytotoxic venom would suppress cell function, haemotoxic would prevent clotting and neurotoxic would attack nervous tissue.

Swelling, bruising and blistering. Nausea and dizziness. This is cytotoxic venom.

'Can you tell what poison it is?' asked Petrov again.

'The most common cytotoxic venom in this area comes from a snake called Koriwala,' said Sujatha. 'It is also called Daboia. These are simply different names for Russell's Viper.'

She looked at the discarded syringe on the floor and then said, 'I'm pretty certain that he's been administered poison of the Russell's Viper. His kidneys will start shutting down soon if we do not give him an antidote.'

Suddenly the doors swung open. Two men from Cracker's security detail, who had been stationed as lookouts towards the rear, barged in.

Petrov's aide was shot down. He fell against the wall, his blood leaving a trail on the white wall as he crumpled to the ground. Petrov cursed himself for having been lax. '*Mu'dak!*' he yelled as he put a bullet through one, then swivelled at the waist and took aim and fired at the second.

Petrov looked over to check on Sujatha, but she was by Vijay's side, completely focused on the symptoms that she was observing. She felt his head. It was burning hot.

The learnings from her days of helping at the hospital came flooding back. The presence of fever indicated that one or more of Vijay's kidneys were shutting down. She had no way to measure his blood urea, nitrogen or creatinine levels. She would have to hazard an educated guess. She gently pressed his abdomen. Then she felt his kidneys by getting Petrov to turn Vijay on his side. It was the kidney on the right side that was in danger. In addition, intravascular coagulation had begun impeding blood circulation and he soon became dizzy and went into a coma.

In tandem, around eight thousand miles away in America, the left kidney of Jean Belanger began shutting down. Intravascular coagulation caused him to become dizzy and to drop into a coma.

From the corner of his eye, Petrov discerned a slight movement at the door. He pumped several rounds into it and was rewarded with a shriek of pain from the other side. Petrov ran to the other side of the door to ensure that the area was sanitized. As he was checking, the door swung open and Sujatha raced out.

'Where are you going?' asked Petrov.

'Into the woods,' she replied. 'I'll be back in a minute. There's no time to lose.'

161

Sujatha reappeared a minute later with a bunch of plants in her hand. '*Nadikalapak*,' she said to Petrov. 'Botanical name Ophiorrhiza mungos. Among its other uses, it also works as an antidote to the venom of Russell's Viper. I'm keeping my fingers crossed that the plants in this region are more effective than the usual. Hopefully, the low-intensity energy exposure over the years has enhanced their efficacy.'

Cure my Vijay. Help me. I need your healing touch. She was desperately trying to send quantum messages to the plants that she held in her hands. She was hoping that Cleve Backster's research on plants was entirely true.

She headed over to the counter on which there were research implements, bottles and test tubes. 'What do you need?' asked Petrov.

'A pestle and mortar to crush this herb,' replied Sujatha. 'And here it is.'

She quickly made a rough paste from the plant and strained it into an IV solution container using a standard gauze. She shook the solution vigorously and ran with it to Vijay who lay unconscious on the table. She asked Petrov to hold the container as she pushed the IV needle into Vijay's vein without worrying about being gentle. This was no time for niceties.

She took the container from Petrov and hung it from the IV stand that was built into the bed frame. She went running back to the counter and scooped up the remnants of the paste that she had made. She applied some of the paste to the area where the poison had been administered and then forced open Vijay's lips to place some into his mouth.

Then she fell to her knees and prayed. And sobbed hysterically as she did.

162

It was a damn long journey and searing hot to boot.

The man had met Henderson at the dark and damp underpass that was called Charles Helou Bus Station in Beirut. They had sat inside a beat-up, filthy Toyota Land Cruiser along with three other men to travel to Damascus. The vehicle then headed to Palmyra before moving northwards to Raqqa. All along the way they were stopped repeatedly at checkpoints for security inspections or paper verification.

The final checkpoint was near the town of Ain Issa and had been fashioned from an abandoned building that sat alongside a dirt track, shielded by a three-foot mud ridge manned by utterly disorganized Arab fighters.

From Ain Issa onwards, Henderson had been blindfolded. He knew that the trip could become a one-way ticket to being beheaded, but it was a chance that he had to take. It had taken patient negotiations to arrange the meeting and he wasn't going to allow fear to get in the way.

Raqqa was a divided city. Mafraqi controlled the eastern parts, while forces loyal to the erstwhile regime controlled the west. The meeting took place at the Hotel Al-Jamia Al-Arabia. Henderson was starving after twenty-four hours on the road and ravenously attacked the meat stew and stale flatbread that was placed before him. Boarded up windows and a creaking overhead fan seemed like luxuries.

Mafraqi walked in an hour later and sat down on a chair opposite Henderson. Behind him stood his two bodyguards, both hardened Arab fighters.

'Why should a wealthy businessman who owns one of the world's largest chemical companies be interested in seeing me?' he asked, staring at Henderson with his deep, penetrating eyes.

'Because I have something that can help you.'

163

Mafraqi laughed uproariously. '*You* want to help *me*?' he asked, attempting to control his laughter. 'Is today the first of April?'

Henderson waited calmly until Mafraqi's laughing spell died down. 'Ironically, both of us want the same thing—extreme polarization. It helps you get more Muslims to feel alienated enough to join your Jihad. But it also helps us to allow Islamophobic elements to flourish. I have a weapon system that can deliver incredible power to your cause. More importantly, I can demonstrate it to you.'

'Why should I believe anything you say?' asked Mafraqi, his expression conveying that he was uninterested in the offer.

'Can we be left alone for a minute?' asked Henderson.

Mafraqi thought about it for a few seconds. Then he gestured for his bodyguards to wait outside.

'The reason that you should believe what I say is because I know everything about the beheading of Abdullah bin Saud in Istanbul following the loss of the First Saudi State to the Ottomans,' said Henderson.

'Why should an event that happened more than two centuries ago between Saud and the Ottoman rulers even concern me?' asked Mafraqi.

'Because you claim descent from one of the people who was beheaded along with Abdullah bin Saud,' said Henderson. 'Supposedly he was a member of the Quraysh, the tribe of Prophet Muhammad.'

'So?'

'Abdullah bin Saud was Wahhabi,' said Henderson. 'He was against wine and music. Apparently, he was forced to listen to the lute by the Ottomans before being put to death. Recent excavations at the ancient prison complex of Istanbul have recovered a lute.'

Mafraqi's face fell. He knew what was coming.

'Your ancestor's name was engraved on that lute,' said Henderson. 'The person that you claim descent from was not beheaded by the Ottomans. He was the lute player of the Ottomans.' *Thank you, Judith, for the tip.*

Mafraqi was very quiet. He was wondering whether to have Henderson killed.

Then Henderson spoke. 'I know your secret,' he said. 'But I have no desire to share it with the world. Your success is also my success.'

164

Vijay stirred. At first it was just a little groan. Then he opened his left eye. The swelling on the left side of his face had subsided but the movement of his eyelid was still obstructed.

Over eight thousand miles away in America, Jean Belanger's rhythms began stabilizing, although he remained in a state of deep sleep. The swelling on the right side of his face had subsided.

Vijay looked at the male figure standing by his side. *Bastard! That rogue Petrov is here.* Then he noticed the other figure. Sujatha! He tried smiling but his facial muscles were incapable of acting upon his emotions. Temporary facial paralysis.

'I thought we had lost you, Vee,' said Sujatha, holding his hand. 'Don't say anything. I will be by your side whenever you want me.'

Slowly but surely Vijay's medical parameters began to stabilize. The swelling on his face reduced and he was able to open both his eyes.

And eight thousand miles away in America, too, Jean Belanger's health inched back to normal, but he remained asleep.

Petrov remained in communication with a small team of men who had landed in a chopper to neutralize any remaining resistance on the outskirts of the Milesian Labs facility. They had succeeded in establishing control over the area but were undertaking combing operations to ensure that there were no nasty surprises. All staff members and researchers of Milesian had been evacuated safely and were being questioned.

'How did you know that you needed to come for me?' asked Vijay, once he came around. He was sipping water from a bottle that Sujatha had taken from the refrigerator in the corridor.

'When information came in that Mikhailov's body had been discovered in Yamuna Nagar,' said Petrov. 'Halfway between our present location and Dharamsala.'

'Mikhailov is dead?' asked Vijay. He was crestfallen. He had grown to appreciate the elder scientist and his vast knowledge.

'Yes,' replied Petrov. 'Could have been killed by Schmidt or Judith's men. But the news about the discovery of his body was a clear signal that I had to get you out of here.'

'Did Mikhailov work for you?' asked Vijay.

'Many years ago he did,' replied Petrov. 'He remained a sleeper asset of the SVR for several years, but we could no longer depend on him. We were in the process of trying to reactivate him when he was killed.'

'Did *you* kill him?' asked Vijay.

There was an uncomfortable silence before Petrov spoke. 'I can assure you that we had nothing to do with his murder. We were interested in using him. Why would we kill him?'

165

'Now what?' asked Sujatha.

'We need to find Brahmananda,' replied Petrov.

'Brahmananda?' asked Vijay. *Wasn't that the name Mikhailov had mentioned to him on many occasions? Mikhailov's guru?*

'The leader of this group of sages,' said Petrov. 'There are one hundred and eight rishis here. Brahmananda is chief among them.'

'What is so special about him?' asked Vijay.

'He is supposedly an elevated soul,' replied Petrov. 'He is being used by Minerva to focus the energies of the other rishis.'

'Focus?'

'Think about what a magnifying glass does,' replied Petrov. 'It can concentrate sunlight sufficiently to burn paper, hay or leaves. That is the role that Brahmananda performs. It is believed that he is many thousands of years old.'

'How can someone live for that long?' asked Sujatha, bewildered by the claim.

'Physics tells us that it should be possible,' responded Vijay, a sure sign that he had recovered. 'Remember we had gone to see the movie *Interstellar*? What was the theory in that film? The higher the gravitational force, the slower the progress of time.'

'I can't remember exactly,' said Sujatha.

'In the movie, the protagonist goes into a black hole that has immense gravitational pull,' explained Vijay. 'Hence time slows down for him. By the time he returns to Earth, everyone else around him has aged, but he has stayed the same.'

'Are you saying that Brahmananda can transport himself to a location of immense gravitational pull?' asked Sujatha.

'There are passages in Hindu texts that explore the very same theme,' said Vijay. 'The *Shrimad Bhagvatam* is two thousand years old, but it explores this idea in some detail.'

'Really?' asked Petrov.

Vijay nodded. 'In the *Shrimad Bhagvatam*, there is a story of King Kakudmi. The king had a very beautiful daughter named Revati. The king was able to take his daughter to Brahmaloka, the plane of existence where Brahma, the creator, resides.'

'Why?' asked Sujatha.

'The king wanted to discuss with Brahma the best possible suitors for his daughter,' replied Vijay. 'When they arrived, Brahma was listening to a musical performance, so they waited patiently until the performance ended. Then the king bowed humbly before Brahma and presented his shortlist of marriageable candidates.'

'And?' asked Petrov, fascinated by the story.

'Brahma laughed,' said Vijay. 'He explained to the king that time runs differently on different planes of existence, and that during the short time they had waited to see him, 116 million years had elapsed on earth.'

'But that's just a story, isn't it?' asked Sujatha.

'Ancient philosophies understood the anomalies of spacetime much before modern scientists did,' replied Vijay. 'The problem has always been the gap between analytical thinking and meditative experience. Meditation or mysticism is an intuitive experience that cannot be learned from books.'

'But how would something like that actually work?' asked Petrov.

'Sages such as Brahmananda simply need to allow their inner duality to play out,' said Vijay. 'Anything and everything can be particles or waves. Evolved beings can convert themselves from particle-form to waveform—just like light—and travel to a dimension of higher gravitational pull. This can give them the additional years that they need. Once this has been achieved, they can return to their particle form, biologically younger than their chronological age.'

'Weren't the lifespans of previous generations longer anyway?' asked Sujatha.

'True, if you go back a few thousand years,' replied Vijay. 'False, if you go back only a few hundred—when famine and disease reduced life expectancy. You see, thousands of years ago, the earth's gravitational pull was far greater than what it currently is. The consequence was that time ran slower. And remember, the rishis used to perform their penance in high-mass areas such as the Himalayas, regions where gravity is fractionally higher in any case.'

'Fair enough,' said Sujatha. Turning to Petrov, she asked, 'But what exactly is achieved by concentrating the energies of these one hundred and eight rishis?'

'Brahmananda insists that his rishis carry out their meditation at the exact spot where the earth's energy meridian lies—along the plateau hilltop,' replied Petrov. 'Using their concentrated powers of perception, they are able to identify a given individual's quantum twin anywhere in the world. For Minerva, killing the quantum twin is far easier than assassinating a head of government. Once the quantum twin is dead, the primary target also dies—of natural causes.'

'So how exactly do we prevent more deaths? How do we convince Brahmananda to stop using his powers to identify quantum twins?' asked Sujatha.

'Let's talk to him,' said Petrov.

166

Petrov, Vijay and Sujatha exited Schmidt's lab and returned to the uphill pathway leading to the plateau where Vijay had first observed the rishis in meditation. Vijay walked slowly, ensuring that he remained stable on his feet. Every few yards they crossed archways leading to yet another winding path or stairway in the forest. Ten minutes later they reached the plateau where the vibrations of *Om* filled the air. Sujatha could almost feel the energy in her bones as they approached the sages.

Vijay ran his eyes over the formation and did a quick count of the rishis who were seated there. He soon realized that he had been mistaken in thinking that the rishis were seated in concentric circles. They were actually seated on eight elevated platforms arranged like the petals of a lotus. All one hundred and eight sages were seated in groups on the petals. At the centre of those petals sat Brahmananda, in his saffron and vermillion robes, deep in meditative bliss.

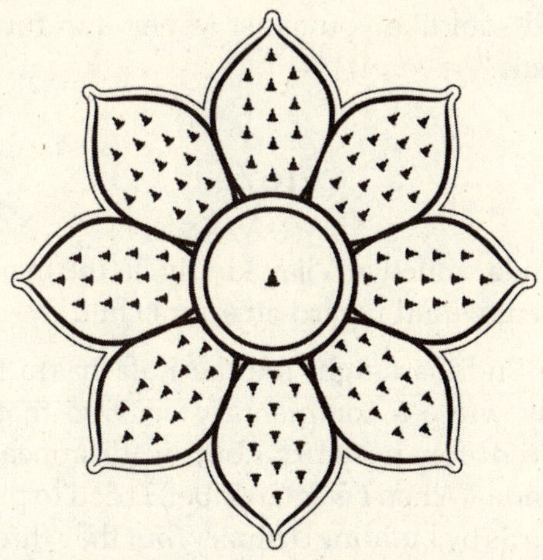

It was Vijay's second look at the fantastic and somehow, deeply moving tableau, but the scene remained as awe-inspiring as at first. It was freezing in the forest, and the darkest hour of the night. Yet these sages remained bare-chested, utterly unmindful of the air around them, or of the fact that they were levitating with each chant of *Om*, so entirely focused were they on their meditation.

Sensing the outsiders approach, Brahmananda opened his eyes. He watched Petrov, Vijay and Sujatha walk up to him as they made their way through the gaps in the petal formations to reach the centre. There was a peaceful expression on his face. He seemed entirely unaffected by the worries of the world.

Both Vijay and Sujatha bowed down to touch the seer's feet and seek his blessings. Petrov continued to stand a few feet away. The rishis around Brahmananda remained in a collective trance. It was as though they constituted a single living organism.

'Ask me whatever you wish, son,' said Brahmananda to Vijay.

'My question is this,' began Vijay hesitantly. 'Why should an elevated soul like you assist Minerva in furthering its sinister plans?'

167

Brahmananda smiled at Vijay kindly, in the manner that a loving parent would regard an errant child.

'When the Buddha taught me the Kalachakra Multantra, I devotedly wrote a commentary on it so that it would be preserved for posterity, but it disappeared,' said Brahmananda. 'When I went to Tibet, I tried to preserve the Terma records by building a library, but they threw me out. When I built my monastery and library in Roopkund, that wretch, Jasdhaval, trampled through my sacred grounds. When Nalanda was ransacked, a veritable treasure chest of records was destroyed in front of my very eyes. And I saw the same sort of wanton destruction taking place at my Hardas ashram near Kargil too.'

Vijay could feel his heart beating faster. He was feverishly attempting to make sense of what Brahmananda had just said.

When the Buddha taught me the Kalachakra Multantra, I devotedly wrote a commentary on it so that it would be preserved for posterity, but it disappeared. Wasn't it King Suchandara who wrote that commentary?

When I went to Tibet, I tried to preserve the Terma records by building a library, but they threw me out. That would have been Padmasambhava?

When I built my monastery and library in Roopkund, that wretch, Jasdhaval, trampled through my sacred grounds. But that was the enraged Guru Astika who brought down hailstones on the king's travel party!

When Nalanda was ransacked, a veritable treasure chest of records was destroyed in front of my very eyes. That would have been the teacher, Shribhadra.

And I saw the same sort of wanton destruction taking place at my Hardas ashram too. That was Brahmananda.

Suchandara, Padmasambhava, Astika, Shribhadra and Brahmananda were not different people down the centuries—they were the same man at different coordinates of the spacetime continuum!

168

Vijay forced himself to concentrate on what Brahmananda was saying.

'Ancient wisdom must be preserved so that future generations can learn from it,' said Brahmananda. 'As civilizations crumble, their records also disappear. That's exactly what I want to prevent. Son, have you ever observed monks making a sand mandala?'

Vijay nodded. He had seen videos in which millions of grains of sand were painstakingly laid into place over several days.

'After its completion,' said Brahmananda, 'the sand is swept away, symbolizing the impermanence of life. Remember, though—the pattern may be swept away but the sand is not destroyed. The pattern is human civilization and sand is knowledge. Humans come and go but knowledge remains.'

Vijay was staring at Brahmananda. He no longer appeared as a single figure. He was multiple hazy figures converging like the alternating bands of light in an experiment. He appeared to Vijay like a hologram with each figure a mere probability function—Suchandara, Padmasambhava, Astika, Shribhadra, Brahmananda and countless others.

'The effects of religious fundamentalism have plagued me down the years,' resumed Brahmananda in his familiar guise. 'Any religion can act like a medicine in small doses but can also act like a poison at higher doses. Ever since Kargil, I pledged to do whatever I could to neutralize the threat of radical Islamism. I have no quarrel with Muslims. Many of my disciples down the ages have been Muslims. The vast majority are peace-loving individuals. But I *do* worry about the effect of radical Islamism on knowledge preservation. It is as virulent as the effect of the Catholic Inquisition on Copernicus and Galileo's work, and as ominous as the Nazi book burnings of 1933.'

'But the predicted apocalypse is still four hundred years away,' argued Vijay.

'The Kalachakra had prophesied that the world will descend into chaos in the year 2424 as a result of the continued religious conflict between Islam and the rest of the world,' replied Brahmananda. 'But the Kalachakra had not factored in the higher Schumann Resonance of Earth.'

'What does that mean?' asked Sujatha.

'It means that Mother Earth is aging faster as she grows older,' said Brahmananda. 'Like a spool of thread that unwinds faster towards the end, Armageddon is just around the corner, not in 2424.'

'But why help Minerva?' asked Vijay. 'They kill people.'

'No one can be killed,' replied Brahmananda. 'Particles and waves appear, then disappear only to reappear. Lifetimes are precisely that. Minerva may choose to believe that they are killing people, but I know better. There is neither creation nor destruction. Only appearance, disappearance and reappearance.'

There was a pause in the conversation before Brahmananda resumed.

'Working alongside Minerva is a small price to pay for preserving knowledge,' said Brahmananda. 'Whatever we sages do for identifying Yamaj, Minerva will have the technology to do it on their own soon enough. At that time, they won't need us.'

He paused in reflection before his next words. 'The library here contains the greatest treasures of the ancients—including the Akashic Records. Minerva has helped us in that endeavour. If you look at the core of a mandala, you will find Buddha and his consort entwined like Shiva and Shakti. They are symbolic of method and wisdom. It is the unity of those two elements that produces bliss.'

Vijay remained quiet. He did not want to interrupt the holy man.

'When Nalanda was ransacked by the hordes of Bakhtiyar Khilji, thousands of parchments were destroyed,' said Brahmananda. 'I lost everything. My books, my scrolls, my pupils ... even the one hundred and eight-bead rosary that I used in my prayers was ripped off my neck. All that remained around me were the smouldering embers of centuries of learning.'

Vijay felt for the rudraksha bindu around his neck. It was inexplicably reassuring.

'Yes,' said Brahmananda. 'I know that Mikhailov gave the bindu to you. It has taken me hundreds of years to reassemble the rosary.'

'Why?' asked Vijay. 'Couldn't you simply get another one instead?'

Brahmananda smiled. 'The rosary in question has special properties. You will understand soon.'

Vijay was pulled out of his reverie because Petrov began laughing maniacally behind him. Vijay turned around and saw that a gun had reappeared in Petrov's hand.

'See?' said a mocking Petrov. 'This group of holy men is the best assassination machine ever invented.' There was a stunned silence as Petrov's words sank in.

Vijay realized that Petrov was no different from Judith.

169

Vijay was shocked when he heard Petrov's words.

'This incredible death apparatus will now be used by the glorious Russian state to eliminate its global enemies,' said Petrov haughtily. 'Why should these chaps work for Minerva when they can work for us? It was the very reason that Russia joined IG4.'

Vijay could visualize his worst fears coming true. Eliminating Judith and Schmidt had only given absolute power to Petrov. And he intended to use Brahmananda, the magnifying glass that could concentrate the energies of the other rishis, to continue identifying Yamaj in order to kill people across the world. Only this time the targets would be enemies of Russia.

Vijay saw Petrov tighten his grip on the gun. He knew that the Russian would have no qualms about using it on him.

He had already experienced being at the receiving end of Petrov's sadistic blows.

What happened next took place almost frame by frame. A bullet grazed Petrov's hand, causing him to drop his weapon. Before he could pick it up, another shot caught him on his right shoulder.

'Stop and put your hands where I can see them,' shouted someone.

Whose voice was that? It seemed oddly familiar. And then Vijay recognized it. A figure stepped into the lotus formation from the shadows beyond.

Sharma.

170

It had been a hair-raising experience getting there. The Milesian facility was monitored by sophisticated radar and air defence systems. The traditional options of being dropped by chopper or parachuting in from an aircraft were unavailable, given that Petrov had taken control of the entire area. So he chose a method that a one-legged man would rarely consider.

Hang-gliding.

Sharma had chosen a hill in Phata that bordered the Milesian facility in Kalimath. As an experienced hang-glider, he knew how to take off from almost any type of slope and then fly for hours. But that had been before his prosthetic leg came into play. He knew that he was taking a massive risk, but he had no choice.

He conducted a pre-flight inspection of the glider, ensuring that all its hardware was in working condition. This included the sail, battens, cables, tubes, bolts and harness connections. Next, he scanned his intended run with practised eyes to make sure it was clear of obstacles.

Sharma lifted the hang-glider—it weighed some thirty kilograms—by grasping the edges of the control bar and ran down the slope of the hill. From his running speed, it was impossible to tell that he was wearing a prosthetic leg.

His glider's sail filled with air as he ran. Tailwinds were soon accelerating his running speed. Sharma felt the hang-glider lift him off the ground when he reached twenty-seven kilometres per hour. He immediately moved his hands from the sides of the control bar to its base. The move reflected his experience.

He knew the importance of sensing small meteorological changes to gain lift to stay aloft. His senses were tuned in to anticipate hot air thermals and wave currents. Soaring like a bird in the sky, he manoeuvred the glider towards the hill that he had seen on the satellite image. He had to maintain a constant speed but there were no instruments to help him. He simply had to sense things through. If he felt he was moving too fast, he pushed the control bar away from himself to slow down. If the glider was moving too slowly, he pulled the control bar toward himself for the opposite effect. He was secure in the knowledge that his altitude was too low to be picked up by radar systems.

He shifted his weight towards the left to guide the machine towards the hilltop. His brain and body were together furiously adjusting his speed and position in real time to make an accurate landing. He noticed the laboratory and office complex to the west, the lotus-shaped meditation platforms in the centre, the reservoir to the south and the cave-library complex towards the east. This was in sync with the satellite map that he had examined earlier. The cave-library area seemed to be the most open and appropriate for a landing, so he nudged his glider in that direction.

He began stalling his glider gradually. As he approached the ground, he pushed the control bar as far out as he could. It tipped the glider nose up and slowed it down, eventually bringing it to a halt.

Sharma landed upright on his feet. A perfect two-point landing.

171

The rishis who were deep in meditation remained unaffected by the commotion, seemingly impervious to the sights and sounds around them, and the unfolding events. The only one among them who was 'awake' was Brahmananda. But he, too, remained still, unmoving and uncaring of the action and drama, although he was at its very epicentre.

Sharma's gaze was flitting between Brahmananda, Petrov and Vijay. But Brahmananda did not appear to him as a well-defined entity. Instead, he appeared as a hazy combination of several figures. Sharma realized what Vijay had already understood some moments ago.

Sharma forced himself to stay alert. He recalled the earlier words of Brahmananda. *Imagine that you are a warrior in a swordfight. Your opponent is equally matched to you. The slightest error on your part could mean instant death. You watch your opponent with utmost vigilance. A crowd has gathered to see the fight. Given that you aren't blind, you can see them from the corner of your eye. And given that you aren't deaf, you hear them in the background. But your mind remains focused on your opponent and his moves.*

He kept his gun and vision trained on Petrov, who was now lying on the ground, bleeding, but Sharma's mind was attempting to communicate with Vijay. *There are one hundred and eight rishis seated here. Each one has a rudraksha bead around his neck. But you—Vijay—are the only one who has the bindu!*

And then Sharma made his first mistake.

172

Sharma momentarily shifted his vision towards Vijay. It wasn't for more than a couple of seconds, but those seconds were the crucial opportunity that Petrov had been waiting for. He picked up the bloodied gun that lay near him and took a clean shot at Sharma. The gunshot caught Sharma in his stomach. He fell to the ground, blood spurting from his intestines.

'No!' shouted Vijay, shocked by the sudden turn of events. But both Sujatha and Vijay knew that it was too late.

Petrov laughed. 'You will now hand over to me that bead that Mikhailov gave you,' he said, pointing the gun at Vijay from where he lay.

Vijay ignored him. Instead, he drew Sujatha towards him, hugging her protectively.

'So touched by your tenderness,' commented Petrov wryly. 'What a beautiful love story. Such a shame that it must end for both of you.'

Brahmananda's eyes were closed once again, and he was leading his sages in chanting *Om*. Vijay and Sujatha remained locked in an embrace like that of Shiva and Shakti; like that of Kalachakra and Vishwamata; like Yin and Yang; like the observer and observed; like any of the billions of connections that made up the universe.

And then Vijay felt the vibrations within him—they were far greater than anything that he had ever experienced. And in the flash of an eye, Brahmananda and the rishis, all one hundred and eight of them, vanished. Poof! Gone.

Petrov was stunned. He couldn't believe what he had just witnessed. Had he been imagining things? Had his mind been playing tricks on him? He felt anger bubbling up deep inside of him and he screamed, frantically looking around him for Vijay and Sujatha so that he could at least derive some pleasure from killing them. But they, too, had disappeared along with the rishis.

And then another shot rang out.

173

'Stay for a few days,' the Dalai Lama had said to Sharma, and he had obliged.

A couple of days later, the pontiff had called him back. 'There's someone I would like you to meet,' he said.

'Who?' asked Sharma.

'You will see,' said the Dalai Lama. 'He will help you decipher these documents.'

Sharma was guided to a room nearby. Behind a desk was a man whose face he had seen before, many years ago at the hospital in Kargil.

Mikhailov!

Except for some wounds on his face and arms, he seemed fine. Sharma stepped forward. The men gaped at one another. 'My operatives informed me that you had gone missing, and here you are!' exclaimed Sharma.

'Schmidt's goons left me for dead at their safe house in Yamuna Nagar,' explained Mikhailov. 'It's halfway between Milesian and here.'

'How did you survive?' asked Sharma.

'I slowed down my breathing to the point that I appeared dead,' said Mikhailov. 'It's a yogic asana that I learnt under Brahmananda. One of the neighbours found me and I was brought here. The Dalai Lama's monks used their miraculous herbal remedies on me. Now, how may I help you?'

Sharma held out the document that Brahmananda had given him. 'It was your guru who gave this to me in the hospital at Kargil. Why he did that, I haven't the faintest clue. Moreover, I have no idea what it means.'

'There is nothing that Brahmananda ever does without a reason,' said Mikhailov. He stared at the document as Sharma unrolled it flat on the desk.

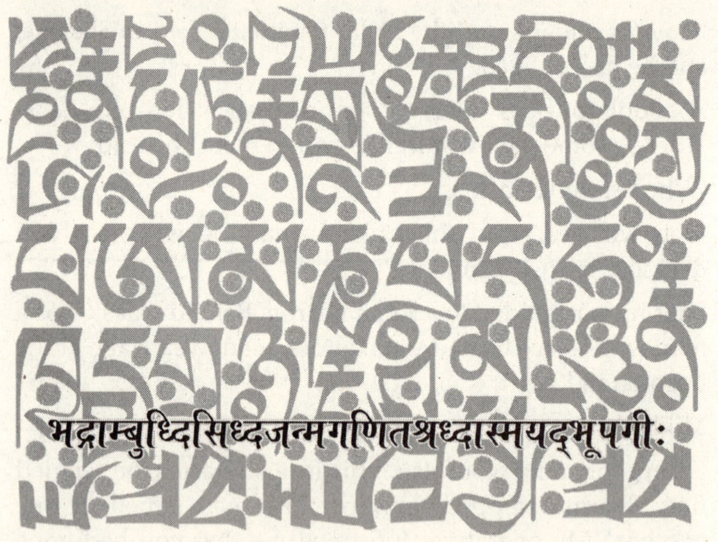

Mikhailov laughed. 'Do you realize what the mantra says?' he asked. Without waiting for an answer he read it aloud. *'Bhadrambuddhi siddhajanmaganita sraddha sma yad bhupagih.'*

'What does that mean?' asked Sharma.

'It's from the Katapayadi system,' replied Mikhailov. 'Brahmananda taught it to me. It's an ancient method of assigning letters to numbers so that one may remember significant values easily through meaningful sentences or verses.'

Mikhailov quickly wrote up a table that provided the numerical values of each consonant.

भ	द्	रा	म्	बु	द्	धि	सि	द्	ध	ज	न्	म	ग	णि	त	श्	र	द्	धा	स्	म	य	द्	भू	प	गि
bha	d	ra	m	bh	d	dh	sa	d	dha	ja	n	ma	ga	na	ta	s	ra	d	dha	s	ma	ya	d	bha	pa	gi
4	-	2	-	3	-	9	7	-	9	8	-	5	3	5	6	-	2	-	9	-	5	1	-	4	1	3

'Any idea what's special about the numbers that you see?' asked Mikhailov.

Sharma tried to make sense of the table, but gave up after a while.

'Reversing the digits, one gets 314159265358979324,' Mikhailov explained. 'If we add a decimal point after the three, we get the value of pi. This piece of paper is telling you to search for a circle!'

174

'That's it?' asked Sharma incredulously. 'Search for a circle? Ridiculous!'

Mikhailov ignored Sharma's outburst. Taking a marker, he blackened some portions of the image. 'Now look at it,' he said, smiling.

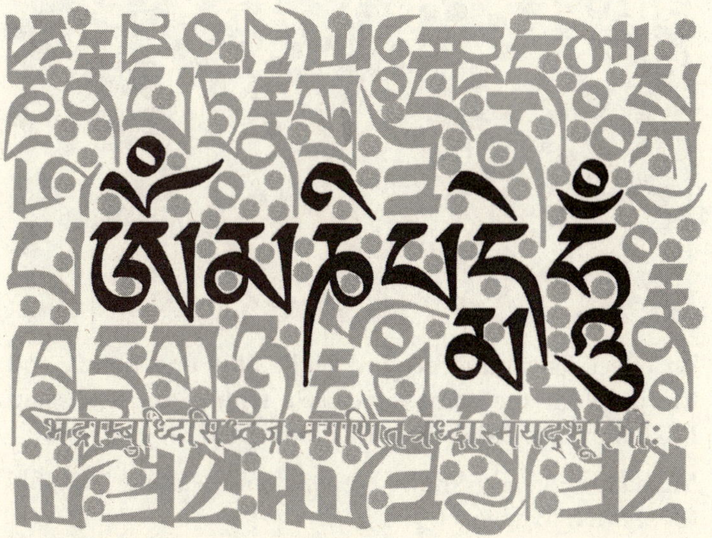

Sharma looked at it carefully. And then he realized that it was a mantra that he had seen hundreds, if not thousands of times at Buddhist temples. '*Om Mani Padme Hum*,' he whispered softly under his breath.

'Correct,' said Mikhailov. '*The jewel in the lotus.* Brahmananda expects you to find the jewel in the lotus, duly enclosed within a circle. One more thing...'

'Yes?' asked Sharma, his head reeling with the information.

'Did you notice the beads in the image?' asked Mikhailov. 'There are one hundred and eight small ones and one big one.'

Mikhailov used his marker to highlight the beads in the image.

'In effect, one hundred and eight plus one points and the jewel in the lotus—enclosed within a circle,' said Mikhailov. 'Any idea what that would be?'

Mikhailov already knew. He was only waiting impishly for Sharma to have a try.

'I give up,' shrugged Sharma. And then it came to him like a flash. Mikhailov chuckled.

'Yes, you are right,' said Mikhailov, picking up on Sharma's thought. 'It's a mandala!'

175

'I also need you to see this,' said Sharma, unrolling the satellite image.

'Do you know the location of this place?' asked Mikhailov, looking at it.

'Alas, I cannot tell you,' said Sharma.

'But I can,' said Mikhailov mischievously. 'Look at the measurements of these land features. The hill is shaped like a pyramid and the ratio of the slope face to half of the base is 1.618—the Golden Ratio.'

Sharma had heard of the Golden Ratio before and recalled reading somewhere that the ratio had been used even in the construction of the Great Pyramid at Giza.

'The Golden Ratio appears almost everywhere,' replied Mikhailov. 'Italy's Fibonacci wrote about the number sequence only in 1202 CE, but this particular sequence was already known to India's Pingala in 200 BCE, several centuries *before* Fibonacci. He called it *maatraameru*.'

Sharma allowed the information to sink in.

'Consider a rectangle based on the Golden Ratio,' continued Mikhailov breathlessly, sketching faster than his explanation. 'The bigger side divided by the smaller side must necessarily equal the sum of both sides divided by the bigger side.'

'And that ratio is 1.618?' asked Sharma.

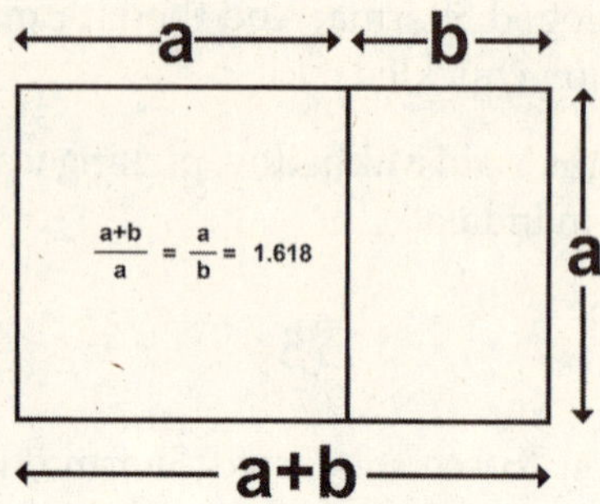

'It is an irrational number,' explained Mikhailov. 'One can only *approach* the Golden Ratio but never fully reach it,' explained Mikhailov. 'The Golden Ratio gives us the Golden Spiral, a logarithmic spiral where the growth factor is 1.618. You can observe the spiral at work in snails, leaves, flower petals, nautilus shells, galaxies and even animal tails. Just Google it on your iPad.'

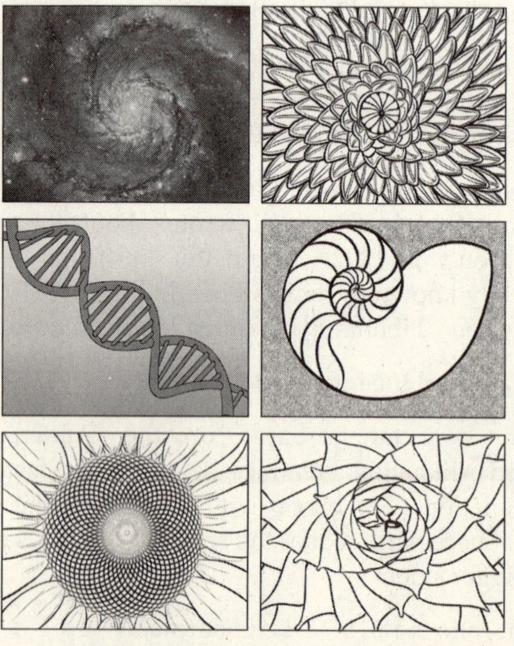

Sharma did. He was surprised to see the results.

'So it is found mainly in plants?' asked Sharma.

'In humans too,' replied Mikhailov. 'The human body exhibits golden proportions, including our faces, our limbs and even our DNA molecules. A cycle of the double helix measures exactly thirty-four angstroms in length and twenty-one angstroms in width.'

'Still brings me back to the all-important question—why?' said Sharma. 'Why is the Golden Ratio present in this hill?'

'It isn't a hill,' said Mikhailov. 'It is a man-made structure.'

176

Sharma exhaled with relief. His gut instincts had been right and Mikhailov had also arrived at the same conclusion independently. The two men continued staring at the high-resolution satellite image in front of them.

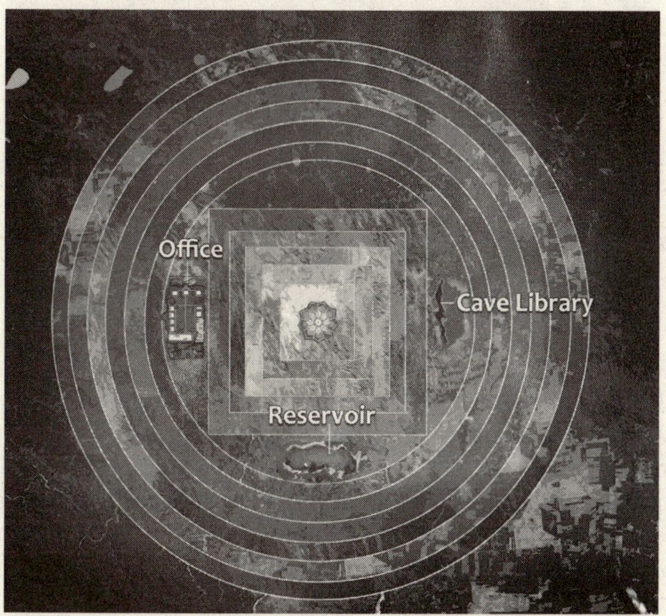

'The formation is quite remarkable,' said Mikhailov, looking at the satellite image closely. 'Six concentric circles enclosing five concentric squares with each inner square at an altitude higher than the outer one. This is almost a perfect representation of the Kalachakra mandala.'

Sharma nodded. He knew that Mikhailov was on the right track. He allowed the Russian to continue.

'The Kalachakra mandala is the wheel of time,' continued Mikhailov. 'It is most revered by Buddhists because it factors in everything: cosmic and astrological, human body and mind. The mandala is actually a two-dimensional representation of a three-dimensional palace—a palace of five floors. Each of the five levels is represented by a concentric square.'

'In your satellite image, we can see that the massive hill has been terraced and carved into five levels so that the innermost plateau is highest,' explained Mikhailov.

Sharma made notes as Mikhailov continued. 'Within the five levels of this palace are various deities, and at the centre is Buddha.'

He paused to scrutinize the satellite image yet again. 'The lowest level of the palace represents the body. The body mandala features twelve large lotus flowers, each having twenty-eight petals. These represent the twelve months of twenty-eight lunar days each. In that sense, the Kalachakra is a representation of both space *and* time. Einstein would be truly impressed.'

'What about the other levels?' asked Sharma.

'The second is for speech, the third for mind and the fourth for consciousness.'

'And the fifth?' asked Sharma.

'The Great Bliss mandala,' replied Mikhailov. 'This is the last of the squares and inside this square is a lotus flower with eight petals. Interestingly, the lotus is one of the flowers in which the petals are also placed according to the Golden Ratio.'

'What is at the core of the lotus?'

'In the centre of this lotus sits Kalachakra—the Buddha—along with his consort, Vishwamata.'

177

'Consort?' asked Sharma. 'I thought the Buddha was celibate!'

Mikhailov smiled. 'Tantric Buddhism emphasizes the union of method and wisdom. It is this union that produces bliss. Just like a father and mother are needed to produce a child, method and wisdom are required for enlightenment.'

'Seems surprisingly explicit for the times,' observed Sharma.

'Please do not get distracted by the imagery of sexual union. Think of Shiva and Shakti. Think of the fact that the universe consists of connections. In Buddhism, too, you have the Bodhisattva, Avalokitesvara, who is also depicted in the female form of Guanyin—the Shakti to Shiva.'

Sharma understood.

'Indian and Tibetan cultures have never been shy about sex,' explained Mikhailov. 'Just look at the carvings of Khajuraho. Prudishness crept in much later.'

'So?'

'They never had any qualms about using sexual imagery that was symbolic,' replied Mikhailov. 'Do not get misled by symbols. Someone unaware of Christianity may see the image of a man nailed to a cross and think that the religion promotes torture! Foolish, right? One must look deeper to understand the true meaning of such symbols.'

Sharma thought about it. Shiva and Shakti were often shown in positions of fervent love in splendid temple carvings that exhibited passion at a level that was entirely unfamiliar in religious art forms of the West. And it was evident that Tantric Buddhism had been heavily influenced by Shiva tantra.

'What is the meaning of the word Shiva?' asked Mikhailov. 'It literally means *that which is not*. In effect, Shiva *is* because of Shakti. Shakti *is* because of Shiva. Neither is complete in and of themselves. The objects that we see around us ... do they exist? No. It's our act of observation that makes them exist.'

Mikhailov studied Sharma's expression curiously to determine if he was on the ball.

'As opposed to Abrahamic religions, sensuous gratification had never been curbed in ancient Hinduism, because the human body was seen as an essential part of the human spirit,' said Mikhailov. 'The Hindu is less concerned with repressing sexual desire and more focused on realizing himself with his entire being—both body and mind.'

178

'Consciousness at a cellular level?' asked Sharma.

'Precisely,' said Mikhailov. 'There are abundant documented cases of organ transplants that show what is called memory transference in patients. For example, a foundry worker who had received a heart transplant found himself listening to classical music, a type of music that he had never liked earlier. It was later discovered that the donor had loved classical music and had died hugging his violin.'

'But surely that's an isolated example,' said Sharma.

'Not at all,' replied Mikhailov. 'A little girl, who received the heart of a murdered ten year-old girl, began to have frequent nightmares about the murder. A liver transplant patient suddenly developed "memories" of herself as a young girl on a farm playing on a swing with her father. She later discovered that those were the actual experiences of the liver donor. In yet another instance, a kidney transplant patient's hobbies and food preferences changed dramatically to match those of the donor. There are countless cases that indicate that thought, memory, intelligence and consciousness are in every cell of our bodies, not just in our brains. The Sanskrit word for body is *tana*—hence *tantra* teaches one the ability to warp or weave one's body into the universe.'

'What about the concentric circles that encircle the squares in the mandala?' asked Sharma. 'What do they symbolize?'

'They represent the elements—earth, water, fire and wind. Beyond that are two more circles that represent space, or emptiness, and consciousness,' replied Mikhailov. 'The Kalachakra mandala is a perfect representation of the interplay between the universe that surrounds us, our bodies, minds and consciousness.'

Sharma absorbed the information and made more notes. 'Is the Kalachakra mandala a representation of Shambhala?' he asked.

'It is more likely that it symbolizes the entire universe,' said Mikhailov. 'Are you familiar with the Hindu symbol, Sri Yantra?'

'Sure,' said Sharma. He had seen it at several temples.

'It looks something like this,' said Mikhailov, quickly sketching the symbol on the pad in front of him. 'Nine interlocking triangles. Four of them pointing up, representing Shiva. Five of them pointing down, representing Shakti. Notice that Shakti is more powerful. All enclosed within a circle. What's interesting is the fact that Shiva and Shakti intersect at fifty-four points. Each point represents masculine and feminine so when you multiply these fifty-four points by two, you get the sacred number one hundred and eight.'

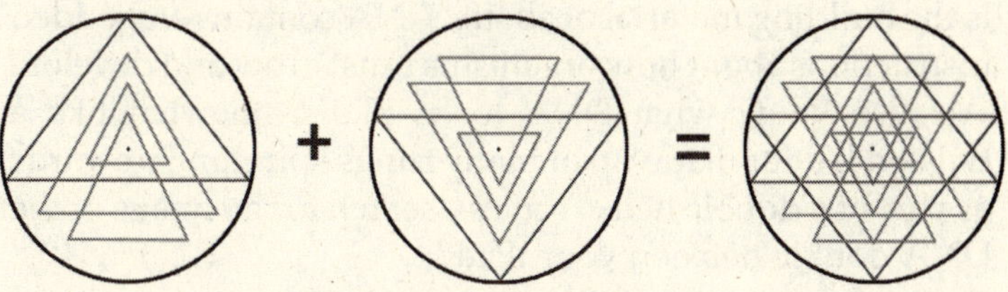

'Why nine triangles?' persisted Sharma.

'It is said that science's best bet to unify the theory of relativity with quantum mechanics is the so-called string theory,' said Mikhailov. 'The theory imagines that reality is composed of coiled strings that vibrate in different dimensions. We can't see these dimensions because they are a mathematical construct of the scientist, but possibly sages can perceive them. Do you know how many dimensions the string vibrates in? Nine! Sometimes the perception of our ancients was ahead of science and sometimes it is the other way round. There was a reason why we described the sacred feminine power as having nine manifestations.'

Mikhailov took a deep breath. 'You know what else is fascinating?'

Sharma waited.

'If a Sri Yantra is correctly constructed, the base angle of the largest triangle will be around fifty-two degrees,' said Mikhailov. 'It is also the angle of your hill in this satellite image. But there is a more fundamental reason why the design of the Sri Yantra is the way it is.'

'And that is?'

'The reason goes back to Deoxyribonucleic Acid,' said Mikhailov. 'What crime shows on television call DNA.'

179

'DNA? How?' asked Sharma, perplexed.

'Let's review the basics, shall we?' asked Mikhailov. 'DNA is the building material of all life. DNA contains embedded instructions about how organisms must grow and develop. We also know what DNA looks like. Somewhat like a twisted ladder made up of many rungs spiralling upwards as part of a double helix. You can search for an image of the DNA double helix on your iPad.'

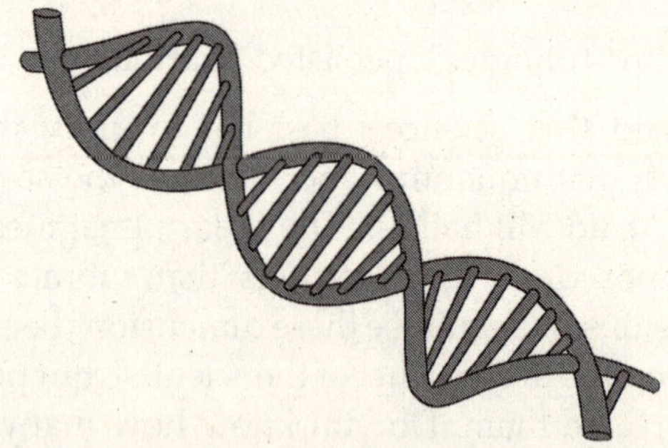

'But most images show the spiral from a side view,' said Mikhailov. 'What if you were looking at the spiral from the top? An aerial view, so to speak?'

'The view would be something like this,' said Mikhailov, sketching an image quickly. 'And you should observe that the Swastika is trying to convey a similar sensation, that of an upward or downward spiralling staircase.'

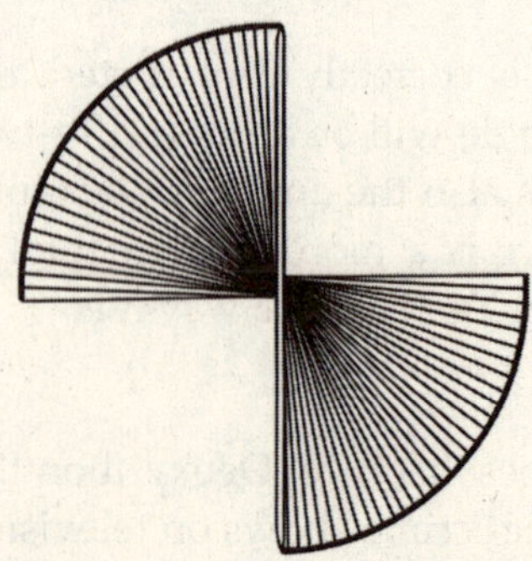

He paused, almost as though he wanted feedback from Sharma simply by watching his face.

'The unfortunate reality is that most DNA research has been sponsored by drug companies,' said Mikhailov. 'These corporations are not concerned about any research that is non-remunerative. But there *is* indeed significant cutting-edge research that has been entirely ignored.'

'What?' asked Sharma.

'The answer lies in my homeland, Russia,' said Mikhailov. 'Some of my Russian colleagues have found that DNA can receive, convert and emit sound and light. These scientists have discovered that DNA can be programmed with lasers.'

'How?'

'I'll show you through an example,' replied the untiring Mikhailov. 'Science has found that diseased rats with deformed pancreatic tissue can be cured by transmitting laser beams through the healthy DNA of pancreatic tissue,' replied Mikhailov. 'The researchers also found that DNA is related to sound frequencies. Russian linguists studied the DNA code in the human genome and they discovered that DNA is almost a language that follows grammar and syntax. This means that DNA can be reprogrammed through frequencies of sound and light.'

'Has that technique ever been used?' asked Sharma.

'Only in alternative medicine,' replied Mikhailov. 'Think Reiki, faith healing or the power of prayer. Our cells are fields of information, intelligence and energy. These methods can bring about a correction in fields that have gone astray.'

'But what does that have to do with the Sri Yantra?' asked Sharma.

'Indian rishis have known for millennia that *mantra, yantra* and *tantra* are a very powerful combination when used together. By chanting sacred mantras—or sounds; concentrating on sacred yantras—or light; and using every cell of their being—tantra—they could elevate their consciousness and heal themselves. Do you see where that goes? Some of these practices could allow one to reprogramme one's own DNA!'

180

'But isn't the Kalachakra meant to lead to Shambhala?' asked Sharma.

'What is Shambhala? Where is Shambhala?' asked Mikhailov. 'The mystery surrounding Shambhala links it to geographical locations such as Mount Kailash, the Sutlej Valley, the Dhauladhar mountains, Tibet, Siberia, China, Mount Belukha, Kazakhstan, Balkh and several other places.'

'What is your view?' asked Sharma.

'They are all wrong,' said Mikhailov. 'Shambhala is a state of mind, a condition of bliss. Not a physical place.'

Sharma was confused. Seeing the puzzled look on his face, Mikhailov explained. 'Tibetan Buddhism, Vajrayana Buddhism, Tantric Buddhism—they are all terms that can be used somewhat interchangeably, because they emerged through the union of Buddhism and Hindu tantra. Now tell me, which Hindu deity is at the centre of tantra?'

'Shiva,' replied Sharma.

'And what is another name for Shiva?' asked Mikhailov.

'Shambho,' answered Sharma.

'Do you now see why it is called *Shambhala*?' asked Mikhailov softly. 'Shambhala is a place where the energies of Shiva and Shakti combine—like the triangles of the Sri Yantra. The mandala is merely a representation of that.'

181

'Have you checked the latitude and longitude of this mandala on the map?' asked Mikhailov.

Sharma reviewed his notes.

'30.5621 N, longitude 79.0846 E,' he replied.

'Now consider these additional coordinates,' said Mikhailov. He dictated the numbers to Sharma effortlessly from memory.

30.7352 N, 79.0669 E
18.8110 N, 79.9067 E
13.7498 N, 79.6984 E
12.8476 N, 79.6997 E
12.2319 N, 79.0676 E
11.5172 N, 79.3194 E
11.3995 N, 79.6935 E
09.2881 N, 79.3174 E

'What are these?' asked Sharma.

'Coordinates of eight Shiva temples—like the eight petals of the lotus within the mandala. It has taken me weeks of research to pinpoint the exact locations.'

'Which temples?' asked Sharma.

'Write them down,' instructed Mikhailov firmly as Sharma took notes.

Kedarnath Temple, Kedarnath, Uttarakhand, 30.7352, 79.0669
Kaleshwara Mukteeshwara Swamy Temple, Kaleshwaram, Telangana, 18.8110, 79.9067
Srikalahasteeswara Swamy Temple, Srikalahasti, Andhra Pradesh, 13.7498, 79.6984
Ekambareswarar Temple, Kanchipuram, Tamil Nadu, 12.8476, 79.6997
Annamalaiyar Temple, Thiruvannamalai, Tamil Nadu, 12.2319, 79.0676

Virudhagireeswarar Temple, Virudhachalam, Tamil Nadu, 11.5172, 79.3194
Thillai Nataraja Temple, Chidambaram, Tamil Nadu, 11.3995, 79.6935
Ramanathaswamy Temple, Rameswaram, 9.2881, 79.3174

'Have you noticed something odd?' asked Mikhailov.

Sharma was not sure what he was missing. He looked at the list again carefully and then it struck him. *All the locations were along the same longitude, plus or minus half a degree.*

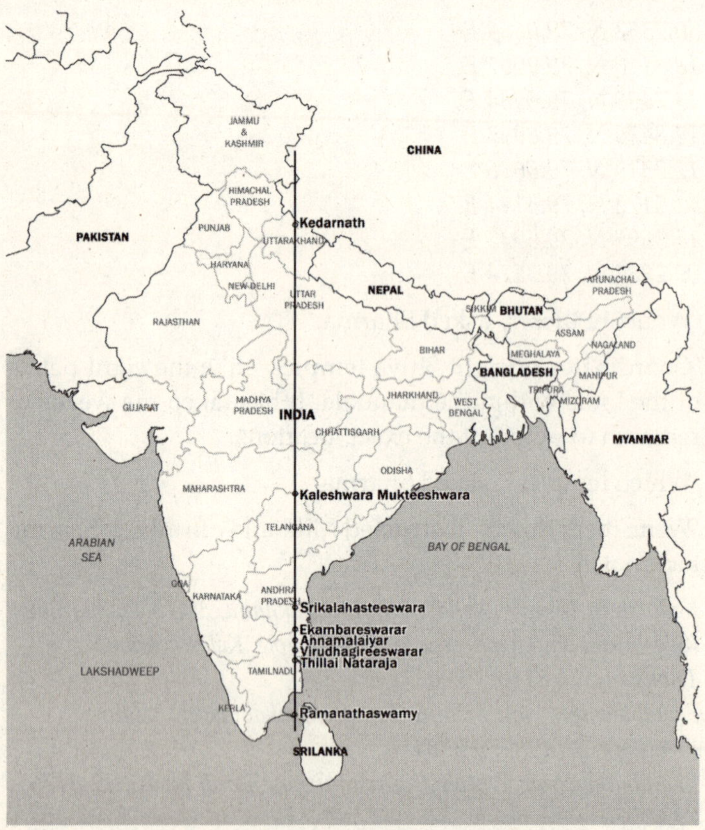

'Very good,' said Mikhailov as he saw realization suffuse Sharma's face. 'Now, string theory is a framework in which the point-like specks of particle physics can also be modelled as one-dimensional objects called strings. Imagine a guitar string that is tuned by tightening it. Musical notes are produced at various points along the guitar neck. Think of particles as those notes. In effect, particles are mere manifestations of a string.'

Sharma hung on to every word.

'You want to know what Shambhala represents?' asked Mikhailov. 'It is the energy produced along this string of eight temples. They lie on the same longitude as your mandala. Each time the mandala vibrates, so do the temples in resonance. Imagine the power!'

'Incredible,' murmured Sharma.

'You haven't heard the incredible part as yet,' said Mikhailov.

182

'What?' asked Sharma excitedly.

'How much do you know about the *Ramayana*?' asked Mikhailov.

'Only to the extent of my reading,' said Sharma.

'Ah, but as Brahmananda told me, there is always a story behind a story. You know the commonly accepted story. What about the real one?'

'What was that?'

'Today's mythology sees Ravana as *Lankanaresh*—the king of Lanka. But we forget that Lanka was the gateway to a much wider continent called Kumari Kandam.'

Mikhailov took a deep breath before resuming. 'Seven thousand years ago, during the period of the *Ramayana*, that region was no longer a single land mass. The ocean had risen and what used to be a single land mass had split into several lands, with Lanka as the crown.'

'How many lands?' asked Sharma.

'Ten,' replied Mikhailov. 'That's why we have the iconography of Ravana's ten heads. It was allegorical. Ravana was the emperor of ten lands. Ten kings of these regions had accepted his suzerainty.'

'That doesn't explain the reason behind Rama's expedition to Lanka,' said Sharma. 'If it wasn't merely exile and the consequent abduction of Sita, then what was the purpose of his trip?'

'Ravana was the greatest Shiva bhakt ever,' said Mikhailov. 'He had been given something very powerful by Shiva. It was called the Atma Lingam.'

'Atma Lingam?'

'It is translated in various ways,' said Mikhailov. 'The most common translation is that it is "the soul of Shiva". It was supposedly an object that could bestow transformative capabilities upon Ravana. Rama needed to take that away from Ravana to secure the borders of his kingdom. *That* was the reason of his trip. Exile and retrieval of Sita was a mere eyewash.'

Sharma's head was spinning. It was too much to absorb in one go.

'After Ravana was felled, why did Rama instruct Lakshmana to sit at Ravana's feet and learn from him?' asked Mikhailov. 'It was to gain an insight into the working of the Atma Lingam.'

'But how does the Atma Lingam relate to this particular longitude that contains the eight temples and the mandala?' asked Sharma.

'Because that longitude also represents the path that Rama would have taken on his way back from Lanka—with the Atma Lingam in his possession on the Pushpak Viman,' replied Mikhailov. 'Hence the power of that particular line. King Suchandara's initiation into the Kalachakra several thousand years later was provided by the Buddha at a place called Dhanyakatakam. The longitude on which Dhanyakatakam lies is the same. *That's* the reason why the initiation had to be done there.'

'Really?' asked Sharma.

'It really depends on what you mean by *really*,' replied Mikhailov.

183

Mikhailov noticed the puzzled expression on Sharma's face.

'The results of a quantum experiment can vary depending on whether or not we choose to measure the results,' said Mikhailov. 'Nature changes its behaviour based on whether we observe it or not. But if the behaviour of the universe depends on whether we observe it, then what is reality? Objectivity is an illusion. The *Upanishads* say: *It moves. It moves not. It is far. And it is near. It is within all this. And it is outside of all this.*'

'I am utterly confused,' said Sharma, forcing himself to stay focused.

'How should I make this easy for you?' wondered Mikhailov. 'Ah, yes. Think of a search engine like Google. You enter a search term in the box. As you type, Google throws up an auto-populated list of potential search terms. How does Google do that?'

'By keeping track of what people search for,' replied Sharma.

'Which means that your own search term will also have an influence on Google's auto-populated list,' said Mikhailov. 'You are not just searching, you are also influencing the outcome. Your own search term also influences Google. The observer influences the observed. To Indian mystics, the observer and observed, the subject and object are indivisible and indistinguishable. There is no division.'

Just as Sharma thought he had understood, Mikhailov threw another idea at him.

'Imagine that a ball that is going round and round in a circle on a plane surface,' said Mikhailov, drawing a circle on a sheet of paper and then placing a dot on it to indicate the ball.

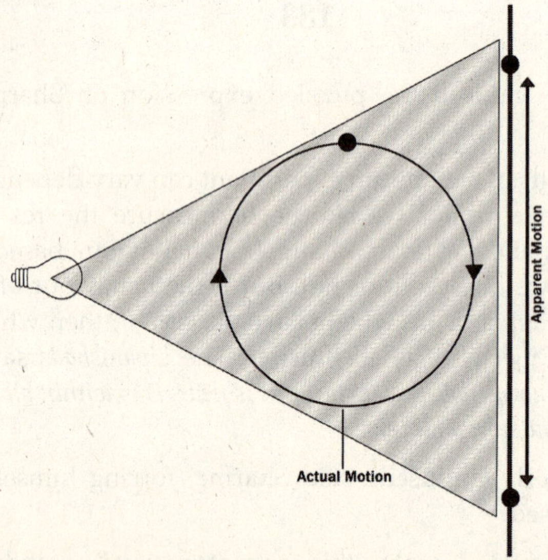

'Now imagine that we shine a beam of light on the ball along the edge of the sheet and observe the moving shadow of the ball on a screen at the other end. Will we see the circular motion of the ball?'

Sharma was not sure.

'No. What you will see is an oscillating motion of the ball on the screen,' said Mikhailov. 'You do not see reality—the circular motion—but illusion, the illusion being the oscillating motion of the ball's shadow. I do hope that you now understand why Milesian's logo is what it is? It may be evil, but it is one of the few organizations that understands the difference between illusion and reality.' Sharma recalled the logo that he had seen on the flags in photographs of the Milesian facility that Petrov had shown IG4 members.

Mikhailov waited for Sharma to absorb this latest revelation. Then he continued. 'A colour-blind individual is unable to distinguish between red, green and blue. He looks at a bright red apple and it appears yellow-brown to him. A person with no colour-blindness sees it as red. Which is real and which is an illusion? That's the key question asked by the Roman Governor Pilate at the trial of Christ—*what is truth*?'

'What is reality then?' asked Sharma. 'And does that mean that Shambhala is also an illusion?'

'The answer lies in being able to experience *nothingness*. I learnt it from Brahmananda.'

'Nothingness?' repeated Sharma, baffled.

'That iPad that you carry,' began Mikhailov. 'Press the power button to activate the screen.'

Sharma had no idea why he was being asked to do it but he played along by pressing the power button.

'It now shows your wallpaper and icons. Look at the screen,' said Mikhailov. 'Can you see your fingerprints?'

'No,' replied Sharma.

'Now put it back into standby mode so that the screen goes dark,' said Mikhailov. Sharma pressed the power button to kill the screen.

'Can you see your fingerprints now?' asked Mikhailov.

'Yes,' said Sharma. 'Clearly.'

'Think of the power-on mode as illusion and power-off mode as reality,' said Mikhailov. 'When you sink into nothingness, you can experience the world as it is. You can see your fingerprints on the screen. Fingerprints that remain invisible when the screen is lit up.'

184

Williams and Henderson reviewed the dossier that had been prepared for them. Listed in it were several instances of hate crimes that had begun taking place in America.

Muslim family garage in upstate New York torched and vandalized. It took five volunteer fire departments to stop the blaze which burned the garage to the ground.

Anti-Asian assault in Brooklyn. The suspect punched and kicked the victim repeatedly while yelling anti-Asian remarks. The victim succumbed to his injuries in hospital.

Connecticut man arrested in Texas following public anti-Muslim rant. A video taken by the family that afternoon showed a man walking over to them, yelling, 'You're a fucking Muslim! Die!'

Ironically, the man attacked was not a Muslim but a Sikh, often mistaken for Muslims due to their turbans.

Man arrested in New York after attack on Asian man. During the assault the perpetrator stated, 'You are a fucking immigrant, go back to your country. What the fuck are you doing here?'

Headscarf reportedly ripped off Muslim teenager near Atlanta. Dunwoody police confirmed that they are searching for a man accused of ripping the headscarf off a Muslim girl while yelling 'terrorist' at Perimeter Mall.

Williams looked at Henderson and smiled. His plan was working perfectly.

185

It was the first time that someone had explained the concept of nothingness so clearly to Sharma.

'But when your iPad is in standby mode, it is still connected to the network, isn't it?' asked Mikhailov. 'That's where consciousness comes into the picture. Think of the network as consciousness.'

'Consciousness?' asked Sharma. 'From outside?'

'The term "outside" implies that there is also an "inside",' said Mikhailov. 'A distinction that doesn't exist. Everything just *is*. We don't know the origin of human consciousness. Is consciousness simply a product of the brain or is the brain just a recipient of consciousness? Have you heard of Pam Reynolds?'

'Who is she?'

'An American singer and songwriter,' replied Mikhailov. 'In 1991, she underwent surgery to remove a life-threatening aneurism from her brain. Because the aneurism was located close to the brain stem, she had no chance of survival. But then she met Dr Robert Spetzler, who decided that she could be operated using a procedure called hypothermic cardiac arrest. Pam's body temperature was lowered to ten degrees Celsius. At this body temperature, her breathing stopped, her heartbeat halted and the blood drained from her head.'

'They killed her?' asked Sharma.

'Technically, yes,' said Mikhailov. 'Her eyes were shut with tape and earphones were plugged in her ears. These earphones produced audible clicking sounds, which enabled the doctors to ensure that Pam had a flat EEG—a non-responsive brain—before the surgery commenced. In effect, she was put into a clinically dead state. The surgery was successful and Pam was restored to life after a seven-hour procedure. She made a complete recovery.'

'How does this relate to consciousness?' asked Sharma. 'What happened—'

Mikhailov held up a finger to stop Sharma from going into full flow with his questions. 'Upon waking, Pam was able to provide an incredibly detailed account of what went on inside the operating room while she was clinically dead—the doctors' conversations, surgical implements used, operating procedures, panic moments and the music in the room,' Mikhailov said. 'If she was clinically dead, where was her consciousness during surgery? It is becoming evident that awareness can exist even outside our bodies.'

'And?' asked the unstoppable Sharma.

'Consciousness could determine whether you observe something or not,' replied Mikhailov. 'The flow of consciousness to you could be determining whether Shambhala is seen by you or not.'

'I still cannot understand why this mandala-like structure built on Fibonacci proportions exists,' said Sharma.

'Energy,' replied Mikhailov. 'Pure and simple energy.'

186

'Some years ago, researchers used cobalt niobate in a study,' said Mikhailov. 'Cobalt niobate is made up of linked magnetic atoms, which result in chains that are very thin, the equivalent of a bar magnet that is only one atom wide. Scientists made the chain of atoms act like a nanoscale guitar string. They found that the resulting notes produced from the spins of the atoms manifested the ratio 1.618. The fact that this entire mandala is in golden proportions tells me that the main aim is to tune into energy vibrations.'

'What sort of energy vibrations?' asked Sharma.

'Energy that concerns life,' replied Mikhailov. 'That is evident from the lotus at the apex.'

'What does the lotus have to do with it?' asked Sharma.

'In Hinduism, the lotus has always been a sacred symbol,' replied Mikhailov. 'This is because the lotus rises from muck to blossom as a beautiful and pure flower. It is almost symbolic of the process of enlightenment.'

'And is related to Brahma too,' said Sharma.

'Absolutely,' said Mikhailov. 'Brahma, the creator of the universe, was born from the lotus that sprouted from the navel of Vishnu while he was in Yoga Nidra. In fact, Vishnu, the preserver of the universe, is depicted sitting within a lotus. He is also described as lotus-eyed, as a sign of beauty.'

Sharma nodded.

'The symbolism of the lotus is also used when depicting the goddesses Lakshmi and Saraswati,' said Mikhailov. 'The lotus is particularly mentioned in the Rig Veda and is referred to several times in the later *Samhitas*. In the Atharva Veda, the human heart is compared with the lotus.'

'Isn't the lotus also sacred to Buddhists?' asked Sharma.

'Yes,' said Mikhailov. 'Buddhism has a special relationship with the lotus. Eight petals of the lotus correspond to the Noble Eightfold Path prescribed by the Buddha, and the Buddhist mantra *Om mani padme hum* refers to the *jewel in the lotus* that is symbolic of enlightenment produced by the combination of method and wisdom.'

'So the purity of the lotus applies across religions?' interjected Sharma.

'It is one of the Ashtamangala—the eight sacred signs. These span across dharmic religions such as Hinduism, Buddhism and Jainism.'

'In imagery too?'

'That came later,' said Mikhailov. 'Once Buddha began to be depicted in images and sculptures, he would often be shown as sitting cross-legged on a lotus seat or sometimes standing on a lotus pedestal. Later tradition holds that lotus flowers would blossom wherever the Buddha placed his feet. In Tibet, Padmasambhava—his name actually means "the lotus-born"—is revered as the second Buddha, having brought Buddhism to that country.'

'So this is definitely a Buddhist mandala,' reasoned Sharma. 'The lotus indicates that.'

'Not necessarily,' replied Mikhailov. 'Take Hinduism's Sri Yantra, and look at it a little differently. Let's shade in some of the triangles. Now focus your attention on the patterns created by the overlapping triangles. You will notice a large diamond—and several smaller ones—inside an eight-petal lotus. The diamond in the lotus.

'In any case, many faiths revere the lotus,' continued Mikhailov. 'In Zoroastrian architecture, the carving of Ardashir II at Taq-i-Bustan shows Mithra standing on a lotus. In ancient Jain sculptures found at Mathura, the lotus appears as the symbol of the sixth *jina* or saint. In Christianity, St Thomas' cross features a lotus underneath a crucifix. Ancient Egyptians noticed that the lotus closed its petals at night and sank into the water, miraculously reappearing in the morning with the sun. So they associated the lotus with the sun god Ra and rebirth.'

'Rebirth?' asked Sharma.

'Yes. Modern scientists are only now telling us about that. Some years ago, a UCLA team recovered a viable lotus seed that was almost 1,300 years old from a lakebed in north-east China. Several others that were 450 to 500 years old were also recovered. They then sequenced and annotated the genome of the lotus, which apparently has a super-efficient mechanism that repairs genetic defects. The lotus definitely holds secrets to longevity.'

187

'Are you familiar with the concept of *Sunyata*?' Mikhailov asked Sharma.

'Something like *Sunnata*?' asked Sharma.

Mikhailov nodded. 'Same word. The former is Sanskrit and the latter is Prakrit. Both mean the same thing—emptiness. In Mahayana Buddhism, Sunyata states that all things are empty of intrinsic existence and nature. Does the name Ernest Rutherford ring a bell?'

'No,' replied Sharma, shaking his head.

'In the early twentieth century, Rutherford's experiments showed that all atoms including solid matter are almost entirely empty space.'

'But if everything around us, including our bodies, consists of empty space, then why are we unable to float?' asked Sharma. 'Or walk through a wall?'

'Actually you *can* walk through a wall,' said Mikhailov. 'All that is needed is a momentary transformation from particle form to wave form and then back.

'But the real question that you want to ask me is the cause of solidity,' said Mikhailov. 'You want to understand what gives matter its solid feel.'

Sharma nodded. 'Yes, that's precisely it.'

'When a particle is restricted to a small area in space, it responds to this captivity by buzzing around,' replied Mikhailov. 'Have you looked at the blades of a propeller?'

'Yes,' replied Sharma. 'As in a turboprop aircraft or a table fan?'

'Exactly,' said Mikhailov. 'When the blades are stationary, you can see them individually. But what happens at high speed? They look like a solid disc instead of distinct blades. It is the high-speed movement of electrons inside an atom, at speeds close to six hundred miles per second, that give atoms their solid feel.'

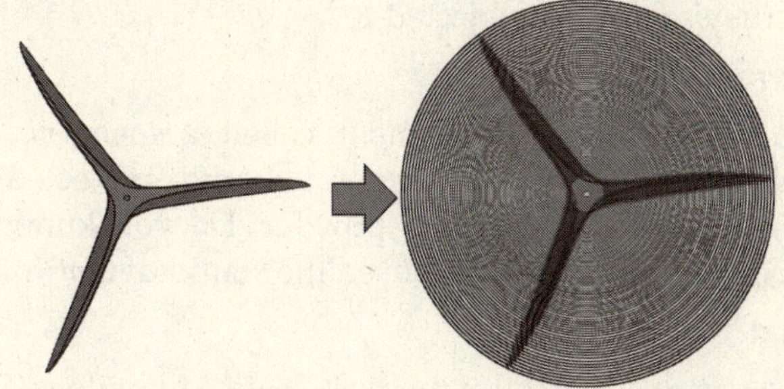

'But that sort of solidity is an illusion,' argued Sharma.

'You are right,' said Mikhailov. 'But then, so is everything else. Consider this. An atom is 99.9999999999999 per cent empty space. An atom's nucleus is around one hundred thousand times smaller than the entire atom, but it accounts for almost its entire mass.'

'What are you trying to say?' asked Sharma.

'If the entire human body were compressed under high pressure to mimic the density of a nucleus, it would be no larger than a pinhead, but the mass would not change,' said Mikhailov.

'And the implication?' asked Sharma.

'Buddhist monks and Hindu rishis are aware of the fact that they can slow down the velocity of electrons within each atom,' said Mikhailov. 'Slow down the velocity, and matter, as we know it, ceases to exist!'

188

'Have you heard the name Hans Jenny?' asked Mikhailov.

'No,' replied Sharma.

'Jenny was a Swiss scientist who created a new field of study called cymatics,' said Mikhailov. 'When materials such as sand, water, powder or metal shavings are subjected to sound waves, they assume different shapes. The shape depends on the frequency of the particular sound wave that they are being subjected to.'

'How is that done?'

'He developed an instrument called a *tonoscope,*' said Mikhailov. 'Sound was generated and projected onto a plate of fine lycopodium powder. Do you know what shape emerged when they used the sound of *Om*?'

'What?'

'Do an image search on the web,' said Mikhailov. 'Search for *Cymatic Om*.' Sharma typed the search terms into his iPad. He was stunned by the images that he saw.

'Precisely,' said Mikhailov, smiling. 'It is the Sri Yantra that emerges. Now, imagine the power of *Om* when it is combined with a physical location that is based on a mandala with someone like Brahmananda at the centre … perfect combination of mantra, yantra and tantra.'

'Brahmananda?' asked Sharma. 'What is so significant about him? I have met him several times since that initial meeting in the hospital at Kargil and he is undoubtedly an enlightened man but…'

'More enlightened than you can imagine,' said Mikhailov quietly.

'There were whispers that he is a few hundred years old,' said Sharma.

'He's far older than that,' said Mikhailov.

Sharma could not contain his excitement. 'Who is he?' he asked carefully.

'He has been known by various names in linear time,' said Mikhailov. 'Suchandara, Padmasambhava, Astika, Shribhadra and, of course, Brahmananda. But he is all of these and more simultaneously.'

'How do you know?' asked Sharma.

'Because I have seen all his forms,' replied Mikhailov. 'It was only Brahmananda who could pull me away from my Russian masters.'

'King Suchandara is said to have lived at the time of the Buddha,' said Sharma. 'So I guess Brahmananda is around 2,500 years old?'

'He has been around far longer than that,' said Mikhailov.

'How long?' asked Sharma, his heart beating wildly.

'Since the time Rama returned to Ayodhya after the battle in Lanka,' said Mikhailov.

189

Sujatha and Vijay were inside the café, seated together on the sofa of a private booth, awaiting a visitor. It had been six weeks since the happenings at Milesian and a bandage around Vijay's upper arm was the only indication of any trauma.

'I still cannot fully comprehend what happened to us,' said Sujatha, as she allowed her head to rest on his shoulder. 'I'm just happy that we still have each other.'

Just then, Vijay saw him walk through the door of the café, looking as spiffy as ever. He took off his Aviator sunglasses and looked around the room before he saw Vijay waving out to him. He walked up to their booth and slid into the sofa opposite them.

'Are you recovering well enough?' asked Vijay.

'The army teaches us to deal with bullets,' said Sharma, smiling. 'The surgeon told me that he removed a bullet and splinters from my abdomen. They found three litres of blood in my abdominal cavity! The surgeon was damn surprised that I had no infection. My wife joked that it was the whisky in my blood that had killed the germs.'

They laughed. 'By the way, what happened to *your* arm?' asked Sharma.

'I fell,' said Vijay. 'Wrong angle. The chip you embedded in my arm is gone.'

'Crap,' joked Sharma. 'And here I was, hoping to keep you under permanent surveillance.'

'Both of us want to thank you,' said Sujatha. 'Words seem inadequate…'

Sharma smiled. 'No thanks required,' he said. 'It was quite an experience. Particularly hang-gliding with a prosthetic leg! I hope that RAW won't expect me to make a habit of it!'

'What happened to Petrov?' asked Vijay.

'I shot the bastard,' said Sharma. 'He thought that he had finished me off. He hadn't. I rose like a phoenix from the ashes!' He laughed at his own dramatic flair.

'But do you know what actually happened to *us*?' asked Vijay, who wasn't prepared to make merry just yet. 'I'm still searching for answers. One moment Sujatha and I were in that forest—standing within the mandala—and about to get shot by Petrov. In another instant, I woke up in a small town called Dungari, some fifty kilometres away. Sujatha was right next to me. We were both lying in a barley field, semi-conscious. How on earth did we get there?'

'It was the bindu that saved you both,' said Sharma. 'You are a scientist. So you obviously understand string theory, right?'

Vijay nodded.

'Isn't a rosary also a string?' asked Sharma. 'A string with one hundred and eight particles and a bindu?'

Sharma waited for his idea to sink in with the couple.

'The one hundred and eight beads that Brahmananda and his sages wore were actually the beads from an ancient rosary at Nalanda,' said Sharma. 'But where did that rosary originally come from?'

'You know?' asked Vijay.

'It was the very rosary that Ravana wore while presiding over war rituals before enjoining in battle with Rama,' said Sharma.

'What do you mean?' asked Vijay, still out of it. 'Ravana joined Rama in rituals?'

'Certainly,' said Sharma. 'While recovering in hospital, I had a chance to read a translation of the *Adhyatma Ramayana,* one among the several versions of the epic. According to that, Ravana was not just a demon, he was a king and a learned Brahmin. Ravana not only conducted the ceremony but also blessed Rama. In fact, he even brought Sita to the ceremony to sit by Rama's side because the rituals in question could not be completed without the presence of Rama's spouse.'

'Seems unbelievable,' said Vijay.

'Makes one wonder whether Ravana was truly the "demon" that he is portrayed to be.'

'But how did the rosary reach Nalanda from Ravana's neck?' asked Vijay.

'Ravana gave it to Lakshmana,' replied Sharma.

190

Vijay took a deep breath. This was a little too much to absorb. 'Why would Ravana give his precious prayer-beads to Lakshmana?' asked Vijay uncertainly.

'We are told that Rama asked his brother Lakshmana to sit at the feet of Ravana when he finally lay dying. Why?' asked Sharma.

'The woman who took care of us at the orphanage used to tell us a story,' answered Vijay. 'That Ravana had been given something very powerful by Shiva—it was called the Atma Lingam. And Rama wanted it.'

'Right,' said Sharma. 'Do you know what the Atma Lingam looks like?'

Vijay did not.

'The Atma Lingam is simply the string of one hundred and eight rudraksha beads, along with the bindu, the one that hangs around your neck,' said Sharma.

Neither Vijay nor Sujatha spoke. Vijay fidgeted uncomfortably with the bindu, feeling he ought to say something. 'But there's that story in which Shiva told Ravana never to place the Atma Lingam on the ground,' he argued. 'And Ganesha tricked him by taking it and doing precisely that!' There were some advantages to having been brought up in an orphanage with a temple next door, he thought, and even a tiny library.

'True,' said Sharma. 'But there are over three hundred versions of the *Ramayana*. Each one has variations. So which one will you treat as the ultimate truth? The bindu that you possess—along with the one hundred and eight other beads—activates the vibrations from eight Shiva temples along the 79 E longitude. It is the aggregate energy from all these locations that the rishis were able to use.'

'How does the bindu relate to the longitude?' asked Vijay.

'Because that longitude also represents the path that Rama would have taken on his way back from Lanka,' replied Sharma. 'Each of the temples along that path was "charged" to resonate at the same frequency as the Atma Lingam.'

'Why did Ravana agree to part with it?' asked Sujatha.

'Ravana had spent thousands of years pleasing Brahma,' replied Sharma. 'Then thousands of years pleasing Shiva. He knew that he had to also please the final member of the holy trinity—Vishnu. And Rama was an avatar of Vishnu.'

'It seems odd that Ravana would cooperate with Rama,' said Sujatha.

'Not that odd if you realize that Rama and Ravana were complementary figures. Without Ravana, there would not be an epic called *Ramayana*. And you know what? There would be no Rama either!'

'You make Ravana sound like a hero,' said Sujatha.

'Ravana was one of the wisest Brahmins ever,' replied Sharma. 'During his lifetime, he made Lanka into one of the most prosperous and advanced kingdoms ever. Moreover, he had the blessings of both Brahma and Shiva. History is written by the victors, and the events narrated in the *Ramayana* merely reflect the opinions and prejudices of the winning side. Hence the negative descriptions of Ravana.'

'What happened to the rosary?' asked Vijay.

'The Atma Lingam was kept with Lakshmana until he threw it away in the forest,' replied Sharma.

'Why would he do that?' asked Sujatha.

'Lakshmana had the unenviable task of leaving Sita at Valmiki's ashram when she was exiled yet again—this time by Rama,' said Sharma. 'As he left her there on the instructions of his brother, Lakshmana flung the rosary away in disgust. He was convinced that the Atma Lingam had brought misfortune on them.'

'And?'

'The Atma Lingam came into the possession of one of the sages at Valmiki's ashram,' said Sharma. 'His name was Sashwata and the rosary remained with him through the various roles that he played over the millennia—Suchandara, Padmasambhava, Astika, Shribhadra, Brahmananda and countless others.'

'Is that why I was seeing him as part of a hologram in the forests of Milesian?' asked Vijay.

'Time is not linear,' replied Sharma. 'Each of his forms is just a probability function, like the bands of light that one observes in a double-slit light experiment.'

'And how do *you* know all this?' Sujatha finally demanded.

'Because it is written in the Akashic Records,' said Sharma. 'While I was recovering from my amputation in the hospital at Kargil, Brahmananda narrated the story to me—the story of Sashwata. The man who refused to die so that he could fulfil his destiny. Little did I know that Brahmananda *was* that man. It is the very story that gave me the will to live.'

'What about the bindu?' asked Vijay. 'How did Mikhailov come to have it?'

'During the Islamic raids on Nalanda, the individual beads went missing, including the bindu,' said Sharma. 'The rosary was a powerful one, allowing a group of rishis to behave as a single entity, a string. The Russians had sent exploration teams to Nalanda in their quest to find the location of Shangri-La and ended up discovering the bindu during their excavations. Mikhailov's grandfather, who had led that mission, passed it on to his grandson.'

'But why did Mikhailov give it to me?' asked Vijay.

'Because Mikhailov knew that both Schmidt and Petrov were after him,' replied Sharma. 'Giving it to you was his best shot at preserving it.'

191

'This still does not explain how Sujatha and I reached Dungari,' said Vijay.

'What worked for you was that hug,' said Sharma.

For a moment, Vijay and Sujatha wondered whether Sharma was joking. But he was in deadly earnest.

'Examine the bindu closely,' said Sharma. Vijay took it from around his neck and placed it on the table.

'Do you notice the dual shading of the bindu?' asked Sharma. 'When you embraced each other, you became whole—a combination of Shiva and Shakti—with the bindu locked in your embrace. You were *de facto* Kalachakra and Vishwamata within the mandala.'

'And then?'

'You became part of the *string*!' said Sharma. 'When Brahmananda and his rishis went into deep meditation and chanted *Om*, the gentle levitation produced was on account of the rishis being at the cusp of particle-wave transformation—being light enough to experience oneness with the universe without leaving the material state. At such times, they would suck energy from the Shiva temples along the string. This was also the reason that the Schumann Resonance would peak at such times, owing to elevated levels of consciousness.'

'That does not explain how we were transported fifty kilometres away,' said Vijay.

'When the showdown with Petrov happened, all one hundred and eight sages transformed themselves from particles to waves, carrying you both along. This was quite normal for them—travelling to a different realm and thus defying time and space. But given that both of you are not elevated souls,' he stopped to grin at the two of them, 'you morphed back from waves to particles within a few seconds. The location simply happened to be fifty kilometres away.'

192

There was a long silence as Vijay and Sujatha took time to absorb all of what Sharma had said.

Vijay was the first to break it. 'What happened to the sages?' he asked.

'They went through a wormhole,' replied Sharma. Vijay nodded, but Sujatha had no clue of what that meant.

'Spacetime is like an infinite sheet, warped and folded in many places,' explained Vijay for her benefit, quickly sketching a figure on a paper napkin.

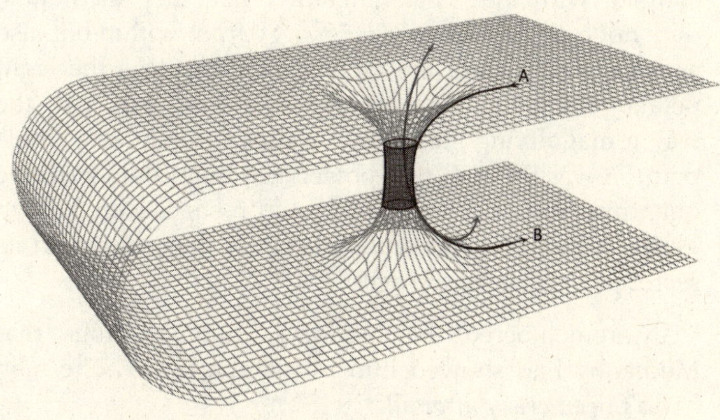

'A wormhole is simply a tunnel that connects two folds—what mythology often refers to as "realms". By going through a wormhole, one can reach another realm almost instantly. It's a shortcut!'

'Why was the Milesian facility shaped like a Kalachakra mandala?' asked Vijay. 'And why were there one hundred and eight rishis at the centre of the mandala, seated on lotus petal-like platforms?'

'Energy,' explained Sharma. 'The Atma Lingam only had power if one knew how to be a true yogi. The Buddha was indeed a true yogi. He assisted Suchandara—Sashwata, Padmasambhava, Astika, Shribhadra, Brahmananda ... whatever—in unlocking the Atma Lingam's power. That process came to be known as Kalachakra.'

Sharma smiled at Vijay and Sujatha. 'The Kalachakra mandala is a representation of the energies of the entire universe. At the core is Kalachakra—along with his consort—seated on a lotus of eight petals. A mandala is based on the Sri Yantra that has one hundred and eight male and female intersection points. Having this mandala located along an energy meridian gave Brahmananda's rishis incredible powers of perception, particularly when coupled with the Atma Lingam. When they meditated, they not only used their own energy from within but also sucked energy from the eight Shiva temples—the eight petals—along the same energy meridian. Much in the way a magnifying glass concentrates sunlight at a single point. It was through that power that they could perceive quantum twins. Brahmananda and his sages were known as the *Keepers of the Kalachakra* because they preserved its secret powers down the ages.'

Vijay remembered the list of latitude readings that Mikhailov had showed him in his apartment. The man hadn't been crazy after all.

'Where exactly is Mikhailov, by the way?' asked Vijay. Sharma had told them that the scientist was very much alive and well.

'Well settled in Dharamsala,' replied Sharma. 'I think he has finally found a place he can call home.'

'And Brahmananda?'

'Could be anywhere,' replied Sharma. 'But most likely near his library.'

193

Henderson took a round of the facilities of the Molecular and Universal Audio along with LIGO's former director Harvey Walsh. The happenings at Milesian Labs had thrown a spanner in Minerva's plans. But Henderson's plans for Molecular and Universal Audio were paying off.

Minerva had poured millions into the cutting-edge research that was being conducted there. The big win had come from Judith successfully headhunting Harvey Walsh from LIGO. The other victory had been Williams securing an ancient document that had remained hidden in the base of a mummified monk's statue. It had been a veritable treasure chest of knowledge to do with utilizing the universe's energy in different ways.

Molecular and Universal Audio was a massive enterprise that boasted the world's best anechoic chamber, a room designed to maintain absolute silence. Typical anechoic chambers provided zero decibel environments, but the one created here was -20.6 decibel.

'How is less than zero even possible?' wondered Henderson.

'Zero decibel only means the lowest volume of sound that humans can hear,' said Harvey Walsh. 'Zero is on a logarithmic scale. It does not mean absolute silence, as you might think.'

'Why do you need an anechoic chamber at all?' asked Henderson.

'Because inside it, we can try multiple variations of sounds that can achieve the results that we're after,' explained Harvey. Seeing the bewildered look on his employer's face, Harvey explained further.

'During my tenure at LIGO, we found that gravitational waves do exist, as stated by Einstein,' he said. 'But at Molecular and Universal Audio, we also discovered what gravitational waves *sound* like. Yes, they do have sound.'

'And what do they sound like?' asked Henderson.

'Like drops of water in a bucket,' said Harvey. 'Almost the sound that an air bubble makes when it reaches the surface of water. Or the sound of an air kiss: *mwahh*!'

It was rather strange to see Harvey puckering his lips to mime a kiss.

'Have you heard the sound chanted by yogic practitioners? *Om*?' asked Harvey.

'Sure,' said Henderson. He was only too familiar with the sound that had been used at Milesian for identifying quantum twins. 'How is that important to your research?'

'You see, *Om* is actually the sound that is produced by combining three different sounds—*aa*, *oo* and *mm*,' said Harvey.

'Why these three sounds in particular?'

'Because when you meditate on these three sounds, each one causes a vibration in a different region of your body,' said Harvey. 'For example, the *aa* sound causes vibrations in your gut; the *oo* sound resonates with your heart region; and the *mm* sound vibrates with the region between your eyes. Thus the idea of *Om* being a sound that accompanied creation is not that strange!'

'And the *Om* symbol itself?' asked Henderson. 'That squiggly shape? What does that signify?'

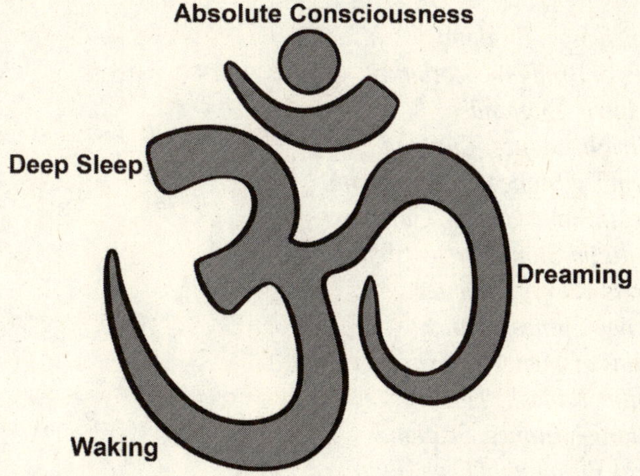

'You will notice that there are three curves that are joined together,' said Harvey, pulling up an image of the symbol on his smartphone. 'Each one represents one of those sounds, but it also represents the three states of waking, dreaming and deep sleep.'

'And the little crescent and dot on the top?' asked Henderson.

'That symbolizes absolute consciousness,' said Harvey. 'Supposedly the state that one attains when one becomes intimately aware of one's own connectedness with everything else in the universe.'

'How is this related to what we're after?' asked Henderson.

'We have found many locations around the world that we can literally *tune to*—almost as with a tuning fork,' said Harvey. 'The world has spent years wondering what is so special about these locations. Now we know.'

194

'Want to see this list?' asked Harvey, pulling out a folded sheet from his pocket. Henderson looked at some of the locations listed on it.

Stonehenge, England
Ring of Brodgar, Scotland
Avebury, England
Rollright Stones, England
Drombeg Stone Circles, Ireland
Wassu Stone Circles, Gambia
Muduma Stone Circles, Telangana, India
Zorats Karer, Armenia
Carnac Stones, France
Taulas of Menorca, Spain
Mount Kailash, Tibet
Callanish Stones, Scotland
Great Pyramid of Giza, Egypt
Mount Shasta, California, USA
Glastonbury, England
Haleakalā Volcano, Maui, Hawai
Mount Fuji, Japan
Lake Titicaca, Peru
Sedona, Arizona, USA
Bermuda Triangle

'You're wondering about the locations on the list,' said Harvey. 'These are energy *chakras* on earth. Ancient man recognized the fact that these locations had unexplainable energy. That's why they created stone circles, pyramids or mandalas at these locations. All these spots can amplify the sounds that we engineer from here,' said Harvey.

'What sound would that be?' asked Henderson.

'If we combine *aa, oo* and *mm*, we get *Om*, also written as A-U-M, the sound that accompanied primordial creation,' said Harvey. 'But the Kalachakra Multantra obtained by Bruce Williams also spoke of nidhane—destruction. The question that we asked ourselves was what would happen if we reverse-engineered the sound of A-U-M to M-U-A? Wouldn't that be the water-drop sound that we heard at LIGO? And using it, would we actually be able to engineer destruction?'

'Could you?' asked Henderson.

'Our experiments have had some unfortunate consequences,' said Harvey.

'Like what?' asked Henderson.

'Sinkholes,' answered Harvey. 'At various places around the world.'

'And you can actually make these happen?'

'With amazing accuracy,' said Harvey. 'Even a single house for instance.'

Henderson was quiet for a minute. Then he smiled. 'Now I know why you insisted on calling this operation Molecular and Universal Audio,' he said. 'It also abbreviates to MUA.'

195

The President nursed his drink as he ruminated on what had happened to Jean Belanger a few hours ago. His mind wandered back to the 530 days that he had spent on his election trail. It had stopped four weeks ago with his inauguration. Around half a million people had attended the ceremony on the West Front of the United States Capitol Building in Washington. The inauguration symbolized the formal culmination of the presidential transition of what was begun when he won the US presidential election. It had been a long and dirty election that had sapped the energy of both candidates.

A few days before the inauguration, the new President had arrived in Washington, DC at Joint Base Andrews on a plane flown by the US Air Force. That same evening, he had been part of a high-profile white-tie dinner in order to meet foreign diplomats along with his Cabinet picks. The next day he had attended a public concert at the Lincoln Memorial. He had then attended a luncheon and proceeded to Arlington National Cemetery to lay a wreath at the Tomb of the Unknown Soldier.

He had spent the night at Blair House along with his family and attended a church service at St John's Episcopal Church on the morning of his inauguration. After the service, the incoming First Couple had gone to the White House to meet the outgoing First Couple. They had posed outside for photos for the White House press corps. The two Presidents had shared the presidential motorcade limousine, as they made their way to the Capitol for the inaugural ceremony.

He had been administered the oath by the Chief Justice of the United States with his hand on a copy of his personal Bible. TV viewership of the event in America alone had been over twenty-eight million and it had turned out to be the most streamed video ever on Twitter. After the swearing-in, the Marine Band had played *Hail to the Chief*. A twenty-eight-gun salute had followed in the new President's honour.

He was looking exceptionally fit for a man of sixty and was clad, as always, in a bespoke suit on Inauguration Day. His lean frame and glasses gave him an air of gravity as he had begun to read his inaugural address.

'Every four years,' he had begun, reading the speech off the dual screens of a teleprompter, 'we assemble here on these steps to effect a peaceful transfer of power.' He had allowed his eyes to pan over the audience and then continued. 'I am truly grateful to everyone who made this possible. We, the citizens of America, must now come together to defend ourselves from the ravages of terrorism and extremism. We will face challenges and we shall confront them head-on. I promise you that, with your support and willingness, we shall get the job done! Together, we will determine the course of America and the world for years to come.'

There had been loud applause as he uttered those words. The President had not smiled in response. There had been too much on his mind. Too much work awaited.

196

Mafraqi's Raqqa always felt under siege. Most people walking the streets looked like they wished they were dead. Many were missing limbs or loved ones, or sporting shrapnel wounds. Surrounding them were broken and bombed-out buildings that had been battered by the forces on either side. Collapsed roofs and pockmarked streets were the norm. Basic requirements such as food, water, clothing, medicines, shelter, sanitation or electricity were luxuries. Added to that was the fear of Hisbah, the religious police, who constantly patrolled the streets to find the pettiest infringements of Sharia. In Raqqa, abnormal was the new normal. The muezzin's call to prayer was no longer an invitation. It was a command. And not heeding that command would attract immediate punishment.

On most days, there were public executions. The loudspeakers today were announcing the forthcoming executions of three people—a rebel, an activist and a suspected informer. All of them had been lined up, duly handcuffed and blindfolded as their sentences were read out. A burly man with a beard that reached his navel swiftly hacked off their heads in quick succession.

Many observers were desperate to leave or to turn their gaze away from the terrible scene, but doing so was dangerous. Mafraqi's spies were always hanging around, searching for faces that showed anger or disgust. Such people would later be singled out for questioning or administered lashes. Arbitrary arrests and torture at detention centres were common.

Mafraqi performed Salah in his cave on the outskirts of Raqqa. Then he sat down on the thick rug and took a sip of black tea. Seated next to him was Habib. In his hands was a satellite phone that had been provided by Henderson. 'The time has come,' said Mafraqi simply, as Habib handed over the Iridium phone to him.

'Will it be the location we discussed?' asked Habib, his heart racing.

Mafraqi smiled in acknowledgment. 'The infidel dog who has been elected President of America has taken it upon himself to destroy Muslims,' he said. 'He has to be our very first target.' He started punching a sequence of numbers into the phone. The numbers were coordinates that would direct all the destructive powers that were available at his command. He punched in the final number and waited for a beep of confirmation. It came a second later.

But accompanying the beep was an ominous rumbling. This was followed by tremors, and the ground beneath the cave began shaking violently.

Both Mafraqi and Habib attempted to run outside but they found themselves freefalling through an abyss instead. The entire mass of rock within which the cave was located came crashing down, massive boulders and debris hurtling through the sinkhole that had opened up inside the cave. One of the rocks hit Mafraqi and fractured his skull. Then both men were swallowed, suffocated and consumed by Mother Earth.

197

'I don't know how I would have lived if I had lost you, Vee,' said Sujatha as they sat in her tiny flat, recollecting their experiences.

'I would have still been around,' said Vijay, squeezing her hand reassuringly. 'Just at a different coordinate in spacetime.'

'What do you mean?' asked Sujatha.

'Think about it,' said Vijay. 'Einstein told us that space and time are intrinsically part of the same continuum.'

'I don't know what that means,' said Sujatha.

'Let's say that I needed to meet you in Delhi,' explained Vijay. 'I would need to tell you where. For example, P83 Connaught Circus, New Delhi. But would that be sufficient information?'

'No,' replied Sujatha. 'I would also need a date and time at which we are supposed to meet.'

'Correct,' said Vijay. 'So if I told you five o'clock in the evening on the following Saturday, then the statement is complete because you now have both a time and place.'

'Right,' said Sujatha. 'What's your point?'

'We normally look at space as Euclidean or three-dimensional,' said Vijay. 'We can identify a point along an x, y and z axis. But what if time were the fourth dimension? What if there were no separate entities called space or time but only one single continuum called spacetime?'

There was a confused expression on Sujatha's face.

'It means that every place and every event would lie in that continuum,' said Vijay. 'You would simply be observing a point along that continuum. It also means that there is no sequential behaviour. Everything that is happening to you has happened before. Everything that has happened in the past will also occur in the future. In fact, there is no past, present nor future. Everything just *is*.'

Sujatha tried to figure it out in her head but gave up.

'Don't even try imagining it,' said Vijay. 'Physicists use mathematical abstractions to imagine spacetime. Mystics simply "perceive" or experience it intuitively. But what it really means is that when you experience a sensation of déjà vu, you are not mistaken. It *has* happened before. It's like a scratched DVD, repeating the same scene over and over again.'

Vijay reached out to hold Sujatha's hand again. 'Millions of connections between sub-atomic particles are happening right now. This moment is infinite. So Sujatha, will you marry me yet again?'

198

Sharma left his wife behind at the hotel in Dehradun when he ventured out. He knew that this was a meeting that had to be one-to-one.

The chopper dropped him at the highest point of the hill, near the cave library complex. He watched his breath fog in front of him. Winter was definitely the best time to be here, because it offered views of lush green forests, snow and sunlight in a single picture frame. Sharma tucked his hands into his jacket and made his way to the solitary bench outside the entrance to the cave.

Someone was already waiting for him on that bench. Sharma sat down next to him, admiring the stunning view of the mountains in the north and the almost limitless stretch of verdant valley in the south. It was a veritable feast for both the eyes and soul.

Sharma pulled his gaze away from the panorama and looked at the man on the bench. He was dressed in his usual saffron and vermillion robes. The only concessions to winter were the socks and shoes on his feet. On his lap was his usual notebook covered in maroon fabric embroidered with a lotus flower.

Brahmananda smiled at Sharma who was rubbing his hands together. 'Feeling cold?' he asked. Sharma nodded sheepishly. He could tolerate the harsh cold of Kargil when he was in battle mode but seemingly went soft when he wasn't.

'Thank you for meeting me,' said Sharma. 'When I stood before the meditating Brahmananda, I saw many faces. And then all of your forms disappeared. Now I have to get my head around the fact that you are Sashwata, Suchandara, Padmasambhava, Astika, Shribhadra, Brahmananda and so many others. Forgive me for saying this, but I am entirely baffled. I have known you only as Brahmananda, my teacher.'

Brahmananda's face crinkled into a smile. 'Have you heard of Pingala?' he asked Sharma.

'I hope you're not going to say that you're him too,' said Sharma. 'My head's too crowded already!' Brahmananda laughed.

'But yes, I know of him,' said Sharma. 'He was the second century BCE scholar who wrote the treatise on poetry metres.'

'Very good,' said Brahmananda. 'But what else was he famous for?'

'Binary numbers,' said Sharma.

'Exactly,' said Brahmananda, approvingly. 'Something that I said I would explain to you one day as the very basis for describing the universe. The binary system is used in computers. Any number can be expressed as a series of zeroes or ones. Pingala was concerned with poetry metres, so he used the concept of short and long syllables, much before the West caught on.'

Sharma wondered anew at the breadth of this man's knowledge. *So what if he'd had centuries to think it all up!*

'Each "1" in a binary number represents a power of two and its position determines the power to which the two is to be raised,' said Brahmananda, writing out a series of binary numbers for Sharma's benefit.

$1001 = (1 \times 2^3) + (0 \times 2^2) + (0 \times 2^1) + (1 \times 2^0) = 9$

$1110 = (1 \times 2^3) + (1 \times 2^2) + (1 \times 2^1) + (0 \times 2^0) = 14$

He paused as Sharma tried working out the examples for himself.

'Now imagine if you could be represented by a matrix of zeros and ones?' asked Brahmananda.

'How so?' asked Sharma.

Brahmananda quickly drew a sketch.

Space-->

Time-->

1	0	0	1	0	1	1	0	1	0
0	0	0	1	1	1	1	1	0	0
0	0	0	0	0	0	1	1	0	0
0	1	0	1	0	1	0	1	0	1
1	1	0	0	1	0	0	0	1	1
1	1	1	1	1	1	1	0	0	0
0	0	0	1	1	1	0	1	0	1
1	0	1	0	0	0	0	0	1	0
0	1	0	0	0	0	1	0	0	0
1	0	1	0	1	0	0	0	1	1

'Imagine that every "0" represents you as a wave and each "1" represents you as a particle along the dimensions of space and time. That's precisely what the Akashic Records are! A description of you at every coordinate.'

'I'm a binary number?' asked Sharma incredulously.

'What is the Sanskrit term for mathematics?' asked Brahmananda.

'*Ganita,*' replied Sharma.

'Correct,' said Brahmananda. 'Etymologically from the root *gana,* which means "to count" or "to categorize". Now, which is the deity that is worshipped by Hindus before all others?'

'*Ganapati,*' replied Sharma.

'Right,' said Brahmananda. 'Notice the common root "gana"? Mathematics is at the very heart of worship. Scholars try to explain Ganapati as "lord of the group" but what if he is symbolic of the numbers that define the universe? What if he represents the fact that each one of us is either wave or particle at various coordinates in spacetime?'

'How?' asked Sharma. 'You had once told me that the Valmiki *Ramayana* and the *Gayatri Mantra* hold the key to my questions.'

'Do you know that there are twenty-four letters in the *Gayatri Mantra* and 24,000 shlokas in Valmiki's *Ramayana*? The first letter of every thousandth shloka from Valmiki's *Ramayana,* when put together, miraculously results in the *Gayatri Mantra*. Mathematics yet again. It's all around you!'

199

Brahmananda poured two cups of hot lemon water from the flask that he was carrying and gave one to Sharma. It felt good in the biting cold.

Sharma tried to make sense of what Brahmananda was saying.

'Why do some people have memories of past lives?' asked Brahmananda. 'Why is it that those memories can be brought to the fore through hypnosis? Dr Ian Stevenson collected data on reincarnation from over three thousand children over forty years. He found that memories, talents, and traits got carried over in addition to the ability to remember names and faces. Lethal wounds in previous lifetimes got carried over as birthmarks in current ones.'

'What explains it?' asked Sharma.

'If we go back to duality, then every particle is also a wave,' said Brahmananda. 'You hit a coordinate in spacetime, manifest as a particle. Then you move to another point in spacetime. In between those two points, you are a wave again. But the wave always has a memory of where it has been. Changing lifetimes are simply the same wave, call it the *soul* if you like, manifesting itself as a particle in a different point of spacetime.'

'But why do I not know where I've come from?' asked Sharma. 'Or where I'm going?'

'In quantum theory there is something called Heisenberg's Uncertainty Principle,' said Brahmananda. 'The principle states that there is a fundamental limit to what one can know about a quantum system. For instance, the more accurately one knows a particle's position, the less one knows about its momentum and vice-versa.'

'How does that explain anything?' asked Sharma, bewildered.

'Exactly what I said! But broadly, it means that the more we know about the particle nature of something, the less we know of its wave nature and vice-versa,' explained Brahmananda. 'If you are focused entirely on your life—your career, monetary status, health, home, romance—the less you would know about where you've come from or where you're going. Hence the need for ascetics and seers like me to step away from ordinary life, and our consequent ability to know about the multiplicity of our lives. Niels Bohr famously called it complementarity. Bohr considered particle nature and wave nature as two complementary descriptions of the same reality, each of them being only partly correct.'

'What about karma?' asked Sharma. 'Is there no cause and effect if all your forms exist simultaneously?'

'At the sub-atomic level, matter does not exist with certainty at definite places. Instead, it shows *tendencies to exist*. Events do not occur with certainty at fixed times but show *tendencies to occur*. Everything is just a probability, all duly encoded in the spacetime hologram of the universe. Karma is simply that. A probability function! I show tendencies to exist at various coordinates, as do you. And there is no sequential nature of time. All my forms exist simultaneously, as do yours.'

'And dharma?' asked Sharma.

'Just because the probability of your taking a right turn along a given path is 80 per cent does not mean that you *will* take it,' said Brahmananda. 'It may very well be a left turn even though it only has a 20 per cent probability. There is always free will. Free will that can influence the probability function is dharma.'

200

There was a lull in the conversation. Both men absorbed the majesty of the mountains in silence.

'The pictures of the Kalachakra Multantra that the Paris art dealer gave me,' said Sharma. 'Why were those documents in the hands of Tibetan immigrants in India? And how did Williams acquire them?'

'The immigrants in question were no ordinary people,' said Brahmananda. 'The mother who was murdered was a descendant of the Rigden kings, the ones who had preserved the Kalachakra teachings passed on by the Buddha to Suchandara. The mummified monk was probably one of her distant ancestors.'

'Why was she killed?' asked Sharma.

Brahmananda shrugged. 'It was certainly not for any monetary gain,' he said. 'Whoever killed her—probably Minerva—knew that she had the Multantra. They knew and coveted its power.'

'Power?' asked Sharma. 'Like your power along with those one hundred and eight sages at the mandala?'

'No,' replied Brahmananda. 'That was positive power. But tantra is the ability to use negative and turn it to positive, like the peacock that consumes poison and uses it to brighten its plumage. What is the corollary to that?'

'That positive can be used for negative?' asked Sharma.

'In the wrong hands, the Multantra can be used for destruction,' said Brahmananda. 'Hence the word "nidhane". In Prakrit, it is an innocent word that means "container", but in Sanskrit it becomes ominous because it implies "destruction". And the Multantra was in Sanskrit, not Prakrit. Whoever took that Multantra knew that they could misuse it.'

'Like Williams,' said Sharma.

'The greatest mistake that humans make is to think that they are distinct and separate from the rest of the universe around them,' said Brahmananda. 'It is that fallacy which the Kalachakra attempts to demolish. Reminds you of the knot that binds you to the rest of the universe.'

'The knot?' asked Sharma.

'Imagine a very smooth rope that is made from many different materials,' said Brahmananda. 'This rope is suspended from the ceiling. Towards the top, it is woven from silk; in the middle, it is nylon; towards the bottom, it is cotton.'

Sharma closed his eyes to visualize it.

'Now imagine that there is a knot in this rope towards the top,' said Brahmananda. 'The knot can freely slide down or up owing to the smoothness of the rope. Imagine the knot sliding down from the silk portion to the nylon portion and finally to the cotton portion. Is it the same knot or a different knot each time?'

'It's the same knot,' said Sharma.

'What is the word for *thread* in Tibetan?' asked Brahmananda.

'No idea.'

'Tantra,' replied Brahmananda. 'And in Sanskrit it means "to weave". In effect, tantra is simply the knot that ties everything to everyone and beyond. The mandala is a visualization of that. Your mind and body, surrounded by your world and companions, surrounded by the wider universe and tied to the wheel of time. Hence the original advice that I offered you at Dhamma Salila—to master the knot!'

Epilogue

The last week of February

The President had taken a weekend trip to Switzerland and arranged a meeting with several European business leaders at his house in Zurich. It was a lovely mansion located in Alstadt, Zurich's historic part of town, featuring cobblestone streets, family stores, restaurants and religious landmarks. The medical team at Bethesda had kept him updated regarding Jean Belanger's condition.

He had then jetted back to Washington, DC, to complete another round of meetings with American business leaders at a reception in the Blue Room of the White House. The list comprised fifty business leaders—CEOs of Citigroup, Walmart, Apple, Blackstone, Mastercard, Microsoft, NYSE, Google, General Motors, Tesla, General Electric and other Fortune-500 companies.

The White House spokesman had perfunctorily announced that the event served as an 'opportunity to discuss policies to create a pro-business climate with top partnership CEOs from all industries'. The discussion was ostensibly on infrastructure, government, taxation, workforce development and improving the business climate. A large contingent of White House officials, including the Transportation Secretary, the House Majority Leader and the Commerce Secretary, were also present.

The Blue Room had windows with a view of the South Lawn and was furnished in French Empire style. On the ceiling hung a nineteenth-century wood-and-cut-glass

French chandelier encircled by acanthus leaves. Sapphire-blue silk fabric had been used for the draperies and upholstery, thus giving the room its name.

'I am delighted to announce that the Canadian Prime Minister, Jean Belanger, has made a complete recovery at the Walter Reed National Military Medical Center and will be flying out from Bethesda later today,' said the President, raising his glass. His assembled guests also raised their glasses and toasted their foreign visitor's health.

The President then went on to circulate, shaking hands individually with his guests and thanking each one for accepting his invitation. He knew most of the guests, given that he had run one of the largest business conglomerates before taking over as President. Each handshake was accompanied by a little remark or gesture to reinforce a sense of familiarity. He was nothing if not a great networker.

He reached the south end of the room and shook hands with an exceptionally familiar face. Mason Henderson of Genchem. To the rest of those present in the room, their handshake was ordinary, but the two men knew otherwise. Each man pressed his forefinger with a slightly greater pressure than was usual against the other's Mount of Venus. A knowing look passed between them.

'Hope all is well, Mason?' asked the President. It was a perfectly innocent remark to others. But Henderson knew that the President was referring to the implications of Jean Belanger's survival.

'Absolutely, Mr President,' replied Henderson to President Bruce Williams. 'How's the golf these days?'

President Williams got up from his desk, stepped out of the Oval Office, and headed south of the Rose Garden. It was the perfect break from an otherwise aggravating day.

The President was a golfer like most of his predecessors, including Eisenhower, Kennedy, Ford, Nixon, Johnson, Reagan, Bush, Clinton and Obama. But these days he rarely found the time to complete a full round on the golf course. So, he did the next best thing—putt on the White House green.

The green had been originally installed in 1954 by Eisenhower but had been relocated to the current spot by Clinton. The President walked the thirty-odd paces towards the green and was handed his putter. He quickly surveyed the line of his intended putt. He stood beside the ball and made a few practice strokes while looking at the hole and then mentally worked out a stroke speed and length that he was confident of. He leaned in the opposite direction of the slope that he was standing on to help him fight visual distortion, shifted his weight to his heels and took the shot. It was perfect—neither too fast nor too slow, and at a flawless angle. The ball effortlessly nestled into the bottom of the cup.

And then the ground caved in. The entire putting green—around two thousand square feet—collapsed and Williams fell inside it. He toppled over as he went in, head first. From above, heaps of earth fell on him. His Secret Service bodyguards fell along with him.

By the time the alarm was raised and emergency teams rushed in to excavate and pull out bodies, President Williams had already suffocated to death.

Henderson opened his closet door and walked inside. He pushed aside the business suits that hung there to reveal a wall mirror. He pressed the mirror gently and it sprang open on a hinge. On the wall behind the mirror was a vault. Henderson placed his entire palm on the scanner and waited for the reassuring whirring of levers as the door unlocked itself.

There wasn't much inside the vault, only a thick manila envelope he had received many years ago. Henderson pulled it out and took it to his bedroom. He sat at the desk in a corner and placed the envelope on it. He unwound the red thread that held the flap closed and peered inside.

He took out the materials from the envelope, placing them on the desk—a single hardcover book, a set of papers held together by a binder clip, a small cream-coloured envelope and a journal.

He looked at the faded green-and-gold leather of the book. *The Holy Qur'an*, printed by Zia ul Quran Publishers, Lahore. He put aside the book and looked at the papers. Right on top was an old passport issued by the government of Pakistan. He opened it to the first page. On it, was the photograph of a beautiful woman. He looked at the details handwritten inside.

Name: Maryam Rashidi
Place of birth: Lahore, Pakistan

The next document was a City Civil Court Petition for Adult Name Change. It requested that Maryam Rashidi's name be changed to Mary Richards. Following that was an Application for Naturalization based upon her marriage to one Mike Henderson. Finally, a marriage certificate that showed her name having further changed from Mary Richards to Mary Henderson.

Henderson looked at the two sepia-toned photographs that were attached to the papers. One of them showed his parents marrying in a civil ceremony. The other showed his parents some years later. In his mother's arms was a baby boy. The child was no older than two, and was dressed in a sailor suit. It was little Mason. In his father's arms was an infant, his little sister.

At the bottom of the bundle of papers was a worn-out Certificate of Baptism issued by a church in Chicago's South Shore. His mother had eventually adopted the faith of her husband.

Distinct and separate from the binder clip documents was a small cream-coloured unsealed envelope. On its face was written *Masoud,* in his mother's handwriting. He had read the letter inside it many times. He gently took it out from the envelope and read it yet again.

My dearest darling Masoud,

The world knows you as Mason, but for me you will always be Masoud, the name that I secretly gave you.

By the time that you read this letter, I will no longer be in this world. As is said in the Holy Qur'an, this worldly life is only temporary, and indeed the Hereafter is the home of permanent settlement. I do not expect you to understand this view, having grown up in America, but I must confess that I betrayed my faith and my people by marrying your father and abandoning my true religion.

These days I am part of a Qur'anic studies group affiliated to the local mosque here in Queens and am realizing that the truth is to be found in the word of the One True God. The people in this neighbourhood know me by my old name and I have discarded all the trappings of my life as your father's wife. The punishment for apostates is very severe and I have told no one of my past.

You must have wondered why I left your father. I shall try to answer that from the very beginning. I was born in Lahore, Pakistan, into a very wealthy family. My father was a landowner and had arranged my marriage to the son of an equally affluent family friend. I knew that such a marriage meant lifelong captivity. So I ran away—unthinkable in those times. I hid in Karachi in the home of a family friend, a commercial pilot working in PIA, the national airline of Pakistan. It was through him that I met your father who was seventeen years my senior. He was employed as a pilot with Gulf Air.

Your father and I fell madly in love and he decided to get me out of Pakistan. This was easier said than done, because my family had initiated a countrywide hunt for me. I was smuggled out to Mumbai from Karachi on a dhow and from there I made it to Dubai. Your father arranged travel documents for me and I was finally able to fly out to New York and join him. We got married shortly thereafter and I delivered you. We then moved to Chicago where your sister was born.

Throughout my life, I tried to be the best wife and mother that I could be. I changed my name, my home, even my faith. I began dressing in Western clothes to be part of the well-heeled crowd and I even attended English classes to polish my accent. I gave up all ties to my ancestral home, my parents and my siblings. There came a time when I could hardly recognize myself.

Your father and I tried our best to educate both you and your sister well and to bring you up with a decent value system. And then one day, both of you kids grew up and left home for college. That's when I realized that the only thing that had been holding me to Chicago was you and your sister. I went into severe depression while I saw your father become a serious alcoholic. Your father and I would incessantly fight with each other and one day he lashed out at me and said, 'Go back to the filthy sewer that you came from, Paki bitch!'

I immediately packed up and left. During my career as a painter in Chicago, I had put aside money in my bank account and I left without demanding a dime from your father. I realized that it did not matter that I had married a non-Muslim, changed my faith, wore stylish 'liberated' clothes or spoke with an Anglicized accent. I would always be a Muslim first. Your father's hurtful words drove me back to my roots.

I have now been living in New York for over six years and have not spoken to you even once after my departure from Chicago. Please don't imagine that I don't think of you. I miss you each day, in fact, every waking moment. But I know that your world and mine are separated by a wide chasm. I have decided to spend my remaining days in the service of Allah. I have nothing to give you except this battered Qur'an that I used to keep in a locked drawer in our Chicago home. Whenever you touch it, I hope that it will make you feel one with me.

This envelope will reach you upon my death through the hands of my lawyer. I am suffering from lymphoma and do not have too many days left to live. I hope that Allah keeps you happy, healthy and prosperous. As-salamu'alaykum, *my sweet son.*

Your loving mother,
Maryam

Henderson used the back of his hand to brush away the tears that were rolling down his cheeks. He thanked the universe for having given him a mother like no other.

He then picked up his journal and began writing.

And it's another day and it's time for me, Masoud, to jot down my thoughts. And you know what? I may have found an appropriate solution to ending world conflict.

Moderate Muslims—the vast majority—have tried their best to convince the world that they are not radical like the extremists of their faith. They have tried telling the world that they do not share the ideology of terrorists, but it's getting more difficult by the day to make the rest of the world believe that. There is nothing worse than being a moderate Muslim these days. The terrorists see you as a non-believer and non-believers see you as a terrorist.

Minerva's solution to the problem of radical Islamism has been to allow the world to descend into an outright war to the finish. It would kill millions—both Muslims and non-Muslims—but I wonder whether such a war will end the ideology that spawned the terrorist?

What is the solution? It has to be a two-pronged effort. On the one hand, we must go after terror havens and exterminate terrorist masterminds. What I did with Mafraqi and Habib—even though Minerva was keen on letting their voices amplify—are examples of that.

It is evident that the Mafraqis of the world accelerate polarization through their words and deeds. But so do the Minervas, particularly under the leadership of bigots like Williams. It was the key reason why I needed to accept the position of Worshipful Master, funnel capital into the Molecular and Universal Audio project, and eliminate both threats.

The second part of any concerted effort has to be to find ways for moderates to reclaim their religion from the hardliners. Islam is not merely a religion. It is also a set of political, social and legal doctrines. Moderates need to pull out the best from the Qur'an and Hadith and let go of the rest. Eliminate the stuff that justifies violence and Jihad; remove the texts that discriminate against women thus making them subservient; shed the material that targets non-Muslims as enemies; cancel out the bits that punish leaving the faith by death; dump the seventh-century Arabic baggage; discard the hatred of gays, Jews and other groups; abandon the guilt that goes with music and painting; dispose of the dated Sharia, and so on. What one would be left with is a subset of verses that enable a follower to pray to Allah without being shackled to the primitive customs and laws of seventh-century Arabia. It would be a reformation like no other, allowing Muslims to get on with their lives in the twenty-first century.

Hinduism, a religion that spans millennia, underwent reformation in the '50s through the Hindu Marriage Act, the Hindu Succession Act, the Hindu Minority and Guardianship Act and the Hindu Adoptions and Maintenance Act. Several other traditions in Hinduism such as child marriage, widow burning and untouchability were outlawed even earlier. Reformation must occur when the time demands it.

People tend to forget that when Europe was in the Dark Ages, significant advancement in science, technology, architecture and arts happened in Muslim lands. The gradual march towards a gentler and more enlightened Islam was halted in its tracks by Wahhabism. Most unfortunate.

Remember that it took around fourteen hundred years from the origins of Christianity for the church to be reformed as a result of forces set in motion by Martin Luther. It is interesting to note that around fourteen hundred years have now elapsed from the founding of Islam.

Maybe the time for an Islamic reformation has arrived?

Acknowledgements

It would be impossible to write the books that I do without the assistance, input, guidance, love and support of so many. Here are some of those without whom this book—and the Bharat Collection—may not have happened.

My publishers, HarperCollins Publishers India—in particular, Ananth Padmanabhan and Udayan Mitra, who have ensured that books reach my readers quickly and efficiently; also my wonderful executive publisher and editor Poulomi Chatterjee, ably assisted by Kartik Chauhan and Shatarupa Ghoshal.

I would be amiss in forgetting the late Prita Maitra, my first editor of the Bharat Collection; Ashok Rajani, my perfectly ruthless fact-checker; and Swati Daftuar, Karthika V.K., Deepthi Talwar, Aparna Gupta, and Meru Gokhale—individuals who helped polish one or more books in this collection. Also, Gautam Padmanabhan, my friend, philosopher and guide who gave me my first publishing break and has encouraged me through several stories including most in the Bharat Collection.

My gratitude to Rupesh Talaskar—my illustrator, who has meticulously executed internal images in several books, Ameya Naik—the versatile composer who conceived the haunting tracks used in the Collection's video trailers,

Ramnika Sehrawat—the talented cover designer for this series, and the team at Oktobuzz for their social media support.

My thanks to Ashoo Naik at Collective Artists, Sidharth Jain at the Story Ink, and Fareen Dossani at SpeakIn for representing me and my work to the world.

Then there are my parents—Mahendra and Manju, and my siblings—Vidhi and Vaibhav, who have always encouraged me to follow my dreams. My wife, Anushika, and son, Raghuvir, have been my constant support in my writing endeavours. Had it not been for their unconditional love, none of my books would have been possible. Also, my little rakhi-sister Farah who has taught me that the most profound connections aren't always explained by logic, but by the quiet magic of the heart.

Then there are the late Ramprasad and Ramgopal Gupta, my maternal grandfather and maternal granduncle, who inspired me with their stories and books. Their blessings prevent the ink in my pen from running dry.

Finally, Ma Shakti, the One who puts power in my pen. I thank you, Ma, for your abundant blessings—forever.

References

I always like to provide a list of books, papers, journals, videos and websites that I have used while developing my narrative. Some of these sources may even express views that run contrary to the story. The idea of any book within the *Bharat Series* is to provide a starting point for further exploration. I am always hopeful that my readers will use the list of sources for further reading and discovery.

1. *A Brief History of Time: From Big Bang to Black Holes*, Stephen Hawking, Bantam, 1995
2. *A History of Saudi Arabia*, Madawi-al-Rashid, Cambridge University Press, 2010
3. *Ancient Observatories—Timeless Knowledge,* Deborah Scherrer, Stanford Solar Center, http://solar-center.stanford.edu/AO/Ancient-Observatories.pdf
4. *Archaeological Excavations at Piprahwa and Ganwaria and the Identification of Kapilavastu*, K. M. Srivastava, The Journal of the International Association of Buddhist Studies, 1980, https://journals.ub.uni-heidelberg.de/index.php/jiabs/article/viewFile/8511/2418
5. *Atlantis—Insights from a Lost Civilization*, Shirley Andrews, Llewellyn Publications, 1997
6. *Black Hole Blues and Other Songs from Outer Space,* Janna Levin, Bodley Head, 2016
7. *Buddhism—A Short History,* Edward Conze, One World, 2007
8. *By the Numbers—The Untold Story of Muslim Opinions & Demographics*, Clarion Project, 2015, https://www.youtube.com/watch?v=pSPvnFDDQHk
9. *Haunted India*, Chandan Sinha, Amazon Kindle, 2014
10. *Historical Rama,* D. K. Hari and D. K. Hema Hari, Sri Sri Publications Trust, 2010
11. *Indica—A Deep Natural History of the Indian Subcontinent,* Pranay Lal, Penguin Random House India, 2016

12. *Introduction to Quantum Mechanics,* J. Griffiths David, Pearson Education, 2015
13. *Introduction to Tantra: The Transformation of Desire,* Lama Thubten Yeshe, Jonathan Landaw, Wisdom Publications, 2014
14. *Introduction to the Kalachakra Initiation,* Alexander Berzin, Snow Lion, 2011
15. *ISIS: Inside the Army of Terror,* Michael Weiss, Hassan Hassan , Simon & Schuster, 2016
16. *It's All About Muhammad,* F. W. Burleigh, Zenga Books, 2016
17. *Knowledge & Representation in Sanskrit & Artificial Intelligence,* AI Magazine Volume 6 Number 1, Rick Briggs, https://pdfs.semanticscholar.org/3be9/3d7d713796ae7f2c1f8e55449f2e530bce2f.pdf
18. *Lost Horizon—The Legend of Shangri-La,* James Hilton, Vintage Classics, 2015
19. *Manusmriti—Text with Sanskrit Commentary & English Translation,* Dr N. C. Panda, BKP, 2014
20. *Manusmriti—The Laws of Manu,* Translated by Georg Buhler, Library of Alexandria, 2012, http://www.hindubooks.org/manusmriti.pdf
21. *Near Death Experience: The Life After Death Explained,* Mark Janniro, CreateSpace, 2016
22. *Radiation Hormesis in Plants,* Morton W. Miller, Marcus Miller, 1987, http://journals.lww.com/health-physics/Abstract/1987/05000/Radiation_Hormesis_in_Plants_.12.aspx
23. *Relativity: The Special and the General Theory,* Albert Einstein, General Press, 2013
24. *Schumann Resonance for Tyros,* Alexander Nickolaenko, Masashi Hayakawa, Springer Nature, 2013
25. *Secret Societies: Gardiner's Forbidden Knowledge: Revelations About the Freemasons, Templars, Illuminati, Nazis and the Serpent Cults,* Philip Gardiner, Career Press, 2007

26. *Shambhala*, Nicholas Roerich, Aravali Books International, 2002
27. *Sound Vision—Patterns of Vibration in Sound, Symbols & The Body*, Rachel Linton, Massey University, New Zealand, 2008. http://mro.massey.ac.nz/bitstream/handle/10179/1018/02whole.pdf
28. *Spies in the Himalayas: Secret Missions and Perilous Climbs*, M. S. Kohli, Kenneth Conboy, University Press of Kansas, 2003
29. *Sri Yantra—The Ancient Instrument to Control the Psychophysiological State of Man*, Alexey Mikhailovna Ramendic, Dina Mikhailnova Ramendic, Indian Journal of History of Science, 1989, http://www.insa.nic.in/writereaddata/UpLoadedFiles/IJHS/Vol24_3_1_APKulaichev.pdf
30. *Sri Yantra Geometry*, Gerard Huet, Theoretical Computer Science, 2002, https://www.researchgate.net/profile/Gerard_Huet/publication/266423316_Sri_Yantra_Geometry/links/0c9605271a498c3cde000000/Sri-Yantra-Geometry.pdf
31. *The Arabs—A History*, Eugene Rogan, Penguin UK, 2012
32. *The Art of Living: Vipassana Meditation: As Taught by S. N. Goenka*, William Hart, HarperOne, 2009
33. *The Birth of Terrorism in Middle East: Muhammed Bin Abed al-Wahab, Wahabism, and the Alliance with the ibn Saud Tribe*, Muhammad Ne'ma al-Semawi, Paragon Publication, 2015
34. *The Clash of Civilization and the Remaking of World Order*, Samuel P. Huntington, Random House India, 2016
35. *The Dancing Wu Li Masters: An Overview of the New Physics*, Gary Zukav, Random House UK, 1991
36. *The Essential Vedanta—A New Source Book of Advaita Vedanta*, Edited by Eliot Deutsch and Rohit Dalvi, World Wisdom Books, 2004
37. *The God Effect: Quantum Entanglement, Science's Strangest Phenomenon*, Brian Clegg, St. Martin's Griffin, 2009

38. *The Golden Age of Indian Mathematics*, S. Parameswaran, Swadeshi Science Movement Kerala, 1998
39. *The Golden Ratio: The Story of Phi, the World's Most Astonishing Number*, Mario Livio, Random House USA, 2003
40. *The Heritage of Nalanda*, C. Mani, Aryan Books, 2008
41. *The Hidden Science of Lost Civilizations—The Source Field Investigations*, David Wilcock, Dutton, 2012
42. *The Legend of Shambhala in Eastern and Western Interpretations*, Victoria Dmitrieva, McGill University, 1997, http://vajrayana.faithweb.com/The%20legend%20of%20Shambhala%20in%20eastern%20and%20western%20interpretations.pdf
43. *The Life of the Buddha*, Tenzin Chogyel, Penguin Books, 2015
44. *The Lost Civilization of Lemuria: The Rise and Fall of the World's Oldest Culture*, Frank Joseph, Bear & Company, 2006
45. *The Lotus-Born: The Life Story of Padmasambhava*, Yeshe Tsogyal, Erik Pema Kunsang, Rangjung Yeshe Publications, 2004
46. *The Practice of Kalachakra*, Dalai Lama & Glenn H. Mullin, Snow Lion, 1991
47. *The Qur'an—A New Translation*, M. A. S. Abdel Haleem, Oxford University Press UK, 2010
48. *The Secret Doctrine: The Classic Work, Abridged and Annotated*, H.P. Blavatsky, Michael Gomes, Penguin USA, 2009
49. *The Secret of Shambhala: In Search of the Eleventh Insight*, James Redfield, Random House UK, 2000
50. *The Speed of Light and Puranic Cosmology*, Subhash Kak, Louisiana State University, 1998, https://arxiv.org/pdf/physics/9804020v3.pdf
51. *The Submerged Kumari Continent: The Home of Ancient Tamils*, Ma. So Victor and Naanjil Amal, Amazon Asia-Pacific Kindle Edition
52. *The Tao of Physics*, Fritjof Capra, Harper Collins, 2007
53. *The Theory of Everything*, Stephen Hawking, Jaico, 2006

54. *The Tibetan Book of the Dead: First Complete Translation*, Graham Coleman, Thupten Jinpa, Gyurme Dorje, Dalai Lama, Penguin Classics, 2007

55. *The Vanishing Hindus of Pakistan*, Newslaundry, https://www.newslaundry.com/2015/01/09/the-vanishing-hindus-of-pakistan-a-demographic-study-2

56. *The World's Muslims—Religion, Politics & Society*, Pew Research Centre, 2013, http://www.pewforum.org/files/2013/04/worlds-muslims-religion-politics-society-full-report.pdf

57. *Transplants, Cellular Memory & Reincarnation*, Larry Dossey, Explore Journal 2008, http://www.explorejournal.com/article/S1550-8307(08)00210-3/pdf

58. *Uyghur Nation: Reform and Revolution on the Russia-China Frontier*, David Brophy, Harvard University Press, 2016

About the Author

Ashwin Sanghi is among India's highest-selling English fiction authors. He has written several bestsellers in the *Bharat Collection* (*The Rozabal Line, Chanakya's Chant, The Krishna Key, The Sialkot Saga, Keepers of the Kalachakra, The Vault of Vishnu, The Magicians of Mazda* and *The Ayodhya Alliance*) and two *New York Times* and *Sunday Times UK* bestselling crime thrillers with James Patterson, *Private India* (sold in the U.S. as *City on Fire*) and *Private Delhi* (sold in the U.S. as *Count to Ten*). His novel *Razor Sharp*, the first book in the Kutta Kadam Thriller series conceptualized by Ashwin, became a national bestseller. He mentors, collaborates and edits several non-fiction titles in the 13 Steps Series on Luck, Wealth, Marks, Health and Parenting. He contributes to the opinion page of *The Times of India*.

Ashwin has been included by *Forbes India* in their Celebrity 100 and by *The New Indian Express* in their Culture Power List. He has won the Crossword Popular Choice Award 2012, Atta Galatta Popular Choice Award 2018, WBR Iconic Achievers Award 2018, the Lit-O-Fest Literature Legend Award 2018, the Kalinga Popular Choice Award 2021, and the Deendayal Upadhyaya Recognition 2023. He has also been awarded an Honorary Doctorate by JECRC University, Rajasthan.

He was educated at Cathedral and John Connon School, Mumbai, and St. Xavier's College, Mumbai. He holds an MBA from Yale University. Ashwin lives in Mumbai with his wife, Anushika, and son, Raghuvir.

You can connect with Ashwin via the following channels:

Website: www.sanghi.in

X: @ashwinsanghi

Instagram: @ashwin.sanghi

Facebook: fb.com/ashwinsanghi

YouTube: youtube.com/ashwinsanghi

LinkedIn: linkedin.com/in/ashwinsanghi

WELCOME TO THE SHADOWY AND ADDICTIVE WORLD OF INDIA'S MASTER STORYTELLER

THE ROZABAL LINE

Shadowed by a clandestine society, which would rather wipe out creation than allow an ancient secret to be disclosed, Father Vincent Sinclair must uncover the secret of a tomb called Rozabal in the heart of strife-torn Kashmir. The tomb holds the key to an ancient riddle, but is time running out for Father Sinclair?

CHANAKYA'S CHANT

Having once averted the threat of invasion by Alexander the Great, the calculating and ruthless Mauryan kingmaker Chanakya emerges two and a half millennia later in small-town India. Will he be able to unite a broken nation once more against the rot that consumes it?

THE KRISHNA KEY

The arrival of a murderer who executes his gruesome and brilliantly thought-out schemes in the name of God is the first clue to a sinister conspiracy to expose an ancient secret—Krishna's priceless legacy to mankind. Historian Ravi Mohan Saini must dash from the submerged remains of Dwarka and the mysterious lingam of Somnath to the icy Mount Kailash in a quest to discover the cryptic location of Krishna's most prized possession.

THE SIALKOT SAGA

The lives of two businessmen, Arvind and Arbaaz, are inadvertently intertwined as they ricochet off one another, playing out their sinister and murderous plots of personal and professional one-upmanship.

KEEPERS OF THE KALACHAKRA

When unsuspecting scientist Vijay Sundaram uncovers a primordial clue to a galactic secret that could accelerate the downward spiral of humankind, he finds himself trapped in a labyrinth, chased by unnamed killers who work with the clinical efficiency of butchers. Can he save humanity—and himself?

THE VAULT OF VISHNU

A young investigator with a complex past races against time to maintain the balance of power in the new world. Across the borders of time and space, from the empire of the Pallavas to the battlefields of the Indo-China wars, myth and history blend into edge-of-the-seat action in another Ashwin Sanghi masterpiece.

THE MAGICIANS OF MAZDA

In this gripping and provocative novel, Ashwin Sanghi travels through epochs of Islamic jihad, Macedonian revenge, Achaemenid glory, messianic birth and Aryan schism—to the Vedic fount from where it all began.

ASHWIN SANGHI

RETURNS WITH ANOTHER

BREATHTAKING TALE

INDIA'S MASTER STORYTELLER 

ASHWIN SANGHI

THE AYODHYA ALLIANCE

'Ashwin Sanghi spins his yarns well and leaves you breathless at every cliffhanger. No wonder his books are bestsellers!'

HINDUSTAN TIMES

BHARAT COLLECTION
MORE THAN 1.5 MILLION COPIES SOLD

An ancient secret.
A forgotten science.
A battle for the future of humanity.

Seven thousand years ago, as he lay dying on the battlefield of Lanka, Ravana whispered a secret to Lakshmana about a mysterious technology that held the key to Ayodhya's prosperity and the world's destiny.

For centuries, desperately sought by explorers, marauders and emperors alike, it has been kept hidden, safeguarded by warriors bound by an ancient oath.

Now, as tensions escalate along India's volatile borders and a crucial defence project teeters on the brink of failure, Indian industrialist Aditya Pillai and South Korean technocrat Somi Kim are thrust into a mission that will upend everything they know.

The two realize they must act fast, but never once do they anticipate that they will stumble upon startling revelations about a miraculous force that once connected Ayodhya to Kailasa, the Pandyan Empire, Rome, Damascus, Thailand and Korea. As the forces of past and present collide, a question looms large: who will harness the power of the ultimate enigma, and at what cost?

The Ayodhya Alliance spans continents and centuries, seamlessly weaving together science, legend and history in a breathless race against time. In this sweeping, unputdownable story of intrigue, betrayal, survival and love, master storyteller Ashwin Sanghi casts his web wider than ever before, spinning once again a riveting, edge-of-the-seat thriller.

HarperCollins *Publishers* India

At HarperCollins India, we believe in telling the best stories and finding the widest readership for our books in every format possible. We started publishing in 1992; a great deal has changed since then, but what has remained constant is the passion with which our authors write their books, the love with which readers receive them, and the sheer joy and excitement that we as publishers feel in being a part of the publishing process.

Over the years, we've had the pleasure of publishing some of the finest writing from the subcontinent and around the world, including several award-winning titles and some of the biggest bestsellers in India's publishing history. But nothing has meant more to us than the fact that millions of people have read the books we published, and that somewhere, a book of ours might have made a difference.

As we look to the future, we go back to that one word—a word which has been a driving force for us all these years.

Read.